Barry B. Longyear

THE HANGMAN'S SON

~ Joe Torio Mystery #1 ~

Enchanteds Publishing
PO Box 100, New Sharon ME 04955
www.Enchanteds.net

ISBN-13: 978-0615483818
ISBN-10: 061548381X

Manufactured in the United States of America

To the Blokes:
Building friendships, rebuilding lives,
and
Dancing with the mountain.

THE HANGMAN'S SON

PADDLE TIME

The huge auto sales and service garage on the edge of Sherman Park squatted in the early January dark, its grimy brick walls black against the fresh white snow banks on Cross Street. No outdoor car lot in this neighborhood. All of the new wares were inside. The building was a flat-topped, post-Depression structure, capped with a twenty-inch thick layer of snow and ice, the temperature hovering around zero Fahrenheit. All but one of the street lights in front of the building were out. From where my partner Al Dockery and I were huddling in the alley on the east side of the building, it was just dark.

Theo and Tony Rizzo were inside the building. Not enough for Lt. Crewe, though. He was waiting for Carlo.

"This stinks," muttered Dock as he shivered in the junker's passenger seat cocooned like a fat butterfly-in-waiting. The wrecked and gutted VW Minibus, buried in snow, was in the alley across from the showroom side entrance. We'd cleared discreet little holes in the snow on the windshield so we could keep an eye on who went in the building.

"I said this stinks," he repeated.

"I'm hip," I confirmed, wishing I had brought some hand warmers. I had both my hand and my gun in my parka's side pocket, only my fingertips inside the heavy ski glove. Dock looked through the cleared place on his side of the junker's windshield. "We're freezing to death, our backup is three blocks away, and the Popsicle King is parked out front telegraphing our punches as we speak. Theo and Tony have to know we're out here." His grump dissolved into a chuckle.

"What?" I asked, my own funny bone in sore need of inspiration.

"You know how Crewe, Stasser, and that news team are hunched down in their seats right in front of the showroom windows making like no one's in the car?"

"Uh huh."

"When I did that walk around I saw they had the engine running."

"You're kidding, right?"

"The engine running, the heater on full blast, windows fogged up, great white clouds of exhaust."

"Just so we still have the element of surprise," I muttered.

"Stasser was resting his foot on the brake pedal, too."

"Jesus."

"I took a quarter and rapped on the window," said Dock. "They're still cleaning coffee off each other."

"Would've liked to have seen that."

Dock's grin faded. "I told 'em about the engine and the brake light, but from the look on Crewe's face, I don't think I was getting through."

"The Five Pees," I observed philosophically.

There were the official five pees they taught at the academy: Prior Planning Prevents Poor Performance. Then there were the unofficial Five Pees we all learned in the squad rooms and on the street: Promoting Pea-brains Produces Piles of Poo.

"You know how you say most good police work comes down to knowing who to ask for help?" said Dock.

"What about it?"

"So, who do we ask now, Joe?"

"You got that Bat signal working yet?"

He nodded toward his right indicating the increasing snowfall. "The dark knight is grounded."

"Didn't know Batman took snow days. You'd think he'd have a Bat Snow Cat." I closed my eyes and shivered inside my parka. "Damn. I should've worn my ski pants, brought my Boot Gloves and Bun Warmers. I'm freezing. Hell. Carlo isn't coming. He's not an idiot."

Dock nodded toward the street. "After Carlo caught a look at that car full of Filberts in front of his showroom, maybe he dropped dead from laughing."

"It could happen," I said.

Dockery turned in his seat and looked over his right shoulder toward the back of the alley. "You ever wonder how Crewe even made it past probie?"

"It never hurts having your uncle as Police Commissioner," I said.

"Which doesn't make Commissioner Graham a bad commissioner," Dock cautioned.

"No," I agreed. "The fact that he can't find his own ass with both hands and a mirror is what makes him an idiot."

Despite Ronald Crewe's all-American halfback, Aryan/Nazi storm-trooper recruiting-poster good looks, our lieutenant had almost no time on the street. His patrol career ended abruptly after the media dubbed him the "Popsicle King." Off duty late one night in August, he had found what appeared to be an abandoned refrigerated truck parked on the shoulder down in East Beverly Division off the Roosevelt exit to the Interstate. The driver was nowhere in sight, the truck still running. Thinking this seemed suspicious, he took the keys from the ignition, opened the doors in back, and investigated. What he found inside were six human corpses all in plastic body bags.

Crewe called in everything but the National Guard, and when the driver came back with a large Coke in one hand and a Philly cheese steak in the other, he found his truck surrounded by cruisers, many heavily armed law enforcement types, news wagons, reporters, and curious onlookers as Crewe grabbed him, spread-eagled him on the street, and put on the cuffs. Then Crewe pulled the driver to his feet and went for the confession. Turned out the truck driver was delivering cadavers to the university medical school and had stopped at a Subway for a sandwich. Crises over. From then on Crewe was dubbed the Popsicle King.

Al Dockery, his gaze fixed on the side door to the building, said, "I'm getting depressed. We need to change the subject, look for the positive." Dock had been my Training Officer back when the fuzz on my uniform blouse was still thick. In both uniforms and the detective

7

bureau we'd grown middle aged and cranky together. The "positives" was how he bitched.

"That chum bucket is half full," I offered.

"You goddamn right, Grasshopper. Like, with all this cold, Joe, they're making a lot of snow for skiing, right?"

"Yeah. Skiing is good this season. Lots of cold, lots of snow. No mosquitoes, either. Hate getting mosquitoes squashed all over my goggles."

Dock nodded. "We're not getting all sweaty. I hate getting sweaty."

"No sunburn," I added. "I can't stand the smell of suntan lotion and sun block. We're not going to get skin cancer tonight."

"We don't have to watch ugly people in thongs or tank tops, either." Dockery nodded his head for either emphasis or additional warmth. "Why is it the uglier people get the more they want to expose? It's too cold for thongs. Can I get an amen on no thongs?"

"Amen," I said. I nibbled at the inside of my lower lip, my gaze still on the alley's entrance. There was a chance Tony and Theo didn't know we were out there. Maybe they were stoned, or running around with black bags on their heads, or taking a nap.

Capt. Finn had gotten the anonymous phone tip that morning while I was grinding my way through the murder books on deceased drug dealers Roy Thoms and Stevie Pillow. They had each been taken out with the Rizzo trademark: a brand-new stiletto left in the heart, the wrapper still on the handle. There wasn't much of a case. There never was. This time, though, Theo Rizzo had somehow left a partial on the blade of one of the two stickers. Aside from making a statement, the whole point of the new knife, wrapper-still-on-the-handle gag, as well as gloves, was to make prints impossible. There it was, though: one tiny partial on the blade. Enough for a warrant. Maybe enough for a needle or three.

After Nicky Batts's lawyer posted half a million bail each to show that they were not flight risks, the Rizzos took flight. Neither the manager at the garage, nor the sales or maintenance personnel knew where they were. Their mother, Brigada, knew but wasn't saying. Then

Finn eventually got a call. He said the anonymous caller reported that all three Rizzo brothers would be at the garage sometime tonight. The collar belonged to Dock and me, but Commissioner Graham ordered a Broadway production: four units, one on each side of the building, six more units in ready reserve out of sight, all under the tactical command of the Popsicle King himself, Commissioner Graham's nephew.

If it was going to be a full-scale assault, it would have made sense to bring in SWAT. However, that way SWAT got the credit, not Graham Cracker's nephew. So we were freezing our butts off and getting ready to blow an arrest or get someone killed in an attempt to rehabilitate the image of the Popsicle King.

Crewe's base unit had Channel Four's Gil Franklin and a camera jock as ride-alongs in the back seat. A successful high-profile arrest would look good on the morning news was the theory. Channel Four didn't want law, order, justice or successful anything, though. They weren't interested unless it dripped red; Gil Franklin was there strictly for the body count. With four previous miscreants stone cold, I had tied the PD record and had attracted unfavorable headlines, all centered around the theme: the hangman's son loves to kill. Learned the ropes at the hangman's knee. Serial killer with a badge. If anyone died tonight, Gil Franklin would have an orgasm and Lt. Crewe would need a divining rod to find his own name in the reports.

"Crewe is a moron," muttered Dock, his stay-positive program down the crapper at last. "Can we call him a moron?"

"The politically correct label is 'reality challenged.'"

"Crewe is an absolute moron."

"This from the sage who teaches that there are no absolutes," I reminded.

"Isn't no absolutes an absolute?" countered Dock.

"Absolutely." I waved the numb contents of a glove in the air. "Dock, what about this phone tip? Who called it in? The Rizzos know we're here, we know they know, they know we know they know."

"Sounds like an invitation to the O.K. Corral, doesn't it?"

"Just a bit. Where's Doc Holiday when you need—"

Dockery's hand shot out, palm toward me, as he nodded toward the street. I looked through my snowy peephole. An instant later, a large man limped into my view. Easily six-foot-six, broad shouldered, and heavy, the man wore a long dark overcoat with fur collar and matching fur cap. He paused for a moment, took a long drag on a cigarette, then flicked the butt in the general direction of the base unit parked in front of the garage. He exhaled, the combination of the smoke and the man's breath blue-gray and lacy in the breeze. It was Carlo Rizzo.

I read Dock's lips as he silently mouthed, "He's made Crewe."

I mouthed back, "Ya think?"

Carlo went to the showroom's side entrance, slightly dragging his left leg as he walked. Years ago he'd gotten his knee tooled by one of Don Scozarri's boys. He opened the unlocked metal door and stepped in, the door closing slowly behind him. I spoke into the open collar of my parka. "Base? Crewe? Carlo made you, lieutenant. They're waiting for us in there. Time to call in SWAT."

There was a crackle from my earpiece followed by the Popsicle King's boyish voice. *"That was Carlo? That means they're all in there, right?"*

"Lieutenant, we're burned. He wouldn't have gone in unless he wanted someone to follow him. They're waiting for us."

"Torio, you and Dockery move in. Backup units, move to Point Bravo. Units One to Four, move in."

"Is this thing working?" I muttered smacking the com unit against the dash. Pressing the talk button I said, "Base, this is Unit Three. Please be advised that the suspects have spotted your damned vehicle and the crowd of morons you have warming up in it."

"That's 'reality challenged,'" corrected Dock.

"Nonsense," replied Crewe. *"We've had no indication."*

"What the hell do you think this warning is?" I replied, a little louder than necessary. Dockery was making a clown face at me, his eyes crossed, his head bobbing from side-to-side.

All of the radio traffic was being monitored and recorded, not to mention overheard by the Channel Four news team, but Crewe hadn't left me any choice. "Sorry about that, lieutenant," I apologized. "I guess Dock only imagined you had your engine running and Stasser's big fat foot on the brake pedal in full view of the showroom windows."

There was a long silence, followed by the Popsicle King's spluttering voice. *"Torio, I don't muck gige a futch ... I don't ... care! We've got them trapped! Now follow orders!"*

Dock spoke into his pickup. "Lieutenant, I believe in the military they call this fighting on ground of the enemy's own choosing."

"Please. Mister Custer," I sang beneath my breath. "I don't wanna go."

"This is the job!" bellowed Crewe. *"Move in! All units move in! Move in, god dammit! Move in!"*

I listened as MacDonald and Rodriguez in Unit Two grudgingly acknowledged the order. Crewe called several times for Carver and Tobin in Unit One to acknowledge, but got no answer. Carver and Tobin were parked in the darkness of the junkyard at the rear of the building. Either their radio was out, they were both out of the unit making their bladders gladder, they had decided to sit this one out, or one of the Rizzos had crept up on them and zeroed out their hard drives.

"Unit Three?" called Crewe. *"Torio? Dockery?"*

"Three," I answered flatly.

"I can't raise Unit One. Torio, one of you go back and see what's become of Carver and Tobin. The other get in that side entrance and back up Unit Two. MacDonald and Rodriguez are already in there. Go! That is an order, detective!"

I felt the acid taste of my stomach in my throat. "How important is that pension, Dock?"

"Tough to enjoy it with your brains splattered all over a new Audi, I gotta admit."

"Yeah. Dock, why don't you go and see if Carver and Tobin are finished with their coffee break while I check some sticker prices?"

Dock glared at me. "Why don't you just paint a big bulls-eye on your ass and play a kazoo?"

"You know I'm a banjo man. Go on, Dock. We can't leave Mac and Pancho in there all alone. Anyway, I'm a smaller target than you and my Velcro is tight."

Muttering obscenities, Dockery pushed open the junker's passenger door and slipped out, his bulk soon swallowed by the shadows and falling snow. I slid out the same side, eased the door closed, pulled the S&W 669 from my parka pocket, moved past the two junkers on the opposite side of the alley, and rushed to the wall next to the side entrance. Feeling the firmness of the brick at my back, I inched toward the door.

The door had a clear glass panel in it. Glancing through it first, I decided, would accomplish nothing but acquiring an extra hole in my head. A deep breath, then I pulled open the door, crouched down, and slipped inside to the right, away from the entrance, my back against the wall. As the door hissed shut all of my senses went to high-receive.

It was dead silent, uncomfortably warm, the scents of new car and old cigarette smoke mixed with a touch of stale car exhaust. As I swept the showroom with my weapon, I searched the shadows. Directly in front of me, highlights from the front window's red neon sign reflecting from it, was a sports utility vehicle on an angle to the door. To my right were two more vehicles, a station wagon and one of the neo-beetles, Adolph Hitler's old design concept still holding up.

Past the beetle was an additional showroom with rows of gleaming imported inventory. Directly across from me, beyond the SUV, was a low slung, glossy black sports car. Beyond that was the establishment's vestibule, which also served as an additional display room for the garage's parts department. On the far wall of the parts department display room, there was an additional red neon sign above a door: "Offices." Through the display window to my left, I noted the base unit, a perpetual cloud of hot exhaust still rising from it's rear, keeping the Popsicle King and media warm and happy. Stasser had, at least, taken his foot off the brake pedal. Always a treat working with professionals.

Satisfied I was alone in the front showroom, I removed my left glove, slipped the Maglite from my coat pocket, and moved to the side of the SUV, squatting beside it. After another pause, I removed my bulky parka and left it and my gloves on the floor after retrieving the squawk. I placed the communication unit in the breast pocket provided for it on the body armor and replaced the earpiece. I waited a beat, then duck-walked around the front of the SUV, pausing for a moment behind the glistening hood of the sports car. It was an Audi R8. Damned good-looking ride. My Mazda MX3 was a 'Ninety-two and about ready to be donated to a demolition derby. I toyed with looking at the sticker price, but putting a light on it would be about as stupid as paying a hundred grand plus for a car that only got thirteen miles per gallon. First things first.

After moving around the sports car, I came to rest next to the entrance to the parts department showroom, the blue neon spark plug casting the floor displays in cold relief. The displays were of Santa and his elves, but in the blue light they looked like a squad of grotesque little space invaders awaiting orders. I studied the aliens for a long time to see if one of them made a move to call home.

Opposite the front doors, running the entire length of the vestibule's north wall, was a thirty-foot long counter. Behind the counter was a door leading to where the parts inventory was stored. The inventory room opened onto the garage's main repair and paint bays where, theoretically, the two uniforms from Unit Two would be working their way toward me from the west side entrance, the Rizzos caught in between. The uniforms from Unit One should be coming in the back of the garage next to the grease racks, if Dockery had managed to waken them.

Putting my lips next to the squawk's pickup, I whispered, "Dock?"

"I can't find Tobin and Carver, Joe. Back on out of there—"

"Negative! Negative!" Interrupted the Popsicle King loudly, making me flinch. Through the display window to my left, I could see Lt. Crewe pounding his fist on the

car's dash. Stasser had his foot back on the brake pedal. The rear window was open and there was a tiny red light moving in the back seat: Gil Franklin's cameraman was taping the play-by-play for tomorrow's broadcast. If his cameraman suddenly turned on the Klieg lights I'd be silhouetted.

"Torio, you get in there and back up MacDonald and Rodriguez!" Lt. Crewe, our leader, keeping on top of things.

"Base, this is Unit Two," called MacDonald. *"We aren't in. The door's got a barrier on it."*

"Uh oh," I whispered to myself.

"Get outta there, Joe," interjected Dockery, his voice rough with tension. *"Tobin and Carver are down. Repeat, Base, Tobin and Carver are down! We need an ambulance, now! We need Torio outta there now!"*

"This is Lt. Crewe. . . . Okay. Okay." A numb silence, then Crewe came back on the net._*"Ambulance is on the way. Torio. MacDonald and Rodriguez still need backup."*

"Negative! Negative, Base. For Christ's sake! This is Unit Two," interrupted MacDonald, his voice tense with frustration. *"We are not in. Repeat, we are not in! The door is barred from the inside. Torio is in there by himself!"*

I whispered into my pickup, "Dock, getting a little lonely here."

I heard the side door rattle and rattle again. *"Joe,"* whispered Dock, *"It's locked."*

That was not good. The door hadn't been locked when I went through it. Hence, if it was locked now, someone had locked it. Maybe I wasn't so lonely after all. I studied shapes and shadows until everything looked like it was hiding someone.

After a long pause, Crewe said, *"Abort. All units, abort operation! Stay in place, Torio! We'll get help to you."* As Crewe ordered the pullout, I caught a glimpse of someone in front of the side door standing behind the SUV.

"Joe Torio, look at you," said the shadow. "I heard it but I didn't believe it. What are you doin' in here, cop?

You must got 'em like brass gongs." The voice was deep, clear. Theo Rizzo, number two son.

I tried to make myself small as an electric prickle ran up my spine. Turning my head, I looked at the showroom window wondering if I ran at it as fast as I could, perhaps shooting through the glass as I went, if I could break through it and escape onto the street. I fleetingly considered that one or more stray rounds might catch the Popsicle King or the TV crew, but before I could finish totaling up the positive reasons for taking a tilt at that windmill, the negative side won with the sound of a pump-action shotgun being cocked.

Springing from my position, I leaped into the parts display room just ahead of a charge of buckshot, rolled to my feet, veered toward the counter, and vaulted over it as the TV camera lights went on. I felt like a bug on a microscope stage. Once I was squatting behind the counter, I pulled the squawk from its pocket, and whispered "Talk to yourself, Dock, and tell the Popsicle King to turn of the fucking lights!"

I ran the volume all the way up and pulled the earpiece jack. Leaving the pocket radio on the floor behind the counter, I crawled toward the inventory room door. Just as I reached it, I could hear Dock's tinny voice beginning a dialog with himself.

"Hey, Joe. Whaddya know?" Pause. *"I'm off today to the picture show."*

"Inspired," I muttered. In the corner of the display room was a large security mirror. From my vantage point I could see a large dark shape moving on the outside of the showroom window toward Crewe's car. Once there the TV lights suddenly extinguished. Another dark shape moved in the mirror but this one was on my side of the glass. As I entered the inventory room door, I saw the shadow with the shotgun ease its way up to the counter, look over, and aim its weapon at the radio. I trained my gun on the shadow. Before I could fire, white hot pain filled my right shoulder as a stiletto was thrust into it from behind. "Dago Frank says 'Hi,'" growled Tony Rizzo's voice.

I violently swung around, Tony's hand on the knife handle stirring things inside as I shoved my gun into

Tony's guts and pulled the trigger. As the shadow fell back, the shotgun fired from the end of the counter, the buckshot eating off the top of the door. I fired twice in the general direction of the shotgun's muzzle flash, then I lurched through the door to the inventory room. The soft red-and-white glow of the exit light in the back through the parts shelves cast deep shadows with diffused edges. I pulled myself to the far wall midway between the door I came in and the entrance to the garage and tried to hide myself in between piles of tires and empty cardboard cartons, the smell of new rubber heavy on the air. Something brushed the handle of the knife letting me know it was still in my shoulder.

Sinking to my knees from the pain, I pulled the Velcro loose on the left side of the body armor but couldn't remove it. The knife had gone through the webbing above the Kevlar. I reached over my right shoulder with my left hand and gingerly touched the handle of the stiletto. Pulling that handle out of Tony Rizzo's hand by turning had moved that blade sideways inside my shoulder, tearing up more things than I cared to think about right then. I couldn't bear even the thought of catching the handle of that knife on something. Biting off my cries, bit-by-bit I eased the narrow blade from my shoulder. Once out, I held the wicked looking sticker in front of my eyes and saw the glisten of its seven-inch blade reflecting though a sheen of my own blood.

"Not again," I whispered, as the blood that wasn't pounding in my head dribbled into my armpit, soaking my shirt. There seemed to be something wrong with the blood flow. Way too much. There was also blood dribbling down my chest. The blade must have gone all the way through, hitting a main line on the way. I could feel the blood pooling at my waist, above my belt. I shrugged out of the body armor leaving it and its added weight on the floor.

There was a noise from out in the display room. Pressing my right arm against my side as tightly as I could, I placed the knife on the floor and took my 669 in my left hand, the sound of my heart still pounding in my ears. The beat seemed to be getting a bit fluttery as a gunshot and its muzzle flash came from out in the showroom.

Carlo Rizzo's low-pitched voice called out, "Tony? Theo? Tony? Theo?"

As I tried to make myself invisible I kept my finger outside the trigger guard so a digit jazzed up on fight-or-flight juice didn't inadvertently pop off an unintentional round. I worked on overcoming my narrow focus by repeatedly checking to my left, my right, up, and down. A wave of light-headedness came and I almost went out.

"Theo! Theo, what—*Mother of God!*"

Theo down? I thought. Theo was the shotgun. That'd have to be the luckiest damned shot of the century. I fought against the blackness. Carlo. I could handle Carlo by myself if I could keep from blacking out.

Scrape, step, scrape, step, scrape.

Carlo paused outside the inventory room door. The big man muttered something. "Tony," then he swore beneath his breath. I guessed Tony hadn't made it either. I would've congratulated myself, but I couldn't see how Theo was dead. Tony was gut shot. That's painful, but lingering. Carlo was acting like they were both dead.

I could hear Carlo's footsteps on the floor, his gimpy left foot scraping the concrete like Boris Karloff in *The Mummy*. Dock was still talking on the squawk. Something about the Policeman's Ball. A shotgun cocked.

Scrape, step, scrape, step, scrape.

"Get ready you rat bastard," said Carlo. "I'm coming for you."

It was dark, the lines of stocked shelves cocked crazily, the lights mixing with shadows, one of the shadows filling the doorway. I tried to aim and squeeze off a shot, but was too weak. Couldn't move my arm. Couldn't see to aim anyway. There was a pause, a small grunt, then another muzzle flash, the sound of it for some reason quite muted.

I felt something hard and cold against the left side of my face. Then it was warm and sticky. Smell of new rubber. Need to replace the bald-headed tires on my MX3. Meaning to get to it for months. I wondered what the Rizzos'd charge for a set of all seasons. Maybe I could get a professional courtesy discount—

Couldn't lift my arm. *Couldn't see.* Great, I was blind. Couldn't lift my head. I tried to squeeze off a few rounds but there was no sound, no feeling, my hand twitching.

Circling the drain, I thought. *Round and round.* Made me think of the big circular staircase. At Pop's house there was the blue rope that held the ornate chandelier in the hall. Went up two and a half stories to a pulley. Nice chandelier. Originally oil, converted to gas, and converted again to electricity. Greenish copper frame set with plates of beveled crystal, twelve pointy light bulbs that looked like fake flames, all on a dimmer switch. The rope that held it was blue.

Billy Roth made a crack about the rope at class. Fifth grade. Said that Joe Torio's father, the hangman, had recycled one of his old ropes.

It was a little funny. Once. Billy took his joke, though, and told it around. And around and around. We fought. Terrible fight. Bloody noses all around.

I felt something at my hand. A nudge. Hand was full of Novocain anyway; shadow over me looking down. Billy Roth, the little bastard.

The chandelier at the Torio's was hanging on a rope that had put twenty killers away. That's what Billy Roth told everyone at school. Jerk. Everybody knows you don't use a rope after three times.

A thump. Another thump. Another.

"Just joking," Billy had said.

King Elementary. There used to be the fat girl, the cripple, the psycho, the computer geek, the Jew, the fag, and the hangman's son: Outcasts all. Billy Roth used to be of our number, but he figured a way out of the few and into the many by throwing me under the bus and rejecting all the other odd human puzzle pieces. Lots of fights and lots of nights filling my head with banal TV shows, hiding in the back of my bedroom closet, cursing the world that had made my father a hangman, teasing my head with ending it all.

The hangman never asked about the black eyes, the split lips, and bloody noses. Instead, one day he took me

18

down to a shack below the tank farm in East Branch to see an ex-con named Leroy Brown, just like in the song. Leroy was shaved bald, had rubbery yellowish-tan skin, a complexion like the surface of the moon, and was one big solid chunk of muscle. After the hangman had left, Leroy said, "I owe you papa, boy. This is payback. Do what I tell you and only the right people get hurt." And then I learned street fighting from a man who used to street fight for prize money and eventually went to prison for killing a man with his fists.

Leroy Brown, every afternoon for two months: Fists, feet, knives, knees, head, dig, slap, poke, punch, stab. I tried some knuckles on the bullies at school, and the beatings miraculously stopped. No more hangman jokes, either, at least not within my hearing. No more beating on the other outcasts, either. Anyone you wanted to pick on had to go through me first.

Wonder if that's when I decided to become a cop. "To serve and protect." That wasn't SRPD's motto, though. On the doors of our marked cruisers, beneath the twin raven logo, our motto read, "Eternal Vigilance." Great photo on the cover of *Nightwatch* a few years ago: A view of two uniforms sound asleep taken through the driver's side window above the SRPD motto: "Eternal Vigilance."

Long shadows, endless caverns of warm, black cotton swimming in oceans of molasses. Urgent voices. Code this, stat that, paper ripping, Al Dockery's angry voice saying something very rude to someone.

Don't piss off the paramedics, Dock. I'm kind of depending on them. Didn't know if I said that or thought it. Meant to say it but it didn't get a laugh. Probably only thought it.

A thump. Another thump. Another.

Puppet jumping painlessly at the end of his strings.

So many running feet . . .

High clouds, the sky between a crisp blue. Saddleback Mountain in Maine. Small ski operation, big mountain. Stayed there in Rangeley with Aunt Cella when being the hangman's son had me running away from home.

Kirby Flagg was dead. Pop hanged him. I couldn't get away from South River fast enough. Hitched rides across country. Aunt Cella wasn't very friendly when I arrived, but I couldn't think of anywhere else to go. After clearing it with Pop and putting up with my moping for an afternoon, Aunt Cella shoved me out of the house and up on the slopes early the next morning to take a skiing lesson. I learned the wedge and in two weeks hammered that wedge into parallel running, a month later doing all the black diamonds on the mountain.

No one in Maine knew I was the hangman's son. No one except Aunt Cella, and she didn't like to talk about it.

Her husband, dead before I was born, used to be a big-time downhill racer and ski instructor. His pictures were all over the house showing a big, robust man, the huge wooden skis he used in the 'Fifties held over his head in one hand. In fifty-two years of skiing, not so much as a sprained toe. Then, according to Aunt Cella, there was a particularly nasty combination of ice, age, ego, and alcohol when her husband was skiing White Nitro over on Sugarloaf. The result was Clifton Roberts dead from one of those fifty mile an hour off-trail spruce massages.

Aunt Cella did all her crying in private. Her only outward expression of affection was to love the snow. She taught me to love it, too. We traveled all over New England and the names became as old friends: Saddleback, Sugarloaf, Sunday River, Mt. Abram, Wildcat, Loon Mountain, Cannon, Jay Peak, Okemo.

The burning wind tearing at my cheeks as I flew down the trails, past and future brushed aside by my rocketing present.

Then New England ran out of snow, Aunt Cella ran out of patience, and it was time to go back to South River and the hangman.

Another thump. Another.

A thought came to me: If all that thumping was paramedics using a defibrillator on me, I'd probably hurt like hell when I woke up, should I live so long.

REUNION

Voices.

Soft Italian accents fading in and out. I didn't want to open my eyes because once I opened them I would have to stop skiing. The snow was red, though. The sky, too. Light on the other side of my eyelids colored by my blood. I'd already had enough of looking at my own blood.

Dry hiss in my nostrils. I opened my eyes to slits and saw a wobbly smear of images. A little focus and on my left was a bank of video monitors, tubing, lights, and dials. To my right was the profile I was second most familiar with in the world: the father of my mother: Round head, tanned face, sunken cheeks, dark-ringed sunken eyes, and what little hair there was, white and fine. Gaspare DeBello. "Hey, Gasman," I whispered, the inside of my mouth dry as leather.

My grandfather's bushy white eyebrows rose as he turned his head. "Joe? Joe? Hey, Nico! Joe, he's awake!"

A door opened and someone came in from the hall. Big man standing, looking down at me. He had a strong jaw, salt-and-pepper black hair above coal black eyes welled with tears. It was the hangman. "Thank God," he said.

"How're they hangin', Pop?" I joked. A little lame humor to lighten the moment. Dying is such a depressing subject.

Pop smiled at the old gag, took my hand, and held it gently. There was a time when I would have withdrawn my hand from his grasp. Those hands of his had done things that repelled and frightened me. This time, though, it was different. Holding Pop's hand was okay. Being able to hold anyone's hand was okay.

"I'm awright, Pop. Li'l dopey—*Lottle* dopey." I seemed to be slurring my words a mite. "Whudda doc say?"

"Lost a lot of blood, but you'll make it, Joe. You need some rest, but you'll make it."

"Thought they lost you a couple times," added the Gasman. "Popped you so many times with those paddles they was about to serve you up with mushrooms and onions."

"What time? What day izzit?"

With his free hand Pop took the familiar gold pocket watch from his coat pocket, and opened it, the beautiful little chimes playing the opening of Bach's *Little Suite*. There were two sayings engraved inside the case, one in Latin, the other in German. Trying to remember what they were made my head hurt and I quit trying. "Twenty after two in the afternoon, Joe. It's Thursday. You been out three days."

Suddenly the bloodbath at Rizzo's Garage came back in a rush and I called out, "Dock!" I sat part way up and fell back on my pillow, the searing pain in my shoulder bringing me wide awake. My shoulder had some kind of soft cast on it.. "My partner, Pop? The uniforms? What happened to Tobin? Carver? Mac and Pancho?"

The Gasman said to me, "You're in ICU. They said not to bother you with this stuff. Don't want to upset you."

"Does not knowing seem to make me calm?. Tell me what happened."

"Dock's okay, Joe," Pop said. "So are the others, mostly."

"What do you mean, 'mostly?'"

"You lost a lot of blood, Joe," added the Gasman. "Surgeon say you had your bronchial artery cut clean through."

"*Brachial*, Gaspare," corrected the hangman. "Brachial."

"Brachial, bronchial," scoffed my grandfather as he dismissed the pronunciation correction with a wave of his hand. "The big pipe in your arm, Joe. Cut up in there pretty bad, too. You got more stitches than my old britches."

"How many?

"Inside and out over two hundred. Doc says they pieced your pipes, muscles, and tendons together. Your arm and shoulder should be all right after some healing and therapy."

"What about the others?" I repeated.

Pop was still holding onto my hand. "Tobin and Carver," he said. "They both have lumpy heads but will be all right. The docs kept them overnight for observation. Tobin he got a bit of a concussion. Somebody went after them both with a sawed off bat."

Someone had been outside, then, stalking the stalkers. Heavy silence. Pop and the Gasman glanced at each other, then began looking everywhere except at me.

"What?" I demanded. *"What?"*

"Everybody else is okay." Pop moved until he was by the head of the bed and stroked my hair. "The Rizzos are dead, Joe. All three."

My head swam. "Who got Carlo?"

"You did," said the Gasman with just a touch of glee. "One of your slugs got him right between the horns. You got Theo and Tony, too."

I shot Carlo? Tony for sure and Theo only barely possible, but there was no way I got Carlo. When he was pumping another round into that shotgun I hadn't enough strength left to blow my own nose. My headache and my shoulder both were putting up a pretty good scream. I looked again at the hangman's face and saw the pain and worry there. I give his hand a squeeze and said, "I'm okay, Pop. At least until the media gets the story."

"Too late," said the Gasman.

My father gave my hand another squeeze. "Joe, on the TV they already calling it the Cross Street Massacre."

"Did Lt. Crewe get killed?" I asked hopefully. "Or horribly maimed?"

"No," said Pop. "He's fine."

I closed my eyes. "Doc give you any idea when I can get out of here?"

"Eight or ten days. Surgeon wants to make sure you're stable—no blood clots—then ease you into PT while you're here. Make sure he hooked up everything right."

I opened my eyes. "Where is Cherie? Does she know?"

"You're going home with me, Joe," said Pop as he clumsily evaded the question.

"What's with Cherie, Pop? She can take care of me, at least in between her real estate appointments, makeovers, and aerobic sessions."

"You're going home with me," Pop repeated. "A friend of mine is fixing up your old room. You'll be fine there."

I glanced at the Gasman for support and caught a frown on the rebound. "You going to need help for a few weeks, Joe," said my grandfather. "When they discharge you, you go home with your papa. You got telephone, cable, broadband, bathroom, pancakes, a chauffeur—everything you need."

"Okay, guys," I said. "What's the story with Cherie?"

"What makes you think there's a story?" the Gasman asked innocently.

"Oh, I don't know, Grandfather dear," I said with mounting frustration. "Maybe it's because *I'm a fucking detective*."

The Gasman almost put his hand on the dressing that covered my shoulder, then lowered it hesitantly to my forearm. "She's not out there, Joe, okay? Give her some time. She's just a little upset."

"The short version, Gee." I looked at the hangman. "Pop?"

"Cherie moved your stuff out of her apartment, Joe."

"What?" The last tingle of anesthetic seemed to dribble out and die. My head was clear and my shoulder felt like it'd been fed through a Cuisinart. "Okay, guys. Enough of the water torture. What's the whole story?"

"She's just a little upset, Joe," repeated Pop. "After you wound up here she didn't come. Kept bawling about not wanting you to be a cop."

"She wants me to sell real estate. Can you see me trying to bully some poor sap into buying a house in this market?" I paused as I realized I had yet to get the whole Cheri Vitamante story. "Cherie?" I reminded them.

24

Pop rubbed the back of his neck. "Internal Affairs dropped in on Cheri five in the morning Tuesday—"

"Whoa! IAB?"

"Yeah. After they grilled Cherie in her apartment and went through your things—"

"Went through my *things*? What are the charges?"

"No charges, Joe. They said it's just for your shooting board."

"IAB doesn't get involved in shooting boards unless there's a scalp they expect to collect." I glanced at Pop, then closed my eyes against the increasing headache, "So, Cherie's upset."

"Mostly about the reporters," added Pop.

I sighed and leaned back against my pillow. My shoulder was definitely getting into drug-seeking behavior. I pushed my call button. "What about reporters?"

"The front of the apartment house where Cheri lives looks like a camp meeting," joked the Gasman.

"The reporters are only there because of the body count," said Pop. "They making a big deal out of you killing more criminals in the line of duty than anyone else in the city cops."

The Gasman snorted and did an imaginary spit on the floor. "They say you the city's designated hitter."

"Good one," I observed.

A nurse entered wearing hospital camo, one of those flowered smocks designed to convey the impression that one's medical care was now in the hands of neoconservative hippies. Wispy blond hair, thin, and carrying an expression that said she just might not go psychotic before the end of her shift. She cycled the blood pressure cuff, checked the monitor bank, and said to Pop and the Gasman, "You two are going to have to leave. Have you been arguing?"

"No," said Pop guiltily.

"Drugs," I said. "My shoulder is killing me. And, nurse, could you dial a number for me? I gotta make a call."

She was playing with my pipes and suddenly something warm and syrupy seemed to fill every extremity of my being. All pain and feeling floated away

25

upon opiated billows. "No, Detective Torio, you don't need to make a call right now. What you need to do right now is rest. I'll get you an ice bag for your shoulder. You two, out. Come back tomorrow."

"Good-bye Joe," said the Gasman.

I mumbled something incoherent in response.

"You go, too, Mr. Torio."

"See you tomorrow, Joe." I felt Pop release my hand and pat it. After several moments swimming in syrup, I said to the fuzzy black creatures surrounding me, "Who the hell killed Carlo Rizzo?"

They didn't seem to know either.

NO VISITORS

The next day Dock dropped by for a hi-and-goodbye call. Winnie Hewitt from Homicide came by bringing a new face I couldn't place. The fellow was olive-complexioned, shaved bald, and dressed very sharp in a blue suit that fit him like he had been born in it. I felt like I ought to recognize him, but I didn't. For a moment I thought he might be Winnie's current honey, but she quickly introduced him as Miles Kieffer of Homicide up from University Division Detectives. He was married and had no designs on Winnie, at least none that he was willing to share. Seemed like a sharp guy. Said he skied, too. We promised to hurt some flakes together should I heal before all the good snow turned to mashed potatoes.

Couple other cops dropped in, Capt. Finn and Chief Harolds made courtesy calls, and Mrs. Crawford from the Homicide floor cleaning crew brought me some homemade chocolate chip cookies the way I like them, warm and a bit soft. Once I got my cookies, I was about to put in a no visitor's request at the nurse's station. Before I could go into action, however, Lt. Roemer of Internal Affairs stuck his head in through the door. "Got a minute?" he asked gleefully.

So many devastatingly rude expressions were fighting to get in my mouth at the same time I got lockjaw. I nodded at him.

Roemer had one of those gray brush cuts, washed-out blue eyes, and a chin like a manatee. Gray suit, yellow shirt, and a pink and blue striped tie. He looked like the Easter Bunny's uncle. Big smile as he sat down in the chair next to my bed. "Glad to see you're feeling better, Joe."

"I bet. Your wife let you out of the house wearing that tie, Bruce?"

"The pink?" he said, looking down at his tie. He shrugged and looked back at me. "I'm secure in my manhood."

"I wasn't talking about your manhood, Bruce. I was talking about your stupid necktie."

"I'm sorry you don't like it. However, I think it goes rather well with my suit."

"It does bring out the blood vessels in your eyes."

Roemer resisted being led astray. "Joe, I wanted to clear up a few things before your shooting board." Although he was smiling, to me the buzzard looked like he was beginning to circle.

"Do I need a lawyer?" I asked.

"Do you?" he responded smugly.

"Asked you first." The temperature in the room appeared to lower about sixty degrees.

"Why do you think you might need a lawyer, Joe?"

"This is a nation of litigators, Bruce." Roemer hated being called Bruce, which is why I called him that: Helping him accept himself. "Everybody wants to go to court, hit the jackpot, and be on TV. Do you want to be on TV, Bruce?"

"Right now, sergeant, this is simply an information gathering interview." Roemer took a recorder out of his pocket, turned it on, and placed it next to me on the bed. I resisted the impulse to kick it off. He said the time and date, identified me and himself, then looked at me. "Shall we proceed?"

I grinned showing all my teeth. "Let's do."

"Let's begin with Charlie Matthews."

I felt my grin fall off my face. "Matthews? The Reservoir Killer? That was almost twenty years ago. Don't you want to go over the Rizzo thing?"

"We'll get to that. Matthews was your first, wasn't he?"

"First. First what? First date? First arrest? First in the hearts of his countrymen?"

"Your first killing."

The scales fell from my eyes. I was once again being sized up for a psycho-killer-cop wrapper. Establish a pattern of killing and make your case that Torio is a pattern killer. I looked steadily at him. "Actually, Brucie, when I was around eleven or twelve I had occasion to kill a hydrophobic raccoon. I believe that was my first intentional killing, unless you also want to include lower life forms. Among Japanese beetle bards in my Aunt Cella's garden, I'm still regarded as something of an ethnic cleanser."

"You shot Matthews."

"Charlie Matthews shot my T.O., Al Dockery, and me."

"What I recall from reading your statement, sergeant, is that you fired at Matthews, striking him in the upper arm, before he shot you."

"Matthews had a piece on my partner when we came to his house to arrest him. He was waving the gun at Dock—"

"Your partner, Sgt. Albert Dockery," Roemer interrupted.

"That's right. We ID'd ourselves and told him to drop the piece and bite the floor. He did neither. Instead he took a wild shot in my direction and missed. I returned fire and winged—"

"Are you that much of a marksman, sergeant?"

"Do you have a lot of success with this interrogation technique, lieutenant? Ask a question then interrupt the answer to ask another question?"

"Answer the question."

"Which one? About the shoot-out with Matthews, or my marksmanship?" When Roemer didn't answer, I cocked my head to one side and said, "I hit Matthews in the arm, trying to disable him, then Matthews fired and hit Dockery, swung on me, fired again, and hit me in the shoulder—same shoulder, too, the son of a bitch. I fired again, killing him. As to my shooting ability, I hit what I'm aiming at."

"With your second shot, where did you hit him?"

"In the head."

"Why in the head?"

"That's what I was aiming at."

"In other words, you were shooting to kill."

"Just as dead as I could get him."

I waited while Roemer adjusted his smirk and then said, "'Rookie Nails Reservoir Killer,'" he quoted from some old newspaper article. "You became quite a media hero when you took out Charlie Matthews, didn't you?"

"Matthews tortured, mutilated, raped, and killed little girls and dumped their remains in the city reservoir, lieutenant. Where do you stand on water quality?"

Lt. Roemer crossed his legs and played with the trouser crease on the uphill knee. "The media also loved you a year later when you killed the Boy Wolf, didn't it? Couple of uniforms and you and Dockery got yourself a genuine serial killer. Did you like those headlines?"

I laughed at him. "You think I'm after ink? Do you have any idea how many nutball calls and letters I got after I dropped Matthews and Hellerman? Jerks knocking on my door at all hours, TV blow-dries stalking me, sticking mikes in my face, IAB slimeballs coming out of the woodwork—No offense," I offered.

He didn't quite carry off a "None taken." He tried, though. A try is as good as a victory to people who don't bet on outcomes.

"I still have a guy who calls me up first thing in the morning every so often with death threats," I said. "I'm surprised he hasn't called me here yet."

"Tell me about Hellerman," urged Roemer.

"Jay Hellerman raped, tortured, and murdered at least seven boys that we know of. He was holding two more hostage in his house on Soldier Heights and was threatening to kill them."

"What about calling in SWAT or Crisis Management?"

"As you know from reading my report, Brucie, I called in both. I also called in a tactical supervisor and an ambu—"

"Hellerman was a lawyer, wasn't he?" Roemer uncrossed his legs and leaned forward.

"—lance," I completed. "Yeah. He did personal injury work."

"You don't like lawyers, do you?"

"I like them a lot more than I like spammers, suicide bombers, or TV evangelists. What's the matter with you,

Roemer? Didn't you go to the academy or put in any time on the street? You're just jealous of real cops, is that it? Those boys and I ran out of time and options. It was either take out Hellerman or sit by and watch him kill numbers eight and nine."

"Those boys were both gay, weren't they?"

"Not right then they weren't."

"I meant—"

"I know what you meant, Brucie, and their lives were still protected under the Constitution of the United States and the laws of this state."

Two beats, then Roemer said, "You dropped Hellerman with a single pistol shot through the head?"

"I did. Very proud of that shot, in fact. Thirty feet, thrifty, and minimal environmental impact."

"Why did you shoot him in the head?"

It was like talking to a jockstrap full of wing nuts. "He was armed and using the boys as a shield, Bruce. His head was the only real killing point I could see."

"You could hardly say you saw his head. Your partner testified that there couldn't have been more than four or five inches between the two boys' heads. At thirty feet you placed a slug between them and right between Jay Hellerman's eyes. Excellent shooting, albeit a rather familiar placement." He waited for a response.

I flashed on that moment. Mean ugly bastard, gun in each hand, screaming at me, the boys crying, and I did a quick threat assessment. If I fired, I might kill one of the boys. If I didn't fire, Hellerman would certainly kill them both while Dock and I stood there and watched.

"I said your shooting was excellent."

I shook off the memory and looked at Breadloaf Mountain through my window. Nice and sunny, the temperature in the teens. The skiing would be great today. "Can you hit anything with a gun, lieutenant?"

Roemer frowned. "Why?"

"Well, if you're a big time Olympic gold medal shooter or a super chief grand master kleagle in the NRA, your compliment on my shooting would give me a glow from my ears to my toes. On the other hand, if you shoot like the usual run of IAB putz, I don't care."

When Roemer's face stopped turning blue, he glanced down at a small spiral pad in his hand. "The year you took down Hellerman, you also dropped a two-bit drug dealer named Eldridge Coumbs. At the Coumbs shooting board you said he came at you with a gun. You were by yourself that time. No partner to back up your story."

"The forensic evidence supported my testimony, however. A drug dealer named Karen Willard had been shot and killed. On a tip, Dock and I were canvassing the occupants of this fleabag tenement on the broken end of Dixon. We were told someone in there had witnessed the killing. I knocked on the door of someone who had a vested interest in not being canvassed: the shooter."

"By chance?"

"If checking out a tip is chance."

"The media was pretty cool toward you on the Coumbs shooting."

"People like drugs a whole lot more than they like their children getting hacked to pieces," I answered. "Go figure."

"You shot Coumbs in the head, too."

"He was shooting at me from around a corner in a dark hallway. For some reason, it was his head sticking around the corner and not his ass."

"If you're so good a shot, why didn't you just shoot Coumbs's gun out of his hand?"

"Is that you, John Wayne?" I laughed at him and shook my head. "I learned my lesson about winging perps and shooting guns out of hands with Matthews. After three months of therapy on my shoulder, I don't do that anymore."

Roemer stared at me for a moment, then looked again at his notes. "Last September a year ago you killed a sixty year old drifter you say came after you outside your apartment and tried to kill you." Roemer glanced up at me. "This homeless old dipso supposedly used a six-hundred dollar Beretta, the numbers conveniently ground off." As Roemer continued, I remained silent. This was the one that still kept me up some nights.

"For some unspecified reason, Torio," Roemer continued, "this bum from down in the Zone took it upon himself to go all of the way to West Beverly to kill you, and managed to pick up a six-hundred dollar weapon for the job along the way. According to the record, you said you suspected an attempted hit by Nick Battaglia, but you couldn't connect Battaglia, or anyone in his organization, with Baines."

"No, I couldn't."

"Three days later," continued Bruce, "Battaglia's guts were spread all over his cell."

"Note that I was nowhere near Books Prison at the time in question," I reminded him.

Roemer nodded. "I know. You were in front of a shooting board when Battaglia was killed."

"Alibis-R-Us," I said. "I cannot praise them too highly."

Roemer pointed a bony finger at me. "At that board, you couldn't explain why a professional crime family would give a contract on you to an old wino civilian, and you couldn't explain how that old wino managed to get his hands on a six-hundred dollar semi-automatic. No one ever could trace that Beretta. A couple of the newspapers and news anchors hinted at the piece being a throw-down. Your throw-down, Torio."

"You don't see anything wrong with that, Brucie?"

His eyebrows went up. "Wrong how?"

"First, treating news opinions as actionable evidence. Second, me blowing away some old bum and planting a Beretta on him. A bum's just a bum, Jack, but a Beretta is a whole lot of handgun. Some thirty-dollar Saturday night special I can see, but did you ever hear of a cop using a Beretta as a throw-down? Before you can afford to do that you need to be making a whole lot more than I get."

"About Baines—"

I was getting tired of the whole thing. "Lt. Rugioli, the investigating officer, was happy with the shoot," I said. "There was GSR on Baines's left hand and he was left-handed."

"You know as well as I, sergeant, that such things can be staged. And if Nicky Batts wanted to push your button, why on earth would he pick a shaky old wino to do the job?"

"All I have are guesses."

"This is informal."

"Isn't that what they told Saddam Hussein?"

His face became dark and angry. "I do not find you at all amusing, Torio."

"Another tragic failure to communicate." I tried to ease my shoulder into a more comfortable position. The tension was pulling at my stitches. "Okay, Brucie, my best guess: Baines was a chronic alcoholic. He was at the stage where he would have tried to shoot the President if there was a bottle in it for him."

"Why Battaglia and why you?"

"It was a clever move. It didn't matter if Baines killed me or not. With me dead, the Battaglia organization wasn't implicated and it had me out of its hair. With the bum dead, though, it looks just like what it looked like and I'm up to my ears in an ocean of bad press and Internal Affairs. Either way Battaglia has my little pebble out of his shoe. It worked, too. Dock and I were taken off the Battaglia Organized Crime Task Force and sent back to Homicide to turn down the heat."

"Then Nicky Batts was murdered."

"He was indeed." I thought a moment. "A setup of some kind, maybe?"

"What kind?"

"This business with the Rizzo brothers might be a part of it. The Rizzos are part of the Battaglia family. Maybe it was someone from the Scozarri organization who tipped off Capt. Finn to have us show up at the Rizzo Brothers' garage that night." I frowned as I recalled Tony Rizzo's words as he shoved that knife into my shoulder.

"What little thought just pranced through your mind, sergeant?"

I frowned. "Something Tony Rizzo said when he put that sticker in the back of my shoulder. He said, 'Dago Frank says "Hi."'"

"Don Francesco Scozarri?"

"Do you know any other Dago Franks?"

"The Battaglia and Scozarri families are blood enemies. Why would one of Battaglia's boys give you a message from Frank Scozarri?"

"I am fresh out of answers. What's your guess, Bruce?"

"We're not here to find out what I think," he shot back.

"Too bad 'cause I'm about out of gas, myself. You want to talk at all about the raid on the Rizzos?"

After a pause, he said, "Very well." He leaned forward to check the amount of tape he had left in his recorder, then leaned back in his chair. "Leave out nothing."

I began with, "It was a dark and stormy night. Somewhere a lieutenant was barking."

Eventually we got through it all without additional medication, illumination, or hostility. Roemer was gone, finally, and I was still out of answers for why the alleged message from Don Scozarri. I also didn't know who shot Carlo Rizzo and why I was still alive. When the paramedics reached me, I already had a tourniquet on my shoulder. I would have put that tourniquet on my shoulder myself had I thought of it. I hadn't thought of it. I didn't have a shotgun for a crank when I was in that parts room, in any event; Carlo was still using it. I could have tightened it up with any number of other things in that parts room, though. Maybe Carlo put that fan belt on my shoulder and used Theo's shotgun for a crank himself. Then, filled with remorse at what his brothers had done to me, he picked up my gun and shot himself between the eyes.

I slowly shook my head as I realized that explanation was the most reasonable one I could come up with for what had happened.

FLEETING FAME

The next day, after a very thin lunch of onion soup, oyster crackers, something unknowable between two pieces of dry rye bread, with simulated raspberry gelatin for dessert, I took a nap and was awakened by a tall thin fellow who looked as though he'd never managed to escape from prep school: long wavy hair, rimless glasses, delicate features, and a faded blue sports coat over faded blue denims. On his feet were beat up black loafers with no sox. In the winter, yet. "Hi," he said as though he had fallen out of a sexual enhancement commercial for nerds. "My name is Wendell Hunt and I'm the story editor for *Criminal Menace.*"

"Does it pay well?" I asked.

His eyebrows went up, then he smiled. "Quite well, actually."

"It's good to have work, especially in troubled economic times. Your mother must be very proud. How is she?"

He looked confused for a moment, frowned, and then continued, "Is it possible you aren't familiar with our show? *Criminal Menace* has been the top network cop show for the past three seasons."

"Sure. I watched a few episodes," I said. "Even saw one last night. You get pretty desperate for entertainment in a place like this. What can I do for you, Mr. Hunt?"

"We're considering doing three episodes based on cases of yours, Detective Torio. There would even be a new character in the series based on you."

"Golly. Can you get Gregory Peck for the part?"

Another frown. "Gregory Peck died in Two thousand and three."

36

"Ought to come cheap, huh? Loved his Ahab in *Moby Dick*. Don't suppose you could have an FBI agent with a leg made of whalebone, huh?. Did you know Ahab's first mate went on to start a chain of coffee houses?"

The confusion on Wendell's face grew deeper. He then recovered by ignoring the reality of the previous two minutes.

"This could be very big for you, detective: The Reservoir Killer, the Boy Wolf, topped off by the terminal clash with the Rizzo brothers. You're interesting and you can cash in on it. Even more important, you can get your true story out there."

I chuckled at that and said, "Go away, Wendell."

His look of confusion redlined. "Go away? *Go away?* I'm talking a substantial sum of money, here, Detective Torio. I came here all the way from Los Angeles to discuss our offer. We're even thinking of Benjamin Bratt for the part."

I laughed until it caused too much pain. "Look, Mr. Hunt—Wendell—I hate to disappoint you, but your show couldn't tell my story or the stories of any of the serial killers I've dealt with any more than it could cure erectile dysfunction disorder."

"We tell the story of a different serial killer every week."

"No, you don't. You tell the stories of imaginary monsters like Bigfoot, Nessie, and Myron the Moose." I picked up my water pitcher and poured myself a healthy dollop of South River Municipal. I took a sip, replaced my cup, and put my head back on the pillow.

Wendell folded his arms across his chest, his body language not very open and affirming according to my old therapist, Betty Grable. "What is your problem, detective?"

"Concerning your show?" I asked, attempting to narrow somewhat the scope of the inquiry.

"Yes, concerning the show."

"Okay. Every week, Wendell, with different faces and almost different words, you run the same yarn over and over again: *Jaws*. There's a shark in the water—eek, eek—lots of blood—eek, eek—with a new wrinkle each week about how that week's shark kills—left fin, right fin, a piece of tail, every other tooth, a thousand cuts using fishing lures, undercooked tuna, whatever. Perhaps the killer's motivation might be some bizarre manifestation of a thoughtless Christmas present the guy got back in '88 that now has him sticking tiny toy reindeer up his victim's butts until they explode. Good *versus* Evil, with our killer, of course, playing Evil trope and your plucky little band of FBI geeks playing Good tropes as they babble out pop psychology maxims and tell each other stuff they already know regarding profiling or evidence-gathering technicalities."

"You're a cop, aren't you? Serial killers *are* evil." Wendell threw up his hands in exasperation. "Can anything be more self-evident than that?"

"You ever read Joel Norris's work on serial murder? *Serial Killers: The Growing Menace?*"

"Who?"

"I was a fool to ask." I pushed my call button. "While we're waiting for my nurse to come and toss your ass into the street, Wendell, I want you to understand that the acting and directing in your show are actually rather good. They cannot rise above the scripts, however. The stories have achieved the absolutely impossible: they suck and blow at the same time simply from sheer ignorance of the subject matter. I wouldn't trust your writers to compose a ketchup bottle label much less any part of my life or career, or the lives and careers of any of the criminals I've investigated. Besides, in none of the episodes I've seen have your intrepid sleuths ever gotten the bad guys."

"What are you talking about? If the serial killers aren't dead by the end of the episode, they're in custody," he insisted.

"I was talking about the bad guys, Wendell."

"Aren't the serial killers the bad guys?" Wendell asked, curling his fingers to make quotation marks around the words: bad guys.

"Don't make quotation marks with your fingers, Wendell. You look stupid enough wearing loafers with no sox when there's six inches of fresh snow on the ground."

He was silent for a good twenty seconds, then he started up again. "Then who *are* the bad guys?"

I sighed as I faced the prospect of casting yet one more pearl before a TV oinker. "Your killers seem to wake up some morning after losing a job or getting jilted by a girlfriend and say to themselves, 'By golly, I know what will perk me up.' Then he takes a Seventeenth Century caulking hammer and begins popping short blond left-handed female Libertarians from Poughkeepsie in the head. Feel free to use that in an upcoming episode."

"What are you getting at?"

"Serial killers don't blossom all of a moment, Wendell, and it's not a free choice. They are made piece-by-piece over years. The makers of your killers are rarely hinted at, almost never identified, and there's no correspondence between the killer's wacky signature and what was done to them. Your show isn't about serial killers. You're doing monster movies and making a fortune out of it. Be happy with that and get the hell out of here."

"Fuck you!" said Wendell as he turned and exited.

"Your welcome!" I hollered after him. "Glad I could help!"

The nurse, a weary-looking brunette in her fifties named Cindy, stood in the open door, glanced at the departing Wendell, then raised an eyebrow at me. "Rehabilitating our media relationships are we?"

"We do what we can," we responded.

That night as I tried to put my nagging shoulder aside and get some sleep, My encounter with Wendell Hunt made me think of my other missed opportunity for entertainment fame and fortune. Years ago Lydia Jenks, the mystery novelist, invited me out for dinner at Beauchamp's in West Bluff overlooking the river. I'd never eaten there before—a shrimp cocktail at Beauchamp's costing a bit more than my best suit—so I agreed. I was flattered and curious. Lydia Jenks was very famous, was researching a cop novel loosely based on the Jay Hellerman case, and I'd never read any of her stuff, which was another reason I agreed to meet with her.

Our discussion never quite made it to dessert. After giving the waiter our orders ("excellent" selections both, Anton said), Lydia Jenks asked me to describe Jay Hellerman. I began with his birth to a migrant farm family in Texas, and once I described the nightmare into which Hellerman had been born, beginning with physical abuse, sexual abuse, incest, drugs, bizarre cultic rituals, the brain damage he suffered from his father repeatedly smashing his head against whatever was handy, as well as the endless procession of radically sick things he was forced to do with bodies stolen from their graves, Ms. Jenks impatiently shook her head. "We can't go into much of that," she said, "if at all."

"Oh?"

"It complicates things. You don't want an action crime story to be immersed in too many facts, too many murders, or too many motives. That kind of confusion doesn't sell. The readers like a clear issue, a simple theme."

"Good versus Evil," I said.

"Exactly."

I held out my hands. "Lydia, there are no simple serial-killer stories—not about real serial killers."

"We can make it simple." She gave me the big smile. "Joe, if I described Hellerman's childhood the way you just did, it would make him into some kind of *victim*—a sympathetic character—not a fearsome killer who needed to be exterminated."

"All of which doesn't alter the fact that Hellerman *was* a victim," I said, not quite hiding the incredulity in my voice. "The behavior he exhibited as an adult is a direct consequence of the kind of punishment and brain damage he absorbed as a child and young teen. It loaded him and aimed him like a gun." From her expression I had the feeling I had just been lecturing a brick wall.

"Sergeant Torio, you brought neither Matthews nor Hellerman in for psychiatric treatment. You killed them both."

"All that is evidence of are the kinds of choices those two men left me. Even so, if you kill a mad dog to save yourself or your community, that doesn't alter the fact that the dog was suffering from hydrophobia."

40

Her eyebrows went up. "You think serial murder is a disease?"

"A symptom of a particular type and degree of abuse."

Lydia shook her head. "No. The readers won't buy it. My editor certainly wouldn't buy it."

"'We're not here to educate anyone or change anything,'" I said, quoting an imaginary marketing director. "'we're here to sell books and dramatic rights.'"

"Be practical, Joe. Look at the commercial difference between the Aileen Wuornos story—the Jean Smart production—where they did go into Wuornos's background and shed a tear for her abusive childhood, against all of the factual and fictional treatments of Ed Gein's career from *Psycho* and *The Texas Chainsaw Massacre* to Buffalo Bill in *Silence of the Lambs*. And no one gives a damn why Ed Gein became Ed Gein."

"Point taken," I said. "Compared to the real Ed Gein, Wuornos had the bigger body count, too." I smiled at her and put down my fork, my crab salad untouched. "Some people can't even catch a break in an auto crash." I got up from the table.

"Where are you going?"

Loudly enough for the entire restaurant to hear, I said in a high squeaky voice, "Sexual enhancement, my foot! I told you those pills wouldn't work, lady." I huffily swished my way from the restaurant and left Lydia Jenks with the check. So much for my collaborative writing career.

Too bad, really. I had been looking forward to the prune whip. Hadn't had any prune whip since Aunt Cella died.

That's dishonest. What I had really been looking forward to was seeing Jay Hellerman's old man finally being held accountable. Still couldn't get it out of my head, that TV ambush interview with Roger Hellerman. *"If he did those horrible things, Jay is no son of mine."* But, you go after Roger, then you have to go after Roger's old man, then his grandfather, and on up the family tree until history runs out. Too complicated.

So the serial-killer prevention tool bag was still going to be limited to finding a bunch of bodies and then eliminating the human weapon who was twisted into finding love, sexual gratification, and meaning through the pain, degradation, and deaths of others. And about the folks who forged and loaded that weapon? Well, how parents raise their kids is none of our business unless they smoke cigarettes in the home or fail to drive green or recycle. Trouble is, there were no "Evil" guys. The parents who made Jay Hellerman into a weapon were themselves victims of the same disease. As another serial killer of my acquaintance once said, "It's a way of life passed down from fist to mouth from one generation to the next."

About ten o'clock I hobbled on down to the hospital's deserted floor lounge and sorted though all the old magazines for something to read. By midnight I dozed off, "Flower Arranging: Bringing Healthful Happiness Into Your Life" but half-read on my chest.

Nearing the end of my stay at Breadloaf University Hospital, I had a visit from Dr. Margaret Grable, a former cop who had taken a bullet on the job and had thereby revealed to her that her life's calling was doing anything other than bleeding to death in a dark alley. She settled on psychiatry, got a student loan, and went to school. Curiously enough, her clientele was about equally divided between ex cons, cops, and hockey moms. Her skin was the color of Tootsie Rolls, her hair left black and cropped close to her skull, her face and figure plump, her eyes very dark and very sharp. She wore a lime green pantsuit with a yellow, black, and orange silk scarf around her neck to hide the scar from the bullet she took. I was sitting up in my chair and stood as she entered the room. "It's Betty Grable," I said.

"Joe DiMaggio as I live and breathe," she greeted with a grin. "Together again."

"All I need is a little piece of paper signed."

"Ah, yes, the little piece of paper. The department wants me to testify to your mental stability before they'll allow you back on the street with a firearm."

"Silly old department. You could write out a note now," I suggested hopefully. "Save everybody a trip."

Then she laughed that special laugh of hers that sounded like a horse imitating a jackass. After the hee-haw laugh, she said, "No, no, no, Joe. A number of sessions, at least. You've been through a traumatic series of events. You've almost died, you're credited with ending the lives of three brothers and leaving their poor widowed mother grieving all over the media, your principle love relationship is down the crapper, and you're going to move back in with your father, the man you blame for most of the troubles in your life. Did I forget to mention the nightmares and the obsession with suicide? Gobs and gobs of important things to chew on before I even get close to signing that little piece of paper, sweetie. Just thought I'd drop on by to see how ready you are to work."

"I'm ready," I lied.

"Excellent. Since that's the case, I have an assignment for you."

"What?"

"I want you to begin by writing the story of your life, from day one to the present. Try and do some every day. I'll check during our weekly meetings and count the new pages."

"Write my—What for?"

"Want me to sign your duty papers, Joe?"

"Is that why?"

She pointed a finger at me. "Sharp as a tack. So, how are you doing today, Joe?"

"Fine."

That jackass laugh again as she turned and walked out of the room. I never should have told Betty about the waiting-for-the-hangman game I used to play as a child. It probably made me sound as though I had issues.

TO MARKET, TO MARKET

Days of decreasing dosages of pain killers and increasing dosages of PT later, I was sent home on a bitter cold day. There was a heavy overcast promising blizzard grade precip, the dense traffic huddling its way down Thirty-fourth in clouds of exhaust and ice dust. The road surface was paved with old ice and sand. I was in the passenger seat of Gaspare DeBello's old gray Pontiac huddled inside the thin overcoat the Gasman had brought with him when he came to pick me up at the hospital. Within the thin wool gloves, my fingertips were curled into my palms as I attempted to conserve warmth. The plaid trousers, yellow mock turtle pullover, and black and orange diamond pattern sweater were thin, too large, and seemed left over from Martha Washington's garage sale. Everything reeked of mothballs, which I thought was supposed to have been banned by the EPA.

The shoes the Gasman brought for me to wear were black and white wing tips a size too large. The green watch cap, at least, fit. I'm never grateful enough for one-size-fits-all. The vehicle moved gently into the Five Corners intersection and stopped at the light, a slight slide to the left as the wheels locked and the car probed the ice chunks and potholes for an entertaining place to come to rest. The tension against possible impact had my shoulder muttering.

"You know, Gasman," I said diplomatically, "they invented anti-lock brakes a long time ago. They really work."

"Lots of good miles left on the Pontiac," he declared as he patted the dash with a gloved hand raising a not inconsiderable quantity of dust. "Are you riding all right, Joe?"

"The only real risk I face is dying of exposure in this rolling refrigerator of yours. When are you going to get a new car, Gee, or at least get the heater on this wreck fixed?"

"Hey, Joe, you want some cheese with all that whine?"

I glared at him. "Don't give me that crap, Gee. It has to be ten below in here. Where's my parka? My ski gloves? You must've lifted this moth-eaten old rag off of Al Capone's corpse."

"Evidence, Joe. Your coat and gloves were on the floor in Rizzos' showroom. CSU tagged and bagged 'em. Those are my clothes from storage."

"Why didn't you get me my own clothes, Gee? This stuff of yours has to be from the 'Forties. I look like I just fell off the boat."

"All your stuff needed to be cleaned, Joe. It's at the house now but that was out of my way. You'll have your own stuff soon enough."

"Cleaned?" I asked. "Everything?"

My grandfather cocked his head to one side, one eye on the traffic ahead. "Yeah. See, Cherie tossed out your Dr Pepper along with all your clothes and stuff. She kept all the cans for the deposit, if you know what I mean."

That shut me up. I never thought my relationship with Cherie Vitamante was ideal, but pouring Dr Pepper all over my stuff revealed an ugly and previously unrecognized facet. I looked to my right and saw the multi-colored side of Gianelli's Five Corners Dairy. The building took up a quarter of the city block. The windows where pedestrians could purchase cones and sundaes were closed for the winter.

Summers the hangman used to take me there for ice cream in a sugar cone. My favorite was black raspberry. Pop always picked chocolate. We would sit at the picnic tables in the shade and watch the setting sun reflect off Breadloaf's west face. Once Billy Roth's joke made me the hangman's son at school, though, all that went away. I hadn't had an ice cream in years.

The light changed and I watched the dairy move from view as the ancient Pontiac crossed Alexander and angled right onto the Old North Cross-town.

"Why didn't Pop pick me up?"

"Nico has a class he teaches at ESCC. When he gets off I'm picking him up so we can go to Cherie's and get your car."

My eyebrows went up. "He teaches?"

"Sure. Part time faculty. You know, adult education."

"Pop is *teaching* at East Shore Community College? What's he teach? Gibbet one-oh-one? Famous Executions? Hemp through history?"

Gaspare DeBello glared at me. "Landscape gardening," he said. He took a breath and calmed down a bit. "Joe, this bad blood between you and your father—"

"Can it, Gee. It's none of your business."

My grandfather hauled off and punched my left shoulder hard enough to make the right shoulder rattle.

"Ow!"

"None of my business?" His face went red as he went into vapor lock for a second. *"None of my business?* Boy, I was tossing cons in the yard before your daddy ever got to play with his first piece of clothesline." He was looking at me and the car was sliding sideways. "I can still bust you like a twig, kid. Are you my grandson?"

"Yeah—" I tried pointing toward the traffic.

"Is Nicolo the husband of my poor dead Angelina?"

"Sure, but—"

"If it's not *my business*, young Snodgrass, whose is it? We are *family.*"

"I'm sorry, Gee," I said, urgently pointing toward the road.

He turned his head in time to miss a bread truck. "You're forty-six years old, Joe. It's damn time you quit sulking because your father isn't a microchip developer or big-time dot-com billionaire."

We rode in strained silence for the next three blocks. Both of my shoulders hurt. The old screw was still pretty strong for being in his . . . *nineties?* I tried to do a little math in my head, but the number kept coming out too high. In two years or so my grandfather would be a hundred years old. Everything seemed to grow a sickening loss of permanence. As the car pulled up at the Thirtieth Street light, I looked at him. "I'm sorry, Gee. I meant no disrespect. But what am I supposed to do? Pop's this guy I used to live with who never let me know him. Every now and then he'd go to work at the Graybar Hilton and break people's necks. It messed with my mind."

"What he did at Books, Joe, was carry out court orders and he did a damned good job of it. You scared of the rope?"

I waved my left hand at him. "After what Pop taught me about the family business, Gasman, I could be a hangman myself. You want to know how old I was when Pop began sharing his craft with me?"

"No."

"I don't remember either. I was that young. What I do remember was a traumatic day at nursery school being dragged in front of the principal and then in front of a counselor because a teacher caught me showing another boy how to make a hangman's knot out of a venetian-blind cord."

The Gasman chuckled and nodded. "Yeah. I remember that one." He shook his head and laughed again. "Nico and I both show up in uniform at her office. When she found out Nico was a real hangman that woman had to go change her panties."

I fought down the desire to laugh. This was serious stuff. "I was the one who had to spend the next year being referred to as, 'that poor child.'"

"What you want? You want a judge, a cop, maybe a lawyer for a father?"

"Better than a hangman."

"They all hang people, Joe. In this state they used to, anyways. Now it's the needle. If I remember right, Detective Sergeant Torio of Homicide, you've used the facilities a couple of times yourself."

"Formerly of Homicide," I corrected.

The executions of Collins and Pruitt flashed through my mind. Collins, lanky and dark, went to the table stiff as a plank. Pruitt, chubby and bald, went screaming and pissing himself. Both were there compliments of Joe Torio and the criminal justice system. They had raped and murdered a twelve year old girl down by the east end of Canal Park, then did it again to another girl four days later in St. George. "If you don't give those two a ride on the needle, who qualifies?" the prosecution had argued during sentencing. Who indeed?

The Gasman was still making his point.

"Doctors, lawyers, Indian chiefs, housewives, all those nice folks on the juries. In this state, they decide if a killer gets a death sentence or not. What about a state senator or governor? Wouldn't you be proud to have a governor for a father, Joe? The lawmakers set the rules about who lives and dies and the governor can stop it anytime he wants. And anytime *they* want, the voters in this state can decide they don't want the garbage taken out anymore. Everybody's got a hand in an execution."

"It's different, Gee. You know that. All of that stuff you talk about in the end comes down to some single individual who actually takes his hands, puts that rope around someone's neck, and springs the trap. Now it's shooting the juice, pulling that trigger, or throwing that switch. It's using those hands to take a life. It's not just a job."

"I seem to recall half a dozen or more corpses with your bullet holes in them, Joe."

"They were all self-defense."

The Gasman shrugged. "That's what an execution is, Joe: society's inadequately slow self-defense."

Approaching Twenty-third, there was some construction ahead that was blocking traffic. As he went past the numbered street, Gaspare veered the car right onto Hollis. There was a crack in the cloud cover allowing a touch of blue to lighten the gray. I stared through the pitted windshield at the parting clouds high over Sixteenth. "You know the thing Pop used to tell the condemned—the 'your life is over' thing?"

"Yes."

"That's what I heard bedtimes instead of *The Cat in the Hat*. I used to call it *The Goose In The Noose.*"

Gaspare DeBello laughed and waved a hand in dismissal. "Ah, Joe, how have you ever lived this long?"

"Amazing, isn't it?"

"What's this 'formerly-of-Homicide' thing you said? You talk to Finn yet? Find out where they going to put you?"

"Yeah. He visited me in my room day before yesterday. I'm on Cold Cases until I can get my arm working and the shrink to sign my papers."

"Any trouble there? Getting your papers signed, I mean?"

I let out a bit of a sigh. "Good question."

"You got a good answer?" my grandfather asked, his bushy white eyebrows arched.

"The shrink wants me to write the story of my life. She didn't seem very flexible about that."

"I will be your personal first reader and in the movie I want the grandfather played by Daniel Craig."

"You don't look anything like Daniel Craig."

"Hah! If I wanted someone who looked like me I'd play the part myself," he said.

As the car reached Pike Street, Gaspare turned right and pulled up to the curb in front of a big white three-story Victorian skirted by a wide veranda, the familiar row of rocking chairs from my youth still there. Five of them.

Spring evenings and summer afternoons the hangman would be out there along with old corrections bulls, old cops, and the occasional old ex-con, all of them passing the time, drinking iced tea and Dr Pepper, rockers creaking on the plank decking. Listening to those stories, that also got me thinking about becoming a cop. First, came the old cops and their stories of standing between the citizenry and the monster. These balding guys with big bellies, half of them divorced and heavily into the sauce, were rough talking, matter-of-fact, covered in scars, and weighed down by the hopelessness of their mission, the media's scorn, and the disrespect of the populace. Yet each one had something to hang onto: A particularly nasty perp taken down, a kidnapped little girl rescued in the nick of time, a gang of toughs faced down and jailed to protect a candy store owner, a destitute old woman's purse retrieved from a punk.

Knights. Author Joseph Wambaugh had named them well: blue knights. That's what I wanted to be. I wanted to pit my worth against the monster and have it take my measure.

"What are you thinking about, Joe?" asked the Gasman.

"Cops. Why I became a cop."

"Regrets?" he asked.

"Only a few thousand," I confessed. I turned and smiled at him. "But there have been a few times when I faced the monster, turned it back, and was glad to have been there to do it. What about you, Gee? Why'd you become a corrections officer?"

He got a faraway look in his eyes and chuckled. "I never did become a corrections officer, Joe. When I went to get a job at Books I signed up to be a prison guard; a bull."

"Why?"

He shrugged. "That was the big-D Depression. I was out of a job and had a brand new pregnant wife. It was getting to be a choice which side of the bars I was going to be on." He nodded to himself. "I always was strong and I spoke English okay, so they took me on. I cracked a lot of skulls, had to kill a few to save a few, met some really great guys on both sides of the bars, and got to do a bit of good here and there. I helped keep a lot of really bad ones off the streets for awhile and retired as yard captain." He nodded again. "I did okay." He grinned and poked me in the ribs. "Faced that monster and kicked his ass." He nodded toward Pop's house. "Go on in, Joe. It's open."

"Thanks for the ride, Gee." I grinned and nodded toward the clothes. "And for the period costume." From next to my feet I picked up the cheap tote bag full of plastic crap from the hospital: soap dish, basin, barf tray, skin cream, talcum powder, toothpaste, toothbrush, a tube of shaving cream, and a disposable razor that cut through whiskers only far enough to get a good grip on them in preparation for mass root extractions. My laptop was also in there.

"When I check in on you two," said the Gasman, "I want to find father and son, not a couple of alley cats." He held out his hand.

"I'll do my best, Gee." Using my left hand I gave his a good squeeze. "Thanks again for the ride."

He nodded toward the house. "Oh, your father's friend Caitlyn is in there putting your stuff away, so don't shoot her."

"I don't have a gun."

He grinned. "I was talking about your mouth."

I got out of the old Pontiac, shut the door, adjusted my sling, and watched as the Gasman pulled away from the curb and drove west on Pike. I loved that old screw. A hundred years old and he'd probably make it, too.

Turning around I allowed my gaze to move over the front of the house in which I had spent my childhood. It still dominated the block. Too big and too expensive for a prison guard moonlighting as a hangman. But Nicolo Torio and his new bride wanted a big house for the huge family they were going to have. That was why my mother did cleaning and the hangman took on landscaping and gardening. The house was all paid for now and the hangman's second job had turned into a money making enterprise. But he lived there all alone. What family he did have had either died or bailed on him.

When I had lived there, the house had been dark beige with still darker trim. With its heavy slate roof, ground floor corner tower, porch roof and French doors looking like the maw of some beast, the house had always seemed to brood. Now it was white and trimmed with bright red shutters. The door was red, too. Very light and happy looking. A snow thrower had cleared the path from the front door all of the way to the curb, as well as the sidewalk and the driveway that went from the street past the west end of the house to the garage in back. I remembered Pop and I doing that with snow shovels a long time ago.

"Joe? Joe?"

I looked at the front door. Standing on the porch in front of the open door was a woman wearing flair jeans, a white blouse, and a fleece vest crowded with warm colors. Her red hair was so dark it was almost brown, lightly streaked with pale gray at the temples. As I came closer, I saw that she was athletically slim and looked to be in her mid-fifties. Climbing the five stairs to the porch, I stopped in front of her. "Are you Caitlyn?"

She stepped aside, smiled widely, and held out her hand. I gave it a left-handed squeeze. "I am and get in out of the cold. You must be freezing."

"Seems to be a nip in the air."

"I just finished putting your belongings away, Joe. You have clean clothes and maybe you want to change."

"Why? Is there something amiss with my apparel?"

"It appears to have been stolen from a Goodwill bin."

"Actually," I said with mock pride, "my ensemble is from the Gaspare DeBello collection." I glanced down at the wingtips. "Neat, huh?"

"The bee's knees," she said. "I especially like the slap shoes."

"So you're Pop's friend?"

"One of them."

"Did you pick the new house colors?"

"As a matter of fact, Nico and I did last summer." As I went in, Caitlyn frowned and closed the door behind me. "Just what is rattling around in your brain pan, little boy?" she demanded.

I smiled at her form of address. "Maybe I was wondering if Pop had gotten himself a—"

"A shackup?" she offered.

"Well, a honey."

She turned, reached to the coat rack and took down a deep purple parka and put it on. "I'm a little surprised you don't know your father's too old-fashioned for that. There's this little ceremony we have to go through first involving a ring, some promises, and a big cake." She turned and looked at me. "Before that, though, there's a son with whom he hasn't yet cleared getting married." She nodded toward the sweeping circular staircase that spiraled around the chandelier, hung still by that thick blue rope. "I put your things upstairs in your old room." She paused, sorted through something, and said, "Your father should be back in a couple of hours." She smiled and looked into my eyes. "You have no idea how much I hope we can be friends."

I watched as she opened the door, stepped outside, and pulled the door shut behind her. Through the heavy beveled glass of the French doors, I watched her cross the porch, go down the path, cross the street, and climb into a red Grand Cherokee topped by a ski rack. As she pulled away from the curb and headed south on Sixteenth, I turned and looked at the staircase coiled around that thick blue rope.

"Home again, home again, jiggity jig," I said as I began climbing the stairs.

AN EVENING WITH THE HANGMAN

On the second floor the master bedroom opened onto the small circular gallery. A hall led off the gallery to my old bedroom on the west side and a sewing room at the back filled with my mother's things. Across from my bedroom was another bedroom where Aunt Cella used to sleep when she stayed here. I always regretted missing her funeral, that I missed saying goodbye to her. She hadn't been a warm and loving soul, but she had been the closest thing to a mother I remembered having. That and I owed her for my skiing and a lot of great days together on mountains. But when she died I was in the hospital with a gunshot wound and the hangman was at my side. Cella died alone and was buried next to her husband with a priest, two funeral home assistants, some skiing friends, and a couple of gravediggers in attendance.

I pushed open the door to my room. Here was where I endured childhood ills to awaken and find the hangman sitting in a chair, waiting, watching over me. Here was where Aunt Cella used to tuck me in like she was shrink-wrapping a slab of liver. Here was where I played the condemned man, waiting-for-the-hangman game. Here was where I cried about Billy Roth's joke as well as the loss of a friend. Here I nursed the wounds from countless fights, and here before the closet mirror I practiced the moves Leroy taught me. As a senior, here was where I dressed, polished and primped for my date with Rita Kwan in high school, and where, afterward, I sat in the dark wondering why the universe had made my father a hangman and if suicide might be a viable answer to anything.

The room was a long space, well lit from the western wall of windows that angled, cutting off the northwest corner of the room, giving it a dual view west and northwest over the garage to the back yards and homes on Elaine Street. My stuff was in the room, unpacked, and neatly placed here and there: Books, tapes, CDs, and field glasses on the shelves, the suits, sport jacket, my bush jacket and fishing vest hung neatly in the corner closet. My ski bag containing my boots, helmet, and stuff was on the closet floor, my old Dynastars and poles leaning against the wall. My thirteen-inch TV was on top of the cherry wood bureau just inside the door, my shirts, sox, and briefs neatly placed in the drawers.

To the left, centered in the south wall, was the small fireplace, the glassed in doors a recent heat-conservation improvement. Centered with its head against the north wall was the platform upon which still lurked the cursed futon I had badgered Pop for then found out, too late, I hated. I'd been too stubborn to admit making a mistake, though, and had spent the last three years of high school sleeping on that lumpy thing at night and doing my homework on the cherry wood desk facing the angled windows.

In the closet's shelves, there were only my dress shoes, hiking boots, slippers, some joggers, an extra belt, a variety of hats, gloves, and a tired necktie collection. Moving to the desk, there was a telephone, newly installed. I checked the number and it was a line separate from the home phone. Next to the base of the draftsman's lamp, in a small flowered china cup, was a shiny new key. In the front of the desk's center drawer was a newly installed lock. A similar lock was installed on the lower right hand drawer.

I slipped off the Gasman's old overcoat, dropped it on the foot of the futon, and sat beside it as I avoided looking at myself in the full-length mirror in the closet door. I felt more weary than I had ever felt in my entire life. Putting my head on the pillow, I pulled a cover up over my shoulder, and buzzed my brain with horrors awake and asleep until Pop got me up for dinner.

My favorites were on the table that night: Greek salad, spaghetti with meat sauce and meatballs, Dr Pepper, and for desert, Gianelli's black raspberry ice cream. "It's good to have you home, Joe," said Pop as he sat on the opposite side of the kitchen table. The spaghetti, already mixed with the sauce, filled the room with steaming hints of oregano, garlic, onion, tomato, and parmesan. "This is great, Pop: All the major food groups. Thanks for getting my car, too."

"Good to have you home, Joe." The hangman smiled and reached for another slice of garlic bread. "That Mazda the same car you got in 'Ninety-two?"

"It gets me where I need to go."

"You're as bad as Gaspare. The radio don't work, upholstery's all chewed up, tires bald, and that back seat's a health hazard."

"Cherie's Rottweiler. He doesn't like to be left alone." I shrugged my unhurt shoulder. "He didn't like me much, either. Got to admit, I never got sleepy behind the wheel with old Cujo in the back seat breathing on my neck."

The hangman nodded as though confirming a matter to himself. "Something I don't understand, Joe."

"What's that, Pop?"

"You and Cherie. I don't get it. You don't like her apartment, her music, her politics, what she eat, the pictures she on her walls, the way she talk to you, her friends, or her dog."

"Pretty, though," I offered. "Cherie, not the dog."

"Cherie *look* pretty, Joe. On the outside. She don't like cops, though."

"She scorns the occupation," I answered. "That's different."

"She don't like cops, she play with drugs. Her friends look down their noses at anyone not foolish enough to pay a fortune for a cup of joe at Starbucks."

"It's not just the beverage," I said. "It's the ambiance. I mean, where else can you go and talk ecology and then drive home in your Lexus."

"Cherie, she also got the meanest mother I ever met," countered the hangman as he shook his head and shoulders in an exaggerated shudder.

"Gloria's a peach, isn't she?"

"No wonder her husband wind up in the funny farm." The hangman shook his head. "Cherie drinks those diet milkshakes, makes gas all the time—"

I burst out laughing. "Yeah. Hell of a carbon footprint for a hundred and fifteen pound real estate whiz."

"Okay. So, why you stay with her, Joe? Because she let you sleep with her?"

I swallowed my mouthful of meatball and frowned as I pondered the question. Taking a swallow of Dr Pepper I lowered the glass and shrugged. "Inertia, Pop. There was a time when I thought it was more. Anyway, she was there. Maybe that wasn't enough, but I talked myself into thinking that was enough."

"So, she let you sleep with her."

"Yeah. She let me sleep with her."

The hangman shook his head and waved his hand impatiently. "Joe, you got to see a shrink as part of your treatment, right?"

"Yeah. My first appointment is tomorrow."

"Who?"

"Same one: Betty Grable. You know, the woman who used to be a cop?"

The hangman nodded. "Good."

"Why?"

"Dr. Grable do some good work on you, Joe, especially after that stuff out at the Reservoir. You know, Charlie Matthews."

"So what about now?" I prompted.

"Look at yourself, Joe. You handsome, like a young Al Pacino, you got a good job, you funny and smart. You feel a lot, too. All things women say they want. I figure you can get any woman you want."

"Honest, Pop, I was really attached to that Rottweiler."

"His teeth in your ankle don't count," Pop said. He leaned back in his chair and thought for a long moment. There hadn't been many father and son talks between us and both of us were rusty at it. I was surprised at how much I was enjoying it.

Pop pushed his plate forward two inches and rested his forearm on the edge of the table. "Joe, what if the woman of your dreams—absolutely perfect—you find her. What you do?"

I reached for another helping of spaghetti, caught Pop's look, and shrugged. "Hell, I don't know, Pop. I'd probably find out who she was seeing and congratulate the lucky stiff." I twirled up a load of pasta and stuck it in my mouth. The hangman was still giving me that look. "Whuh?" I said, talking around the mouthful.

"I know you feel left out of everything when you was a kid. Maybe that's my fault. It's up to you now though. You deserve better and maybe Dr. Grable can help you get it." One of his eyebrows went up. "You should stop calling her Betty Grable, too. It's disrespectful. Her name is Margaret."

"She calls me Joe DiMaggio," I countered.

The hangman grinned as he turned back to his spaghetti. "Now I just wonder who was first at the plate with the smartass remarks."

I looked innocent for a moment and then laughed. "You might be right." I leaned back in my chair and thought of the old fashioned picture of my mother hanging in the dining room where we never ate. "Pop, was Mom the perfect woman for you?"

His face grew serious, then he smiled. "You remember her at all?"

"A little. It's pretty vague."

Pop glanced at the dark outside the window. "She loved you so much. She would've known how to bring you up."

"You miss her."

"Every day. She loved me, too," he explained. "I thought life was over when she died." He looked up at me. "But I had a son. You kept me alive."

Things were getting a bit morose for a first get together, so I changed the subject. "What about this Caitlyn?"

Pop's eyebrows arched. "Caitlyn. What you think?"

"What I saw I liked a lot. She said something about you waiting on my blessing to get hitched?"

"Sure."

"Are you crazy?"

"You think it crazy wanting your son's blessing?"

"Quaint, maybe. Offhand I can't think of a single soul who wouldn't just go ahead and do what he wanted, especially since I bailed on you. You sure don't owe me anything."

"You are my son, Joe. Family is important."

"From what I've seen, Pop, Caitlyn is terrific." I thought for a moment, then nodded. "If I get to be best man, you have my permission to get hitched."

He smiled broadly. "She made this spaghetti sauce."

"I take it back, Pop. If she made this sauce, I'm going to marry her myself."

After dishes and the news, we watched a CD of an old favorite: *The Life of Brian*. We both did a lot of laughing. It was good to be home.

That night I dreamed of childhood faces, beatings, cruel words, and Leroy Brown answering the question I finally had worked up the courage to ask. *"What's the payback for, Leroy? What'd my father ever do for you?"*

"Your daddy hanged my daddy," answered Leroy. *"Done it good, too."* And then Leroy snapped his fingers. When he was twenty-two Leroy had been one of the witnesses at his father's execution.

After dreaming about Carlo Rizzo coming for me in the dark, I screamed myself awake and couldn't get back to sleep. I stared at the ceiling until the hangman knocked on my door at three. He had made blueberry pancakes and we ate them in the living room as we watched an old Kirk Douglas political thriller, *Seven Days In May,* in which things are not as they seem.

BILLY ROTH

Much later that morning, still packed with Pop's pancakes and the sun finally up, I showered in the hall bathroom, half a plastic garbage bag taped over my right shoulder to keep my dressing dry. Back in my room I put on faded black jeans, a tan pullover, black joggers, and an olive colored sweater. I left off the sling and gingerly sat at my desk. Taking the key from its china container, I opened the center drawer where I used to keep my ruler, pencils, pens, and the occasional *Playboy*. In there now were holsters, cleaning equipment, boxes of practice and working ammo, and my Colt King Cobra .357 Magnum with a four-inch barrel. I hadn't cleaned the Cobra in months. I checked and it sparkled. The hangman's new girlfriend, Caitlyn, had cleaned it.

I pulled the shoulder holster out of the drawer and contemplated the rig. The thought of having that elastic strap wrapped around my right shoulder forced me to place it aside. Also in the drawer was a fabric pancake holster with the restraining strap cut away. It fit the Cobra and I slipped it on my belt at my left side just forward of my hip. I made an experimental cross-body draw with my right hand, felt the stitched tissue in the back of my shoulder cry out, then did it again, v-e-r-y slowly. It pulled, but I could draw the piece. I loaded it with hollow points, rested the hammer on an empty chamber, placed it in the holster, stood, and put on the loose-fitting fleece-lined leather bush jacket from the closet.

I put my badge in my pocket, closed the closet door, looked at my image in the mirror, and decided that the jacket concealed the carry adequately. As I turned back to the desk, wondering if it was too soon for me to try and return to work, there was a movement.

It was something outside the window, across the back yard, high, white, and small, jerking up and down. I turned and looked through the window. Over the garage, and across another back yard to a pale yellow three-story home, the white thing was moving in the window to the room where Billy Roth used to sleep. I took the field glasses, looked through the window, and saw Billy Roth's mother, her upper body leaning out of Billy's window. She was waving a white towel with one hand and holding a similar pair of field glasses to her eyes with the other. She looked as though she was trying to get my attention. With my left hand I pulled up the sash and leaned out. As soon as I appeared, Mrs. Roth smiled and motioned for me to come over.

I lowered the glasses, stood frozen for a second, then nodded and waved back. After closing the window I looked at the field glasses. Old, cheap, low powered. They were almost opera glasses. Billy Roth had given them to me for Christmas two years before the joke about the rope. Billy bought himself a pair, too, so we could communicate through our bedroom windows. Morse code. In the days we used mirrors. At night, flashlights. I was surprised I'd kept the glasses all these years.

I replaced the glasses on the shelf, took a black fleece watch cap and a pair of ski gloves from my ski bag, and left the room.

"I was so scared when I heard about what happened, Joe. The TV, night and day, day and night. I tried to call at the hospital, but they were keeping out everyone who wasn't family." Mrs. Roth poured the tea, brought the steaming cups to the kitchen table, and sat opposite me. The tea was touched with jasmine and honey. She looked awfully old.

The walk to the back gate, across the alley, into the Roth's back yard had pulled away the years. The memories were intensified by seeing Billy's mother and sitting in that kitchen, at that table once again, the site where Billy and I had consumed many bowls of chicken noodle soup, slices of watermelon and mince pie, and sandwiches of precious peanut butter and grape jelly on Wonder Bread. The room smelled like a bakery.

"I'm okay, Mrs. Roth. They patched me up and told me I'll be good as new in a few weeks."

"The TV, Joe. All this business about those Rizzo brothers. They're talking about putting you in jail. What are you going to do?"

"It's just news hype," I said. "Nothing to worry about. Once the shooting board clears me, it'll all blow over."

Her eyebrows capped blank eyes. "Shooting board?"

"A review panel, Mrs. Roth," I explained. "Every time an officer fires a weapon, a panel made up out of police officers, lawyers, and a couple civilians looks into it to make sure everything was kosher. That's all."

Looking to change the subject, I nodded around at the blue-flowered wallpaper, slightly yellowed with age. "It looks just the same."

She nodded sadly and looked at her cup. "Funny. I never did put in a modern kitchen. There just wasn't enough money. Then in 'Ninety-five Harry died and I didn't have the heart to change anything." She reached out a hand ribbed with blue veins and placed it on my wrist. "Thank you for coming to the funeral." Before I could respond, she nodded indicating the kitchen. "Now the real estate agent tells me not to touch a thing. This is a perfectly preserved prewar something-or-other. He assured me the yuppies will go into feeding frenzy once the housing market picks up again."

"Are you moving?"

"That was my plan before the housing market fell to pieces. There ought to be a buyer at some price though. That's what the real estate man says." She nodded as she sipped at her tea. "This place is too big just for me. No family, no grandchildren." Her voice drifted off wistfully, her eyes glistened, and she put down her cup. "You know, Billy felt terrible about losing his best friend."

My eyebrows climbed at the abrupt change in subject. "He had a funny way of showing it."

"He did a bad thing, Joe. Making fun of you wasn't right. He knew that."

"Then why did he keep it up? Did he ever tell you?" Embarrassed at having snapped at her, I shook my head. "Sorry. That wasn't meant for you."

She leaned back in her chair, took a breath, and let it out, suddenly looking older and very frail. "It doesn't change anything, Joe, but understand that Billy was the only Jew in King Elementary. For a long time you were his only friend. His religion was no obstacle to you. That was one of the things that made you so special."

She dried her eyes with a tissue and looked at the clouds through the window above the sink. "I remember when you two got those binoculars and used to talk to each other with the Morse code." She glanced back at Joe. "We could see the flashes from your window. Harry told me it was Morse. I asked him if we should learn it too so we could eavesdrop, but he said what you two had was more special than whatever mischief you might be hatching."

I shook my head at the memories. "Big state secrets. 'What'd you see on the tube? Did you hear about Wendy holding hands with Paul? You going to watch the game Saturday?'"

Mrs. Roth clasped her hands together on her lap and smiled sadly. "Billy was all alone at school, except for you, Joe. Bullies would tease him, call him names, get rough with him. But then he found he could make people laugh, and if they were laughing he was a part of things. He was so desperate to belong." She looked down at the table. "It was that business about the chandelier rope. He made a joke about it, everybody laughed, and suddenly Billy stopped being an outcast. You must know what that meant to him."

Before I could say anything, she grabbed my right wrist, making my shoulder throb. "I know that's when you became even more of an outcast, Joe. Then you two fought." She released my wrist and slumped back in her chair. "It was almost like permission for him. More jokes, a bigger audience, more acceptance." She glanced up at me. "It was a drug, making people laugh. He fed off it. He was a part of things, invited to parties, chosen for team sports, later on he even had a couple of girlfriends."

"Mrs. Roth, I'm trying real hard to be sympathetic, but you just listed everything I *didn't* have at school."

Her voice became haunted. "I know. No one knew that better than Billy. When he died—"

"Come again?" I sat back in the chair, stunned. "Died?"

"July eleventh, nine years ago."

"Nine ..." I searched my memory. July was when the old bum came after me with the Beretta. Nightmares, depression, on the rubber gun detail with Betty Grable, the shooting board, endless packs of reporters and public officials trying to lynch me. Not a time for reading obits.

"I'm sorry, Mrs. Roth. I missed it." I looked into her eyes. "Honest. I would've been there for you if I'd known. What happened?"

"Billy was murdered. He was performing at a club down in the Zone. He was a comic, you know. They call it stand up."

"Stand up?" I frowned as I thought. Standup headliner killed outside a comedy club down on the west end of Wilson next to the tracks. A club called Chuckles. "Manny Logan? Billy was Manny Logan?"

"He changed his name for the stage, Joe. He used to say Manny Logan was a name you could invite into your home for a couple of laughs. Billy Roth sounded like he might have had something to do with stealing atomic bomb secrets."

I smiled. "He was a funny man."

"The police, I heard one of them call the killing 'boiler plate.' On my own I figured out that meant they fill out the form, file it, and forget it. Did you ever see him perform?"

"Yes. Ten, twelve years ago. I took a date to a club. Chapin's. We caught his act." I shook my head. "I didn't recognize him."

Her voice sounded quite hollow as she asked, "Did he make you laugh?"

Chapin's was a jazz club on Beverly between Lincoln and Booth, which drew a joke from the comic, even though the Booth wasn't John Wilkes and the Lincoln wasn't the former President. The girl was a wannabe Goth from Records who thought she'd try on a hangman's son for a cheap thrill. I didn't remember her as well as the show we'd seen at the club. That night my ribs ached I laughed so hard. Jokes about being jealous of his wife's gynecologist; a book he'd written about the rough neighborhood in which he lived: *A Bullet Runs Through It*, being attacked by a bear in Alaska: a Kodiak moment.

"He made me laugh, Mrs. Roth. A lot. That was a great night when I saw him at that club, and later that year when I saw him on television. The Letterman show?"

"David Letterman," Mrs. Roth confirmed as her gaze wandered to the window again. "How he treated you was his big regret. His big shame. You don't know how he punished himself over it." She looked at me. "Can you forgive him, Joe? Can you find it in your heart to forgive Billy?"

"Of course." I felt the edge of tears teasing my eyes. I stood and hugged the mother of my dead childhood friend. "Of course." In my mind I was wondering who had wanted Billy Roth dead nine years ago, besides me.

DEEP AND DARK

Later, back at Pop's house, I used the new telephone on the desk in my room and called Police Park Tower. After a computerized run-around I tracked down the status on the William G. Roth a.k.a. Manny Logan killing. Det. Louis Rockland pushed buttons and read me the dope. *"Killing took place outside a rathole called Chuckles, Ninth and High. He was popped in the back of the head with an ice pick. His wallet, cards, ring, and watch were taken, no sober witnesses, not much in the way of clues. In and out. Wallet was found in an alley two blocks away, no money or cards, no prints. The watch and ring never turned up. Neither did any of his credit cards."*

"Cold Cases?"

"At the bottom of the freezer, Joe. Anything else?"

"Switch me over to Cab Nelson, would you, and thanks."

"Sure thing. About the Rizzo Brothers, Joe, the lodge is with you."

A click and a buzz then a gruff voice came on the line. *"Det. Nelson."*

"Cab, this is Joe Torio."

"Hey, Joe," he said, the gruffness removed. *"They say you're going to join me on the big fat paper mountain. Is that permanent or only until you heal?"*

"In *any* case, it's only temporary."

"When do I get to dump half this load on you?"

"Tomorrow, maybe. I'm not good at sitting around the house. Still trying to figure out how to use my arm, though. Cab, can you dig me out the stuff on a killing?" I read the name and case number I'd gotten from Rockland.

"This Roth a friend of yours?"

"Long time ago. Just curious. I wanted to see if anything would shake out if I went through the book."

"Everybody's got one."

"Got one what?"

"A case," answered Cab. *"A relative, a friend, someone you know, a case that stuck in some detective's craw. A lot of butts have filled the chair on the other side of this table, Joe, and every one of them brought an interest in at least one old case. Something to keep you up nights."*

"You have one, Cab?"

"Had," he corrected. *"I cleared mine. I'll have yours waiting for you."*

After hanging up, I stared at the phone, wondering if tomorrow was too soon to take up the Big Blue Burden. The phone rang and it was Dock. After some preliminary jests regarding my loafing around and my cushy new desk job at Cold Cases, Dock said, *"I wanted to let you know they bumped me up to lieutenant."*

"About damned time, Dock. Do Ellie and the girls know?"

"I'm telling them tonight at Fratiano's. Going to have a bit of a celebration. Want to come?"

"Hey, Dock. Thanks but that's for you and your family. Besides, Pop and I have catching up to do. I guess the department can't screw up everything. Congratulations on the promotion. What'd they do with the Popsicle King." There was a moment of silence that was growing long enough to get awkward. "What?" I asked.

"Crewe is still in Homicide. The Police Commission decided to go ahead with the Major Case Unit, Joe. It's under Capt. Finn. They put me in charge of training, organization, and field operations."

"When did the brass hats start listening? We've been pushing that for years. This is terrific."

"Yeah," said Dock, *"but you were supposed to be there, too, Joe."*

"Bad timing and seven eighths of a loaf, Dock. Once you get that bunch of super cops up and running, we'll be able to hit the big ones with everything we've got. Maybe when I get bored with this cushy spot I have in Cold Cases, I'll let you hire me away from Cab."

A pregnant pause. *"Will do. See you."*

I hung up, glared at the phone, and said to the silence around me, "Son of a *bitch!*"

Dock and I, along with a few other cops had been mulling the creation of a permanent major case unit for years. Up until then the maximum gore, high body count, super profile cases stumbled through the usual channels: Try and put together a task force, work out the kinks and incompatibilities, try and figure out who would be in charge of what, reinvent the wheel one more time, then go after the killer. Then Gerald Soams hit South River, the bodies kept dropping while we worked out the kinks, and the media headlines kept screaming about the police not doing anything.

The Gray Eye Killer killed only a certain kind of boy: very young male prostitutes with gray eyes, then he would knife the victim to death and keep the eyes for trophies. Homicide, the South River County Sheriff's Office, and the State Troopers put together a task force at last, pulling cops off other assignments here and there. Before the cobbled together assortment of equipment, experience, and expertise staggered into motion, special detail cops from Vice managed to bait the killer and end his run with maximum prejudice. Finally the media joined the call for a major case unit. It would be a standing task force, already trained with local, state, and Federal units, communications, and facilities. Everything already in place and working: a solution waiting for a problem. Dock and I wanted to serve in such a unit. Half of us made it, at least.

Son of a *bitch.*

That night on Jerry Starr's freak and dementia show, Cherie Vitamante appeared speaking on "the Joe Torio I know," proclaimed the tease. It had taken every last ounce of will not to watch. Starr wouldn't have had Cherie on unless she had lurid tales to tell, and I didn't want to see her tell them. I didn't know if I had ever loved her, but I was sure I didn't want to hate her.

I went up to my room, wrote for awhile, then flopped back on the futon, closed my eyes, and tried to fall asleep. Something, though, kept me awake, and it wasn't my shoulder, the lumpy bed, or thinking about Cherie. There were very familiar sounds coming from downstairs.

Ludwig. It was the Fifth Concerto. "Emperor." The pageantry and power lifting the soul through different times and alternate dimensions. The hangman would be in the room with no windows, where he could relax, be himself, and fill his reality with Beethoven. The music he loved most was Beethoven, which, I suspected, had to do with the mysterious German who figured somehow in my father's life. In the fourth grade when I was sick with the flu and had to stay home from school, I was bundled up with blankets on the couch in the music room watching an old rerun of *Hogan's Heroes*. Pop was watching it with me until everybody's favorite character came on: Sgt. Schultz played by actor John Banner. I was divided between laughing and coughing but there was nothing but silence from the hangman. I turned to see if he was enjoying the show. His eyes were welled with tears. Finally he got up and left the room.

Swinging my legs to the floor, I put on my slippers, pulled on a faded black ESCC hoody, and walked in the dark through the hallway, around the landing, down the stairs and into the living room, curiously pleased that I still remembered my way in the dark. From the southeast turret with its circular array of curved windows, the light from the street spread cold and blue across the carpeting. That was where Pop placed the Christmas tree every year. There was always a Christmas tree. There were always presents. When I wasn't at home, he'd send them to me the next day or so after they'd put in their time beneath the tree. The hangman wasn't a Christian, but he believed in St. Nick and Christmas trees. By New Year's the tree was always gone.

There was an opening from the living room into the music room where stood an upright piano that I hadn't heard played since Aunt Cella died. Her music was still piled on top. As a child I had taken a few lessons, enough to make it all of the way through the first movement of Ludwig's "Moonlight." Pop and Aunt Cella were my only audience. When I was done, Aunt Cella clapped her hands and gave me a peck on the cheek. High praise from the Wicked Witch of the East. The hangman had tears in his eyes. After seeing my father cry for the second time, I never played that piece or anything else ever again.

In one of our old sessions years ago Betty had asked me why it had been so hard for me to see my father cry. *"I can't see him with tears,"* I had told her. *"He killed people with more deliberateness, less emotion, and more frequency than most mob button men. It's easier to believe he isn't human. When I see tears in Pop's eyes, I have to admit his humanity."*

I entered the music room. Opposite the windows on the east side of the room, behind a couch facing Pop's HD flat screen and next to a rack holding a baseball bat signed by the Yankee Clipper himself, was a door slightly open. I pushed it open all of the way.

The hangman was in his big green leather chair, his right elbow on the armrest, his hand holding up his head. The room was not much larger than a walk-in closet. It was crowded with shelves full of books, pictures, and old LP records. Next to the records were rows of compact discs. In the corner was a desk with an old Dell PC on it, the stock starfield screensaver running two hundred on slow.

The stereo system was within arm's reach of the chair in which the hangman sat. A single floor lamp three-way on dim illuminated the room, the old paper shade casting everything in soft yellow light. There was a tan leather wing-back across from Pop's chair, and I lowered myself into it. The creaking of the leather as I sat down caused Pop to look up.

"Was I playing the music too loud?"

"You can't put in too many onions, use too much marjoram, or play Beethoven too loud," I answered. I cocked my head toward the player. "I'm not familiar with the recording."

He turned town the volume to a comfortable background level. "Deutsche Grammophon came out with everything of Beethoven's a few years back. This

70

piece is done by Maurizio Pollini on piano with the Wiener Philharmoniker."

The hangman paused and cocked his head toward the music room. "Cheri was on the TV."

"Did you watch it?"

"Only a little."

A big fat pause. "Why didn't you watch, Pop? It was my fifteen minutes of fame,." I quipped in a lame attempt at lightness.

"Joe, anything true you want me to know you'll tell me. The stuff that isn't true, I don't need to hear." He lowered his hand to the armrest and raised his eyebrows. "Did you watch it?"

"No. That's not the way I want to remember her." I studied the hangman for a moment. "You're quite a guy, Pop."

The hangman smiled, then the smile lessened by degrees until the corners turned down into an expression of concern, guilt, worry, deep thought. I couldn't tell for certain. "Gaspare told me about the talk you two had."

"Hard to believe he's Sicilian, the blabbermouth."

The hangman stared into a dark corner for so long that I wondered if he had fallen asleep. His jaw muscles flexed, though, then he nodded and gave a resigned shrug. "What do you want to know, Joe?"

"Are you serious?"

"The reasons for secrets sometime die a long time before the secrets do. Maybe now all's left are secrets without reasons."

I studied the mystery of the man before me. I leaned back in the chair. What the hell. This was my chance. "Okay. Tell me about the German."

The hangman's eyebrows arched as his mouth fell partly open. "How do you know about him?"

"I'm a detective, Pop. Slower than most, but a detective nevertheless. I know there was a German, and that he was a large, elderly, blond man like Sgt. Schultz in *Hogan's Heroes.*"

Pop nodded. "What else, Joe?"

I smiled. I was being tested. "Okay, the German gave you that pocket watch, taught you to love Beethoven, Christmas, and Christmas trees, and he taught you your

71

drops in early Nineteen forties Sicily. I'd say it had something to do with the German occupation. That's where I run out of guesses."

"Smart boy," he said. "Such a smart boy. You were right, Joe."

"About what?"

"About becoming a police officer. You are quite a detective."

"Well, right now my shoulder is telling me flipping burgers at Wendy's makes more sense."

"What about being happy, Joe? Are you happy?"

"Happy?" I thought on it. "No. Being a cop is like trying to bail out the *Titanic* with a thimble and taking the blame for all the wet feet. You were right, Pop. There is no such thing as a happy cop. Not on the streets; not in this chair. There are a few war bonnets up in the top of the Police Park Tower who are having a good time, but they're pretty corrupt. They stopped being cops a long time ago."

"Any reason to keep at it then? It's tough to do work that makes you feel small."

"It doesn't make me feel small. Frustrated a lot, hopeless every now and then, but I get in a lick every so often, Pop. I've taken out some real bad garbage and saved a few lives. Enough to make it worth it."

We sat silently for a time, then Pop reached up and turned out the light. What light there was in the room came from the power light and readout on the hangman's CD player, the screensaver, and a green light from beneath the desk that was probably a backup power supply for the computer. The volume on the stereo was turned down some more, probably with a remote. Then Pop began talking. "The German, his name was Claus Ruger, and he looked very much like Sgt. Schultz."

Then Nicolo Torio told me about Capo, Fili, Messina, the streets, and the man from Germany they brought in to do drops. He told me about learning his ropes, the death of the German's son, hanging Capo, then the horrible death of Claus, the end of the war, and coming to America where he met Gaspare, went to work at Books, got the job of hangman, and about the love of his life: my mother.

It wasn't all of the hangman's secrets, but it was a start. Most of the men he hanged he had known for years. In a strange sense, he had been their friend. They told him things they never told the cops or their lawyers or loved ones. He couldn't share all that. Not quite enough hours in a single night for that.

The Beethoven CD had finished sometime before. Pop and I sat in the darkness. I stood, went to Pop's side and placed a hand on his shoulder. The hangman gave a small laugh and turned on the floor lamp. "What's this, Joe? I almost expect you to say, 'Great. Not only is my father a hangman, now I find out he's a war criminal; an illegal immigrant.'"

"I'll save it for my memoirs." I leaned over and did something I hadn't done since I was seven years old. I kissed my father and said, "I love you, Pop."

The hangman's big hand found mine and held it. "I should have told you a long time ago."

"You had a jerk for a son," I said.

"No. You weren't a jerk."

"I missed out on a lot of Christmases, a lot of ice cream cones at Five Corners. That makes me a jerk."

"Gianelli's." Nicolo turned on the light. "Good ice cream. My cardiologist calls Dario Gianelli the antichrist selling heart attack in a cone."

"Come spring, Pop, I'm going to take *you* there and get you a three-scoop chocolate cone."

"Three-scoop. My cardiologist would have a heart attack." He shrugged. "I could use a triple-scoop chocolate cone. Black raspberry still number one with you?"

"You bet." I cocked my head toward the door. "I better try and get some sleep. I'm going to try and go to work tomorrow and see if I can warm up some of those cold cases. Can you drive me in? This shoulder of mine isn't going to be happy working my car's floor shift for awhile."

"I'm leaving about four in the morning, Joe. A contractor up in Camp Charles wants to go over a landscaping bid. I'll ask Caitlyn. She should still be awake. Maybe she can drive you in."

"Great."

We fumbled for a moment. Hugging takes practice, but it felt as though an important piece of a very old puzzle had fallen into place. Half way up the big staircase, my eyes even with the chandelier, I heard the beginning of Ludwig's *Romance cantabile in E Minor*. In bed, I listened to the music, watched the ceiling, and pointlessly speculated on the missing piece of the puzzle. When I tired of that, I began making up speeches I'd never deliver before the shooting board. When I begin making speeches, it's time to get up and do something else. And there was something else I wanted to do. At my desk I cranked up my laptop and began on my father's part of my story. When I was well into it, I gave in and logged onto the SRPD site and went to the duty roster, Police Arms Discharge Incidence Review Board. The hearing time and place hadn't yet been scheduled, but the board membership had.

It didn't look good for me. Not only could I not explain how all three Rizzos had been dispatched, I had no witnesses, and the gang who would be going over the bones of the incident and ruling upon the righteousness of the gunplay as well as my fitness as a detective could have been drawn from the Spanish Inquisition.

Shooting board membership rotated every quarter, and this quarter's ranking board member was Lt. Trask from IAB. He looked like Joe Biden before the hair plugs. We'd tangled in the past. After the Baines shooting, he threatened to resign if I kept my badge. Unfortunately he withdrew the offer before anyone could go into action.

The second cop was a uniform from Sherman Park Division, Sgt. Lana Hubert. Medium height, brunette, with the face that sank a thousand ships. I knew her from when she was in Public Relations. Bad press on the Baines matter thoroughly soured her on me.

The criminal defense attorney who was functioning as moderator and arbiter of the applied laws and regulations was Matt Ventnor. He always sported a face coated with designer stubble. Maybe he was trying for the Manly Man look, but to me he always looked like he was coming off a three-day bender. He was the attorney who the Coumbs family had hired to sue me and the city after their murderous drug-dealing offspring, Eldridge, had answered my canvassing questions with a gun. Killing Coumbs had left me one short of tying the department body count record—not something Sgt. Huber and Public Relations wanted to occur right in the middle of their "the police officer is your friend" campaign. Matt Ventnor lost his civil case, too. Maybe it would make sense to hire a platoon of lawyers to get these guys to recuse themselves. That wasn't in the bylaws, though. To get anyone off the shooting board it would be necessary for me to prove to a specially and inconveniently convened appeals board actual fraud or malicious intent on the part of said board member. For some reason, no shooting board member had ever been forced to recuse him or herself.

The other lawyer was City Council hopeful Tracy Stiles who looked like Hillary Clinton after forty cans of Red Bull. "What the citizens of South River need is more law and less enforcement!" she had once said in a television interview. That was followed by weeks of, "What I really meant when I said that, was . . ." In her campaign to promote South River as "America's Home Town," she had proposed, among other things, disarming the police. Once the police put down their weapons, she was convinced, the gang members and mobsters would follow suit. I'd never had a personal run-in with Stiles, but her views on the Police Department and its personnel were, to say the least, extreme.

Rev. Jules Hollis was half the civilian team. He'd been on one of my boards before. To me he looked like a skinny Reverend Wright but sounded a lot like Alvin the Chipmunk. Whatever the hearing covered, his view always depended on his current agenda, which depended a lot on who was paying his bills. On our previous encounter concerning my dispatch of Jay Hellerman, the famed "Boy Wolf," the fact that I had saved the lives of two boys with my single pistol shot was irrelevant. His focus was on the fact that, in making that shot, I "had carelessly placed the lives of those young boys in jeopardy." I had also sent "the wrong message" to the city's youth. He never was very clear about what the "right" message would have been.

The final member was Prof. Arthur Dumont. Arthur's bio said he taught sociology at Breadloaf U. He had piles of money and was said to have flirted with the radical student movement back in the 'Seventies. Dock used to say Dumont had been born with a silver hand grenade in his mouth. I hadn't had any personal run ins with him, but at the risk of generalizing, he didn't sound like a candidate for the police pep squad.

It was after one in the morning. This was not helping my slumbers. Beethoven was done for the night and Pop must have gone to bed. I needed to get some sleep. If I don't get at least two hours a night, I hallucinate all the next day.

Desperate times called for desperate measures. This was never a step I took lightly because of the possible risk of brain damage, clinical depression, and eventual suicide. I took my copy of *Windows XP Inside Out* (Second Edition) and paged to where I had left off the last time I'd needed big help in clubbing myself into unconsciousness: Page 409, nearing the exciting conclusion of "Tweaking the Windows XP Interface." By Page 412 I was comatose and well into a nightmare filled with blood, screaming, error messages, and seized applications.

Bill Gates hovered before me, wagging his finger. "This program is not responding," he chided. "If you choose to end the program immediately you will lose any unsaved data, *and we'll get your little dog, too!*"

DEATH TO JOE TORIO

The phone awakened me at three. I groggily answered it with a grunt and was treated to thirty seconds of my usual caller threatening to kill me, *"just the way you took out the Rizzo brothers, you cop cocksucker."* The guy sounded really upset, but I had to interrupt him. "Hey, thanks. You reminded me about my appointment with the shrink today. You didn't quit therapy, did you?"

Silence.

"Anyway, nice to hear from you." And I hung up.

What the hell; It was someone to talk to.

I could smell the pancakes from the kitchen. Pop must have heard me screaming in my sleep. Pop's cure for sleeplessness was to move up breakfast and get an early start on the day. I stumbled downstairs and began packing my face with blueberry pancakes drenched in butter and real maple syrup. While I worried about the weight I must be putting on, I was surprised to learn from Pop that the landscaping job he bid on would net almost three million to his firm if the deal went through. It would be the biggest contract Torio's Landscaping had ever done and would mean a number of additional names on the payroll. Never can tell what's going to happen when you pick up a pair of pruning shears. I promised to keep my fingers crossed for him and he was out of the house by four.

At half past six, Caitlyn picked me up in her Cherokee. It was sunny and cold and there were moldy oldies from the 'Fifties on her CD player: Duane Eddy doing "Rebel-Rouser" followed by the suggestive "Great Balls of Fire," by Jerry Lee Lewis. As we crossed Jefferson, I moved the passenger sun visor to shield the side window and glanced at Caitlyn. "Thanks for putting away my stuff and for cleaning my gun."

"Nice piece," she said. "A little chunky for me, but a nice piece."

"Where'd you learn about guns?"

"I grew up in the mountains above Stover's Wells. My father was a hunting guide and he taught me how to handle guns."

"A good man?" I asked.

She nodded. "He was a good, sweet man, and a career Marine." She glanced at me then shifted her gaze back to the rush-hour traffic as she turned off the radio. "Also, my mother, still living, is at the North Valley Living Center, I graduated from Mary Baldwin College, served in the Marines, did therapy work in private practice and in the prison system, am now retired, and have been married before—another good man, now deceased—no children, and I want to get married to Nicolo in January or February. I have other plans already made for June. Anything else?"

"You're not going to be one of those assertive, straight from the shoulder, no nonsense types, are you?" I asked.

"I'm a cream puff."

"I noticed the ski rack, Caitlyn. Is that current or a leftover."

"Skiing is what I do when I'm not praying for snow. I understand you're pretty good on the planks yourself. Want to go up sometime when your shoulder's better?"

"That'd be really great. If I could figure out how to make a living being a mediocre skier, I'd be out of the crime business altogether."

"What do the slopes mean to you, Joe?"

"Mean? I don't know." I thought on it for a few seconds. "Everything seems to make sense the second my skis touch the snow. Every problem I have becomes manageable, my focus is sharpened, the blood gets pumping, and I'm happy dancing with the mountain."

"My ski instructor used to call it fun with physics."

We rode in silence for awhile, our thoughts on packed powder, rushing winds, and gravity. When she spoke, her voice was clear, unfaltering. "Joe, I don't usually hand out unsolicited advice. My judgments, when they occur, are few and far between and made only after acquiring a lot more information than I have about you."

"But," I added.

"But?"

"I heard a definite 'but' in your voice."

She smiled, and it was a smile that warmed her entire face, making it easy to see what had attracted the hangman. As we left the bus terminal behind, approaching Sherman, the traffic on Sixteenth looked jammed. Immediately Caitlyn swung right onto Sherman and got into the lane to make the left onto Seventeenth.

I moved the visor to the front, shielding my eyes.

"You're never going to know until you ask," she said.

She pulled the car up to the Seventeenth Street light, stopped, and put on her left turn signal. "Okay, Caitlyn. Where do you stand on solicited advice?"

"If I think I can help, I help. If I can't help, I can usually aim the inquirer at someone who can. In any case, I'm there." The light changed and Caitlyn turned the Cherokee onto Seventeenth. She had guessed well. The traffic was much lighter. "I'm not a visiting therapist, and I can't take the place of missing parents, Joe. I can be a friend, though. Can you use a friend?"

I nodded. "Yeah. I could use a friend."

When we reached Pine, Caitlyn turned left and the sight of the greenish silver spike of the Police Park Tower filled the windshield. Suddenly my throat was so choked I could hardly breathe, my chest tightened and filled with stabbing pain.

"Are you okay, Joe?"

I nodded my head in the direction of the park across the street from the tower. "Pull in there."

She pulled into the traffic, cut across the street with a minimum of conflict, and steered down the winding tree-lined lane into the park. I watched the leafless trees pass, the sleeping flower beds and shrubs buried beneath a thick blanket of snow. Toward the center of the park, the black granite obelisk of the Police Memorial thrust into the sky, the Romanesque horror of City Hall on

Alexander facing the park from the south. Caitlyn pulled into the north parking lot, put the vehicle into park, and turned off the ignition.

I opened the door, stumbled out of the car, and hurled my O.J. and flapjacks all over the snow-covered trunk of an undeserving maple. Two deep breaths, shuddering all over, filling my lungs with the bitterly cold air, and I felt my head clearing. When I opened my eyes, I was looking at the memorial. Caitlyn was standing to my left holding out a freshly opened bottle of water. I nodded my thanks, took a mouthful, rinsed, and spat. I took another mouthful and swallowed it. "I might've jumped the gun a bit on going back to work."

I stepped around her and walked the footpath down toward the memorial, the cold air clearing my head as I fixed on the black granite structure that was the park's focal point.

Not many residents of South River cared for Police Memorial Park and its monument to fallen officers. The Tower looked down on it like a disapproving parent. The joke in the squad rooms was that Herbert L. Quayle, the architect of both the Tower and the park, secretly hated cops. The original plans called for all cop award and memorial ceremonies to be held in the shadow of the black obelisk. It was too open and cold in the winter and too crowded with mosquitoes, bums, drug dealers, muggers, weenie-wavers, and sun bathers in the summer. Even so, on those few days in the spring and autumn perfect for outdoor pageantry, no one wanted to crowd a memorial ceremony on top of a funeral each time a cop dropped. For simple award ceremonies, in addition, it simply required too much bother in the way of preparation, attendance, and transportation to hold them in the park. No one except a cop's family cared when a cop got a commendation, and the chief or the mayor didn't want to spend all morning at it. So, such ceremonies were held on the steps outside Chief Harolds's office, or across the park on the steps outside Mayor Howe's office. A grin, the thirty second attaboy speech, the pin, the photo-finish handshake for the odd reporter who might show, then it was back to the graft.

The park and its memorial sat there, then, providing only a midnight challenge for weeded-out frat boys at Breadloaf U. and ESCC to see what could be hauled to the top of the obelisk, strictly in good fun mind you, to humiliate authority. One year it was a toilet. Another year it was an entire pickup truck. One year a twelve-foot high monocled statue of Mr. Peanut was impaled on the obelisk's point. The obelisk had been painted and acid-stripped so many times the dedication carved into it was getting hard to read.

Mounted on the pedestal of the memorial, engraved on dozens of little bronze plates, were the names of officers who had been killed in the line of duty. The street punks and cops both called it the Scoreboard.

I stopped before the memorial, the monument for once unadorned by either vehicle, appliance, or graffito. At eye level was the scoreboard. Many of the names meant nothing to anyone but the record-keepers. Some of the names were known only by surviving family members. The few I knew I hadn't been close to. One name, though, stood out of the crowd: Capt. Abe Levin, former commandant of the police academy. Old at-the-end-of-the-day, go-home-alive Levin. He had been mugged outside his home in West Bluff and beaten to death. Unsolved. Probably somewhere in the Cold Cases heap.

"Strange place to go if you're having an anxiety attack," said Caitlyn.

"It was handy." I glanced at her, then looked up at the sky. "Carlo Rizzo is coming at me in my dreams every night," I said. "I'm dead. I know I'm a dead man. Helpless, I can't lift my arms, move, defend myself, nothing. Carlo is dragging that gimpy foot of his across the floor, telling me he's coming, chambering another round in that shotgun." I exhaled a ragged breath. "It's mixed up with another nightmare I've had ever since I can remember. In that one, too, I'm helpless and can't do anything, but I can't see anything but colors and fuzzy shapes. There's this endless screaming, everything covered in blood." I took another breath and let it out. "When I wake up I feel like I really don't know what I'm doing. I'm already dying, there's something I need to do to save myself, and I can't figure out what it is. About then there's this asshole who calls me on the phone to threaten me with death. He's at least real."

"What do you want to do right now, Joe?"

"I want to run. Run back home, hide in my closet, turn on the TV, and fill my head with noise."

"How would you feel if you ran home?" she asked.

I frowned and began walking around the memorial just to be doing something. How would I feel? "Pretty goddamned small and useless, is how I'd feel. Probably do a lot less puking, though." Little brass plates, some filled with the names of dead officers, many more blank. I glanced back at Caitlyn. She was looking down at the base of the memorial.

"Joe?" Caitlyn pointed with her finger at the bottom row of blank plates. "Look."

I bent over and saw that something had been scratched into the surfaces of five of the plates. One word per plate: "Death-To-The-Hangman's-Son."

"Probably couldn't figure out how to spell DiMaggio," I speculated. I glanced at Caitlyn. "Pop ever show you his watch?"

She grinned and nodded. "'It is all a joke,'" she quoted in translation. "Do you believe that?"

I looked back at the message scratched into the scoreboard plates. "The world almost has me convinced. It could use some funnier material, though." I turned, gave her arm a squeeze, and said, "Thanks for the ride, for the talk, and for the loan of the ear. I really appreciate it. I'll get one of the uniforms to give me a lift home." I glanced again at the "Death-To-The-Hangman's-Son," turned, and began marching toward the Tower.

SIBERIAN LULLABY

The elevator door opened on the third floor and I waited as a custodian, a couple of painters, and a uniform got off. I followed them and the doors silently closed behind me as I took in the new decor of Room Three Hundred, the Robbery-Homicide Division's bullpen, the remodeling finished while I had been in the hospital. The harsh overhead lights had been replaced by soft, indirect energy-saving lighting, which had already caused most of the occupants of the twenty-four steel double desks to import their own desk lamps so they could see what they were doing probably producing a net gain in energy consumption. The old tan linoleum had been replaced by gray-green asphalt tile. The dingy grayish-tan walls were now eggshell white, and the old white ceiling was now a rich plum. It looked like the cashier's office at a high-end bordello. None of the usual faces were there.

I went to my desk and someone else had already moved in. The ID plate on the desk said the new tenant was one Det. Robert Stoss. I'd never met him. He had been brought up from St. George Division just before I went in the hospital. The stuff from my desk had been placed in a lidded box and the box marked with my name and placed on the top of a low divider between Stoss's desk and the desks next door. I peeked in and my paperclips were safe. Taking the box I moved down the desk aisle and took a right into a wide hallway before reaching the Field Commander's office, currently occupied by Lt. Jessup. He was on the phone and didn't notice me.

On the right were back doors to the large meeting rooms used for morning case conferences and to headquarter task forces when they were created. The first Room, three-thirty, housed the Jennings Kidnapping Task Force, organized to retrieve from whomever was holding her, Misty, the sixteen year old daughter of newly elected Congresswoman Madeline Jennings. Keyboards were being tapped, calls made and received, the different jurisdictions attempting to stake out their own turf before the FBI arrived as Congresswoman Jennings hovered before the local TV cameras "To keep everybody's feet to the fire," as she kept putting it. With all that going on Dock was going to have a job hammering together a functioning Major Crimes Unit. My suspicion was that the kidnapping was a big hoax perpetrated by Misty with the aid of her current hunk, part-time high school student and full-time druggie Tyrone Plummer. Not my case.

Facing the back door of three-forty was a large space which was designated room (or more properly "space) three-fifty, according to the stenciled notice on the wall. On the left were four double desks arranged two by two, three of the pairs dedicated to research and secretarial work. The fourth, in the left rear, backed by a caged set of floor-to-ceiling shelves filled with dusty old manila folders, was the Cold Cases table. Sitting with his back toward me was a white-haired, stoop-shouldered man sitting at his computer with his shoes off. Cab Nelson was in his late sixties with dark leathery skin spotted with tan blotches. He looked a lot like Edward G. Robinson in *Key Largo* minus the cigar and plus about thirty years.

"Tell me, Cab, is it true when you retire with fifty years you get pay-and-a-half?"

"I'm only hanging in here until I get my Dirty Harry tie tack," he said. The old man turned around and grinned, his face crinkling up at the eyes and corners. "Hi, Joe. Welcome to Siberia. Did you see your girlfriend on TV? The Jerry Starr show?"

"Missed that. How was it?"

The old cop shrugged. "Depends on whether you're trying to sell peas or find out what happened."

"Sold a lot of peas, huh?"

"Green Giant should have you on retainer." Nelson held out his hand indicating the seat at the desk facing his. "Saved it just for you."

I looked at the dust on the seat. "When's the last time you had a partner, Cab?"

"Memory fails," he said. "That's why we have computers."

I hung up my coat, brushed off the chair with a couple sheets of wastepaper, and sat down. Cab Nelson then got up and guided me in my descent into the electronic, dust, mold, and paper quagmire reeking of frustration, hopelessness, and despair called Cold Cases.

Take a failed investigation, crack it open, see if it still has what it takes to fail again, flunk it, go on to the next case. At the end of each file I got to check off what Cab referred to as the Siberian Lullaby: "No new clues. No new witnesses. No new suspects. No new entries since last review." Then, the kicker: If the file was from after 1988 it would be electronic and that was the end of it. If the file was before '88, it needed to be entered into the computer in the hopes someday the lullaby would be sung automatically by a piece of software.

After an hour of hopelessness, I looked away from my monitor, leaned back, and said to Cab. "Now I know what made you so old and ugly."

"I'm only nineteen," Cab responded deadpan without looking away from his screen. His gnarled fingers efficiently took the data from the bulging manila folder to his left and entered it into the computer. He raised one white eyebrow. "It's been a hard life."

Cold Case reviews: beating dead horses to see if you can raise flies. Thousands of computerized files, and that number again jammed into dusty folders and packing boxes behind the wire on the secure shelves. Should we ever work our way through those, everything before 1975 was down moldering in the Police Park Tower basement.

Old crimes, old dust, old pain, injustice, and horror scabbed over by time and faded by death. Homicide cleared three out of every five cases. That made the homicide dicks feel superior to Robbery, Vice, Narcotics, Juvenile, and the other non lethal and domestic beef units who only cleared on average one out of six cases. We were at the bottom of the pond. Cold Cases had cleared three whole cases so far that year. That was three out of around four thousand. Not exactly the satisfaction of a job well done.

For the computerized files, it was call it up, compare it to the active files data base to see if anything new had been entered, maybe make a phone call to the detectives who had worked the case, an old witness, see if the missing relative ever turned up, check off the lullaby, and go on to the next case. For the pre-'88 files that were not computerized, first it was necessary to sort the rat's nest into the proper piles, call up the program, and then enter the works into the computer. What could be scanned was scanned, which was very little. Handwritten notes on scraps of paper, forms typed by gorillas wearing boxing gloves, creased, wrinkled, smudged and adorned with coffee rings, pizza sauce, and cigarette burns.

Case number thus and so, four years old. Homicide. Three dead on the upper end of Rutherford between Twenty-Seventh and Twenty-Eighth. No new clues. No new witnesses. No new suspects. No new entries since last review. Next case number so-and-so, eight years old. Rape-homicide in Canal Park, check off the lullaby, go onto the next case number. In the end I cheated and detoured to the Billy Roth a.k.a. Manny Logan case I had asked Cab to leave out. Same old song, though. Case number so-and-so, nine year old mugging-homicide in the Zone.

The crime scene photos showed the comic stretched out on his back in the street in front of Chuckles. He was wearing a heavy dark winter overcoat, leather gloves, and there was a thin coating of snow on the street. Not much in the way of footprints. Billy Roth's eyes were open, staring up at a cold night sky. ME's report said the victim had been stabbed in the back of his head with an ice pick-like instrument and his brains actually stirred. Time-of-death placed at between midnight and one in the morning, the snow on the street having been deposited shortly before twelve.

One thing that bothered a cop named Leska bothered me, as well: Why was an ascending comedy star like Manny Logan doing a gig at a dive like Chuckles? The vic's mother had answered, _"That was where he'd gotten his very first break. Chuckles asked him to come back for a reunion of performers who'd gotten their starts there. He was glad to do it."_

Happy reunion.

Something else. South River wasn't New York or L.A. A comedy reunion with a few name headliners would be a big deal. Saturday night, too. There would have been a crowd. There almost had to have been witnesses worth more than a note or two.

Irving Harriman, owner of Chuckles, confirmed that Manny Logan had indeed gotten his start there, but knew nothing about a reunion. When Manny showed and told Irv he was ready for the show and who else was going to be there, Irv had been perplexed. That was the first he'd heard of it. That was also the first he'd heard about any assistant named Nate—the one who had supposedly rendered the bogus invitation. "Manny went and did twenty minutes anyway, gratis," Irv was quoted as saying. "That's the kind of guy he was."

Crime scene photo of the victim's gloved right hand palm-down on the street. The crime scene technician who took the picture wrote, "Note the marks probably made by the victim's hand in the thin snow cover on the asphalt just beyond his fingers." The crime scene dude referenced an additional low-angled shot that showed more contrast. From the photographer's point-of-view it looked like four dots and a dash. If the victim had indeed made those marks, from Manny's point-of-view it would have been a dash followed by four dots: in Morse Code, the numerals four and six respectively. In the detective's opinion, in Manny's death throes, brains all scrambled, the victim momentarily rested his fingers on the snow and twitched.

Watch stolen. His senior class ring from West Beverly gone along with his wallet. Nothing but the empty wallet ever recovered. No new clues. No new witnesses. No new suspects. No new entries since last review.

It took less than three hours for me to feel absolutely crushed by the sheer volume of the city's unavenged blood and treasure. My shoulder throbbed from typing and my eyes ached from screen glare. During the break in the bullpen coffee room, as he leaned against the soda machine sipping at a Diet Coke, Cab said, "Joe, do you think you might have come back to work a little early?"

"I can't imagine ever being ready for what you do, Cab."

"What *we* do," he corrected maliciously, one brow ascendant. "Find anything interesting on the Roth case?" he asked as the brow descended.

"Siberian Lullaby. Big comedy showcase reunion invitation at Chuckles that never happened."

"Setup?" suggested Cab.

"Looks like he was invited to his own funeral. No clue who, unless it's the number six written in Morse in the snow."

"Your man know Morse?"

"We both learned it as kids. We were pretty good at it."

"Number six mean anything special to him?"

"We used to use it as slang for 'ass' and 'tail.' Other than that, it means nothing to me. Dave Leska, detective on the case out of East Branch, didn't think it was anything."

Cab finished off his soda and held the empty aluminum can in his hand. "Joe, the Cold Case table's a lot easier to hack if you just look upon it as record keeping. Make the entries, cross the tees, dot the eyes, and if there's nothing new, go on to the next file. Don't look at the clock and don't look at the pictures."

I tossed my empty soda can in the blue plastic "cans & bottles only" recycle bin next to the soda machine, went back to my desk, made my appointments for physical therapy, and confirmed my appointment with Betty. It was time for me to take action. If I didn't get the hell out of Siberia soon, I risked dying of extreme paperbite. I was back on the lullaby until I was interrupted by Lt. Roemer from IAB poking his gray brush-cut around the corner. "Torio," he called. "Call your lawyer. Shooting board, One PM, Room 505. Good luck." He grinned and slithered back under his rock.

Most cops who wind up in the Internal Affairs Bureau get there either because of pathological ambition or they were caught dirty. When you have something on a cop, it's easier to recruit the fellow into becoming a rat on his fellow cops. It's sort of like doing police recruiting by giving muggers and killers a choice between prison or the Police Academy. It results in a peculiar work ethic.

Apparently Roemer had made my career his personal white whale. He was convinced I was a psychotic killer who had figured out how to feed his demon legally. "A good cop," he had said to me and about me on more than one occasion, "almost never has to draw his weapon." The last time he said that in front of a shooting board of mine, I pointed out to the board that over half the names on that ugly monument down there in the park were of officers who either didn't go for their pieces or were too slow in doing so. Then I heard a click come from Roemer. He had a hand in his pocket and had been recording me. Might be useful in a future hearing or trial.

It's good to be dedicated to something greater than oneself.

FLEXIBLE BATON

As I entered Room 505, Lt. Trask pointed at a chair at a table facing the board. I sat in it and looked at the panel facing me. Sgt. Hubert sneered. Everyone else was looking with some confusion at the crowd of reporters and media blow-dries filling most of the spectator seats. Also in the spectator section was Chief Harolds, Al Dockery, the detective I met when Winnie Hewitt brought him to the hospital, Miles Kieffer, and attorney Mike Hogg. Hogg was the big surprise. Whenever Mike Hogg defended a cop, two things could be taken for granted: First, Mike believed the charges to be bogus, and, second, the cop was going to get off.

I hadn't hired Mike and no one else had, as far as I knew. I hadn't been charged with anything yet. My old Third Eye kicked in, though: Dock had brought in Mike Hogg. He had also invited the media. Both were intended to send a message to the shooting board that getting rid of Joe DiMaggio Torio for anything less than actual, flagrant, and well supported infractions of important police regulations would be messy, embarrassing, time-consuming, and very, very expensive both to the city and personally among the board members.

I noted that Commissioner Graham's nephew, Lt. Crewe, wasn't in the room. Graham's flunky, Dieter Linge, however, was there sitting in a front seat, wearing a natty charcoal gray three-piece suit, a blue shirt with matching tie, black leather gloves on his hands, both hands resting menacingly upon a black leather attaché case flat on his lap. Blond, blue, and slender, Dieter always looked to me like a Gestapo agent impatiently awaiting clearance to resort to harsher measures. As Trask called the board to order, Dieter stood, went to the table across from the chairperson, took an envelope from his attaché case, handed it to Trask, and stood there to make certain Trask read it. Mission accomplished, he turned abruptly and left the hearing room. For a brief moment Trask looked like a little kid whose favorite toy had been confiscated by an unreasoning parent. He passed the document around to the other members. When everyone had read it, the board members covered the mikes and mumbled among themselves. That concluded, Trask again called the board to order.

They played the recording of the call to Capt. Finn in which the anonymous tipster disclosed the location of the Rizzo brothers. The caller's voice had been altered electronically to disguise it and had been traced to a pay phone on the corner of Cross and Twenty-seventh down from the Rizzo brothers' auto dealership. After that, the board invited me to state what I thought had happened, which I did to the best of my ability. Although I drew several strange looks from board members and Lt. Roemer, nothing else was done, save for entering into the record such things as reports from Ballistics, CSU, and the ME's office. No questioning, no cross, and they didn't even have a report from Crewe, who never showed. Among the things not entered in the record was the recording of the operation's wireless chatter before and during the event. I couldn't have rigged the hearing better had my own family manned the board. The fix was in. Trask at last asked me if I had any questions. They probably wouldn't have responded to a "What in the hell is going on here?" kind of inquiry. But, maybe someone could help fill in a blank.

"Who put the tourniquet on my shoulder? When the paramedics got to me, there was a tourniquet on my shoulder using a fan belt and a shotgun. Who did it?"

They had no answers. The spectators had no answers.

There was a vote.

The killing of the Rizzo brothers was unanimously deemed righteous and I was cleared. When I looked over at him, Dock was nodding to himself. "I don't get it," I said to him. "Even when they liked me, I never had a board that went under three hours. They didn't even call

Roemer." I looked at the expression on Dock's face then Kieffer's. "I don't suppose someone arranged for Commissioner Graham to hear a recording of the operation radio transmissions the night of the raid." I arched my brows.

Dock looked at Kieffer. "Well?" he said.

"A possibility," Kieffer replied with a straight face.

Dock studied where the board members were standing and milling around. He pursed his lips, stood, and said, "Enough fun and games, Kieff. Back to the salt mines."

Kieffer stood, turned, and followed Dock and the crowd of disappointed reporters out into the hall.

Later, in Betty Grable's waiting room, her receptionist, Roscoe, told me I'd have to wait a few minutes. "Here you go, sergeant," he said as he handed me a frosty cold bottle of Dr Pepper.

"Thanks, Roscoe. I'm surprised you still have a supply."

"Nobody but you sucks down that crap. Bet that bottle's a couple years old." He headed back to his desk.

Roscoe Wu was the size and shape of a refrigerator and looked like the product of a passionate night of love between Arnold Schwarzenegger and Charlie Chan. Former resident of Books State Correctional Facility, having finished seventeen out of a twenty stretch for murder two, he had dragon tattoos on the backs of both hands and a master's degree in psychology on his wall. Next to his degree was a framed wire photo of him in chains between two broad-shouldered corrections bulls on his way into Norden Hall at Breadloaf University to give his orals. I always had a mental picture of his examiners pointing out to each other that, even if he did the full twenty years, Roscoe would still be out in less than four years. *Pass or fail? Hmm?*

I took one sip of my Dr Pepper, sat down in one of Betty's comfortable chairs and pondered what I wanted from the upcoming session.

I wanted my walking papers. Before I could go back on the street, I needed some responsible mental health professional to attest to my sanity. There wouldn't be much point in picking at my nightmare collection. It would take months just to go through the highlights. My fears and self-esteem issues could take forever. Hi, how are you, I'm fine, get my papers, and goodbye. It looked like Kieffer had been grabbed for the Major Crimes Unit and unless I could hurry things up, I was going to miss out altogether.

Time passed and then passed some more. I got into looking through the jokes in an old issue of *Reader's Digest*. My eyelids grew heavy and I yawned. Long before reaching the end of an article on some horrific disease, I yawned again and drifted onto the train to dreamland.

Helpless, I cannot move, there is light all around me, the universe is filled with screaming. Blood everywhere I look, blood. The screaming—

I opened my eyes and Dr. Grable was looking down at me, a very deep frown on her face. She withdrew her hand from my shoulder and the frown morphed into a wry smile. "So, Joe, getting psyched up for your session?"

I tried for a comeback, but my tongue was as dry as leather from sleeping with my mouth open. After I finished saying something that resembled someone talking with a pair of pliers clamped on his tongue, I got up and followed her into her office.

I sank into her couch and after a bit of arm twisting I told her the dream. More arm twisting and I told her about the night at the Rizzo brothers' garage. She brought up the hanging of Kirby Flagg on her own, remembering it from the first time I graced her couch. I did have one positive thing to report, which was my forgiveness of Billy Roth, once I'd found out he had been murdered.

"Let's hope your remaining resentments can be resolved less drastically." She leaned forward in her chair and placed her hands on her knees. "Don't take time out to think up a wisecrack, okay, Joe? Just answer my next question."

"Okay."

"How do you feel now about Billy?"

I frowned. "Gypped. I feel gypped out of a friendship, a childhood, a chance to make things right." I uncrossed my legs, sank back in the couch, and shook my head. "I had lots of chances to make things right with Billy. I always figured, though, it was his job to come to me first. Many wasted opportunities."

"Own your own part of it, Joe," cautioned Betty, "but don't take on the responsibility for the whole thing." She glanced at her watch. Must be getting close to quitting time.

"Betty, I was wondering if you were planning to certify me fit for full duty."

"You've got time, Joe; use it. It's going to take awhile for your shoulder to heal. Meanwhile, we can work on your head."

"If you certified me fit for duty, I could at least go back to Homicide and help work cases doing research, phone tag, canvassing, that kind of stuff. Finn has me on Cold Cases."

Betty nodded. "That's a great place to do research and play phone tag, Joe. Is Cab Nelson still running that unit?"

"Cab Nelson has been running Cold Cases since Millard Fillmore was President."

"It keeps a paycheck coming in, you'll be abreast of what's going on in the department, and we can begin something I've been trying to get you to do since I first saw you after the Charlie Matthews thing."

"What's that?"

"Joe Torio is going to join the human race."

"What, did Visa revoke my card already?"

She leaned back in her chair and unconsciously tucked her deep purple scarf up around her neck. "Who is your best friend, Joe?"

I shrugged. "Al Dockery, I suppose."

"You suppose?"

"We've been together close to twenty years. I have dinner with him and his family now and then, we work cases really well, and I like him a lot. He taught me most of what I know about being a cop."

"You have just described a good partner, not a friend. Who knows your deepest darkest secrets and still likes you?"

I was getting that trapped rat feeling. "You?" I offered.

"I'm your shrink. Although I have been trying to know you for a number of years, I don't know your deepest darkest anything. I'll bet you my next year's salary against that piece of junk you drive that the young woman you were living with doesn't know anything about you except that you're a cop, you tell a lot of jokes, and you're heterosexual."

"She knows I like Dr Pepper," I said lamely.

She smiled that wicked smile. "Let's try it from the other end, shall we? What is Cheri's deepest darkest secret?"

I stared at a pale green wall for a moment while I gave it a thought. "Her favorite color is powder blue," I said at last. "I think it is," I added.

"I'm just guessing, Joe, but Cherie Vitamante's store of issues is probably a bit deeper than that."

"She worried about me being a cop."

"As I recall, that wasn't much of a secret."

"She worries about getting fat."

Betty curled her lip in scorn. "You just described fifty-one percent of Americans, the remaining forty-nine percent already are fat." She clasped her fingers over her belly and leveled a gaze at me. "Your assignment between now and next week is to go make a friend, Joe: Male, female, old, young, love interest, a mutual passion for skiing or movies, I don't care. Begin making a relationship—an *honest* relationship. Remember: friends know all about you and value you anyway. Those from whom you withhold things you are regarding as potential threats, not friends."

Fresh out of wisecracks, I eased my shoulder into a more comfortable position and nodded at her. "I may have made a start in that direction with my father. Maybe even with his intended, Caitlyn." I smiled ruefully. "Joe Torio the open book," I cracked.

She smiled. "Not to everyone, Joe. Just those with whom you desire a relationship."

"Then you'll sign my walking papers?"

"We'll see, Joe. How is the life story coming?"

"I don't know. I got around a hundred and fifty pages."

Her eyebrows went up. "Really?"

"Yeah. The stuff kind of bubbles out. Want me to send what I got as an attachment?"

"The last time I handed out my Email address to a patient I wound up getting spam from every porn peddler on Earth." She narrowed her eyes and thought for a moment. "In any case, no. When you have it finished I'd like to see it. Right now, continue as though no one will ever look at it. It's just you communicating with you."

"Me communicating with me. Join the human race," I muttered as I walked back to the Tower. "Bah, humbug." In a mental nod to Groucho Marx, I asked myself if I would want to belong to a race that would accept me as a member? "Good question," I said out loud in the elevator causing the young woman who was standing next to me to smile nervously and edge away. "Sorry," I said without explanation. Telling her I was returning from a session with my shrink where I was being treated for mental issues after killing a few folks probably wouldn't have eased her mind.

THE LOST KNIGHT

I settled into a routine of sorts. I arranged with Cab to pick me up for the first couple of weeks. While we had all this togetherness time on the road, I began trying out my human-race-joining wings on the world's oldest cop. I sent forth a few probes in the feelings *qua* deepest darkest secret department, and Cab Nelson finally raised a hand and put on the brakes: "Joe, my generation invented sucking it up and stuffing it. As it was put to me, if I can't handle my feelings, go eat a gun or teach them to swim."

"Gee, thanks for sharing, Cab."

"Anytime. You like to play poker?"

I became Cab's "friend," by his definition. I did my job, was amusing, rooted for the Yankees, and played poker with him and a few of his cronies Wednesday nights. The old Third Eye turned out to be very useful in poker playing until how much I won began pissing off Cab's poker cronies. Cab and I became really close friends, by his definition, when he found out my father actually had named me after Joe DiMaggio and I showed him my father's autographed bat.

Betty Grable judged this "friendship" a start, albeit somewhat feeble. The papers remained unsigned, but I still had time, as Betty kept pointing out..

A little over three weeks of this and some really painful physical therapy at the Sports Center at Riverside General, I could drive my Mazda with a minimum of agony and took over wheeling myself in to the Tower in the mornings and back at night. Pop was right. My back seat was a health hazard and I still hadn't done anything about that mouse that had died in the AC. When I ran the defrosters it still smelled like strange bacon. I began considering the possibility of a new car. With the auto industry on the ropes and the economy in the crapper, there should be some great deals to be had. All I needed was some assurance from the department that I wasn't going to be fired or tossed out on a medical pension. For that, I really could use Betty signing my walking papers.

Cab's buddies were convinced I was somehow cheating at cards and unceremoniously uninvited me from the Wednesday night poker game. Cab quit in protest. As Betty put it, "So you're not really making any new friends but are costing your partner his old friends."

"Progress, not perfection," I told her.

Then one day the next cold case file up for review was someone I knew: Rita Duke. I didn't recognize the name at first, but when I opened the file and scanned the identification block, I saw the victim had been born Rita Kwan. It slammed me like a brick between my eyes.

High school. Time for West Beverly High's senior prom and the hangman's son didn't have a date and didn't want to stay at home with the hangman and watch old movies. I wanted to go to the dance and I didn't want to go alone.

Perhaps I was insane to go for the most beautiful girl I knew. No one at my school would go with me so I asked a girl from another high school to go to my senior prom: Rita Kwan, the queen of Vadalia High. I first saw her at a game we played with Vadalia the year before when I was a junior. She was head cheerleader, luxurious long black hair, honey complexioned, mischievous dark eyes, a body that made me want to crow like a rooster, and she'd never heard of the hangman's son.

The famous ten-minute date. Rita had just broken up with her boyfriend and wanted to make him jealous. Why not go to a dance with this fellow, Joe. I had two eyes, all my own teeth, and my own car which was a cool Thunderbird pieced together over two years from several wrecks, painted a sporty red. Speaking of deep dark secrets, when she asked me what my father did, I told her Nicolo Torio sold hemp.

There was a brief moment, when I entered the gym with Rita Kwan on my arm, when all of the jokes about hangmen and recycled ropes were forgotten while the jokers tried to keep from stepping on each other's tongues. Rita glittered, she flowed, she glowed. She looked so goddamned beautiful it hurt.

Then music and we danced. It was a slow one to an oldie, "You'll Lose a Good Thing" by Barbara Lynn. Among the dimmed colored lights, the delicious scent of her filling my imagination, it was like having a heated cloud in my arms. She snuggled up close and it seemed like my entire life had been suffered to lead up to this one perfect moment.

And then that dance was over. There was nose powdering to be done and a few of the girls from West Beverly took Rita aside and let the queen of Vadalia High in on the truth about the hemp salesman. There was no second dance. Rita vanished. When I called her home her mother informed me that Rita had called for her father to come and pick her up.

Rita didn't like ghosts. She especially didn't like ghostmakers and sons of ghostmakers. She probably wasn't terribly fond of liars, either. I went home, hid in the dark safety of my closet, and toyed with tears and suicide. Couldn't remember if I'd told that one to Betty, but decided that I probably should. And now Rita was dead.

I read the rest of the file. I didn't look at the pictures.

Cause of death: penetration in the back of her head with an ice pick-like instrument, the victim's brains stirred somewhat by the movement of the narrow blade.

Something sick seemed to be crawling up my spine. So, what did a standup comic from West Beverly and the wife of the chief financial officer of Century Tools now of Collier have in common? They both died the same way. Oh, and in the past they both had done wrong to Joe DiMaggio Torio.

Scientific method: time to test the hypothesis.

"So," I muttered to myself, "Who was the person I hated the most in school?"

Who cost me the most blood and pain? Looking from the outside, who was Joe Torio's nemesis: Ed Derek. No doubt about it. Two years ahead of me in grade school, he was the ringleader and chief bully. I donated a lot of blood on account of his newly assumed opposition to capital punishment until Leroy Brown showed me how to fight. Ed Derek certainly fit in the set of childhood associates, such as Billy Roth and Rita Kwan, who had done me wrong. I entered his name to see if he had an old case in the freezer.

A bit of a search and there it was: Edgar Derek, washed up on the east bank of the South River between the Interstate and railroad bridges. Cause of death: the familiar ice pick-like instrument in the back of the skull plus brain scramble.

I felt myself getting ill. Billy Roth, lower middle-class, working family, Jewish, graduate of West Beverly High, funny man, single. Rita Kwan, upper middle-class, managerial father and academic mother, Catholic, graduate of Vadalia High, graduate of Dartmouth, stunning beauty, married to Elliot Duke, CFO at Century Tools. Edgar Derek, lower low-class, alcoholic family, atheist, dropped out of West Beverly High before his senior year, thug, junky, divorced. Like three peas in a pod.

I got the hard copies out of the stacks, poked through them to confirm the information I'd gathered, then walked around the desks until I was standing next to Cab. I dropped the files on top of the one he was entering into the computer.

"Like me to look at something, Joe?" he asked, a wry tone in his voice.

"I got three vics there, Cab, all died the same way—ice pick in the back of the head, their brains stirred—and as near as I can tell the only thing connecting them is me."

Cab dropped his reading glasses from his forehead onto his nose and scanned the first sheet on each file. "What's their connection with you, Joe?"

"At one time or another back in my school days, each one of these victims done me wrong."

"How'd you learn about them?"

"I came in with Billy Roth. Heard about his murder from his mother after I got out of the hospital. I ran across Rita Duke doing routine case reviews. I picked Ed

Derek as a cross check because I hated him more than anyone else I knew in school."

Cab glanced up at me. "If someone was bumping off people you hate, you figured the killer had to include Derek."

"No hit list of mine would be complete without him."

He dipped his head toward the files. "So, how did each of these persons do you wrong?"

Getting into deep dark secret time for real, now. One-by-one I told him. Cab listened, absorbing everything. When I was done, the old cop settled in and began reading the files, checking the information in the manila folders against what had been entered in the computer, examining all the reports and photos, while I logged out the stuff on the three cases from the evidence room. After dropping the boxes off with Cab, I went to the pogey bait palace, got him a Diet Coke and myself a Dr. Pepper. When I returned Cab was well through the second file. I sat in my seat, sipped my beverage, and marveled as the old man scanned each sheet, apparently missing nothing and digesting all. When he was finished with the third file, he closed it, pushed his reading glasses up on his forehead, sat back in his chair, glanced at the three evidence boxes, and folded his arms.

"Well?" I prompted.

"It seems pretty damned obvious, Joe, you are our prime suspect."

"Should I detain myself for questioning?"

"Probably what would be helpful is if you made a list of everybody you hate—or hated. You haven't seen any of these vics since school, right?"

"I saw Billy Roth when he was performing at a jazz club a few years ago, but I didn't know it was him."

"Concentrate on people you hated in school, Joe. I don't think the ones since then are at much risk."

"What makes you think so?"

Cab grinned. "Last I heard, Lt. Crewe is still alive."

"Good point."

"Let me have the names when you've compiled a starter list. Meanwhile, I'll go through the evidence boxes on the first three."

"You think we'll find more?" I asked.

He raised a single eyebrow. "Don't you?"

"Yeah. Okay, begin with Anthony Steckard," I said and spelled the last name for Cab. Tony had been Ed Derek's second banana in the punch-on-Joe Torio hit parade. I wrote the name down at the top of a piece of lined paper and began adding more: other bullies, whisperers, icy shoulders, cruel practical jokers, teachers into ridicule and unjust punishment, and school administrators who seemed to blame me for scarring up all those students' knuckles with my face. I was beginning to think I ought to call Betty Grable for backup. It was getting to be a long list, and I already knew how short the list of those I loved would be.

"Joe," said Cab.

"Got another one?" I asked expecting the worst.

"Not yet. Anthony Steckard was killed in a traffic accident in Toledo four years ago."

"Lucky him."

"Lucky you. As soon as you finish your hit list, Joe, make a list of anyone you helped or who might have regarded you as kind or helpful when you were in school."

"Why?"

He looked up at me. "All we have to work with right now is possible motive and the SODDI defense."

"Some Other Dude Did It?"

Cab nodded. "If you didn't pop these guys and scramble their brains, which is our working theory, someone else did them for you."

"A guardian."

He nodded. "Shark in the water," he muttered. "Three is minimum qualification to be a corn flake." He took the names I had on my list and began running them, making our case that we had a serial killer on the board and it wasn't me.

By the time we were done for the day, I had a migraine and was so depressed and bone weary I left my car at the Tower and had Cab drive me home. We had tracked four more unpleasant childhood acquaintances of mine who had gone onto a better world with scrambled brains, two of them from out of state. Nancy Wrangle had been president of the Drama Club and had been the moving force behind keeping me out of the club and any school theatrical productions. Her successful argument was that my "penchant for violence" made me a "disruptive presence."

Charles "Chuck" Ballinger had been captain of the West Beverly high school football team, had gotten an athletic scholarship to Northwestern, and had gone on to do assistant coaching at Wayne State until he got the head coaching slot at ESCC (yay Ravens) long after I had graduated. Back at King Elementary, though, he had been third banana in the punch-a-thon.

Constance Biddle had been the English III teacher when I was a junior at West Beverly. During the first semester I couldn't get more than a D minus on any written paper I turned in, although I maxed the exams and quizzes. I finally took the papers to my English II teacher, Jane Draper, and asked her to look at them. It was Miss Draper's opinion that none of the papers deserved less than an A- and she went to Ms. Biddle about it, the confrontation advancing rather rapidly to the hammer-and-tongs level. It went to a hearing before the English Department as well as the principle. Ms. Biddle lost and I got my grades upped. After that, and for the remainder of my time at West Beverly, I was Constance Biddle's private whipping boy. Endless jokes, little digs, "accidents" of various kinds, a constant whispering campaign in the faculty break room. As the new chemistry teacher, Arnold Betts, had put it to me the first time we met, "So you *don't* have three heads. For the longest time I thought your name was 'Watch out for that motherfucker.'"

The Jesse Masterson matter involved my father. Pop hanged murderer Roger Cobb and Assistant Principal Masterson was chairperson of the Save Roger Cobb committee. Mr. Cobb was tried and convicted of the premeditated murder of two soldiers down in the Zone. The Save Roger Cobb defense committee's premise was that capital punishment was immoral. On top of that, Roger Cobb was perfectly justified in killing the two veterans of the Vietnam era, since they were "agents of a criminal enterprise engaged in an illegal war." It probably wouldn't have been a big deal except that Mr.

Masterson shot off his mouth during a school assembly. I did a little research, found that neither one of the soldiers in question had ever served in Vietnam. The only enterprise they had been engaged in down in the Zone had been tossing down a few beers while watching scantily clad dancers do their stuff at The Score, then a go-go club.

I took my information to Mr. Cobb in private. He chose to respond, however, during the next student assembly by branding me and anyone who believed as I did "an immature, ignorant, blood-hungry war hawk." I got to hear variations of that quotation, by the way, at all but the most recent of my shooting boards.

After arriving at Pop's, my debate with myself concluded, I called Lt. Roemer's office and was told he was at his home. I called him there. What Cab and I were working on was officer involved and I was still my most likely suspect. We had to call in IAB and Cab had left it up to me. Roemer's daughter answered, and I got out "This is Detective Ser—"

She screamed, *"Cop, Daddy!"* then apparently dropped the receiver onto a hard surface. When Roemer answered, I said who I was and began telling him the situation. He cut me short and told me to make an official report to Internal Affairs in the morning. He didn't want to talk about it right then. Old Bruce sounded half in the bag and rather troubled. I would have asked him what was going on, but I don't converse well with chemicals.

After hanging up, I looked in the phone book and called Jane Draper's number. A woman who identified herself as Marie, Jane Draper's daughter, answered. I identified myself, and Marie let me know that for the past two years her mother had been in Riverview Assisted Living Center. A broken hip complicated by diabetes, poor circulation, and some "female problems." Marie said her mother had mentioned me often, particularly since my hospitalization after the Rizzo brothers thing, as her most famous student. She gave me her mother's number at the nursing home and said to be sure to call: her mother would be thrilled to hear from me.

I punched in the number and, indeed, Jane Draper seemed very happy to hear from me. *"You had such a hard time growing up, Joe. When you were in my class I was convinced you were going to be a writer. Well, you've certainly gotten in print being a detective."*

"I have such a low tolerance for alcohol I decided against a writing career."

She laughed, sounding the same as when I was a high school sophomore and in her class. She really had been the one bright spot in high school. *"When it was announced in the paper you had entered the Police Academy, it was such a perfect fit it was like a light bulb went on over my head. It was so obvious you were to be a police officer I don't know why I never saw it when you were in school."*

"Well, it wasn't all that clear to me. Miss Draper. Why I called, recently I've had to do some thinking on the past," I said. "I wanted to thank you for all your help back when I had to go up against Ms. Biddle about my themes and research papers. You put a lot on the line for me and that took a lot of guts. Thank you very much. For me, your class was a comfortable stretch in a depressingly long and bumpy road."

"Well, you're welcome and it's kind of you to say so, Joe." A couple of beats. *"How have you been doing?"* she asked, her voice quite serious. It wasn't a how-are-you-I'm-fine kind of question. She wanted to know.

A mess of jokes and diversionary prattle immediately came to mind. While I struggled with shoring up my protective walls, she said, *"The papers wrote about the Rizzos being killed, their wailing mother, and tons more on how this event will affect the department, the city administration, possible Federal funding, and the morals of the children of South River for the coming millennium. They never said how you are."*

"Not so well, Miss Draper." It just popped out.

"Tell me what's going on, Joe," she said, followed by, *"and I think you're old enough now to call me Jane."*

I sat down on my bed and it tumbled out. I told this woman I hadn't seen or spoken to for over twenty years what was going on with me—the unabridged edition. Then I wanted to know how she was doing, so I asked.

The aging process is quite a challenge, she confirmed. We talked some more. By the time we closed out I'd promised to visit her out at Riverview. It seemed that the friend making thing I was so afraid of wasn't as hard as I was making it out to be.

TOO MANY MURDERS

The next morning Cab and I filled out an official report and went over to IAB to see Lt. Roemer to turn it in. Cab had on his Yankees cap in honor of Lt. Trask, who was a notorious Red Sox fan. We were informed Roemer hadn't come in. No estimated time of arrival. We managed to get in to see Lt. Trask, but Trask was preoccupied with something else. He cut our narrative short, told us to dump the report on his secretary, and get out of his office. After the bum's rush, we stood outside the door to Internal Affairs staring at each other. "No cautions, no removal from the case, no removal from duty, no nothin'," I said. "Hey IAB, Torio in possible trouble again. I thought it'd be like throwing a live steer in piranha infested waters. In there it was more like throwing a dead piranha in the middle of a cattle stampede."

Cab scratched the back of his neck. "I'm guessing IAB has other fish on the griddle. Never seen it like that before."

"So, what do we do now?" I asked.

"Until we get thrown off the case, Joe, we work it. Since we have this little extension, I was wondering what we'd come up with if we worked it the other way."

"You mean put in a search for all ice pick in the head killings and see if any of the victims offended me sometime in the past."

"Well put, my boy. Let's run it through VICAP, too. Some more of your old persecutors could have been nailed outside our jurisdiction."

Unlike cops, sharks often roam outside meaningless political boundaries. The FBI's Violent Criminal Apprehension Program was a lot of paperwork, but once the Feds had all the information regarding the crime, the Bureau number crunchers would be able to provide details on the crimes closest in kind to our murders. It was covering a base.

We returned to Cold Cases, began running the search, and gathering the files. The program wasn't refined enough to sort out the knives from the ice picks, ice axes, and other sharp instruments, and no distinction had been made between the brain-stirred victims and the simply stabbed. Hence, we had to collect all the terminal head stabbings and go through each file. We came up with fifty-one occurring post my time in school. At the end of the day we had tentatively credited three more homicides to Joe Torio's Guardian account for a nice round total of ten. The newcomers were Steven Kale, William Price, and Lyle Saunders. I had forgotten all about them.

That evening Cab and I left the Tower together and had dinner at Fratiano's in Sherman Park. We asked Papa Orsino for one of his secluded back rooms, listened to the barely audible Italian background ballads being piped in, packed in the pasta, and talked murder. Cab wanted to know about the most recent additions to Guardian's list.

"All one incident. I was classmates with Kale, Price, and Saunders at East Shore Community College. My junior year they played a trick on me. Steven Kale was throwing a party at his family's estate up in Randolph Circle. He invited me to attend. William Price and Lyle Saunders were friends of Kale's and were there, as well."

At the time I didn't even know why I had been invited or why I accepted. Kale and I had never been friendly. I think at the time I looked upon the invitation as a friendliness gesture from Steve. I was hardly ever invited anywhere, so I decided to go.

Randolph Circle up in Glenn Heights was like a different planet. There were more trees, expensive shrubs, flowers, and well-tended grass than I had ever seen outside a cemetery. Inside the Kale mansion there had been a lot of good booze, acid rock, questionable pot, and unquestionable coke. Lots of really good-looking guys and girls. I had been wearing my best, but as I stood on a very thick, very white carpet self-consciously sipping at my Dr Pepper, I could almost feel clumps of dung dropping from my polyester. A look, a comment, a few shared snickers. Finally it dawned on me that I had been invited in to entertain Steven Kale and his friends. "I say, Muffy-poo, let's watch the hangman's son try to blend."

"Then I left," I said to Cab as I leaned back from my half-eaten shrimp carbonara. "I didn't know anyone else there. If Guardian was there, I couldn't guess who he was."

"Maybe he just heard about it," suggested Cab.

"Man, I don't know where we go from here," I said.

Cab smiled and said, "Sure you do."

Yeah. I knew: The list of all those I might have helped or been kind to during my school and college days. Someone who felt obsessively grateful and who wanted to balance the injustices of Joe Torio's life with a sufficient pile of blameworthy corpses. We kicked around bringing it all to Homicide, but none of the cases we had were active. Major Cases wasn't up and running yet, and squealing for the FBI was way above our pay grade. For the moment, the mess was ours.

Cab drove home and I called Jane Draper to see if she was up for a visit. She was. I took the old Collier Street Bridge over the river to West Shore, went up West River Drive to Cortina Street, and turned right into the Riverview Campus, which replaced the former designation, Riverview Nursing Home. I wondered when the marketing whizzes would get to renaming Books. When I was a kid it was Books State Prison. Even before Pop quit hanging them in the Dance Hall, they changed the name to Books State Correctional Facility. Could Books State Involuntary Reeducational University, South River Campus be far away?

Riverview was housed in two modern brick buildings each one looking like a huge piece of red toast stuck in the ground parallel to the river. The imaginatively named Building West was higher up on the river bank and offset about seventy-five yards north of the even more imaginatively named Building East, allowing an overlap of about fifty yards. I parked in the South Parking Lot and entered the motel-looking lobby of Building East, which by virtue of being closer to the river had the better view for the residents on that side. Half of those on the opposite side had Building West for a view. The remainder had varying views of picturesque West Shore, the meat packing capital of Lincoln County. Luther Stebbins, Dock's old partner now a resident in Building West, once said that on a warm summer day the residents of Riverview could hold pieces of bread out of their windows and bring in ham sandwiches.

Jane Draper's room was on the third floor on the river side. From her window she had a great view of the river and Middle Island Park. On the opposite side of the river was where East Branch joined the one. Toward the south she had a terrific view of the Interstate bridge, the railroad bridge, and the Collier Street Bridge. She had a nice looking room one wall of which was covered with pinned-up letters from her friends, relatives, and former students. There was a hospital bed that looked very motelish and three comfortable overstuffed chairs. She had TV and a laptop computer. Jane herself had white hair and a big smile I would recognize anywhere. She was wearing a lavender pantsuit over a pale yellow blouse. On her feet were black leather flats and on her nose rested a pair of shaded glasses with gold frames. Her eyes were "a bit sensitive to bright lights." Beside her chair was a walker.

We talked about this and that, catching up, until just before eight. There was a movie she wanted to catch on TV, *El Cid* with Charlton Heston and Sophia Loren. I asked if I could watch it with her, and she sent me down for sodas and popcorn from the building kitchen. We settled in and watched this fictional retelling of the story of Spain's greatest hero. There were commercials, and they ran the gamut of pills, exercise equipment, investment opportunities, wrinkle creams, and booze. As my sweet old hostess put it, "Everything to make your noodle limp and then give it backbone." During one of those breaks, Jane killed the sound and said, "Joe, the first time I saw this movie was on tape a few years after you graduated from West Beverly. When I saw it that time, I thought of you."

My eyebrows went up. "Me?"

"You were something of a knight in high school, you know."

"I never thought of myself that way."

"True knights never do. A number of the kids did, though. You were a fighter and good at it."

"That got me a few sessions with the principal; Cops on two occasions."

She leaned forward. "You didn't pick fights, though. The only fights I heard about were ones where you were defending kids who were being bullied. That's why when I learned about it the Police Academy seemed like such a good fit for you."

"Can't bear a bully," I said with a bit more conviction than I intended. I looked at her. "Can you remember any of the names of the kids who might have felt I helped them?"

"You don't remember them?"

I shook my head. "Not a one, and remembering them has recently become something of a need."

She studied me for a moment, turned off the TV, and said, "What's going on, Joe?"

I told her. It was close to eleven by the time I'd told her everything. Finally she said, "Horrible." She gave a slightly wicked smile. "Exciting, too. Especially when you think about how much some of your ten victims really deserved to get their brains Mixmastered with a sharp instrument."

I laughed. "Jane, are you looking for a place on my suspect's list?"

"If the victims could move faster than a snail and were stronger than a dish sponge I have a terrific alibi." She reached up, got a pad of paper and ball-point pen, then turned the TV back on. While I caught the last hour of *El Cid*, she pondered and wrote down names.

When I left a little after midnight, I had a list in my hand with fourteen names on it along with my deeds then in reference to them. As I first scanned the list, a few of my incidents of chivalry came back. Retrieving a hat for a girl named Rosalind Davies from a bunch of

111

clowns who were playing monkey-in-the-middle was one. Getting back lunch money for two freshman, Gil Carpenter and Mickey Ryan, taken by a three hundred pound senior named Lom Ravines was another. I smiled when I saw Greg Castro's name. I had come upon Jason Brewster trying to force Greg into a hall locker. His efforts thus far had cut Greg's lip and torn his shirt. With Greg's help we put Jason in the locker instead, and without his pants.

Most of the names, though, rang no bells. I was taking the Fishkill Underpass on my way to Boundary and debating with myself about calling Cab and letting him know about the information Jane had supplied, when my cell phone played Wagner's *Ride of the Valkyries*. It was Cab. Without ceremony, he said, *"You got an alibi for the past couple of hours?"*

"Rock solid. I was visiting an old teacher of mine at Riverview. What's up?"

"Capt. Finn just called me. Our Guardian pile of cold cases just got moved over to Homicide. They also found Lt. Roemer's body thirty minutes ago."

My stomach seemed to flip and sink to my knees. "Ice pick?" I asked, recalling the troubled way Roemer had sloughed off my call the day before.

"No. He caught a bullet through his head. In and out. The crime scene geeks figure a long distance rifle shot."

"A sniper?"

"Yeah. They dug the slug out of Roemer's wall and they think it's good enough for a match. It doesn't fit with the others, but he does have a connection with you."

"True."

"Do you own a rifle of any kind?"

"Nope."

I heard him sigh with relief. Cab's voice dropped to about half volume. *"Even so, roll up your pant legs, partner. The shit is about to run very, very deep."*

It didn't take long. The next morning Capt. Finn took my badge. I was indefinitely suspended without pay pending the outcome of the IAB investigation. Since it was mine, I got to keep the .357 Magnum. The S&W 669 was also mine, awarded to me for shooting perfect scores on both target and combat ranges when I was at the Academy, but IAB continued to hold that in evidence concerning the Rizzo brothers' matter. My alibi for the Roemer sniping checked out, and it seemed I also had rock-solid alibis for all of the ice pick murders supposedly done by my self-appointed guardian. If I wasn't in the hospital from injuries received in the line of duty, I was getting a commendation from Chief Harolds or being interviewed by some reporter, which Lt. Trask apparently thought remarkably suspicious.

"Before the media begins asking why you are still a detective, Joe," explained Finn, "Upstairs thought it would be prudent to give you a little time off."

"Without pay."

"Yes," said the captain.. "To avoid the impression the big blue wall is somehow supporting you."

"No risk of that."

Finn looked like an ad from the Robert Hall's over-the-hill catalog. Gray suit, TV-red tie, gray topcoat, what remained of his graying hair blow-dried into something resembling a honeydew melon hiding beneath a fur-lined toilet seat. Finn had a moderately slim build that attested to many hours upon Tread-slave, Stair-demon, Thigh-buster, and Butt-kicker. He grinned. "Heal that shoulder, Joseph, and get your clearance from the psychiatrist," he said. "Let Internal Affairs investigate and clear up this matter so when you're ready to return to work, it won't be in the middle of a media storm."

"The department still paying for the shrink?" I asked.

He frowned and thought for a moment. "Your condition is duty connected, your treatment ordered by the department. Yes, I believe the psychiatrist is covered. The union would insist."

If I had been in Finn's shoes, I wouldn't have suspended me; Instead, I would have run my butt into an interrogation room and grilled me until I came across with the name of my accomplice—he who shot Lt. Roemer in the head while I watched old movies with a retired English teacher. So, just as well no one asked me.

I hadn't really unpacked my box from getting moved out of Homicide so I topped it off with my Cold Cases paperclips, bid farewell to Cab and the lullaby, and drove home. I half expected the front to be crowded with reporters, but my possible connection to ten or more slayings was overshadowed by the new administration's efforts in Washington to continue the old administration's efforts to end the recession by turning it into a Roosevelt depression. There was only one reporter waiting. He was keeping warm in his car and listening to his radio as his 401k turned into bubble gum change. By the time he noticed me, I was in the house and refused to answer the doorbell.

I called Betty to broach the possibility that our future sessions might have been rendered pointless by my suspension. Before I could get to it, she interrupted by saying, "What a wonderful opportunity to work on yourself." She also decided we would now double up on our sessions. Every cloud do have a silver lining.

The doorbell rang again, I peeked through a window in the turret which had a good view of the front door. It wasn't the reporter. Standing there were Lt. Jared Trask of IAB, Det. Sgt. Beaumont of Homicide, and two other trench coats I didn't know. "Hoo boy."

I mentally rolled up my pant legs and opened the door.

They didn't have enough for probable cause and didn't have a search warrant. Would I, however, give them permission to toss the house and take into evidence whatever the hell they felt like?

I said I wasn't the legal owner of the house and couldn't, therefore, grant such permission.

Did I own a rifle, they wanted to know.

No. Don't own a rifle and never did.

"Someone who can shoot like you, Torio?" said Beaumont. The guy looked like Charles de Gaulle with hair. "And you don't go hunting? Not even once? C'mon." He really had a big nose.

I told them about the rabid raccoon I shot in Maine. The rifle, however, had belonged to my Aunt Cella.

"Where might that rifle be?" asked Trask.

"Not a clue. Last I saw it was in Rangeley, Maine."

"Do you recall the caliber of that rifle?"

I frowned. "It was a Remington 700. A thirty-oh six, I think."

That lit them up. "Could we have your aunt's telephone number and address so that we could question her?"

I pointed up. "She died quite a number of years ago. I believe the number is unlisted."

"What happened to the weapon?" asked Beaumont.

"I don't have a clue. Her heir was a nephew of her deceased husband. Never met him. If I ever knew his name, I can't remember it."

"Did she leave you anything?" asked one of the unnamed trench coats, a heavy young man with a three-shaves-a-day shadow and a knowing smirk.

"Her music. She was heavily into Chopin. Anything else, guys? I need to begin looking for a job."

Trask's eyes almost glittered as he asked, "Would you, at least, let Computer Forensics go through your laptop, in a cheerful spirit of cooperation? It would make you look better, for purposes of the investigation," he added.

I pointed up again, using a different finger, and closed the door in their faces.

SUICIDE BY JUSTICE

What could possibly put the cherry on top of my day? It would be only a matter of time before Trask patched together enough BS and found a judge who would give him a warrant. Who knew what they'd find if they tore the house apart. Pop was at risk, too. I was sure he had a few things that wouldn't look so good in the media or in front of an investigation. Maybe we could get adjoining cells. I called his number. *"Morton's Salt,"* he replied enigmatically.

"Come again?"

"'When it rains, it pours,'" He quoted. After a long silence he let me know that the three million dollar Camp Charles deal had fallen through. The contractor was going to have to file for bankruptcy.

"Good man, that Peter Blaylock," said Pop. *"Done a lot of business with Pete over the years. Shame. Over forty men and women work for him."*

"How about you, Pop? Are you okay?"

"Charlotte Costa, my accountant, wants me to lay off at least four of my own crew. She'd prefer six. I told her to figure out what cut everyone would have to take to keep everyone on."

"Can you find enough work for them, Pop?"

"Things are tight, but grass, weeds, and trees keep growing. Come spring a lot of places going to need to be cleaned up. At some price we can all keep working."

"I can help out for awhile, Pop. I've been suspended," I said brightly.

"With pay?" he asked.

"No."

A silence. *"Joe, that's not really good news, is it?"*

116

"Depends on how you look at it, I suppose. Betty Grable was thrilled. We need to talk when you get home, Pop. I'm about to be investigated."

Pop was hip enough to presume our lines were tapped. *"Well, while I try and figure out where our next meal is coming from, maybe you should go write a book."*

"Maybe I'll do a script for *Police Academy XVI.*"

Long silence, then he let out a breath. *"I'll be home in a few hours."*

I ended the call and looked around the living room. Pictures of me, of my mother, Aunt Cella, the Gasman, my godfather Bill Mack, my class photos from King Elementary, West Beverly High, and East Shore Community College. I looked at the photo from King Elementary wondering if the Guardian's young face was among the hundred and twelve shown in the picture. Amazing how many faces I couldn't connect to either a name or a memory. Some of the names from Jane Draper's list had been in classes other than my own. Right then, though, not having Pop dragged off as a war criminal was the priority.

I had no idea where my father kept anything except his collection of recordings. But I did have a bit of training on searching a building and began doing so. I started in the basement and learned that my father had tried his hand at furniture restoration. In the music room bookshelves I found more than a hundred books on the American Civil War, and more than that on true crime. Pop even had a paperback copy of Lydia Jenks's book on Jay Hellerman ("the unauthorized case study"), unauthorized by me, she meant. A lot of books to go through page-by-page. I flipped through them but found nothing.

By half past four I'd made it to the second floor and was in the sewing room creeping myself out by going through my mother's things. Clothes, dress patterns, letters, files, some stuffed animals, boxes of fabric and sewing stuff, and books. My mother was a Baroness Orczy fan as well as an L. Frank Baum enthusiast along with a lot of Agatha Christie and Rex Stout. Sticking out from the crowd was a book on the American Civil War:

<u>Life And Death in Rebel Prisons</u> by Robert H. Kellogg. It was an 1865 edition which described former Sergeant-major Kellogg's experiences in Andersonville and other Confederate institutions of incarceration. In that volume was where I found a piece of white ruled paper, folded in quarters, yellowed with age stuck between the pages. Why it wasn't with my father's other Civil War books in the music room was a bit of a mystery. The volume had been inscribed to Pop by my godfather, Bill Mack. The date was four months after I was born.

The paper had the name Wm. Edison Fuller written in cursive script over and over, as though someone had been practicing Mr. Fuller's signature. A tingle skittered across the surface of my skin as a number of things that had no intention of coming together locked onto each other with death grips. Dock called it my Third Eye and the unconscious links ran me headlong into a brick wall of conclusion. Now it made a lot more sense why the hangman hadn't wanted me to be a cop.

I never did have the confidence in my intuition that Dock had, except when playing poker. It was in my important papers file along with my diplomas, commendations, and such. I went to my room, dropped into my desk chair, opened the drawer and took out the file. My birth certificate had supposedly been signed by State Registrar Wm. Edison Fuller. Chances are Wm. Edison himself wouldn't be able to tell the difference between this signature and his own. My godfather had the pick of the very best forgers in the state from whom to choose. Never hurts to have the warden owe you one. Didn't seem right, though. Bill Mack was too smart to have used a professional—particularly one who could cause him a lot of grief. I put that aside for the moment and thought about the little field trip the hangman took me on when I was in the fourth grade.

October day, the trees full of color, a math test coming up, but the hangman took me out of school for the day. I asked him why and he said we were going to see a session of superior court: the retrial of Kirby Flagg.

Flagg had been all over the papers and TV. The retrial was in its second week and the media, engaging in its usual manufactured hysteria, were shaking before

118

villagers the possibility that Flagg might indeed get off, although there had never been a chance of any such thing happening. When Pop and I entered and sat in the back, a police forensics expert under direct examination was rambling on about conchoidal fractures and a broken pair of eyeglasses. At the defense table, seated two places away from his attorney, was Kirby Flagg, seemingly disinterested in the legal proceeding. He was a former state trooper who, in an alleged rage, allegedly slew his wife, his three daughters, and his grandmother with a double-edged ax. It had happened long enough ago that his legend had some really sick parents threatening to send Kirby Flagg to tuck them into bed if their children didn't behave themselves.

At one point in the trial Kirby Flagg turned around and let his gaze wander among the spectators, picking them out one at a time, until his eyes found the hangman, and then me. The man's hair and eyes were dark, his lashes quite long. The eye contact made me feel like the killer had physically reached out and touched me. I couldn't look away or breathe.

The eyes and the man's expression were hard, pitiless. It was as if he could not afford emotions of any kind. Still, he nodded once at me. I nodded back. The man then turned around and appeared to slump and snooze in his chair. I went home having learned next to nothing about the justice system, my head buzzing with a thousand questions, and no one to ask who would give me a straight answer. In the middle of winter Pop put the noose around Kirby Flagg's neck and pulled the floor out from under him.

"Angelina and I couldn't have children," said the hangman. I turned my head and Pop was standing behind me, looking over my shoulder at the page of practice signatures.

"I didn't hear you come in," I said.

He pointed at the paper. "When Kirby went crazy and butchered his family, his brand new son, Kirby Bernard, escaped the slaughter. He was only a few weeks old. The day before, Kirby Flagg had been called in and had to spend all night in Stover's Wells helping to investigate the murder of a woman and her two daughters."

"Mandy Parker," I said. "Her daughters, Nancy and Amber." I shrugged and refolded the paper, replacing it in the book. "A year or so after I joined the detective bureau, I looked into the Kirby Flagg thing." I looked back at Pop. "He was a top cop: Medal of Honor, five commendations, lieutenant in the state detective bureau."

"That's right."

"He was sick, conscientious, and dedicated," I continued. "Flagg also cared about the people he was supposed to protect."

"Kirby always kept his feelings bottled up," said Pop. "It was like that in those days." He sadly shook his head. "Then it all landed at the same time: sleepless nights and one gory senseless murder after another."

"Then he snapped," I said.

Pop nodded and sat on my bed facing me. He looked very tired. "Kirby told me it was the only way he could protect his family."

"By killing them?" I asked.

"Yes. He should've been put in Temple Glen, but he wouldn't let his attorney plead insanity. He told me I was the only one who could save him."

"Suicide by justice," I remarked. I glanced up at Pop. "How did he miss killing me?"

"You were so new, Joe. In his insanity he simply forgot about you. You were so quiet. Bill Mack said that was what saved you. Joe, you never said anything or even cried until you were almost two years old."

"And you hanged him."

"I did."

I rubbed my eyes, the investigation and getting suspended long forgotten. "So, you hanged my father and how did I wind up as your son?"

"Kirby knew I didn't have any kids. He said he wanted me to have you." Pop rubbed his eyes, leaned forward, and rested his elbows on his knees. "When I told her, Angelina didn't think at all. She said to do whatever I had to do to make it happen. Warden Mack fixed it up through friends and contacts. A few records adjusted, a few more burned, and Angelina and I went away for about four months. When we came back, we had a son."

"Why? Why did Kirby Flagg give me to his executioner?"

"I don't know. Maybe you should ask Dr. Grable." The hangman shrugged and held out a hand. "Kirby was broken in his head. Maybe he thought it was a way of making up to you what he did."

"Do you believe that?" I asked him.

"No."

"What, then, Pop?"

"You messed up his plans to save everyone he loved through death. I think Kirby was trying to punish you for surviving, Joe. Maybe he could punish me, too, for hanging him." He was silent for a long time and then asked, "Remember when I took you to court that time?"

"I do. I always knew it had nothing to do with learning about the justice system."

Pop nodded. "Kirby wanted to see you. He threatened to blow the whole thing up in our faces if I didn't cooperate and bring you by the trial. He wanted to see the kind of boy you had become. Later, back in Books, he told me you were a nice looking boy." Pop smiled sadly. "He also told me never to let you become a cop."

Pop took the Civil War book from my hands, opened it, and removed the folded sheet of paper, unfolded it, and let his gaze wander over the practice signatures.

"Not smart, Pop, leaving evidence like that lying around. Who was the forger who phonied up the birth certificate?"

"Bill Mack's friends in the registrar's office got the form and filed it when it was done. Angelina was the one who forged the signature. Bill said she had a real talent." He nodded at the piece of paper. "I should have thrown this away when I discovered it among your mother's things. I simply couldn't do it."

As it turned out, I couldn't either.

The next morning at ten o'clock, as I lowered myself onto Betty's couch, she asked me, "So, Joe, how are things going?"

I started giggling and couldn't stop. Tears streaming down my cheeks, then I laughed out loud until it was difficult to catch my breath. Roscoe got my coat off and rolled my sleeve, Betty gave me a shot of something, and Roscoe drove me home. He was there when Pop showed up.

I didn't ask Roscoe if Betty was going to sign my papers. It would've started me giggling all over again. I went to bed and Pop and Roscoe went to the kitchen and talked for a long time. They were, after all, old friends.

THE FERRYMAN

A couple of weeks later, most of my squirrels back in their cages, I went out to see Kirby Flagg's grave. Curiosity, mostly. Answers from the one person I was certain couldn't supply them.

The eastern end of Books prison grounds was a long, narrow, triangular lot of about sixteen acres, the point formed by Canal Street and the Heights Road as it swung south around Soldier Heights. Prisoners and staff at Books referred to it as the Corner. It contained the prison cemetery. The Corner was enclosed by a low masonry wall topped by wrought-iron spear points, more for decoration than security. Outside the masonry wall was a twelve foot high chain-link fence topped with three rolls of razor wire. That fence was to keep vandals and souvenir hunters out. Above it all was an angry dark overcast that promised more snow.

The keeper of the Corner was a fellow named Len Smith who everyone called Tombstone. I knew him from back when my father ran the Dance Hall and Tombstone was glad to see me. He was a heavy set man with a wide, deeply lined face, his complexion deep olive, his eyes dark brown and curiously serene. He wore a thick blue goose-down parka and insulated work gloves.

If you died inside and paid your bread before you were dead, Tombstone would carve you up a slab of white marble with your name, dates, and whatever else you wanted, within reason. Last gasp messages to the warden, guards, or certain prisoners were not allowed. Those who left their eventual dispositions to the state, however, got a pressure treated wooden stake with a laminated bar-coded ID card tacked to it. The earlier markers were cedar and didn't have bar codes. About a tenth of the graves had marble markers. Paths had been cut through the snow with a snow thrower across the graves. "Lots of visitors this winter," Tombstone explained. He pointed out Kirby Flagg's marker. I didn't really know what I was doing there, but Tombstone left me alone to do it.

Kirby Flagg's grave was close to the Canal Street side, the road noises making me flinch as I looked down at the weathered cedar marker, the plastic covered ID card tacked to it containing his name, prison number, and dates. And what do you say to the unhearing monster who stalked my nightmares ever since I could remember? Hi? Here I am, father dear? Is there a special place for cops who bust their mainsprings or are you wandering the same circles of Hell as everyone else?

I dug the remaining snow away from the front and back of the marker. On the back of the cedar stake I noticed something scratched into the wood. I bent over and looked.

They were words: "Beloved Son, Husband, and Father."

As unexpected tears came to my eyes, I abruptly stood and looked over the wall at the traffic on Canal, the buildings on the far side of the street backed by the mountain as it eagerly awaited the new snow.

"Want me to chip loose a little dirt?"

I turned and looked at Tombstone Smith. He moved quietly for a big man. "What?" I asked him.

The keeper pointed with a thick calloused finger at the grave. "I can get a hammer and chisel, get under the ice, and get you a bit a dirt. A lot a family come by here like that. Get a little dirt from the grave, you know, as a keepsake."

"No." I pointed at the marker. "On the back of that plank someone scratched some words."

Tombstone nodded. "'Beloved Son, Husband and Father,'" he said. "Killed his whole family, you know."

"Yeah. You know who scratched those words into the marker?"

He shook his head. "Nope. It's been there for about twelve years, though. Lots of markers here have sentiments scratched in 'em." He pointed west in the direction of the inmates' educational center that now stood where the old Dance Hall had been. The wide end of the Corner's triangle backed up against it. "Over there on Jack Dolan's marker is scratched, 'Here lies an unforgiving rotten son of a bitch.'" He shook his head. "Can't disagree. Prob'ly was the only way some poor bastard could hit back."

"Did you ever meet Kirby Flagg?"

The man's heavy gray eyebrows rose an increment. "Never did, not face to face. He was up on the row when I was doing my fifteen stretch. Condemned prisoners got their own exercise yard, you know. He send word to me, though, to carve up a proper set of stones for his family out at Avon Gardens. Proper set, he said, and the design was left to me. He could pay, too. I worked it out with the warden." Tombstone frowned and nodded. "Warden Stafford in those days. Anyway, I figure it up, pick the stones, carve 'em up, and Avon comes, gets 'em, and sets 'em. You ever been out to Avon Gardens?"

"No."

"Beautiful place. You go on out there. Take a look at what I done. Biggest job—best job—I ever did. Avon done a real good job settin' the stones, too." He smiled as though he were laughing at himself. "That's a lot of pride workin' my mouth," he said. "Sorry."

"What did you think of him?"

"Who?" he asked.

"Kirby Flagg? What did you think of him?"

"Never met the man. I don't judge anyways." He waved both his hands indicating the entire cemetery. "Cain't know enough to judge any o' these cons." He stuck his gloved hands into his coat pockets. "The man I killed, detective, deserved killin' more'n anybody who ever walked on dirt. The jury and that judge didn't agree, though. Got me my job here. Don't suppose they have to agree if I was willin' to do the time."

I nodded toward Kirby Flagg's marker. "How come he doesn't have a headstone?"

"Sent him a note askin' that same thing. He come back with a note o' his own and the rest of the bread he owe, sayin' he couldn't think o' nothin' more pitiful than a man who has to go order and pay for his own headstone." Tombstone turned down the corners of his mouth and nodded once. "The man, he got a point there. Hope for him, though," Tombstone said as he grinned widely. "Go lookit the stones I carved out at Avon. They's hope for everybody."

Avon Division is on the heights northwest of the city next to the river. St. George University and Lanford Academy are located there, along with some of the oldest homes in the city and a few working farms. The cemetery overlooks the river and is considered to be something of a showplace because of its many gardens, widely spaced impressive monuments, and the occasional ancient tree. You always hear someone say "What a beautiful place to be buried." Personally, I thought it would be tough enjoying all that beauty with all that dirt in your face. There was a light wind blowing up from the river raising little ice-dust whorls around some of the headstones. Here and there an individual, a couple, visiting the graves of those long past caring who showed up or how often.

The temperature seemed to be dropping. After I got directions from the gate house, I drove in and found the location. Turning off the ignition, I left the keys, and looked through the windshield at the pride of Tombstone Smith. The Flagg family monument designed and carved by the Corner keeper was simple, stark, and beautiful. It was a wall, eighteen feet long, three feet high, and a foot thick made from polished black granite, the ends of the wall bent toward the graves like the embrace of two huge black arms. It had to have been made from a number of blocks joined together, but it looked like a single gleaming piece, the name Flagg carved in the center. I got out of the car, put up the hood on my parka, and walked over.

The names were all there, except for Kirby's mother. Inez Flagg had been buried next to her husband, Kurt, in their own plot next door.

I studied the cleanly carved letters and frowned as I read the names from left to right: Chana and Tasia, my twin sisters. Alicia Marquez, my mother. A wide unmarked space, and then my eldest sister's name,

Felicia." It suddenly dawned on me that I wasn't really Italian. I was English-Mexican.

Something else I noticed: That wide blank space. "Tombstone left a place for Kirby," I said to the silence. I was both touched and startled by the liberty the stone carver had taken. I wiped my palms over my face and turned away. There was a small party in the distance visiting a grave, their mumbles swallowed by the wind. A single mourner, a man, was standing on a rise, looking in my direction.

I looked back at the Flagg family resting place. Was Kirby Flagg a beloved son, husband and father? Tombstone didn't judge, but I had a different investment in the answer. Those four children came from somewhere. His mother didn't live with him because he hated her. Would they like to have Kirby back with them again? Were they beyond caring? The media could make some hay out of it, though, if they knew: The ax murderer now resting amidst his victims. I'd just have to have it done without the media finding out about it, I decided. Maybe being together again would heal a wound that would allow all of them to rest. Come spring I would have Kirby Flagg placed with his family. It seemed like the right thing to do. Have to get Tombstone to carve the inscription.

My life had been spared by a forgetful madman and saved by a childless hangman and his wife. Standing there, I think for the first time, it got through to me that I wasn't condemned to die. Improbable as it was, I was alive. I was *still* alive. Somehow I knew that I would never again take my own existence for granted.

SHADES

No good deed goes unpunished.

Three weeks, several hearings and fruitless investigations, multiple shrink and physical therapy sessions later, and that's what woke me that April morning: No good deed goes unpunished. It was just after two in the morning. Pop wasn't making pancakes so I hadn't screamed him awake.

Who said that first: No good deed etc.?

I wasn't sleeping anyway so I cranked up my laptop and found out the Wikkies didn't know either. Origin unknown. One more fruitless investigation. Homicide had chewed on the "Guardian" murders for a few days, called in the FBI, and now everyone could say with all honesty, "It's out of our hands."

I had my badge, Betty had grudgingly signed my papers with the proviso that I continue our sessions, and I would officially return to the Cold Cases desk in the morning. Normalcy. I had no doubt that the whole Guardian thing would wind up back in Cold Cases before May. Cab and I continued investigating my Shining Knight list, begun by Jane Draper, but everybody had alibis for at least six of the murders. The ones who had alibis for all of them were deceased.

There was a feel to the whole thing I couldn't shake. Shades. That's what Dock calls that creepy feeling that the puzzle makes no sense at all without that one important piece, and that most important piece you should already know because it's so damned obvious.

My phone rang and I looked at the clock on my nightstand. A little before three. Death Threat Charlie never called before five. I picked up the cordless handset and said, "Yeah?"

"Joe, it's Dock." His voice was about as dead serious as I'd ever heard it.

"What's up, D—" I wrestled down my usual greeting. "Hi," I said at last.

"Come to 762 Booth down in the Zone. Be ready to go to work."

"What's up, Dock?" It simply came out.

"You want back in the bigs?"

"Yeah—"

"762 Booth. Now," and he cut off the call.

The temperature was in the low teens, snowing, and a steady fifteen mile an hour blow coming off the river. The cross town streets on the way to Booth were slick with the new snow on old ice. No one was out on the street who didn't have to be there. I came into the Zone on Faulkner and took a right onto Booth. Pulling my MX3 up behind one of the blue-and-whites, I shut it down, put on the brake, and looked through the windshield. Where I'd parked was half way to the intersection with Randall where rose the Egypt Hotel, its red neon letters reading Egypt Ho**l the same as they had for the past five years or more, earning the fleabag establishment its nickname, the Egyptian Hole. It was a busted down neighborhood prettied up a little by the freshening snow. The windows in the rundown row houses were dark, a curtain here, a blind there, twitching. Here and there were buildings that had been rehabilitated through mass infusions of well laundered funds. The address Dock had given me appeared to be one of those.

I noticed a figure move in the shadows. It turned as it looked at something in its hand, a dull glint of light reflected from something on its chest. A badge. It was a cop. I popped the seatbelt, opened the door, and got out. Pulling the collar of my overcoat up against the icy wind, I walked over to the police officer who was keeping the crime scene log. "Move along, buddy," he warned. "This has nothing to do with you." His nametag identified him as of the Bradleys.

"Sgt. Torio," I said to him as I flashed my tin. "Lt. Dockery wants to see me."

"Sorry, sergeant. I thought I saw you get out of that shitheap Mazda over there and mistook you for a local."

"I *did* get out of that Mazda."

His eyebrows went up as he shook his head and leaned it toward his shoulder mike. "Then I really am sorry."

While he called it in and checked his watch, I looked around. The curbs on Booth were lined with parked cars, a couple of them up on blocks, one burned out, at least half a dozen out of my price range, a couple out of Bill Gates's price range. Drug dealers, players, pimps. A sort of late night, late morning kind of street.

Every police vehicle crowded around the entrance to the green-painted row house had its Christmas lights on and the out-of-sync blue strobes were at once hypnotic and nauseating. Between the hour, the weather, and all the blues there were no curiosity seekers. There was a plainclothes cop in a dark overcoat across the street, knuckling doors. He looked like Stan Brooks. I'd known him from back when I was in Homicide. Dock had moved him over to MCU. Stan was in his low thirties and looked like a self-indulgent Mr. Clean. He was wearing one of those multi-colored Laplander hats with the ear flaps down.

No media, yet. Dock finally appeared beneath the light over the house's stoop looking like a giant double scoop of pistachio ice cream topped with a chocolate bonbon. Big-top sized pale green coveralls, shoe covers, and latex gloves. Dock pulled off the covers and gloves and tossed them into a red and yellow plastic bin by the door. Emerging from the door behind him was another, much smaller figure: a woman in crime scene coveralls wearing a black baseball cap, the bill forward casting her face in shadows. Didn't recognize her. Dock saw me and launched himself down the three steps to the sidewalk. The woman remained on the stoop, watching.

As Dock slowed, those big browns drilled into me. "You look better, DiMaggio."

"I see that high-fat, high-carb diet is working out for you, Dock."

"What am I going to do with you, Joe?"

"No one ever seems to know unless they have a knife or a gun."

Dock nodded at Bradley and the officer lifted the crime scene tape. I went beneath, Dock took my arm, and led me toward the door. "Tell me you're okay, Joe."

"I'm okay. Papers and everything."

Dock looked into the shadows, frowned, and pulled the palm of his hand over his closely cropped hair. He looked at the moisture on his hand. "Dr. Grable told me you've come a long way but you have a long way to go."

"What ever happened to doctor-patient confidentiality?"

"Margie used to be a cop. We served together in East Roosevelt Division. She's not going to saddle a fellow cop with a nut case."

"Does this mean I'm not a nut case?" I asked.

"She tells me she can pull your papers any time she feels like it. So, don't miss any appointments, Joe. You think you can handle some work?"

"What? Are you kidding? Major Crimes? Let me at it."

"You look a little shaky."

"The streets are sheets of ice and I'm standing in the middle of a snowstorm," I protested.

"What about your shoulder?"

"I finished physical therapy end of March and it's fine." I gave my arm and shoulder an impatient demo wiggle. "Want to arm wrestle?"

"Counter productive. I'd rip off that little twig at the shoulder." Dock rubbed the back of his neck and nodded toward the green-painted row house with the mysterious woman still standing on the stoop, still watching. He was getting to the point of the exercise. "Dust off your Third Eye, Joe. I need a reading on this situation. There are shades all over this thing and I can't put my finger on them. I need to be sure."

The way the woman stood on the stoop— something—said to me that she was as much of an odd fit here as I was. "One of yours?" I asked Dock.

He turned his head and glanced at the woman he had left behind. "No. She's a PI working for the male

131

vic's father." Dock leveled his browns on me. "Frank Scozarri."

Francesco "Dago Frank" Scozarri, head of the Scozarri family, lord of the west side mob, including all of the Zone. Don Scozarri of the many missing bodies. Prostitutes, protection, politics, and labor relations. Scozarri only had one son, even though Frank never married the boy's mother. I could feel my own eyebrows climbing. "Vince Polizzi is one of the vics?"

Dock nodded.

I could almost hear the champagne corks popping over at the Organized Crime Task Force. Vince Polizzi brought up a whole pile of questions. Why wasn't the Scozarri family over in Sherman Park right now stacking up Nicky Batts's boys like cordwood? And, speaking of the OCTF, why weren't they running this investigation? And the woman on the stoop. Dago Frank's club had certain rules: Number one was it handled its own problems. A mob boss hiring a private dick? Biggest question, through: who was bad enough to take down Vince Polizzi?

Dock nodded toward the open trunk of a police cruiser, and said, "Suit up. You can toss your overcoat in there next to mine."

"You sure this is okay with Finn?" I asked.

"It is for now; I didn't ask him."

I took off my topcoat, dug into the trunk, picked out pale green coveralls, latex gloves, and shoe covers as Dockery pulled out new gloves and covers for himself. Pulling on the coveralls, I carried the rest. Dock led the way up the stairs to the stoop and entered the vestibule without introducing me to the PI. I paused, held out my hand and said, "Joe Torio."

She took off her right glove and turned her head slightly. The light from the vestibule momentarily illuminated her face. A great face, but she'd thrown herself together in the middle of a cyclone. Late twenties, early thirties, plus or minus. There were gray sweats on beneath the coveralls. Straggles of light colored hair framed tinted glasses and a mouth with a grim set to it. "I'm Julia Powers," she responded, shaking my hand. Her fingers were warm and dry, which wasn't easy fresh out of a latex glove in sub zero temperatures. Strong grip.

"Have you been through the crime scene?" I asked her.

"Yes, but you don't want to hear about that."

My eyebrows went up in surprise. "I don't?"

"Not yet." She had a delicious little smile. "That's not how you work."

"What do you know about how I work?"

"That much time you don't have." She cocked her head toward the door. I followed the direction of her gaze and saw Dock frowning back, his gaze repeatedly jumping from the woman to me, back-and-forth. That was when I remembered: Julia Powers was the Bait, the Vice cop who had taken down Gerald Soams, the Gray-eye Killer. Did I ever have a bunch of questions for her.

"Joe? You ready?" urged Dock.

"Yeah."

I glanced at Julia, saw an enigmatic smile, turned and put on my shoe covers.

THE FACE

The vestibule was a small wood-paneled enclosure illuminated by a single overhead bulb. The wood paneling was missing trim. Graffiti was scratched into its surface, varnished and painted into illegibility. A white painted wooden chair was next to a small green plastic table, both of them to the left of the entrance where someone could rest a couple of bags of groceries while fishing for their keys. Opposite the front door was the interior door: heavy-duty steel, knob lock and two dead bolts, one a foot above the knob, the second a foot below. It had three small glass panes in a row at eye level. Green tinted. I looked at the glass on an angle, checking an edge. Not green tinted. Bullet-proof.

"This is a cartel hatch," I said.

"Used to be a cutting operation in here four years ago," said Dock. "This property was seized in a bust and put up for auction. The new owner kept the door, for all the good it did her."

Dark print powder was visible on the table, the door, the door molding, and the tarnished brass handle that served as a doorknob. On the floor were two tiny black drips that could have been paint, blood, or something else. They were marked with chalk.

"All done in here," said Dock. "Inside we need to move some things and take a few more pictures, but by and large the scene's been worked. Do what you need to do."

I was at the end of a long, brightly lit hallway, the walls papered recently with tan-and-cream vertical stripes, the wood trim new and done in satin-finished birch. Dining room to the left, living room to the right, blood on the refinished hardwood hallway floor directly

134

in front of my feet. A flight of stairs on the left side of the hallway past the dining room entrance. More blood. Beyond the stairs and past a mail-littered phone table was the entrance to the kitchen.

Directly in front of me was a pool of blood, smeared by the motion of the body that had leaked it. Beyond the limits of the pool and smears were spatters, both high velocity and low velocity, the low on top of the high. The high was back spatter from slugs striking living flesh. The low came from drips as blood pumped out from dying flesh. No irregularities in the low velocity drips. No struggles, no running, no dramatic death throes. Bang, you're dead. Good shot and knowledgeable about where to hit. The smear had been caused by whoever moved the body. The blood that wasn't smeared was separated into clots and serum, the clots dried to a day-old brownish-black color.

Next to my right foot, in a curiously small group, were sparkling brass cartridge cases, eight in number, all of them circled and given the number seventeen, indicated by a yellow and black plastic marker. The cartridge cases had been polished. "The brass?" I asked Dock.

"Nine millimeter Lugers."

I squatted down to look. Each brass casing had been shined like a jewel. I'd never seen a semiautomatic or automatic weapon eject its spent cartridges in a neat little pile. Had the shooter swept them together after killing the two in the hallway? But, having done that, instead of taking them with him he leaves them behind?

I looked again at the blood near the front door. No forward spatter beyond the pooled blood. No exit wounds. I mentally filed it, stood, and noted a very young green-clad Medical Examiner's Assistant wearing a mist mask playing a UV light across the floor of the hallway to the kitchen. A detective in coveralls stopped next to her and spoke before he passed her and moved into the kitchen.

"You got chalk fairies bumping into each other?" I asked Dock.

"The techs, ME's and detectives, as well as the uniforms assigned to MCU, all have been cross-trained so everyone knows enough about all the jobs to make the other guy's job easier."

There were thin, intermittent low-velocity blood trails that appeared to lead from everywhere to everywhere, a safe-passage corridor marked on the floor beyond and to the right of the near pool. The vics had dropped where they stood: One at the front door, the other in front of the dining room entrance. Then the killer began moving things.

"I have to go see a man, Joe," said Dock. "Be a minute."

"Go and see your man," I answered as I pushed away from the wall, turned, and stepped into the living room. Avoiding the chalked evidence marks in the center of the carpet and their contents, I worked the room from the walls in. Pastel yellow painted walls, more birch trim. Cream colored overstuffed couch backed up against the curtained windows overlooking the street. Potted jade trees on the sills. Do-it-yourself K-mart coffee table and end tables, three remotes, TV listings, and a copy of the current *Video Movie Guide* on the coffee table. Two easy chairs sharing a satin varnished pine end table. Imitation weathered brass Wallyworld lamps, and a big, beautiful flat-screen HD Sony on the side of the room facing the couch with stud-shattering surround sound, VCR and DVD players. The last time I'd seen a price on that model television it had been on sale at Gold Medal Mart for two grand and change. A heap of TV. The vic was not rich but put what money she did have into video entertainment.

To the left and the right of the Sony were unfinished homemade shelves packed with paperbacks, pictures in cheap frames, and row upon row of DVDs, old VCR tapes, pro and off-the-air copies. *Fargo, Seven, Manhunter, Night of the Generals, Silence of the Lambs, Sunset Boulevard*. A taste for murder. I pulled the *Fargo* tape cassette from its shelf. There was a white pressure sensitive label on the cover with tally marks. Twenty-three. She'd played the tape twenty-three times. I replaced the tape.

On the far wall were two posters, each one advertising a different gentleman's club. The poster on the left was an expressionistic view of a dancer on her knees caught in a spotlight, everything around her in smears of fuchsia and turquoise. The artist had not included the legally required g-string. The poster advertised The Score, now a gentleman's club on Wilson. The poster on the right, same artist, was similar except the dancer was standing and looking back over her left shoulder, again no g-string. The poster on the right advertised a club a few blocks up on Booth at the broken end of Beverly called The Scarlet Letter. The posters were excellent. I looked: By Eyota, just the one name. Gentlemen's club dancers painted by Eyota, South River's answer to Toulouse Lautrec.

The pictures on the shelves and end tables were the usual framed parents, aunts and uncles things, with one of them being a recent one of Don Scozarri's late son. I'd never noticed before, but Vince Polizzi looked a bit like Al Pacino in *Godfather I*, but with his eyes all the way open. Taller maybe. A little heavier—all in the shoulders. Another photo: Vince and a stunningly beautiful face at a party. They both looked very happy. I looked at her image again. Her face drew me like a grappling hook. A cloud of black curls framed features with smoky dark eyes above scarlet lips. Another photo, Vince and the beautiful face down in Orlando posing with the big rat. The heir apparent to the Scozarri family was wearing mouse ears. Vince Polizzi, the made mouse. No doubt about it, Vince had been in love—head-over-heels, make-me-look-like-a-fool in love.

One final eight-by-ten shot of Vince, by himself, a big smirk on his face appearing just above his name and booking information. Any cop would recognize that particular artist's work. It was a mug shot. An inscription at the bottom: *Dear Juna, I'm just a prisoner of love. Vince.* A row of Xs and Os along the bottom of the shot. Hugs and kisses.

Polizzi: enforcer in love. Who else gets booked and asks the booking sergeant for eight-by-ten glossies? The frame was even one of those toothpick and Popsicle stick things they sold in the prisoners' craft shop at Books. Prisoner of love.

There were several pictures of a beautiful dark-haired girl at various ages from three or so to her teens.

Various takes on that incredible face. Vince's love in her early years and I frowned. Vince had every reason in the world to have a couple dozen shots of Juna all over *his* house. Her face was a dream. But all those photos of herself in her own house? You don't lay out two grand for a TV if you're all that happy with what you see in the mirror.

I turned and looked again at the tape collection. *Spartacus, The Man Who Came To Dinner, Blade Runner, Outlands, Lawrence of Arabia.* The irony made me sigh. Vince's one true love would have made a better match for me than Cherie Vitamante. Cherie didn't care for movies. She had been indifferent to anything that didn't involve running, sweating, eating tofu, saving the radishes, selling real estate, or catering to Pansy, her pet Rottweiler.

In the center of the floor was a mostly blue imitation Persian rug and, in the center of a chalk circle next to a yellow evidence marker, there was what appeared to be two pairs of eyeballs staring at each other. I burst out with a laugh it appeared so comical.

I squatted and examined the eyes more closely. Two sets of apparently real eyeballs, both sets slightly flattened from fluid loss. I shined my Mini Maglite on them. Both sets were brown, the corneas a little milky, scraps of muscle attached to the sides.

"Joe?"

I looked over my shoulder at Dock. He was standing next to Miles Kieffer. Kieff had on the uniform: coveralls, gloves, and shoe covers, a mask down around his neck not quite covering his plum colored tie. Windsor knot with a dimple, matching shirt. He was the one I'd seen talking to the MEA near the kitchen. I stood.

"Hi," I said.

"Kieff," Dock said to the man, "I'm teaming you two up for the time being. Joe is senior, so he's in charge." To me, he said, "Kieff's been with me since we cut the ribbon, so do what says. Any problems?"

"No problem," said Kieffer. "I like a circular chain-of-command." He looked at me.

"You never have to hunt down anyone for permission," I added.

I'd looked up Kieffer since he came to visit me in the hospital and helped save my butt from the shooting board. A prize-winning reporter for the *South River Herald,* one fine day he up and quit the paper. A week later he entered the police academy and made detective in just under three years—a department record. A year later he maxed the sergeant's exam and was made detective sergeant fourteen months after that. When Dock got the green light to put together the Major Crimes Unit, Kieffer had been a natural first pick.

Dock looked at me. "Are you going to be long? The ME wants to finish bagging the other parts."

"More than just these?" I asked, pointing down at the eyes.

"All over the house," said Kieff quietly. He started to say more but Dockery put a restraining hand on his arm.

I looked down at the eyes on the carpet. Posed body parts meant a message. I walked back to the shelf where Juna kept her tapes and DVDs. A lot of old favorites: *The Thing* with Kenneth Tobey, Chuck and Sophia in *El Cid.* "The MEA can finish up in here," I said to Dock. "As for the rest, I won't be long. Vince's bodyguards. What happened to them?"

"Bodyguards? There weren't any."

I looked up at Dock. "Ever since he got his first Kevlar diaper, Vince Polizzi has never left the family compound without protection. Remember *Il Mano Negri?"* I held up my right hand in the shape of a claw.

"Yeah. But we haven't found any more bodies."

"If his boys aren't here, Dock, they're someplace else."

He stared at me for a moment and raised his eyebrows. "Let me do a consult with the private eye."

Dock headed for the stoop, leaving me alone with Kieffer and the eyeballs. I crossed the hall and went to the dining room entrance, pausing briefly to look at the blood there on the hall floor. It was almost completely separated into shiny yellow serum and islands of clots, low velocity spatter on top of high velocity. Body smears. Looking back at the front door, I fixed the doorway and both puddles of blood in my mind, then turned into the dining room. I stepped over the drip trails and walked the safe strip to the left side of the entrance.

Eight foot eggshell white ceilings brought the cast-off blood spatter down close. Swing after swing making the interior of the dining room into a two-tone wrap-around Jackson Pollack. I'd never seen cast off spatter that looked like that. Something else, too. The scene, all of that blood, should've been shouting rage at me. What I was sensing, instead, was loss, sadness—another something else: guilt. The disembodied eyes, however, were saying love.

A CSU tech in white coveralls was dusting down the smoked maple mantel above the closed off fireplace on the far wall. Mike Ijumaa. He always reminded me of Eddie Murphy in a foul mood. We'd worked a few together in the past, and when you were feeling out the edges of a question mark, Mike was the one you wanted sprinkling the dust. I had dated his sister Cathy once, the results of that particular experiment being the principal supporting argument for inflatable rubber companions. Mike's face was drawn tight and he didn't look like he wanted any small talk, which meant he wasn't finding what he wanted. A curt nod which I returned then I faced the center of the room.

The table was a large tan maple thing—relatively new—placed longitudinally in the room. Chairs for six. Three of the chairs had been tossed carelessly in front of the street window and the remaining three had been tossed into the opposite end of the room, leaving the ends and sides of the table clear. The debris of papers, clothing, and junk on the floor was ankle deep in places, dumped there when the chairs were tossed and the table cleared. Juna didn't entertain. The dining room set had been her filing system. There were two heavy tracks of blood across the debris and the hardwood floor beneath. One track—a combination of partial foot impressions and low velocity blood spatters—went to the near side of the table. The second track—also partial foot impressions and spatters—went to the far side. The foot impressions were wet origin positives of bare feet. The killer worked in the nude. Almost. The toes also had wrinkles. "He have something covering his feet?" I asked Mike Ijumaa.

"Plastic," Mike answered without turning. "Fairly heavy gauge, but nothing sophisticated."

"Like freezer bags?"

"Yeah. The feet are size ten, medium, he appears to have all his toes." He turned and faced us. "I can do linear dimensional characteristics. Nothing useful in the way of skin ridge patterns, though."

"What's your feeling?"

Mike grinned. "You're the only one who ever asks for that, Joe."

"Maybe I'm the only one who wants to know."

He pointed down. "The perp hauled bloody pieces of meat all over this floor and the floor above, yet the only clear foot impressions are right here. He must have had slippers or something like them in his murder kit." Mike pointed at the impressions on the near side of the table. "My feeling is whatever we manage to find is only what this dude wants us to find." He pointed up at the ceiling. "We have backswing spatter and no evidence of violent repeated stabbings."

"So, what is it?"

"More will be revealed." He went back to work.

So Mike Ijumaa was impressed. That meant an unusually high level of forensic awareness in our boy. That was one of the shades that had bothered Dock. Possible cop? ex-cop? I faced my new partner. "Kieff, this crime scene is at least a day old. Who discovered this mess?"

"An anonymous second-story man. He broke in upstairs after midnight, checked out the body parts up there and the ID on the dresser, figured out Vince Polizzi was one of the vics, and called Frank Scozarri."

"A great deal of community spirit for a masked man."

"Hi-yo Silver," he said.

"I stand corrected."

"I figure the second-story man wanted to get in front of this with the don in one big hurry. After he got it on record that he was not the one who whacked Vince, he went out the way he came in and probably joined the Peace Corps and got himself sent to Palookastan. We don't have any evidence that he made it downstairs at all."

I frowned. "And then Don Scozarri steps outside their thing and hires a PI to call it in to us and work the scene? A woman?"

"He brought in cops, too. Scozarri wants this guy, Joe, and I think he understands that this killing is way outside his experience. He wants to be on top of the investigation, and he knows we're not going to work with Tommy Zee, or any of his other buttons, so he sent Julia Powers."

"Why Powers?"

"Ex cop, she's worked with us in the past, and she did some work for the don, too. Remember Dion Orgoglio?"

"Goggles. Went off his nut and started killing willy-nilly without compensation."

"Or permission. Took a hit man's holiday."

I poked through the memory pile. "Orgoglio drowned, didn't he? In Canal Park?"

"There was definitely too much H^2 in his O."

"You think Powers clipped him?"

Kieffer held out his hands and dropped them to his sides. "Rumors."

"Do you believe them?" I asked.

"Oh, yeah. I believe them."

I turned back to the table. The top looked like a prop from a Civil War battlefield surgery reenactment. Blood. Lots of it: Smears, puddles, serum, clots, and spatters among the knife and saw gouges and hair wipes. Here and there, among tiny bits of flesh, were scattered pinkish-white granules.

"Mike, is this bone dust?"

"Yeah. Very coarse, like from a heavy coping saw or keyhole saw. Our boy is no surgeon." He glanced up at the spatter pattern across the ceiling. "Heaps of gusto, though."

LOVE NOTES

Before I reached the kitchen door, I could see part of the kitchen table and what was on it. Kieffer tapped my arm.

"What?"

"You can blow your chunk in the kitchen sink, if you like, Joe. It's been cleared."

"Don't talk about that with me. Ever."

"Talk about what?"

"What you were talking about, Kieff. Don't talk about that."

"Sorry."

"It's simple science, Kieff. The body listens to what it's told, and if everyone is conversing about chunk, then it chucks chunk. If flinging the feed doesn't exist, then the body acknowledges that and the pudding stays put."

"Nice alliteration," said Kieff with a deadpan nod.

Ignoring his comment, I entered the kitchen, my gaze hard to the right. Personally, I was regretting the pudding imagery in my caution to Kieffer. The appliances were late 'Seventies stuff: chocolate brown, beat up, chipped. The fridge carried an assortment of magnets holding up recipes, coupons, a menu from The Tori Gate, and a movie schedule for Cinemania torn from a newspaper and a movie schedule for The Flik, an art theater in Roosevelt Notch. *Casablanca* again. Cabinets, white-painted oak, scratched, and missing a couple of knobs. I forced my gaze by slow degrees to what was on the table.

On the white-and-gold Formica surface, beneath an adjustable lamp hanging from the ceiling, were two upper torsos, heads and arms removed and cut through the spines just below the rib cages. They had been placed chest-to-chest, one male, one female, the female on top.

I closed my eyes. "Kieff, who's the regular MEA on the team?"

"Mattie Chala." Kieffer's voice was thick. He glanced at what was on the table. "Doc Kratzer's here, too."

"Can we get both of them in here? I want to get these separated."

Kieffer passed the word and I studied what I could of the female torso's back. Clear, no scars, bruises, or tattoos. Hard to think of that beautiful face once being attached to this lump of meat. Doc Kratzer's heavy steps came down the stairs. He was the city's Chief Medical Examiner, Burl Ives with a scalpel. He was an old-timer dating back to when my father stretched necks at Books. When I was twelve the doc gave me a biology dissection kit for Christmas complete with dead worm, grasshopper, frog, fish, and rat, each preserved in formaldehyde. He'd made up the set himself and it had turned me off biology for life.

Kratzer filled the doorway as he leaned in, the gray stubble of his beard more a fashion statement than a neglected shave, his pale green coveralls unbuttoned above the second button. "So, Joe, returned from the dead, have you."

"For the moment. How are you doing, Doc?"

"Another fascinating instant in a spectacular career. Wait 'til you get a load of what's upstairs. It'll make a fond memory of that dead rat I gave you that Christmas." The ME nodded toward the table. "Ready to pull them apart?"

"Please."

"Mattie!" he called out as he navigated his bulk into the room, an MEA in his wake. Mattie Chala was tall with Sophia Loren eyes above the mist mask she continued to wear over her nose and mouth, her hair wrapped tightly in a black scarf dotted with tiny blue roses. She exchanged looks and nods with me, reached into the large black shoulder pack she was hauling, and passed out new latex gloves all around. Kratzer had Mattie lay out two child-sized white body bags on the floor and on the end of the table she spread a new white

144

wrapping sheet. Carefully, Mattie on one side and the Doc on the other, they lifted the female upper torso from the male's, a slight ripping sound as the coagulated blood between the lumps of flesh protested the separation. They placed the female lump on the sheet, anterior side up. As Kratzer scanned the freshly revealed surfaces, he muttered his favorite old line: "Dead men tell tales."

Mattie went at the female torso with a brace mounted camera. Each time she put out the L scale and took an exposure with the two and a quarter inch camera, she followed by rotating the camera's mounting frame, putting a digital camera where the two and a quarter had been, then taking another shot. While she worked the female, I checked out the male.

Big guy, Vince. Wide shoulders. A couple of ropy old knife scars that had healed without stitches high on his left shoulder. A healed gutter wound where a slug had bounced off his right collarbone, probably fracturing it. Vince was in a tough line of work. He was smart and experienced enough to be his father's enforcer and out of jail for the past seven years. Street smart, certainly armed, and accompanied by bodyguards. So why was he on Juna's kitchen table doing impressions of cold cuts?

"Do you have an approximate time of death?" I asked the ME.

"Four minutes after seven, yesterday morning."

"You talking to your crystal ball?"

"Different kind of crystal." Kratzer held up the back of his left wrist, the cuff of his latex glove covering his Timex. "Defensive wound. Look on the back porch. The male vic got his Rolex nicked. Everything else seems to support that."

Kratzer stepped back removing the benefit of his bulk in obstructing the view, revealing once again those two mutilated lumps of flesh, the flashes from Mattie's camera work burning the images into my mind.

Ready for this, Dock had asked.

Yeah, Dock, I'm ready for this.

I looked at the Polizzi lump. Four entrance wounds in Vince Polizzi's chest, the lowest near the tip of his sternum, the highest two went right in the pump. The lowest wound was the reentry from Vince's wrist *via* his

145

Rolex, ragged with an abrasion ring shaped like a fat lip. There were four entrance wounds in the female's chest on the right edge of her left breast, just above center. All four through the pump, all with regular abrasion rings and a light stippling connecting the wounds.

"No exit wounds," I said.

"None." Kratzer's bushy brows rose above his eyeglass frames. "The male was the distance shot. The female's wounds are intermediate—within two or three feet of the muzzle. There would be more stippling except the vic was wearing a light bathrobe. We—"

A low moan seemed to come from one of the bloody lumps of meat on the table and we all jumped, including Kratzer. Again the moan. It was coming from behind me and Kieffer. We both turned to see one of the MCU detectives, a stocky woman in her forties wearing a black beret, a bit of a black jacket appearing above her coveralls. Her face was round, grim, dark, and going gray around the edges. Eyes wide, also going gray around the edges, her gaze fixed on the female torso. Her cheeks appeared to be inflating. I gave Kieffer a panicked glance and he nodded toward the front of the house. "Clair, are Brooks and Hewitt done with the canvass?"

Her eyes attempted to wheeze up a spark of dignity. "I'm as good as anybody in this unit, Kieffer," she whispered loudly, covering a small belch. There was a guttural rumble, more vibration than something audible. Clair Turner's stomach sounded like a garbage disposal eating last Thanksgiving's turkey bones. Her eyes rolled back in her head for an instant and I began edging away, convinced she was about to blow.

"No one's questioning your competence, Clair," Kieff insisted calmly, backing away, as well. "That's why I'd like you to check how the witness interviews are progressing. They need to be supervised. Go supervise."

Det. Turner hovered on the edge of obstinacy for a tantalizing moment, then she turned about and rocked from foot-to-foot toward the front door.

Relieved, I glanced out in the hall, poked Kieffer's arm, and pointed to the right. "Back porch?"

"Yeah."

"Is she going to be all right?"

146

"Turner?" Kieffer nodded. "Yeah. Dock brought her up from Records. She's a wizard with paper, but that's just about all she's ever done, so she queases up some at the icky bits."

"Unlike us," I said, giving myself permission for a swallow.

Kieffer held up a gallon-sized plastic evidence bag, as yet unoccupied. "Unlike us," he confirmed with a grin.

I leaned back into the kitchen without looking in that direction. "I'm done in here, Doc." I cocked my head toward the back porch, and nodded at Kieff who opened the door.

A single yellow bug light left over from an earlier summer illuminated the back porch casting everything in high jaundice. Two overgrown hemlocks in the back yard had kept the killer's work private from the neighbors across the alley. There were drifts of fine snow in the corners of the porch, the snow from the roof piled up beneath the roof edge as high as the porch railing. Kieff flicked on a flood array bringing the scene into sharp focus.

On the deck were two pairs of arms and legs—minus hands and feet. They were arranged in love-making, this time positioned such that the male was on top, missionary style. Another love note. "Okay to move these?" I asked Kieffer.

"Yes. All done out here."

I put on clean gloves, squatted, and picked up the male's left arm, holding the severed wrist close to my face. Vince's left wrist still had the steel-cased Rolex on it held there with a wide black leather strap. The slug had gone through the strap beneath the left side of the wrist and had exited at the edge of the watch casing, deforming it, shattering the crystal, and stopping the movement. Replacing the amputated limb, I took out a pen, marked the entrance and exit wounds on the latex covering my own wrist and watch.

I stood, held up my hand, palm away from my body, and tried to line up the two wounds with the tip of my sternum. "Vince's palm couldn't have been even chest high when that slug bent his timepiece."

147

"Fast shooter," Kieff remarked.

"Juna has the tight group in her heart," I said out loud. "She's closest to the door, she opens it, the shooter puts four in her pump, and down she goes. By then Vince knows what's going on and begins lifting his arm. The shooter shifts his aim and squeezes off another four into Vince. He only got his hand up to here," I said, indicating the tip of my sternum.

"There's more than that."

"What?"

"You sure it's okay? Third Eye and all?"

"Yeah, Kieff. What?"

"Vince was armed and he never even got off a shot."

"Armed—"

A clatter from the back yard interrupted me and I stepped to one side in time to see Capt. Finn. A uniformed officer was leading him along the shoveled back path toward the back porch stairs, both of them sneaking in the back way. As he came up the stairs, Finn saw me.

"Joseph? On the job?"

"Sort of visiting, sir."

"You look much better."

Finn looked down at the arms and legs on the porch floor, the realization of what they were suddenly registering on his face. He looked at me, turning to assure that the body parts would be out of his view. "The front is filling up with reporters, Joseph. I'm glad I managed to get to you before they did." He leaned in toward me. "You haven't talked to the press yet, have you?"

"No, Cap."

"Good, good. Very good." He actually rubbed his gloved hands together. "The Chief and I have reconsidered our talk with Lt. Dockery. I know how important it is for you to be back to work, but given the current circumstances, we think that it probably wouldn't be in the best interests of the department or MCU for you to speak to the press in any capacity."

"Mum's the word," I said.

He faced Kieffer. "We were thinking that Joseph might even want to sit this one out. I know I told you and Lt. Dockery—"

"Cap," I interrupted quickly.

"Yes?"

"I apologize for barging in, Cap, but Doc Kratzer has been looking high and low for you."

"The ME? What about?"

"That's way above my pay grade, Cap."

Finn's eyebrows went up then he sighed resignedly. "Where is he?"

"In the kitchen." I pointed at the back door. "Through there, first door on the left. It seemed pretty urgent. Mind the safe strip and ask someone inside for shoe covers, gloves, and such."

Capt. Finn gave another sigh, nodded his thanks, and marched through the back door, the unidentified officer following in his wake. Kieffer leveled his black-eyed gaze on me, a smirk on his face. "That was cold, brother Torio."

"Cap needed something else to think about. Back to what you said before: How do you know Vince was armed?"

He shrugged a mite sheepishly. "Well, we don't know for certain. But upstairs on the bed are where the hands are. One of Vince's is holding a gun."

"Right or left hand?"

Kieff paused for a moment, his brow furrowing. "Right."

"Any bloodstain evidence on the gun?"

"Nothing visible. Dock wouldn't let us move it until you got a look. Mike will go at it with all the tests after you've had your peek."

"Vince wasn't armed when the door was opened." I pointed at the arm with the Rolex. "Vince was left-handed. When he died he wasn't trying to shoot with that arm, he was playing catch with a submachine gun."

"How do you know he was left-handed?"

"I watch a lot of TV, Kieff, and Vince has been on a few times. Channel Six had a clip of him signing for his stuff once as he was being released on bail." I pursed my lips and frowned. "But the shooter still put that gun in

Vince's right hand. Why's he lying to us?" I frowned. "Bigger question: Who could've been at the door that Vince would've been down there without his weapon or any other protection?" My well was dry. I glanced at Kieffer. "Let's look at that bedroom."

As we passed the kitchen on our way upstairs, Cap Finn had his head in the sink while his knees sagged and Doc Kratzer explained to his assistant, mostly for Finn's benefit, why it was important in closing a body bag not to catch in the zipper such things as pubic hair, nipples, noses, and various other appendages.

APOLOGIES AND AMENDS

The master bedroom on the second floor was at least thirty degrees cooler than the rest of the house, due to an open window that overlooked the hemlocks in back. There was a large poster on the south wall next to the closet door showing an almost nude female figure dancing against an abstract background of colored lights. In the lower right corner printed in red reflective foil was the name of a gentleman's club: The Score. Different artist than the pair of posters downstairs. There were more framed photos on the bureau beneath the poster. Many repeats of the photographic cast in the living room. Parents. Papa Salvati reminded me a lot of the Gasman. That dried-up, wrinkled squint came from decades beneath a molten white Sicilian sun. Of course, you got the same look if you breathed near a plastics factory.

High school yearbook photo of Juna. Beautiful young woman. Half a dozen more photos of herself. I shook my head. The gears were beginning to grind loudly. I turned and looked at the bed.

King-sized. Remotes on the bed's left nightstand: one for the TV and players, one for the mattress. The dual electric blanket controls were hard wired. Covers pulled to the foot of the bed, the bottom sheet taut and printed with Disney characters. The bed was positioned with the head between the two windows. The one on the right was open, its sill dusted with print powder. "Kieff, if they've got everything they need off that window, I think we can have it closed."

While he went over to shut the window, I looked at what was facing the foot of the bed. On the low dressers that filled the space from the bedroom door to the adjoining wall, was a twenty-five inch Sony flat screen, a VCR, a DVD player, and next to them, a shelf holding yet another collection of tapes and discs. *Pride and Prejudice, Conagher, Cotton Goes To Harlem,* the whole Godfather set, the whole Alien set, *The Matrix, The Horse Soldiers* as well as *Conan the Barbarian. Seven Days In May* and the Star Wars starter trilogy. She even had a pro copy of the Lew Ayres version of *All Quiet on the Western Front.* I picked up the cassette from the shelf. Nineteen tally marks.

I felt a very strong attraction to what Scozarri's son had loved. Juna. Her face and her movies: That's all I knew about her. That and she loved a wiseguy. I glanced toward the door. Kieffer was looking at me, frowning. "Powerful movie," I said as I held up *All Quiet on the Western Front.*

"Evidently."

I saw that my hand was trembling. I put the cassette back and turned toward the bed. On the carpeted floor next to the bed, about four feet away from the window on the right, was a puddle of what appeared to be vomit, circled in white chalk and accompanied by a marker. Next to it was another circle and marker, a faint outline of a positive foot impression where someone had landed after stepping in the lunch. I looked up.

The hands and feet from both victims were arranged on the bed, her fingertips pointed toward the head of the bed, palms down, his left hand pointed the same way on top of hers. Rear entry. Another love note. The right hand was also atop her right hand, but held loosely by the fingers was a gleaming nickel-plated Dan Wesson .44 Super Magnum. At the foot of the bed, Vince's heels were tented together, toes out and positioned between her feet, also with toes out, outboard ankles up.

I pointed toward the vomit. "Ours?"

"It's a deposit made by our anonymous burglar." Kieff nodded toward the phone on the nightstand, a white wireless, now smudged with print powder. "He called the don from there."

"He wear gloves?"

"Yes. Those prints appear to be Juna's."

I shifted my gaze to the vomit. "I wonder which made our intruder puke: the mutilation or that one of the vics was Vince Polizzi."

"If I was in his sneakers I know which would make me sicker." Kieff pointed at the window. "He went out the way he came in: back porch roof. As near as we can tell, he didn't take a thing with him."

"He *was* upset."

"We figure the extent of his influence on the crime scene is confined to the window, the telephone, Vince's wallet on the nightstand, the Ralph McMuffin on the carpet, and that foot impression after he stepped in his greens. Nikes, eleven extra-wides, according to Mike."

I looked at the bureau. Next to the TV was Vince's shoulder holster, a rig for a left-handed draw. I turned back to the bed. The scene was starting to talk. What it had to say, though, wasn't about sex, hatred, and rage. Instead it was all about love, guilt, regret, and obsession. Something else, too, represented by the gun being in Vince's hand: Misdirection. Or was it a warning?. All together it was a reach for something—a number of somethings. It was a stage set for a fantasy play. Whoever the perp saw as the male lead in his bloody production, though, was right-handed.

I looked toward the open doors of the closet. "Anything in there?"

"Yes."

Stepping around Kieffer and the foot of the bed, I walked over and looked into the closet. It was filled with the smell of lavender. In it were street clothes, dress clothes, sequined costumes, a red-and-black woman's ski outfit. Juna skied, too. This son of a bitch had butchered my ideal woman.

On the floor among the shoes were the tongues of the vics placed tip-to-tip. Another love note.

"Jesus," I muttered as I felt my skin prickle and my stomach flip. "Kieff, is the bathroom clear?"

"If you're preparing to orbit your Oreos, man, stay out of the bathroom. Trust me on this. Want me to get you one of the large plastic evidence bags? Let me get you one." He began waving frantically at someone in the hall.

"Maybe later." I took a deep breath and exhaled slowly. "I'll take a look at that bathroom, though. Lower torsos?"

"Going to need the MEs to separate the parts?"

"Yeah. I'm done in here."

Kieffer passed the word along and I stepped into the bathroom off the master bedroom. No more than a half-dozen photons could have hit my retinas before I shut my eyes and turned away. Lower torsos, buttocks, and upper thighs of the couple, the male sitting on the toilet, the female straddling the male, like two intimate containers of guts.

When Doc Kratzer and Mattie Chala lifted the female torso to put it in the already spread wrapping sheet, the guts partly spilled. It looked like an illustration out of *The Divine Comedy:* Dante's Inferno three days into the garbage strike.

I took one of the offered evidence bags and kept it handy. Kratzer pointed out the absence of any additional entrance wounds. He found the cuts interesting, though. "No stabbing, or hacking, no chopping. Just long, sure-handed incisions with a very sharp knife."

"Not a scalpel?"

"Longer blade. More like a filleting knife. Like all the bones that have been cut, it looks like he went through the spine with a coarse saw."

There was a very clear, almost complete, hand print in blood in the center of the female's left glute. I glanced at Kieff. "Gloves," he said. "Mike Ijumaa says heavy, non-skid gripping surfaces like kitchen gloves. No chance for prints. Takes a large sized glove, though."

"Anything else?"

"Yes. Look at this." Kieff pointed to each lower torso in turn. The genitalia had been removed from each one. I turned and stood for a full minute in front of the bathroom sink, focusing on the pink toothbrush, the tube of Colgate Total squeezed from the middle, Listerine Mint—

—A voice, crying, begging, swearing that it was sorry. *Anything. I'll do anything. I'm so sorry.*

So sorry—

154

"Are we done in here?" asked Kieff.

I turned, nodded, and staggered toward the door.

LISTEN TO ME

Upstairs hall, leaning against the wall, trying to ease the tension in my neck, I looked at Kieffer. "I hate throwing up," I said. "I think I hate nausea more than getting cut or shot."

"Joe, is it true that Doc Kratzer gave you a dissection kit for Christmas when you were a kid and you gave all the specimens a full police funeral as soon as the ground thawed?"

"I'm the only kid I know who ever got a dead rat from Santa." I looked at Kieffer. "This stuff doesn't bother you at all, does it?"

"I've seen worse, like those burned corpses they pulled from the Bentley Building back a few years ago, or the pieces they swept up after the Regional Express air crash out at Soldier Heights." A haunted expression brushed over his face, his gaze shifting to something down the hall. "I was on both of those stories."

"I read those pieces you did for the *Herald,* Kieff. They were great, especially that one on the REX crash, the cadets from the military academy helping the police and the Feds hunt for remains, the passenger profiles, the follow-up on the cadets. Really great."

"Thanks."

"So, if you can write like that, why are you hauling tin and shuffling body parts?"

"Better working conditions?" he joked. After a slight shrug, he looked down at the floor. "Nothing profound. I did a police beat until I had my nose rubbed in what's happening to this city—to this country. It's my city and my country. It was time to pick a side."

"You didn't think you could do that as part of the media?"

"I kept running into editors who wanted to pick the team I supposed to root for. We disagreed."

The sounds of heavy footsteps came from the stairwell followed almost immediately by the appearance of the back of Dock's head. Dock turned his head and looked over his shoulder as he came to the top of the stairs. He grinned. "Kieff, what can you do with a Pulitzer you can't do with a police commendation?"

"Buy groceries."

"True, but you don't get all that free garbage thrown at you with a Pulitzer." He came to a stop facing me. "The PI put in a call to the don. Polizzi had two bodyguards with him named Edmondo Pitone and Paulo Casale. They're Vince's boys, but they work for Dago Frank. According to the don, they had a job to do. They would not simply take off on their own and grab a couple of brews. The bodyguards are either dead or in the wind with Battaglia money in their pockets. I put Clair on seeing what kind of paper she can find on them."

Kieff nodded. "Good. That'll keep all those Fruit Loops Clair ate from decorating the crime scene."

Dock looked at me. "You look puzzled, Slugger."

I nodded. "I am puzzled. Gruesome as it is, our boy here is very polished in what he's done. Everything has been worked out to the last detail and practiced until it's almost on an instinctual level. This guy has done this before a number of times."

Dock nodded, nibbled on the inside of his lower lip, and said, "Outside when you're done." Dock swiped a hand through the air in our general direction and turned toward the stairs. "I gotta go. We had to send for an ambulance for Finn. You two know anything about that?"

"Nope," Kieffer and I both mumbled.

"He was chucking his cheese in the kitchen sink when he tripped, and fell backwards into a body bag which was already partially occupied." He frowned.

"Really," I said.

Dock continued down the stairs. "He has his peculiarities, but it would be good to remember Finn is one of the good guys."

Kieff was looking accusingly at me. "Capt. Finn was about to send me home," I said. "I'll make it up to him. Honest. What's next?"

Kieff nodded toward the bathroom. "That was the worst of it. All that's left is in the hall closet: a pair of ears."

"Ears."

"Mattie says they belong to the female vic."

"Just the one pair? Show me."

In between the door to the master bedroom and the door to the guest bathroom was a linen closet illuminated by a single forty watt bulb mounted in the ceiling. The back of the closet was lined with deep shelves stacked with sheets, pillows, spreads, blankets, and such. It smelled like cedar and laundry detergent. I stood on a footstool that was kept there for reaching high places and looked. On the top shelf, there was nothing except the aforementioned ears. Pierced, no earrings. Outside edges outboard and set apart like a pair of stereo pickups. "What about Vince's ears?"

"Haven't found them. Same with the heads and genitals. Trophies?"

"Pretty heavy and awkward to toss in a backpack. Possible, though." I looked around at the shelf. It was large enough to hide a small child. I climbed down off the footstool. "Is there an attic?"

"Just a crawl space full of rock wool. Nobody had been up there in decades. The trapdoor we went through out in the hall was painted shut, and that was old paint. What are you thinking."

"This boy—and he's thinking as a child as he does this—this boy wanted his mother's attention. He wanted it back. Our boy had been pushed aside. He was probably the means by which his mother got her rocks off between lovers."

"So," said Kieff, "he was the center of the universe one moment, a discarded dildo the next."

"Well put. He was a joke to himself. You can't survive for long being a joke to yourself. He had to take action. Where would the lover have to be so that our boy

158

could talk to his mother without fear of discovery? The basement," I said.

"We didn't find anything down there."

"Vince's ears are in the basement."

Kieffer cocked his head to one side. "Joe, we went over the place with the proverbial fine-toothed comb."

"They're in the basement."

My new partner studied me for a second, one eyebrow raised, then he nodded and held out his hand toward the stairs. "After you, swami."

The basement was well lit and relatively neat and clean. A garden hose hung on a peg near the stairs. Built into the side of the stairs was a new workbench with a few basic tools as well as a fourteen inch TV that was taken apart. There were half-finished interior walls testifying to at least one owner's unrealized plans to finish off the basement. Naked studs, some new wiring, nothing hooked up. I started with the workbench room and began making my way clockwise around the basement, probing the darker corners with my Maglite.

Broken furniture, musty boxes of old clothes, a box of dust encrusted canning jars, three sheets of drywall, the bottom edges mildewed and crumbling from floor damp, half of a motorcycle next to a set of stairs leading to a padlocked door to the back yard. Finally, the furnace, an old coal-fired forced hot air arrangement that had been converted to oil. I began checking the air ducts when I noticed something. "There. Fresh tape."

As I moved a wooden box beneath the taped joint, I heard a click behind my back. I turned and Kieffer was holding up a needle-pointed switchblade knife in his left hand. "Did I violate some subtle point of unit etiquette?" I asked.

"For the tape, swami."

"I knew that." I took the knife, climbed up on the box, and ran the point around the joint. Without touching the tape, I took one side of the duct and shook it back and forth until the two ends parted. With them separated I shined my light into the end leading to the furnace, and there they were. "Bingo."

I got down and Kieffer took my light, climbed up, and looked into the open end of the duct. "Missed that fresh tape," he said. "I'll get Mike down here and see if he can lift anything off it." Kieff looked down at me. "Okay, Kreskin. You have any guesses about the rest of the missing parts?" He climbed down off the box and traded me my light for his knife.

"Not at the moment."

Kieff closed the knife and put it in his hip pocket on the left side while he scanned the joints on the remaining ducts. Something was feeling strange to me and I had to poke at it. "Kieff? I got a question."

"Go."

"You're Dock's number two. You been with him ever since he got the okay to start the unit."

"Right."

"You're being awfully nice for someone who's had an untrained senior partner dumped on him that he has to baby-sit."

He turned from examining a duct and smiled broadly. "Joe, Dock said you two used to talk about setting up a unit like MCU all the way back when you were both in uniforms. It's always been understood by all of us, if you ever stayed alive and out of a straight jacket long enough, Dock was going to bring you in to run things. Besides, you found the ears, man. You found the ears." He turned and headed toward the stairs.

I sat down on the box, grateful to get off my feet for a minute, and began trying to work a minor ache out of my shoulder. Major Crimes: Big challenges, good, smart people, a boss who liked and understood me and how I worked. And there was Kieffer: sharp, a modicum of wit, and I liked him a lot. About all that could screw this up for me would be Betty pulling the conditional work permission she had granted. I'd have to be especially sane from now on, at least as far as appearances went. Something of a challenge, that.

Shades.

Dock said the case had shades on it. I glanced up at the open end of the heating duct. That voice still in my head and growing stronger: *Listen to me. Don't let him hear us. Please. This time. Listen to me.* Begging, pleading, useless cries flung into an infinite void. The ears were different than the rest. They had nothing to do with his love notes. They had to do with listening—a lack of listening, rather. There was at least one missing love note, though. Heads and genitals—

"Oh. Of course."

I stood, climbed the stairs, and made my way outside to where Dock was standing on the stoop. Plenty of bright lights. The media was there in force. "Dock, has anyone checked out the cars?" I asked, pulling off my gloves and shoe covers.

"Cars?"

"Up and down the street. The cars. On the seats? For the missing body parts? Weren't you ever a teenager?"

"I was a different kind of cut up in those days."

I pitched the gloves and covers into the scene exit can, went down the stairs to the curb, pulled out my Maglite, and shined it through the windows of the nearest car. I brushed away the new snow and looked in. Nothing but candy wrappers and an old road map. Dock called for two uniforms to check the cars on the opposite side of the street while he took the same side I was on but in the opposite direction, Powers walking with him.

I turned to my right and went to the next vehicle, a five-year old Toyota. On the rear seat, jumper cables, empty packs of Camels, a Thermos jug. The next car, nothing. Absolutely clean. As I was checking the next, a tan Lexus, I heard a voice call out, "Lieutenant! *Lieutenant!*"

I looked over the snow covered hood of the Lexus and saw Bradley standing across the street beside a bluish-looking Lincoln, his light shining into the car, his face aimed away from the car's interior. There was the squeak of a strangled scream as another uniform angrily hustled a few civilians away from the car. A third uniform came running with more crime scene tape. Dock, Kieffer, Powers, and I made it to the car at the same time. I bent over and shined my light through the rear side window.

Between the flakes falling on the recently cleared glass, I could see the heads on the back seat, driver's side. Hers on its left cheek facing forward, his on its right cheek facing toward the rear, empty eye sockets open, their lips touching in a long, final kiss. On the passenger side of the back seat were the genitals. His and hers.

"Tab A inserted into slot B," Julia Powers remarked flatly.

"Shit!" said Dockery as he straightened up, glared at Powers, tottered a bit, and nodded once just before he bent over and aimed toward the center of the street. As Dock ralphed his roni onto the centerline, at least half a dozen camera flashes went off. It was a Kojak moment.

SHADE BLUE

"I've been on the force twenty-six years." Dockery looked out the passenger side window of the cruiser. The car was within the expanded crime scene boundary, as was a good segment of the street now, mainly to keep the media at bay. The sky was clearing and growing light, only a lone flake or two falling every so often, less than two inches of new snow on the ground. I was sitting in the rear seat behind Clair Turner. Kieffer was to my right, sitting behind Dock. Powers was in the house doing the scene one more time.

"Before that, six years in the MPs," he continued. "I've seen worse than what we have here a dozen times at least. Never quite this deliberate, but worse. Nothing quite like an abdominal maggot mass on a hot summer's day."

"That's what I always say," I chimed in.

Dock turned his head forward and looked through the windshield. He shook his head, muttering, "Tab A inserted into slot B. Jesus. Where is Powers?"

"In the house," Turner and Kieffer answered in unison.

"Blew my greens right in the middle of a crime scene. I can't believe it." Dock glanced back at me, raising his eyebrows. "Media get footage of that?" he asked.

"Living color and surround sound. It'll probably be a miniseries by tonight."

"I want one of the tee shirts," said Kieffer.

"This is no joke," said Dock. "Wait until you see the questions at that press conference." He raised an eyebrow. "What the hell. Maybe it's my fifteen minutes. Get me a morning TV spot: 'Breakfast with Al.'"

163

We burst out laughing, the horror in combination with our lack of sleep making it seem funnier than it was.

"In the chef's corner this week," announced Kieffer, "tossed salad."

That *was* funny, and we roared. Dock waved his hand for quiet. "All right," he said. "Jesus, they'll think we're doin' weed in here." He pulled out his handheld, flipped open the cover, and began fingering his way through the electronic pages. "The ME's preliminary report: probable homicides—"

"Probable," muttered Turner sarcastically.

"Worst case of suicide I ever saw," said Kieff, doing a credible W. C. Fields impression. More giggles. Dock held up his hand and the tension-relieving mirth faded.

"Okay, cause of death in both cases: gunshot wounds to the heart, mechanism—" He lowered his handheld to his lap and looked through the window toward the house. "Really big holes in the heart tissue with subsequent leakage and pump malfunction. Manner is homicide. Time of death approximately seven yesterday morning. The weapon appears to be a fully automatic nine, most likely an Uzi. Stan Brooks and Ballistics promise everything but the serial number and bill of sale by noon." His gaze drifted slowly across the faces behind the yellow tape. "Is Ward getting shots of the crowd?"

"That's right," answered Clair. She cocked her head to the left and I could see a man in his thirties making like a shutterbug. I knew him slightly. Ward Staples had been a PI before getting behind a badge. Next to him, Stan Brooks in his stupid hat was looking for a place to ditch an abused cigar butt.

"Okay, Clair, as soon as the ME gets the remains out of there, have your neighbor do a walk-through. See if anything is missing."

"Right."

"Was she close to the Salvati girl?" I asked.

Clair looked down at her own handheld. "Loraine Puser, sixty-eight, she's known the female vic for around fifteen months. She used to get a few dollars to watch the vic's place while Juna was at work at The Score. She said she knows what should be in the downstairs."

Dock turned and glanced back. "Okay, Kieff, run down the vics."

Kieffer pulled out his own handheld. "The female vic is Juna Salvati, white, twenty-six, single, black and brown, five-seven, one twenty-four. No exes or children. She's six weeks into dancing at The Score, that gentleman's club up on Wilson. Before that, she danced at Yancy's Cravat in Magena. This is her place free and clear. Her parents' number was on the refrigerator. I called and reached her father, Marco Salvati. I got his address."

"Rough?" I asked.

Kieffer frowned. "He didn't even ask what it was about, which I thought was a little strange."

"Did you tell him?"

"Nope." Kieff tapped his screen with a finger. "As we all know, the male vic is Vince Polizzi, white, thirty-one, single, black and brown, five-eleven, two forty. No exes or children we know of. He lives with his family—if you'll pardon the expression—out there in West Bluff where he was employed as Don Scozarri's enforcer and heir apparent."

"This killer is toast," said Clair, her expression deadpan. "He got the mob on his young ass, now."

"God knows how many taps the Feds have on Scozarri's phones," said Dock. "We'll leave it up to Powers to keep the godfather informed." He looked toward Clair. "The bodyguards?"

"Pitone and Casale are still among the missing. They're out of New York and have been with Vince less than a year. We don't have any paper on them and neither does the NYPD. Probably imports."

"If they don't have records," I interjected, "we won't have prints or any current pictures."

"The PI said she already asked Scozarri, and photos are on the way. We can dust their homes for prints if we want. Dago Frank, says Powers, is convinced the bodyguards would not desert their posts. They must be dead. The Lincoln, where we found the last of the body parts, is Vince Polizzi's." Dock gestured with his hand in the general direction of the back seat. "Joe, you and

Kieffer take Juna Salvati's parents. Bring Powers with you."

"Why?" I asked.

"The godfather doesn't trust cops for some reason."

A cynical chuckle came from all of us.

"For the moment," Dock continued, "he's willing to let us handle this matter. Scozarri seems to trust this PI. As long as Powers sees this is a serious investigation, Dago Frank will stay on the reservation."

"You want us to toss the Salvati place?" asked Kieff.

Dock held out a modifying hand. "They've got a gob to choke down. If they keep a room for their daughter, you might ask if you can take a look. For now, nothing that requires a warrant and a pry bar." He faced me. "Wheels?"

"My own."

"Why didn't you pick up a pool car at the Tower?"

"You just said show, you didn't say you had—"

"You still in that crapheap Mazda?" he interrupted.

"It's a classic."

"So's the *Titanic*." He frowned. "Clair, Brooks, and Hewitt need this car and I'll need the car Kieff and I came in. Powers doesn't have wheels, Joe, so I guess it's your sardine can. You ever get that hatch fixed?"

"Two years ago. It broke again."

"How do you keep it open?"

"An old ski pole."

"You ever notice you and your grandfather are cut from the same bolt?"

"I disagree. My heater works."

Dock exhaled the sigh of eternal burdens. "Okay, DiMaggio, grab the CSU kit from my car before you take off." He turned farther, winced, and looked at Kieffer. "Mike Ijumaa is still on call, so if there's anything that needs an expert to collect, you bring him in."

Kieffer nodded, glanced at Clair Turner, and held up his handheld in her direction. She bumped his with hers, they each poked again, then came a couple of tiny beeps, the address information successfully copied. Robot sex. I half expected them to take out smokes and light up. I looked at Kieff's handheld and saw that Juna's parents lived at 1440 26th Street in Sherman Park.

I felt my hands grow clammy. Where Juna Salvati's parents lived was less than two blocks from Rizzo's Volkswagen-Audi. I hadn't been within a mile of the place since that night.

"Joe?"

"Hah?" I jerked my head up, the images about me shifting focus, wowing in and out. Dockery was sitting sideways in the passenger seat looking back at me. "What?" I asked.

"You okay, Joe?"

"Never better."

"Maybe you ought to tell your face." Dock tapped a finger on the center of his forehead. His sign for the Third Eye.

I rubbed the back of my neck, sorting it out in my head as I talked. "It's there: The need; especially the pattern. We got another shark in the water. Hard to believe this is the first time he's ever been noticed. These aren't his first killings and he is long from finished. His message is mixed: mostly love and guilt. He's got his formula down perfect. Vince Polizzi was the most careful and most suspicious man on earth, and with good reason. Even so, the vics trusted this shooter completely."

"You think our boy knew who he killed?" Dock asked.

"If he carried tin in this state anytime during the past ten years or so, he did," Kieffer answered before I could. He glanced at my questioning look and said, "More than one of us thinks we're after a cop."

Dock aimed his unwavering gaze at me. This was the question he had been waiting all night to ask. "Is he a cop?"

I nodded. A little tan and white dog was begging snacks from the spectators and I watched it until the dog went under the tape and was intercepted before he got to Dockery's breakfast. I looked at Kieffer. "If our boy had shown up in a uniform, though, Vince wouldn't have even come down the stairs. On the other hand, we know that the killer wants us to think that Vince was armed."

"Why does he want us to think Vince was armed?" asked Dock, "and why would that make him part of the Blue?"

"To warn us off; to protect us. He's telling us to stay out of his way." I looked at Dock. "He's either a cop or former cop and, as I said, these are not his first efforts."

"The FBI Field Office is sending over Kagen," said Dock. "He's their criminal profile coordinator. We have until eight tonight to get our information together for him. Why do *you* think he's a cop, DiMaggio?" Pressed Dock.

I frowned as I mentally pieced together the reasons for my gut-level assessment. "This guy's routine is studied, practiced, and formed within an unusually high degree of forensic awareness. I'd be surprised if we find a print of his or semen, hair, skin cells, or anything else he doesn't want found."

"What about those foot impressions and that glove impression?" asked Kieff. "We got his foot and glove size. From that we can make a guess at a physical size."

"Nothing about this guy is what it looks like, Kieff, not even to himself. The evidence shows he's a psycho with a submachine gun, but that's not what Juna Salvati saw through that window in her door before she let him in. If he shows us a footprint size ten, my hunch is the one size foot our boy cannot have is a ten."

Kieffer looked irritated. "Maybe he figured obscuring the friction ridge skin impressions with the plastic was enough."

"So, Kieff, leaving us with a size ten foot, he lets us exclude eighty-six or eighty-seven percent of all American males?"

"Maybe you give this guy too much credit."

"Maybe." I rubbed my eyes and then lowered my hand. "But I don't think so. "

Turner faced Dockery. "A possibly delicate matter, boss."

"What's that, Clair?"

"The cop angle: Do we bring in Internal Affairs?"

Dock nibbled at the skin inside his lower lip, rubbed the back of his neck, and looked through the windshield at the street. "Right now all we have are suspicions."

He glanced at me. "We got nothing we can take to court."

"But you're sure."

"Sure enough."

He looked forward. "Shit. I'll have to get together with Trask and negotiate something," he said at last.

"Want me to take care of it?" asked Kieffer.

"No. I'll give the Slime Squad a buzz and see if Trask wants to get on this train. IAB has Roemer's murder and Joe's Guardian Killer to sort out so they got all they can handle right now. We've got no direct evidence it's a cop, so Trask might just go for being kept informed for the time being." He squinted as he paused for a thought and then glanced at Kieffer. "Our boy is awful good with that submachine gun."

"Ex military?" suggested Kieff.

"Maybe. It might also just be a lot of practice." Dockery pulled his lips into his mouth, thought a second, and released them. "Up until 'Ninety-two, licensed collectors used to be allowed to own functioning fully automatic weapons in this state." Dock punched at his handheld. "I'll put Brooks on checking out the old authorized ranges. Maybe he can come up with a name."

I looked and Dockery was looking straight at me. "What?"

"Your expression, DiMaggio, says checking the ranges would be a big fat waste of time."

"Well, yeah. You have to check it out, but this guy knows how we do what we do, Dock. He's not registered and neither is his weapon. I'll bet you a week's worth of donuts against your Jenny Craig payment he's never been within sight of a public or club shooting range."

Dock glanced at Turner. "Lots of wilderness up in Lyon and Washington Counties. See if the Sheriffs over there have any reports of automatic weapons being used."

Turner nodded. As she wrote she said, "Boss, what about that lieutenant who comes to the range out at the academy to put on those demonstrations?"

"Carlton. He's the SWAT commander."

"That's the one." She looked at Kieffer. "Carlton. You ever see him with a Thompson?"

"I hear he's pretty good," said Kieff. "Can't hurt to run him for an alibi."

"Joe," said Dock, "you in our boy's head at all?"

"Some." I tried to gather the few thoughts I had. "We're cleaning up after a shattered love and sex triangle: Mother, son, and at least one adult interloper; probably more"

I frowned as the edge of a thought managed to peek through the fog. "That first adult rival—first to our killer anyway—might have been a police officer. There were probably numerous rivals over the years. I'm thinking our boy had enough one day and took back his place—probably by force—and it had unacceptable consequences. I think our boy is trying to make up for it."

"Sexual? With the mother?" asked Turner, her eyebrows upraised.

"Without a doubt."

Dock pointed a finger-gun at Clair Turner. "As soon as your gang returns to the Tower, get busy assembling the case information for Kagen. Also, I want that VICAP report filed yesterday."

"Right."

"Okay," said Dock to Kieffer. "I'll have the uniforms, Brooks, and Hewitt keep the neighborhood interviews moving, finish collecting the evidence, and brief our contacts at county, state, and fed to see when we can put together our organizational. Anything else? Joe?"

That neat little group of eight polished brass cartridge cases teased my mind. Juna was only a couple of feet away from the shooter. There had been high velocity blood spatter on the floor there between and to the sides of Juna and her shooter. Nothing on the polished shell casings, though. And two touches on the trigger, four rounds apiece. In-and-out without leaving a neighborhood ripple. I closed my eyes. "Imagine how cool, how focused, how deliberate and controlled this guy has to be. Four-and-four right on the money. No shaking, no hesitation."

"And?" prompted Kieffer.

"It doesn't fit with all those back swing spatters in the dining room. There he appears to be telling us he's enraged, deranged, hysterical, out of control. But he doesn't leave us any latents, DNA, nothing. And we have back swing spatters but no stab wounds. You got no stabs, you got no back swings. No back swings, no backswing spatter."

"Staged?" asked Kieff.

I thought for a second then shrugged. "It doesn't feel like it, Dock. Maybe it's not even meant to be interpreted."

"What then?"

"I don't know. It's not part of his message, though."

We all looked and Julia Powers was standing and waiting in the doorway to the green-painted house. "What about her, Dock?" asked Turner.

"Officially, Clair, Julia Powers is a private consultant on the case. She actually is a victim profiler. Unofficially, she's Dago Frank's price to sit back and let us do the dirty work." He looked back at Kieffer and me. "She's with you two. Keep Powers up to speed, let her go where she wants unless it compromises the investigation. She used to be on the job, so she'll be cool. If she wants to help, let her help. She's not on our clock. Be sure to maintain the chain of evidence on whatever you collect."

"That wasn't what I meant," said Turner whirling her right index finger around her right temple.

"I know what you meant," Dock answered. "As far as I know, she's as sane as anyone in this car."

Clair Turner glanced back at me and I restrained myself from sticking my thumbs in my ears and waving my fingers, although I did cross my eyes. She laughed.

Dock rubbed the back of his neck again, turned his head, scanned the crowd outside, closed his eyes for a moment, and said, "I'm going to have to wade though those damned reporters to get to my car. 'No comment,' gang. That's your exclusive for the media: 'No comment.'"

Powers came down the steps and began walking toward us, the bill of her hat down and the collar of her coat up, obscuring her face. She wasn't looking for a spot on the evening news, either.

"Very well, children," said Dock. "Tote that barge, lift that bale, get those warrants, give those rights, and do

171

not talk to the media." A beat. "Let's get at it." He climbed out of the car into an unintelligible storm of shouted questions from the police line. He signaled for Kieffer, Powers, and me to follow him. Long before we reached his cruiser, the shouts shifted focus from Dock to me.

THE THREE AMIGOS

"The hangman's son—"

"Sgt. Torio, have you killed number eight, yet?"

"New record, sergeant—"

"—true that the last three numbers on your badge are six-six-six?"

Dock had the trunk open, he snatched out an aluminum CSU kit and handed it to Kieffer. Dock said something to Powers, then nodded at me. The three of us headed for the Mazda.

"Sgt. Torio! How do you feel about breaking the city's record for killing—"

"Aren't you ashamed—"

"Is this crime connected—"

"What about the Guardian? Is he an ex classmate—"

"Do you regret—"

"—Called you a butcher. How do you respond—"

"Bianca Devlin, detective. Is your assignment to the Black Gang a demotion?"

As I reached my mostly red MX3, I grabbed the handle of the driver's door as a microphone with a Channel Seven bug on it was stuck in my face far enough for the foam cover to mash my nose before it withdrew. Holding it was a little red-headed geek hunter in a lime-green pantsuit with enough lip-liner around her fat-injected lips to make her look like she'd spent the morning sucking a Baby Ruth. I popped the car's hatch, tripped the seat lock, and stepped back to allow Julia Powers to climb into the cramped back seat while Kieffer lifted the heavy hatch, propped it open with the ski pole, and put in the CSU kit. He threw in some packaged coverall outfits for the three of us, just in case. More microphones were gathering.

"Have you been demoted from Homicide, sergeant?"

"Was Lt. Dockery sick out there?"

"Sergeant Kieffer, how do you feel working with the hangman's son—"

"You'll have to talk to the case supervisor," said Kieffer to a reporter as he tried to get in the car.

"Sgt. Torio," called out Bianca, she of the fat lips and green pantsuit. "In light of the deaths here, are you in favor of gun control?"

"If you own a gun," I said, "I am definitely in favor of you controlling it."

I nodded for Kieffer to shut the hatch and had to shoulder Bianca out of the way to get back to the door, and I did so. She landed with her butt on the snowy wet asphalt and said something that would make an interesting bit of tube candy, if Channel Seven had the guts to use it.

"Sorry," I said and pulled the seat back as the hatch closed. I held out my hand to help up the reporter, but she simply glared at me.

I got in the car, and as soon as Kieffer climbed in and shut the passenger door, I buckled up, cranked it up, nudged a few folks out of the way backing up, then dropped it in low and squealed northwest through the crowd up Booth. An old car, perhaps, but the motor still had plenty of pickup. At Randall I hung a right and took Ninth north once we hit the Cross Town. As the heater began scenting the air with mouse bacon, I noticed Kieffer staring at me with his mouth open. "What?" I asked.

"Just a suggestion, man: Either put out a Kojak light and make with some wah-wah noises or slow this piece of shit down."

"Sorry." I eased off the accelerator and glanced in the rearview. "I guess old Bianca there was getting to me."

"You know what Bianca Devlin's real name is?" asked Powers.

"No."

"Drusilla Butts."

"How do you know that?" Kieffer asked.

"She was a year ahead of me at Lanford," Powers answered.

We laughed on that until I turned to Kieff. "What was that crack about my car?"

Kieffer and Powers both laughed at the same time. "Are you shitting me, man," he said. "I've been in dog pounds smelled better than this." He turned and looked back at the PI. "What do you say we go rent a car?"

"And miss a ride in this classic?" she remarked. "Hey, Joe, what tore up these seats? Do you drive for Grizzlies On Wheels?"

Kieffer and Powers were really enjoying themselves. I couldn't think of a good comeback so I asked a question. "Julia, who was it who gave you the ride to Booth Street?"

"Tommy Zerilli. You know Tommy?"

"You must be charmed. You're one of the few persons who ever took a ride with Tommy who are still around to talk about it."

"He's sweet."

"Yeah, for someone who does brain surgery with a Glock," remarked Kieffer. "Does the don know the name of the second-story man?"

"He says he doesn't. I believe him. His boys are looking, though."

"Did Tommy Zee take you straight there or did you talk first with the don?"

"I talked with the don on my cell phone. I was right in the middle of my morning run when he called and Tommy was there twenty minutes later. He must've done ninety all the way from Booth."

"You go running at two in the morning?" I asked.

"When I can't sleep. I hear you watch old movies and eat pancakes."

"How did the don seem?" asked Kieff.

"He sounded like a father who just lost his only son. Let me save you more groping around the edges, boys. As far as my client is concerned, I am to cooperate fully with the police insofar as this investigation is concerned, as long as you folks keep at it and keep me informed as to your progress. Anything else?"

"As a matter of fact, there is something," I answered. "When the alleged second-story man called Scozarri,

175

who did he talk to? Did he talk to the Don directly or did someone else take the call?"

"Tommy Zee took the call. Do you have a first-man-in thing smoking your fedora?"

"First day at the Academy: the guy who reports the murder did it, three-to-one."

"Which would be the second-story man."

"If there is, indeed, a second-story man."

"You saw the barf, Joe. If you think that belongs to Tommy, you don't know Tommy. Stuff that would gag a pathologist wouldn't interrupt Tommy's chili dog, pickles, and mayo."

"Anyone else talk to the second-story man?"

"I don't think so. A survival thing, Tommy thinks."

Kieff slouched down in the passenger seat. "I have a question, partner." He glanced at me to see my reaction to the term.

"If it's about the smell and torn up seats, that's no mutt; that's genuine seven-hundred dollar Rottweiler."

"Something else."

"I'll answer if I feel like it."

Kieff grinned. "Okay, man. Did you get drunk one night and make obscene phone calls to *every* media story editor in town?"

I smiled sheepishly and shrugged. "I do not recall any such event."

As I took a right onto Canal, Kieffer said, "What else?"

I looked at the rearview and Powers was listening. "It's a number of things. That business at the Rizzo brothers garage. It's brought out some strange opposition."

"Some even stranger support, I bet," added Julia.

"That's no lie. But my body count plus Pop being a retired hangman has a bunch of the fantasy news writers spinning rather fanciful explanations for my behavior. Me being a possible serial killer myself sells copies."

Kieffer looked at me. "My father was a corrupt cop." He looked back at the PI. "Yours?"

"Air Force general and microchip tycoon—also corrupt."

Kieffer shrugged and looked through the passenger window, scanning the street from habit. He placed his palms over his face, ground the sleep out of his eyes, and gave a tremendous yawn. "Long day."

"It's just getting started, gang," I said. You want to take a seven and grab some breakfast?" I talked over my shoulder to Julia. "How about it? Some food?"

"You can eat?" She asked it like I would have to be some kind of carnival geek to be hungry after our tour of the recent crime scene.

I considered it for a second. "I guess not. Let's hit Jolly's 24 Hour on Stanley and grab a Dr Pepper. You want some coffee?"

"With milk," said Kieffer.

"A Dr Pepper sounds good," said Powers.

Before I could properly react to finding another Pepperhead, she asked, "How do you two want to handle Juna Salvati's parents?"

"I don't," said Kieffer. "I mean, I do *not*. No good at that stuff at *all*. Tears, screaming, all that hair-pulling. I'll work the room while you two handle the bereaved."

"You're an algebra man," observed Powers.

"Say what?"

"Take the known quantities, drop them into the appropriate formula, then solve for X. Algebra man. No emotional entanglements."

He shrugged. "First day at the academy, right? Get emotionally involved and sooner or later you eat a gun. Right, Joe?"

"Wasn't that the same day they told us about equal justice under the law?"

"Yeah, okay. And equal opportunity, the coming pay raise, nobody's on the pad, corruption upstairs is history, and the satisfaction of a job well done." His voice became more serious, but still with a touch of amusement. "So, how do you do it, Joe?"

"I suppose I still count on my fingers. All we deal with is information, Kieff. We find it, sort it, grade it, refine it, and present it. All of the whys—the motives— are the roadmaps to everything else, and all the whys are on a feelings level. So that's what I try to find: feelings. When I sort through the evidence I try to feel what a witness, a suspect, a perp feels. Without judgment—Get in there and ride the monster until I can see life, the world, and the situation the way the monster does."

"Why?"

"That's where the answers are."

Kieffer stared at me, his eyebrows up. "Man, how have you lived as long as you have?"

"Amazing, isn't it?"

"What about getting lost?" Julia asked me, her reflection in the mirror dead serious.

"It happens," I answered reluctantly. We were getting awfully close to deep and dark time.

"And?" Kieffer prompted.

I shrugged. "And then they find me and bring me back for the next job. I don't sleep much, but I never did. And I get to see a lot of great movies." I glanced to my right and Kieffer was shaking his head. "What do you feel about our boy, Kieff?"

"What? Feel? The killer?"

"Yeah. How do you feel about him?"

"He kills and butchers citizens. He disgusts me, makes me sick, outrages me—I hate him." He raised his right eyebrow at me. "How do you feel about him?"

I thought for a moment, attaching labels to those nebulous things that rode me every night, making sleep a ridiculous fantasy. "Fear. I'm afraid of him. I'm afraid of his pain, his guilt, his love—both the degree and intensity. I'm also afraid for him. I feel sorry for him."

"Sorry for him?" repeated Kieff, both eyebrows now arched.

"Yes."

"What about feeling sorry for the vics?"

"I feel sorry for them, too. Look, this killer didn't just drop out of the sky, Kieff. He was made brick-by-brick. Genetics, environment, all of those little coping choices we all make. I don't know what all those things are yet, but there are things that bent him and aimed him like a weapon." I grinned at Kieffer. "Which one of us, do you think, is closer to understanding, hence catching, the sonofabitch?"

After that we talked about Kieffer's wife, Miriam, and his daughter, Mona. His wife and daughter both hated that he was a cop, but suspected he was only on the job to gather material for a book. If he wound up on the *Times* bestseller list, all would be forgiven. I asked if MCU had ever gotten the kidnapping of Congresswoman Jennings's daughter cleared.

"It fizzled, first, as it happened," said Kieffer. Turned out that Tony Plummer took a cell-phone photo of Misty in the buff at a resort in Palm Beach and Emailed it to a friend of his, whose communications were being monitored for various controlled substance transactions. Before Plummer's buddy could Email the photo to all of *his* buddies, he was up to his eyeballs in cops. Apparently Tony and Misty planned to get the ransom money and vanish. The busted friend, their confident, blabbed all.

Neither Kieffer nor I were uncool enough to grill Julia about the Gray-eye Killer—for about ten minutes. She volunteered a few things, but nothing new. It had wound up with her being taken off the job and in therapy, so it was a spot still sore.

At the red-nosed Jolly Clown drive-in speaker, I bellowed the order into the thing three times before Julia noticed the City Health Department's ptomaine tag hanging from the clown's nose. Jolly's was closed cutting off the nutritive support to at least thirty-seven percent of the city's vermin population. We proceeded without sustenance.

ANOTHER LOVELY FACE

"My daughter was a slut, detective. I ain't surprised at all she got herself killed."

Marco Salvati, Julia, and I sat at Salvati's kitchen table, the familiar scents of oregano, garlic, browned beef, peppers, onions, bacon, and tomato in the air. Sauce simmering in a large stainless steel pot on one of the gas stove's back burners. The room was pale-yellow 'Sixties, spotlessly clean. Salvati was staring at the tan-painted table top as his big gnarled hands rubbed the sleeves of his gray wool shirt as though warding off a chill. Hard expression, his jaw set. Not indifferent, though. He was doing Sicilian macho the way my grandfather had after Mama Elisa had died: Full of pain and cut off from his feelings as far as any outside eyes were concerned. Still, there was something beyond that in Marco Salvati. Hard to read. It was like talking to scar tissue, not an open wound.

Kieffer was as far from the table as possible, hiding in Juna's old room with the CSU kit. After looking at Juna's room herself, Julia had come into the kitchen and seated herself across from Salvati.

Marco looked up and smiled at her. "You see pictures of my daughter?"

"Yes, Mr. Salvati," Julia answered. "She was a very lovely young woman."

"Movie star. She could a been a model or movie star, famous dancer—a *real* dancer. Theater. Even opera. She had a sweet voice." The smile faded, his gaze drifted back to the table top. "All those lessons, good grades, go to church. Marry some big shot, maybe. Anything she want." He nodded to himself and shrugged. "Well, she

180

did what she want. Watch TV her whole life and shake her fanny in front of a bunch of drunks."

"Did you keep in touch with her at all?" I asked.

"She had nothin' to say to me." He looked up at me, his cloudy gaze sad and moist. He shrugged. "Sometime her mother talk to her. Don't know when the last time was. She don't tell me." He frowned as though the mention of his wife recalled his duties as host. "You want somethin' to drink?"

"Sure. You got a Dr Pepper?"

He grimaced. "Nothin' like that. Beer. Coffee. Water. Some apple juice." He looked at Julia. "My wife drinks this soy milk stuff. Supposed to pump up her hormones."

"Thanks, no," she answered for both of us. "When do you think your wife will be back?" she asked.

"Mass is done at ten." He glanced at the electric clock over the sink. It was a quarter to eleven. "She went to pick up a few things. The grocery is close by." He gave a slight shrug and put out his lower lip. "A few more minutes maybe."

"Do you know anything about your daughter's boyfriends, her boss, other friends? New friends? Enemies?" asked Julia.

"She was nothin' but new friends, miss. Boyfriends. John this, Michael that, Abe somebody else, and that last one, that Renzo," He shifted his gaze back to Julia. "I even met that Renzo." A bitter little laugh. "Renzo the wiseguy; Like wearing a black shirt and watching *The Godfather* four times makes you hooked up. What a empty suit. Iowa Neapolitan is what he was." He shook his head, "Corn-fed Cosa Nostra. Tough enough, maybe, but two dates with my daughter and he's calling me *goomba* like he paid my way over on the boat." He waved a hand and muttered something in Italian that sounded very rude.

"Any of those have last names? Renzo?"

In return I got a really strange look from Mr. Salvati. "DeStefano. Renzo DeStefano."

"Do you know where he works?"

"In Hell, I expect. Before, he work for Tri-County Construction out of Baldwin. Foreman."

"Is this Renzo dead?"

Salvati frowned. "As dead as Julius Caesar." After a moment of that, he fixed his gaze back on the table top. I set aside Renzo DeStefano for the moment. "Did you ever hear of Vince Polizzi?"

"Sure. Francesco Scozarri's bastard." His bushy eyebrows went up in a momentary gesture of respect. After all, Polizzi was a real wiseguy. "My daughter knew Vince Polizzi?"

"Yes."

Then the eyebrows came down again. "I don't get none of this." He looked at Julia Powers. "They never said nothin' about Vince Polizzi. This other stuff, though, I gave it all to the cops last year. Why's the Polizzi boy come up now?"

Julia looked at me. I looked at the old man as Kieffer entered the kitchen holding something. "In connection with what, Mr. Salvati?" I asked.

"What are you talkin' about? What's goin' on here?"

"Who were the police officers?" asked Julia. "What were they investigating?"

I saw Kieffer waving at me, attempting not to be noticed by Marco Salvati. In his other hand he was holding a framed photograph of what was by then a very familiar face. As the bottom of my stomach dropped out, I remembered all of those pictures in Juna Salvati's home. I had been right after all: Juna hadn't been a narcissist and my famous third eye had a big fat finger stuck in it.

"Baldwin cops," answered the old man. "About my daughter Lacy and this Renzo DeStefano. Murdered."

I glanced at Kieffer. After a Bambi-in-the-headlights glance back, he held out his free hand in a lame gesture of apology. I looked at Juna Salvati's father as I felt at least a liter of acid dump into my stomach. "No, Mr. Salvati, we're not here about Lacy." My mouth was as dry as kitty litter. "We're here from the South River PD about your daughter Juna."

"Juna? *Juna?*" His voice was hollow, his eyes seemed to sink back into his face.

"Yes. Juna Salvati and Vince Polizzi. I'm very sorry, but they were both murdered yesterday morning in Juna's home on Booth Street, here in the city."

182

Marco Salvati seemed to decompose before our eyes. Motionless, his face reddening, his lips drawn tight, his eyes narrowing. He dug at his cheeks with his fingernails as though his face was caught in a maddening itch. Finally, his eyes closed, his shoulders slumped, he hung his head, and hot fat tears slipped down his face.

"They weren't discovered until early this morning, sir, which is why—"

He howled. It was a cry that ripped out the bottom of the universe.

"—why it took until now to let you know," I finished lamely.

A long, low, cooing moan filled the room. Julia reached out a hand and placed it on Marco Salvati's hand. His hand turned and gripped hers, and she held his with both of hers. I looked at Algebra Man, but that particular superhero was covered in more chicken feathers than Frank Purdue, his face turned in the opposite direction, his hand rubbing the back of his neck.

The moan was cut short by a ragged intake of air, followed by the old man repeating, "My babies, my babies, my sweet little babies."

As the father of Juna and Lacy Salvati dissolved on the table, Kieffer, Powers, and I all jumped as the lock on the front door turned. Kieffer cocked his head to one side, closed his eyes, and looked like he was about to get sick as he turned back through the door to intercept the mother of the two dead dancers.

I sat back in my chair, rubbed my temples, pressing, trying to excise my advancing migraine like popping a pimple. There was more wailing coming, and after the wailing, there would still be questions that needed answers: the old ones, and a whole bunch of new ones.

FUNTOWN

After filling in Dock about Lacy Salvati and Renzo DeStefano, he ordered us to Baldwin to see what we could shake out of the Baldwin PD. After passing Books, I turned down Louise and took the Heights Road south. Before getting on the Interstate we stopped at Chocko's, got gas, and loaded up on Twinkies, moon pies, cashews, coffee, and Dr Pepper.

Baldwin, about forty minutes east of South River, was in the heart of red clay country, known for cabbage, bricks, strip mined gold, and night crawlers. The town had a population of around twenty-eight thousand, a sixteen badge police force, one pretty good ski resort north of town, Eagle Mountain, and a Western theme park named Silver City that everyone in the state called Shakedown City. The billboard on the city limits proclaimed Baldwin "Funtown—A great place to play, work, and live." The sign was riddled with bullet holes.

Once we got in town we could see Baldwin's budget committee had somehow sneaked a shovel-ready deep-pocket earmark past the voters. The PD were headquartered in the old municipal building on the Perry Street side of Madison Square. Brown sandstone, big double hung windows flanked by illusory columns, the whole thing encrusted with scaffolding and hung with tarps. A sign announced that, once the renovations were completed ("Your tax dollars at work."), the structure would be known as Baldwin City Police Center.

Inside the future Police Center, a haze of dust hung in the air on its way to settling out on drop cloths, stacks of new flooring, and packing crates that appeared to contain new computers and office furniture. The smell of ammonia was thick and the desk staff cranky. After half an hour of Kieffer and I being double-talked and bounced around between a couple of particularly irritable paper wizards, Julia Powers leaned out of a doorway and whistled at us. We followed her into the chief's office.

Scott Poleman was in his late fifties, a spectacular comb over on top, a face that reminded me of Yasser Arafat, and a butt that reminded me of a clown I once saw at a Shrine Circus. He had a coarse tweed suit that looked like it was woven from gray and black twigs, a white shirt, and a black string tie. Chief Poleman eyed Kieff like he ought to take an antibiotic. His inventory of Kieffer complete, he appeared to be having a hard time making up his mind about whether he ought to go to bed with Julia or throw us all out. When she opened her coat revealing her baggy gray sweats, her option waned. Leaving the door open in case he chose to exercise the other option, the chief pointed to a couple of straight-backs and a red leather upholstered chair that was so low the only way a woman wearing a dress and sitting there could keep her color and style of undergarments secret was with a staple gun. Julia flopped into the red chair, slouched down, let her knees fall apart in the Chief's direction, and interlaced her fingers across her belly.

Poleman's office looked like a set from *Judge Dredd Meets Police Academy*. Flags, banners, displays of weapons—pistols, knives, and rifles including an M-14, an M-16, an M1928 Thompson, and a wicked-looking machine gun I couldn't place. There were framed photos of the chief with sundry politicians, celebs, and cuffed alleged criminals above a bank of modern communications, security, computer, and entertainment equipment. He had three screens facing him from the wall behind his desk, and, just before he punched off the center screen with his remote, I noted that the chief had been watching a women's body-building competition. He did not stand to greet us so Kieff and I sat down. He looked from Julia's crotch to me.

"Chief," I began, "we have a double homicide that may be connected to an old double homicide here in

Baldwin. We'd like to look at the DeStefano-Salvati file and evidence and compare your murders with ours."

Poleman' skin momentarily appeared to lighten. He then frowned deeply and smiled widely at the same time. "Now, son—Sgt. Torio, is it?—You used to have a big rep up there in South River Homicide, didn't you? Now, how did you ever wind up in the Ghetto?" He glanced at Kieffer. "That's just what we call your Black Gang here— Major Crimes Unit? We call it the Ghetto." Big smirk. "No offense."

Kieffer and I exchanged incredulous glances. Without changing expression, Kieff fixed his gaze on Poleman's face. "Ah'll jest set heah, suh, 'n' moldertate 'till yawl needs me."

As the comment sailed over Poleman's head and Julia suddenly discovered something in her eye, Poleman raised an eyebrow at me. "Now, don't go getting all sensitive on me. It's just I never heard of nobody white bein' in South River MCU. You're sort of a white sheep, right?" Big yuk, for Poleman, at least. A fellow fraught with irony. "Y'all call it the Black Gang, right?"

"I don't," I said, "but I'm new."

"I heard some South River uniforms call it the N-squad, although they sort of spelled it out a bit more, if you get my drift." Dead air from our side of the room. "G'wan, Torio, tell me it don't bother you."

"What bothers me?"

"That you're the only white in MCU."

"What makes you think I'm white?" I asked him.

"G'wan." Big pause accompanied by an intense stare. "You're not white?"

"What? You need a hearing aid to go with your new eyeglass prescription?"

His expression went from stunned, to disbelieving, to suspicious, to studious, at last arriving at something approaching an epiphany. He glanced at Kieffer's upraised eyebrows, and shifted his gaze to me. "I never would've guessed. Name like Torio. I mean Eye-talians, they're white, right?"

"Well, there *was* that unpleasantness with Carthage," Julia offered. She looked at Kieffer. "Is Eddie Murphy really Irish?"

"Possibly. Robert E. Lee, though, was Chinese."

"Now don't you smartasses all get off on an ethnic thing. I'm just asking." Poleman frowned as he leaned forward and studied me more closely. "Well." He moistened his lips and shook his head. "Okay. Yeah. I can see it now. The eyes. You can see it in the eyes. And the fingernails. I wouldn't of noticed if you didn't mention it, but I see it now." Poleman raised his eyebrows as he leaned back in his chair. "I guess it don't pay to take too much for granted."

"You can't judge a book by its cover," added Julia with about a yard of tongue in her cheek.

"Double your pleasure, double your fun," concluded Kieffer.

Leaning forward, I attempted to get back to the DeStefano-Salvati murders. "Chief, about that case—"

"And lookie here, you got this rich-girl PI in tow." He nodded toward Julia still sitting in his Sharon Stone chair with her knees apart. "Now, I never seen anything like that."

"C'mon, Joe Bob," Julia said to me, but still looking at Poleman, "The manure truck is double parked 'n' Kieffer Bob 'n' me gotta git back to the slurry pit."

"Sho 'nuff," Kieff agreed.

They both looked at Poleman with straight faces.

"Now, there is no need for anyone to become overly sensitive," said the chief, his face now quite red.

"No risk of that," I said.

"Now all you just hold on. I am no racist. I got three of 'em here on the force."

"Racists?" I asked.

"No. Blacks. *African Americans*. You know. Look, one of 'em's even a sergeant. I mean, I didn't mean to offend anyone's ethnic or occupational preference, Torio."

"We're beyond offense, chief. Now—"

"But when they started up that Major Crimes Unit, it was supposed to be somethin' special, right? The best of the best, the elite? In all the papers 'cause that Gray-eye Killer ran you boys around for so long."

"Gerald Soams killed a couple of Baldwin boys, too, as I recall," said Julia with a deadly calm expression.

"The point is, your Major Crimes Unit is somethin' of a joke, isn't it?. They're hacking your original budget in half, right? 'Cause of the economy? Disband the unit in a year or so? That's what it said in the papers."

"Oh," interrupted Julia wide-eyed as though she had discovered an unexpected treasure. "You read the papers?"

"Of course I read the papers," he retorted. "Black Gang? I mean, even down in East Branch Division all the cops aren't black."

Kieff leaned forward, his elbows on his knees. "What makes you think I'm black?"

Chief Poleman's eyebrows went up, then down. "Now, I've had just about enough of you assholes. If you don't have any questions I can answer, then I'll just have to ask you to leave."

Smoke and mirrors. Poleman really did not want to talk about the DeStefano-Salvati murders. I took a patient breath. "About those murders—"

"Torio. With that name and your face, I bet back in school you got lots of dates with white girls."

"You lose. Now, about those homicides—"

"I don't see how we can help you." Poleman interrupted again. "We cleared that one a week after the, uh, bodies were discovered."

"Cleared it?" repeated Kieffer as he got to his feet. "Who'd you collar for it, Chief?"

"It was in all the papers. Fellow named Doyle." Poleman scratched behind his ear, checked beneath his fingernail for trace evidence, and leaned further back in his chair. "Wilson Doyle—"

"Scabby Doyle?" burst out Julia. "You hung a double homicide on the Confessor?" The chief's face was reddening.

"Man, that is desperate," I added. "How'd the papers let you get away with it?"

Chief Poleman feigned uncomprehending injury, but couldn't carry it off. "Doyle confessed, Torio. His con—"

"Scabby Doyle has confessed to everything from the White Chapel murders to Bernie Madoff's bank account. Everybody knows his train doesn't exactly stop at all the stations."

"He described things about the crime scene that weren't released to the press."

I leaned forward in my chair. "Had to close those murders yesterday, eh, chief? You're heavily into shares of Shakedown City and there's simply too much blood and too many body parts scattered around to keep Funtown looking like fun in the media."

Poleman's eyes went very narrow. "What do you know about body parts?"

"A lot more than the media did, it appears."

"How'd you keep the lid on it, chief?" asked Kieffer.

The chief's mouth shut tight and he simply glared at us.

Julia held a finger beneath her chin and looked at Scott Poleman as though he was a specimen on a slide. "I've never seen the like before, gentlemen. The subject has an absolutely astounding inability to draw a line from A to B. I believe they call it forensic dyslexia."

Kieff nodded and held out his hands. "I owe you an apology, Chief Poleman."

"Oh?" He looked warily at Kieffer.

"At first I thought you were simply some kind of Jiminy Cracker sociological throwback, then it was beginning to look like you were running some sort of cover up for police misconduct, but you're just as dumb as sock full of rat turds, aren't you?"

"I still like him as a racist crook," said Julia.

Poleman leaned forward, more worried than offended. After staring at me for a moment, he said, "What was that case again?"

"DeStefano-Salvati."

"And what does this have to do with you folks?"

Kieffer exhaled an enormously impatient sigh, crossed his arms, thrust out his lower lip, stood and walked slowly toward the door. "Well, chief, we have trouble. Back there in River City." He closed and latched the office door. Kieffer walked back and stood before Poleman's desk. "The person who made our bodies dead left what we call a distinctive signature. You probably covered crime signatures in your correspondence course."

"Now, look here—"

"He's done this before, chief," said Julia, getting to her feet and positioning herself off the left end of the chief's desk. "In fact, our trail leads right to the murders of Lacy Salvati and Renzo DeStefano here in Funtown, where, if the real killer had been caught a year ago, he wouldn't have made dead the bodies in South River. I do believe some eager assistant district attorney could probably put together a convincing charge of criminal facilitation on what you did—excuse me—*didn't* do."

"A fact that won't get lost on the media, should we have to make a point of going to them," added Kieffer.

"Media?"

I got to my feet and stood next to Kieffer. "Part of that signature," I said, as Kieffer pulled out his handheld, "involved the dismemberment of the corpses, and the transportation and pairing of body parts to various locations about the crime scene. Perhaps you recall the pattern."

Holding his handheld out so that Poleman could view the screen, Kieffer said, "Like that."

Chief Poleman did a great impression of someone who had been suddenly smacked in the face with a frozen mackerel. "I swear, to us it looked like the perp went drug-crazy. Some crackhead cut up a couple of people, then played with the parts. A one-time thing. It couldn't have been any kind of serial nut. That was our expert's opinion."

"FBI? Who?" demanded Kieff. "Who was your expert?" Poleman mentally juggled a few lies and rationalizations until Kieffer said, "It was you, wasn't it, Scotty? You were the expert."

"Dammit. It's just not the sort of thing that happens in Baldwin. Anyone can tell you that. This is a good town with good people."

Kieffer frowned, his expression astonished. "I don't know, man. Do you sleep at night hanging from your neck? Have you been getting your smokes out of the evidence room?"

"What did the VICAP report say?" I asked. Poleman's chin lowered slowly to his chest. He certainly didn't supplement his income playing poker. "You didn't file, did you?"

"Feds," he grumped, in a pitiful attempt to invoke the local-cop brotherhood bond against the credit-sucking agents of the FBI. "It's a lot of paperwork." He shrugged with only his left shoulder and stared at the top of his desk. "See, we already had— You know, Torio."

"Yeah. You already had a confession. Tell me, which one of your stooges knew about Scabby, came into South River, and put a bug in Scabby's ear?"

"I resent that, detective!"

The fronts of my thighs leaned against the edge of Poleman's desk making it move toward Poleman half an inch and making Poleman jump. "Chief, I think you recognized something when brother Kieffer there showed you that image on his neat little handheld. You've seen ours. Now we'd like to see yours."

"If we'd had any idea—"

"See, Chief, that's how VICAP works," said Kieff. "You don't get an idea until you know, you don't know until you *ask,* and you can't ask unless you file." He paused for a beat then observed. "You didn't even call in the state crime lab team."

"Of course," added Julia, "If you call in the staties or file with the feds, you risk bringing in the PR people, the media, and the whole circus, don't you?"

"All those images on *World's Grisliest Crime Scene Videos,"* I added.

Kieff nodded toward all of the electrical equipment on the built-in behind Poleman's chair. "Very up to date. I am quite impressed with the improvements being made around here."

"Did you notice the wireless attachment?" asked Julia. She looked at the chief. "Would you say that the Baldwin Police Department has everything on that computer?"

Warily, Scott Poleman nodded. "That's right. We just completed entering our backlog last month. Cost a bundle."

"Excellent."

Awareness suddenly registered on Poleman's face. "You think I'm going to copy you our files on the DeStefano-Salvati murders?"

"That's just what we think," I said. "You see, not only is it going to help us take a shark out of the water, it's going to make a whole heap less noise to copy us the file in the spirit of inter-jurisdictional cooperation than it would for us to have to work it through the DA's office, the State Inspector General's Office, the State Police, the courts, and the media."

"All those terribly unfair questions and headlines," said Kieffer.

"The talk shows, the columns, 'Police Cover-up Puts Greed Before Justice,'" Julia announced for effect.

Kieffer leaned forward. "What say, chief? Want to help stop a killer?"

I placed my fists on Poleman's desk top and leaned on them. "We're blue, through and through, right chief? Same color, same side, after the same thing."

He gasped out a staccato heh-heh-heh like a nervous Elmer Fudd.

Julia held out a hand. "And, while we're at it, chief, we're going to want to look through the physical evidence and check out the crime scene, as well. We'll probably want to borrow a few things from your evidence room, too."

PATCHES

309 Choy Street was five blocks northwest of the future Baldwin Police Center. The neighborhood looked like the Zone back in South River, just smaller. The brand new aluminum siding on the house was Big Bird yellow, garish against the brown, gray, and dirty-brick drabness of the surrounding houses. After being invited inside by the residents, a couple of working girls, we learned that the entire house had been redone from the basement to the upstairs closet. Larisa and Chantelle said that the all-new interior was in place when they rented the house with an option to buy at a ridiculously low figure, which they exercised this past October. The seller was the City of Baldwin. She told me the figure and it was low by even post real-estate market crash standards.

After we did a walk-through of Lacy Salvati's former residence, determined that anything blood might have touched had been either bleached out or bodily replaced, we went back to Police Central to go through BPD's evidence room. The place was organized essentially by putting things wherever they could be jammed, stuffed, or stacked. There was no evidence clerk, simply a patrol officer who handed us a key and told us to enter in the log anything we opened or wanted to remove from the premises. He also urged us to lock up when we were finished and return the key.

"If I ever get caught for something illegal," said Kieffer, "I hope it's in Baldwin."

I nodded. Bevis and Butthead could've gotten Saddam Hussein off on Baldwin chain-of-evidence alone. We wouldn't be able to use it in court either. Still, we might be able to glean some answers from it. We loaded what we could find in the back of the Mazda, particularly the cartridge cases, recovered slugs, DNA samples, hard copy photos, state ME reports, and portable room content inventories. The cartridge cases were 9mm Lugers, but with months of tarnish on their polished surfaces. Fingerprints etched into their surfaces, too. Poleman's probably. The chief's prints were in the state database so, regrettably, it wasn't necessary to hold him down to roll his fingers.

It was getting late. I called Dock about Baldwin PD's noteworthy paradigm of inter-jurisdictional cooperation, then the three of us loaded into the already packed car and headed back to the city, whatever sunset remaining obscured by a new front moving in. As I drove, Julia examined a slug and cartridge case with a ten power lens and latex gloves she'd taken from the CSU kit, and Kieffer fingered through the DeStefano-Salvati file on his handheld.

After twenty minutes, Kieff closed up his handheld and put it in his pocket. "Change the address and a couple of names and this could be the Polizzi-Salvati murder file." He shook his head. "I can't believe that hick bastard gave this case the easy close just to keep the local Chamber of Commerce happy. How did he think he could get away with it?"

"Scabby's a South River character," said Julia, putting something back in a box and removing something else. "Poleman figured over in Harris County, with no trial, playing it all down, leaving out the gritty details, he could bury it on the back pages and make it all go away."

"He had to know, sooner or later, it would blow up in his face," I said.

"Only if he could add two and two." She leaned back and rubbed her eyes. "He didn't seem real good at that. By the way, the marks on the shell casings appear identical to those at Booth Street. He's using the same gun."

I glanced back at Julia and shifted my gaze to Kieff. "I like how you both handled yourself back there. The three of us together did a great job processing the contents of that nightmare Poleman calls his evidence room."

"We were brilliant," confirmed Kieffer glancing back at Julia.

"But," said Julia expectantly, eyebrows raised in Kieffer's direction.

"Okay," he said, turning to look back at her. "Make me feel good about this connection you have with Frank Scozarri."

"He's my client. That's the only connection, and if it wasn't for that, I wouldn't even be here."

"So, what exactly have you been hired to do?"

"I explained that." She thought about it for a moment, then nodded to herself. "There's no confidentiality to protect here, guys. As far as Frank Scozarri is concerned, I'm here to keep you guys honest."

"Why wouldn't we be honest?" asked Kieff.

She smiled. "Try looking at it from the don's point of view, boys. Why *would* you be honest? Every level of law enforcement from public school hall monitors to Interpol have been trying to nail the Scozarri family for decades. The don remembers some of the choicer scams that have been pulled in the past to try and take down Vince Polizzi."

Neither Kieff nor I said anything in defense of law enforcement's occasionally half-witted efforts to break the Scozarri family by breaking the law themselves. There had been shenanigans with the IRS, the State Police kidnapping the family attorney at a crucial moment, manufactured evidence that blew up in the D.A.'s face, and the famous illegal listening devices in Vince's bedroom. When the don's boys discovered the bug in his son's bedroom, they set up a tape player next to the bug and delighted in playing audio tapes of the rawest porno they could find around-the-clock for the benefit of their listening audience. After a week of that, they fed the story to someone at the *Herald*. After that one hit the papers, there was a rash of early retirements and unavailable-for-comments.

"In his heart," Julia continued, "Frank Scozarri knows this isn't family business. He's had a little experience in this area."

"Dion Orgoglio," I tossed out.

A beat as she studied me in the rearview mirror. "The don wants his boy's killer caught. He'll do anything to achieve that end. Are we all buddies, now?"

I felt a finger poking my right shoulder, which was still a bit sensitive. It was Kieff. "What?"

"While we're being honest here, homey, do you know why Dock put you and me together?"

"I thought you were the one who pushed Dock into taking me on."

"True. But that didn't mean he had to partner us up."

"Okay. Let me guess. Dock thinks I should be on a leash and you're supposed to hold the other end." I glanced at Kieffer. "Getting too heavy for you?"

"I can hold up my end." He faced me. "Piss you off?"

Two beats. "Yes and no."

"You must be great on a witness stand."

I looked in the rearview, and the PI was looking back. "Yeah, Kieff, it pisses me off that I'm treated like some kind of mental basket case when all I want to do is put all this behind me, put in my eight, and go home alive. No, it doesn't piss me off because it all isn't behind me. I've given the department, and Dock too, some reasons to be concerned. I had a rough patch back there."

"Rough patch," snorted Kieffer. "Your girlfriend dumping you: that's a rough patch. Having hemorrhoids: that's a rough patch. Having to shoot and kill three of Nick Battaglia's goombas, being stabbed and dropping dead, being cut up and sewed back together in the hospital, then being put through the media sausage factory for it: that's not a rough patch, partner. That's sliding down the big razor."

I started giggling, caught a glimpse of Julia looking back, and burst out laughing. Kieffer was looking confused.

"What?"

"That too. What you said about the rough patch."

"Hemorrhoids?"

"The other pain in the ass. While I was in the hospital, my girlfriend *did* dump me."

"Oh, man."

"She put my stuff in the hall and poured Dr Pepper *all* over it."

We all laughed and Kieffer put a hand on my shoulder. "What happened?"

"Oh," I waved a hand in the air and dropped it back on the wheel. "I'm a cop, I'm emotionally unavailable, I watch too much TV, I hated her mother and her friends, I didn't get along with her Rottweiler, and I dropped dead in the hospital. Did I already mention that I'm a cop?"

"You did say her Rottweiler did your car's interior," said Julia.

"As Cherie used to say, 'My doggie has housebreaking issues.' That was her attempt at police humor. The dog ate my seatbelts, too. Cost a hundred and fifty to buy a used set."

"You installed these?"

"Yeah."

"You want to slow down?" urged Kieffer. "This spot here on mine is old blood, isn't it?"

"It was very simple to do and I did a good job. The only problem was getting the rubber cement to hold."

"Thank god for hot-glue guns," said Julia. "Lots of good car deals available these days, Joe."

"In economic chaos," added Kieffer, "there is opportunity."

"I'll think about it."

The reservoir, Looking Glass Lake, was in sight off to the right, snowmobilers out on the ice making tracks in the new snow. Above them were Glenn Heights and the mountains beyond. I could just see the south tip of Breadloaf, the ski trails white and ripe.

"Julia, do you go with us to the Tower or do you want to be dropped off at your place?" Kieffer asked her.

"Drop me off on the way to my place. I want to finish my run and grab a shower. Joe, do you ski?"

"Why?"

Kieffer burst out with a laugh. "You got that look, man," he said.

"What look?"

He nodded toward Breadloaf. "A need for slippery places."

"Yeah. I ski and haven't been out this season at all. Do you two ski?"

"My first pair of shoes were Lange boots," said Julia.

"I took it up a few years ago and all my priorities changed," said Kieffer. Deadpan he held up a power fist. "White is beautiful."

"As soon as we put this killer away, we are all going to go and hurt some of those little flakes."

"Do you have anything else, Joe?" asked Kieffer.

"Anything else?"

"You got the slopes and the job. Do you have anything else?"

I did a quick scan of the car's interior and noted that I had the PI's attention, too. The deep and darks were coming at me again. "Good lord, Batman," I said, "I *am* the only one in this town who didn't minor in psychology."

"I took my degree in it, actually," said the PI.

"Get over here, man, and nudge your toes into my Nikes," said Kieffer. "Dock put me on you because he's worried about you. He's worried about you because Capt. Finn, the police psychiatrist, your father, your ex-squeeze, and even your father's girlfriend are worried about you."

"Gee. You know everything."

"Not everything." Kieff turned and looked into the back of the car at Julia. "Are you worried about him?"

"No."

"There," he said. "I didn't know that."

"But now you do," I answered. "What's it matter what my off duty recreations are?"

"I like you, Joe. I like the way your head works, mostly. I think you're going to be a big part of MCU, and I think we'll do okay together. I think we're going to be terrific friends. But I want to go skiing with you and the PI some weekend instead of getting tooled by some psycho with a submachine gun while I'm wondering if my back is covered when we go through the door. Is that clear enough?"

"Okay, partner," I said at last as I glanced back at Julia. "Both of you. I admit I still have a few corners that need cleaning." I looked at Kieff. "I've had a couple of partners shot up, but all of my old partners are still alive. I may cry on you, bleed on you some, or bend your ear into a pretzel, but when Dodge City comes down, your back is covered."

"Cool."

We rode in silence for an uncomfortable minute then Julia pointed at the car's tape deck. "I haven't seen a car tape player in years. What's on the machine?"

The psych evaluation was over. "One of my pop's tapes. Beethoven's Ninth."

"Not exactly traveling music, is it?"

"Ludwig's okay. I was raised on it. But I'm a blues man, myself: B. B. King, Delbert McClinton, Louis Jordon, Ray Charles—"

"Ray Charles," repeated Kieff.

Kieff held out a hand toward the tape player. "You talk fine names, homey. Where are your tapes?"

"Like I said: They have Dr Pepper *all* over them." He winced in sympathy. "So, I made this tape from Pop's collection so I'd have something to listen to. It's my favorite. Should I put it on?"

Kieffer nodded. "Play that funky music, white boy."

I pushed in the cassette, there was a moment of silence, then the heavy opening crashes of the Ninth dropped on us, imploding eardrums and rattling the windows. *Berliner Philharmoniker, jah?* The soft passages were too difficult to hear over the road noise unless the volume was most of the way up, making the loud passages something out of a Gestapo basement confession session. That's what the hangman used to use to lull me to sleep when I was little. I never could relate to anyone who knew the words to "Rock-a-bye Baby." As I turned to take the Heights Road exit, the three of us were conducting the orchestra of the air.

CHOPPING SQUID

At the Tower in Room four forty-seven, the darkness outside advancing, Kieffer and I registered our trophies with the evidence room clerk, updated Dock, raced through the Baldwin materials with him, then listened as Dock filled us in. Brooks had finished with the only three shooting ranges in the state where authorized owners of fully automatic weapons used to be able to shoot. The weapons were mostly antiques from the World Wars and Korea fired by collectors every so many years just to see if the things still worked. Now outlawed. Not an Uzi on record. Lyon and Washington Counties were no help. After a few housekeeping things, Dock got me by himself in his office, pointed at a chair in front of his desk, and sat down.

"Sit."

I sat.

"So, what do you think of Kieffer?"

"If I don't like him you're not going to take him out and shoot him, are you?"

"Not with his union."

"I think we'll make a great team. I like him a lot. You thinking of splitting us up?" I leaned forward. "Has he said something?"

There were two palms facing me. "You're swinging before the bell, DiMaggio." He lowered his palms to the top of his desk. "He hasn't said anything because I haven't had a chance to talk with him yet. I'm talking with you first."

"Okay," I answered warily.

He studied me for a moment then clasped his hands over his belly. "You're senior to Kieff."

"And?"

"I'm at full strength now, Joe, the full budget is coming up, and there are a few housekeeping chores to do."

"Just so I don't get swept out the door."

"What would you think if I offered you the number two slot in MCU?"

I slumped back in the chair. "I'd think you needed to be put away in a home, that's what I'd think. You would need a whole new rubber gun squad all to yourself. Maybe a rubber howitzer squad."

"Why?"

"For openers, Dock, I still don't have my duty papers clear yet. Betty Grable can pull them at any time. Also, unlike everyone else in the unit, I'm not cross-trained for MCU. In addition, almost the entire department top chain of command would like to see my badge back in Finn's desk permanently, and there's not a blow-dry in the media who isn't after my scalp. My name on the list as deputy field commander is the kind of lightning rod this unit doesn't need. On the other hand, Kieffer has been with you since the beginning, he's been through all of the cross-training, the media loves him as one of their own, he is very sharp, and, more importantly, has paid his dues. He's earned the number two spot."

"If the budget gets approved, Joe, Finn goes back to doing nothing but heading the Detective Bureau. I'll be bumped up to captain."

"I'll still call you Dock."

He scratched his chin and sent his gaze up into the shadows. "The deputy field commander will be a lieutenant."

"Wow. From doghouse to porterhouse on two murders a day."

"You sound like you don't want the promotion."

"Look at what being a lieutenant's done for you."

"I'm not kidding, DiMaggio."

"Lieutenant, huh? Department funerals, staff meetings, and award ceremonies, right? Getting in front of the media and answering all those gotcha questions with the current spin. Thanks all the same."

"You could get a new car."

"There are a lot of really good car deals out there right now. If I wait until the economy is really in the crapper I ought to be able to pick up a stretch Hummer for a song."

"You couldn't afford to fill the tank."

"There's that."

"So, you're not going to jump off a bridge or go eat worms if I make Kieffer official."

"You know I'm afraid of heights. I just want to work the cases, Dock. Honest. That I can handle."

He rubbed his eyes, put his feet up on his desk, and lowered his hand to his lap. "I missed you, Joe."

"I missed you, too, Dock. Do we go pick out curtains now? I prefer earth tones."

He grinned. "What'd you think of Julia?"

"I like her. She's sharp, seems to know who she is, isn't trying to prove anything. You should've seen her with Poleman. She helped Scott do the right thing. The Scozarri connection seems straightforward. The don wants Vince's killer taken down."

"Julia Powers has been cleared all the way to the chief's office for this job," said Dock. "Still, if the media gets onto the Scozarri angle, that's the end of Rico. Got me?"

"Check."

"You like her, though? Her and Kieffer both?"

"Yeah." I thought a second and nodded. "Yeah. I like them both. In fact, we plan to do a little skiing together as soon as we get a chance. The answer to the question you really want to ask is, I'm doing just fine."

There was a sharp rap on the door and Kieffer came in carrying a large manila envelope. "Dock, we got some mail from a friend of ours, if you'll pardon the expression." With the thumb and forefinger of his right hand Kieffer folded over an ear and pushed his nose aside.

"Our thang," said Dock, swinging his feet to the floor. "What is it?"

"Must be important. Dago Frank had *Il Mano Negri* himself deliver it." Kieffer dropped the envelope on Dock's desk. I stood and Kieffer and I crowded around for a look while I pondered Don Scozarri's delivery boy.

Il Mano Negri, aka Hank Sinito, probably the best brain in the local underworld, carried every aspect of the Scozarri family's financial empire, from bets and investments to bribes and payoffs, in his head. He earned his distinguished nickname because of the black leather glove he always wore on his useless right hand. It was said that Nicky Batts's boys once kidnapped Henry Sinito, and held his hand in a vat of molten candy to encourage him to reveal sensitive information regarding the Scozarri family business. He didn't even cry out. If Hank Sinito was delivering the mail, Frank Scozarri considered it important.

The envelope contained several pictures of two men. Head shots, full-length shots, formal, and informal. Full face, profile, coming and going. Bright yellow Post-it notes identified the two men as Paul Casale and Ed Pitone, Vince Polizzi's bodyguards the morning he was murdered. Casale reminded me of comedian Lou Costello. Pitone reminded me of Sean Penn. Another Post-it note indicated that the car they had been using was an '07 silver Chrysler Aspen, along with its tag number registered to Pitone. We picked the best head shots for the all points bulletin.

"Funny," said Kieff. "I never thought of the godfather using Post-it notes." He shook his head. "Can you see Don Francesco pushing his shopping cart through Staples buying office supplies? A new cartridge for his printer, a bottle of gun solvent, a rubber finger? Post-it notes?" He turned toward the door. "It's ruined the whole mob experience for me."

"Kieffer," said Dock.

He turned at the door. "Yes?"

"It's official now. You are number two: Acting lieutenant, MCU Deputy Field Commander."

He frowned and looked at me. "Joe?"

"Hey, man, ever since I was in first grade I've known what the number two stands for." I got up and shook his hand. "You do the paperwork and bear all the responsibilities, I crack the cases and get the girls."

"An offer I can't refuse."

Back at our desks, Kieffer updated the data by syncing the information on his handheld with the computer. There was a handheld waiting for me in before another terminal which was on my new desk. After showing me how to sync the thing, loading it with the current files, Kieffer spent a few minutes showing me how to get around in the MCU applications.

An hour later, I was home sitting in the music room of Pop's house eating a salad preparatory to working on a sausage and peppers pizza that was warming in the oven. There was the Mayor's Day charity something or other on the tube. It was a spine-crushing bore two seconds into the Police Academy chaplain's invocation. I switched to an ancient *Law & Order* rerun for background noise—the frozen-baby evil-landlord episode. While NYPD's two-seven took down the wicked proprietor, I practiced looking up and entering things in the handheld.

It was going to be a different experience having all the case materials with me in my pocket, excepting the physical evidence. The tiny computer could hold an incredible amount of material. In addition to the murder book, a calendar, things-to-do list, calculator, even some games. I got out the pizza, and after playing games on the handheld for about an hour, I ventured into the Baldwin case and began comparing it to the killings on Booth Street.

Fingering through the crime scene photos, a few minor differences: the kitchen table was in the center of the kitchen instead of against the west wall; instead of in a linen closet, Lacy's ears had been found in a cardboard box in the back of a small bedroom upstairs being used for storage. They'd never found Renzo's ears. I suspected they were still in the basement of Lacy Salvati's completely remodeled house, the working girls there still wondering what that strange odor of bacon was every time they turned up the heat. I made my first note on the handheld reminding myself to have the State Crime Lab collect Renzo's ears. Lacy Salvati's video tape and DVD collection put her sister's to shame. Over four hundred movies. Lacy even had a small TV/VCR combo unit in her upstairs bathroom. Brochures showed she was looking into another flat screen HD. That would make one each in bedroom, living room, and kitchen.

Renzo's car, with its consignment of body parts, had been found in the garage in back rather than on the street. Everything else was similar: type of neighborhood, layout, drip trails, blood spatter in the dining room, parts groupings, poses, placements, tab A inserted into slot B. No forced entry and virtually instant demise. The front door had a window. They let the killer in after seeing who he was. An absence of DNA, hair, and latents. Pictures of a beautiful size-ten foot impression with plastic-wrap wrinkles.

Scott Poleman had sent the slugs off to the State Crime Lab to ID the weapon. It turned out to be a 9mm Micro Uzi. A few brown fibers imbedded in the slugs: wool. I moved to the images of the body parts. The five inch long stitch from the tip of Vince Polizzi's sternum to his heart was actually a pretty crappy group for this shooter. The Baldwin four and four were both in groups each one of which could be covered with a coaster. Almost no ride at all. It made me wonder if, as she dropped, Juna Salvati had bumped into our boy while he was perforating Vince. If so, she might have left some of her blood or hair on the shooter. Perhaps something of his on her. Another note.

Near Lacy's door, on the carpeted hall floor, was a neat group of brass casings, each one polished like a little jewel. The brass was strange enough of a clue that it even drew the attention of the Master Sleuth of Baldwin, Scotty Poleman. Several pictures and a note that said, *"Ask about this."* No record of an answer. That oftentimes happens when you're your own consultant.

By the time I went home, "GQ" was what the media was calling the killer: GQ for *Gentleman's Quarterly*. All the vics were either employees or customers of gentlemen's clubs. And quarterly? Well, there had been some quartering done. It was a sick stretch, but the news writers liked it. We did too. We used it.

Other things the same: the victims. Lacy and Juna Salvati were strikingly beautiful women, smoky eyes, billows of rich black hair framing faces filled with delicately sensuous mischief that promised to erupt into copulation frenzy at any moment. And bodies. The publicity shots of Lacy from The Scarlet Letter, and of Juna from The Score, showed forms that must have had those gentleman clubs packed to the air vents. While we were in front of Turner and Hewitt looking through the publicity shots, all of the men in the unit frowned and were teddibly clinical, playing into the feminist fantasy that worthy men only become aroused as a result of true love preceded by a politically correct analysis of a woman's intellectual potential and socio-economic contribution to the global village.

Freed from that chilling influence, I let it fill me: the dream, the lust, the separation of form and substance, the flight into image-driven fantasy. Incredibly beautiful bodies, but the images in my mind kept being drawn back to their faces. The Salvati sisters would sit around the house weekends and school vacations watching TV. If they had the money they went over to Roosevelt Notch to lose themselves in old movies shown on the big screen. Very little dating in school. Both sexually promiscuous afterward.

Marco Salvati would go after his daughters about why they didn't get out, do things, become something. At the beginning, at least, as with all children, they'd try to explain. But no man, especially a father, could look at those beautiful girls and believe that his children had no confidence in themselves, that they believed themselves to be unlovable, the normal world a place in which they didn't belong.

It must have driven the old bricklayer nuts. And what would make such beautiful girls into self-demeaning sofa spuds? A parent? An uncle? Next door neighbor? Teachers or bullies at school? The parish priest? That last was swami's guess. Children don't naturally think of themselves as inadequate, worthless, or evil. That has to be learned. They don't become promiscuous and even exhibitionistic all on their own. Whoever it was who had bent their twigs had unwittingly placed both of those girls in the path of GQ's juggernaut. I made a note to find out who the parish priest was back when Mama Salvati used to bring the girls along to mass.

206

Of course, the killer wasn't interested at all in why those girls were the way they were. He was completely visual himself and running on his own motivations. It was that face that was the key to entering his mind. GQ and I were both drawn to the same face.

There were still those back swing spatters that were made without back swings. The Baldwin photos showed the same band of spatters in the dining room extending from near the center of the ceiling, across it, down the wall, and about two feet back toward the center of the room on the floor. The guy would have to have had a back swing like Tiger Woods to come up with patterns with that degree of arc. It was blood: Juna Salvati's. None of Vince's. Same thing at the Baldwin crime scene. The spatter arc had been composed entirely of Lacy Salvati's blood. That it was a message was clear. The meaning of the message and whom it was for, though, were mysteries.

Noises at the front door ripped me from my thoughts. Pop and Caitlyn were home. I put away the handheld and picked at an uneasy little feeling that was crawling over me. I felt the lump of the little computer in my breast pocket as I realized the big drawback to the handhelds: no way to get away from the job. Not for me, not for anyone involved with me. Bringing the murder book home was like chopping squid for a living and never taking a shower. And Kieffer wanted to know if I had anything besides skiing and the job. Well, there was television. The movies. Joe DiMaggio Torio, Vince Polizzi, Renzo DeStefano, the Salvati sisters, and GQ— We all had the movies.

I thought a moment about trying to date someone. Betty had suggested it: Get out, eat dinner, dance, go to a movie. The PI in the sweats and sneakers was a possibility. She dug the blues, liked Dr Pepper, and she seemed to like me. A peek at the Internet, though, was enough to discourage me. Besides her high-end PI firm, she owned Hood Semiconductor, Riverside Hospital, and about a dozen other health related institutions from rehabs to ambulance services. Estimates of her wealth put her just a little too high to notice someone in my bracket.

Maybe I could try Winnie Hewitt. I remembered her from when we were both in Homicide. She always reminded me of Halle Berry, but with Kathleen Turner's voice. Smart, sharp looking, sexy to those who with a high verbal abuse threshold.

Footsteps. The hangman came into the living room and stood in the music room door. He was solid, dark, his heavy face smiling like a friendly old piece of leather. "You eat yet, Joe? We got Chinese."

"General Tso's chicken?" I inquired.

"Extra hot and spicy."

"You have a sale."

"We got it," called Caitlyn from the hall, "to celebrate your new job. I'll have it ready in a minute." Pop turned back to help her. Pop was hooked. I'd have to see what I could do to move that wedding along.

I was hungry. I leaned forward, grabbed the remote, and as I punched off the TV, something came through the double-paned window between the TV and the piano while a familiar whump sound came from behind me followed by the distant crack of a rifle shot. I stupidly turned and looked. There was a bullet hole in the back of the couch

I looked for Pop and the hangman was back in the doorway, his eyes like hubcaps. "Joe?"

I waved at him. "Turn off the lights, Pop!" Quickly he swiped at the switch plunging the room into relative darkness, the only light coming in from the door to the living room. On his own, Pop shut down the living room lights, as well.

"Nico? Joe?" called Caitlyn.

"We okay," said the hangman quietly. "Shut off the hall light." The room became even darker, a streetlight from the front of the house providing the only illumination.

I picked up the wireless phone from the coffee table and punched in the number for the SRPD dispatcher. After calling in the gunshot, I had the dispatcher switch me over to MCU. Winnie Hewitt was still there and I told her what had happened. I also passed on the possibility that some of GQ's DNA might be on Juna Salvati's body parts. When that was done, I moved over to the window. The slug that had gone through the double panes had left grapefruit-sized holes. I edged around until I could see out at the night.

The first thing I noticed was that three of the streetlights along Sixteenth, the three nearest the house, were out. I looked across Sixteenth at the old Peters place on the corner. The whole house was lit up. Greg and Mandy Machado were having a party. Glancing back at the couch, I eyeballed the line between where the bullet had punctured the leather and the holes through the window panes. That would put the shooter across Pike and above any of the houses that fronted on the south side of the street. The only thing left was the steeple of the South Street Baptist Church, the red warning beacon on it cycling at lazy intervals. I called in the West Beverly Division cops to land on the church.

While I moved out to take a quick peek at the signal beacon, a tiny yellow flash appeared beneath it —I jumped to the left into the TV as a second slug flew through the glass followed by a second crack of a rifle shot.

"He's got a night scope!"

"I got an idea," shouted the hangman angrily. "Keep running around in front of the window. Maybe you run him out of ammo before the cops get to the church!"

"No need for sarcasm, Pop."

"Just stay down, Joe. You okay?"

"Yeah. I'm not sure about the TV, though."

"Oh no, not that," said Caitlyn dryly. She had moved up next to Pop. "Joe, what have you gotten yourself into now?"

"Why do you think it's me?"

"Call me crazy, but you seem to be the one attracting all the lead."

I heard brakes squeaking at the side of the house facing the sniper. I ducked beneath the window and came up on the other side, looking through it without getting in line with the church steeple.

"Is it the police?" asked Caitlyn.

It was a white van with an uplink dish. Unbelievable. How could Channel Seven arrive before the police? Getting out of the van's passenger seat was a redhead now wearing jeans instead of her lime-green skirt. "Well, well. Drusilla Butts, as I live and breathe." It went against the grain, but I called out and warned her to stay behind the van until the police cleared the church.

After Mike Ijumaa and the Crime Scene techs were finished digging slugs out of the couch, making measurements, cleaning up glass, and running off with the remains of the double window pane, there was a pair of detectives from West Beverly Division. After considering what little he had and watching Pop and me board up the window with a piece of old plywood, it was Det. Stanker's opinion that the sniper was a Lee Malvo wannabe after random victims to see how big a splash he could make on the evening news. It was way after four before all our visitors cleared out of the house. While I was on the sidewalk seeing Stanker off, Drusilla Butts came out from behind a tree and wanted to know if I thought the sniper might be a relative of the more than half a dozen persons I had killed in the alleged line-of-duty, and what did I think of that. I asked her if it was true her real name was Drusilla Butts. While she was frantically arguing with her cameraperson about wiping that particular bit of tape, I went back in the house and went to bed, wondering if the slugs out of Pop's couch would match the one that went through Lt. Roemer's head.

THE SPARK

The next morning I got up late, skipped breakfast, and drove up to the Sherman Park substation at Twenty-eighth and Chandler to see a detective there I knew named Rose Pinsky, a good cop who reminded me an awful lot of Betty White. I had worked with her a on a couple of homicides in the area, and for whatever reason she looked kindly upon me. I told her about the Salvati sisters and my suspicions of possible priestly girl diddling at St. Helen's fifteen or so years ago. She promised she would look into it.

By the time I got to MCU it was after nine and things were already in gear. In the bullpen the chairs were filled and Roz Kagen from the Bureau's South River Office was discussing the Bureau's current profile of GQ: white male, black hair, brown eyes, middle thirties to early forties, highly intelligent with probably some college, heterosexual, capable of having a family and holding down a fairly demanding job, probably not a current or former police officer.

Kagen's argument was twofold: First, the amount of forensic information available through TV cop shows and documentaries: "Anyone who watches *CSI*, the cop shows, or *Forensic Files* on Court TV can pick up enough to foil an examination for trace." Second: "The gun in Vince Polizzi's hand. Cop kindergarten: the perp is down, what's the next thing you do before you stop his bleeding, your partner's bleeding, or your own bleeding?"

"Clear the weapon," said everyone in the room, but me. I was wondering, if that was the case, why put the gun in the wrong hand? Vince's shoulder holster was there on the dresser, and it was a rig to hang beneath his right shoulder for a left-handed draw. The gun, however, had been in the right hand. It wasn't the kind of thing a compulsively careful fellow like GQ would overlook. It was a message and the message said, stay out of his way. The only ones being warned, in addition, were cops. GQ was a cop.

I let my gaze wander around the assembly. If you threw out that meaningless "white" word that began Kagen's profile, it fit an awful lot of the men in that room.

Ward Staples, the one who had been taking the pictures of the spectators at the Booth Street crime scene, was bent over his handheld. He was male, black hair, brown eyes, middle thirties to late forties, highly intelligent with some college. So was I, as far as that went. Staples was sitting next to Stan Brooks, and although Stan was the poster child for pork chop control, he fit the rest of it. His long drooping moustache showed that his hair had been black before he began shaving his head bald. Hetero, brown eyes, and some college. Very smart.

Mike Ijumaa was behind them, looking no worse for the hours he'd put in the night before. He was sitting next to Mattie Chala, comparing notes. Mike fit Kagen's profile like a carbon copy. And if you let go of this insistence that GQ was male, Mattie fit, as did Winnie Hewitt sitting across the room from me making notes in her handheld. Clair Turner, too, I thought as Clair chased down some pills with a Canada Dry Ginger Ale.

I turned and looked at Kieffer. Male, black and brown, middle thirties blah, blah, blah. Unless Roz Kagen was willing to climb out on a limb with more specifics, his profile wasn't going to be much use. Of course, Kagen was convinced GQ was not a cop.

"Will you blink?" whispered Kieffer.

"What?"

"Blink. You've been staring at me for the past five minutes without blinking. It's creeping me out, man."

"Don't wet your panty liner. I was thinking about something."

"What'd Ballistics turn up at your father's place?" he asked.

212

"The sniper uses a .30 caliber, full metal jacket round, six with a right twist. In the church steeple there was nothing but an open window."

"What about access?"

"West Beverly Division is working through all the key holders. Dozens of church and self-help groups, and the keys get passed around from hand-to-hand depending on who is handing out the cupcakes any given day. I suggested to IAB that they compare the slug to the one that got Roemer."

Kieff thought on that for a moment then asked, "Joe, what have you been working on recently?"

"Nothing but GQ. Somebody might be trying to collect belated payback for the Rizzos. Snipers aren't a Battaglia family thing, though. They like the up close and personal."

I turned my head and resumed scanning the faces in the room. Faces I didn't know. One was a uniformed lieutenant from Baldwin PD. There were sheriff's deputies from South River, Harris, and Polk counties, as well as a detective and a couple of troopers from the State Police barracks. In addition to the MCU team, there were detectives from West Shore, Exeter, and Magena. Lt. Trask was in back trying not to look a part of things.

Kagen was still working the house. "Out of the ten sets of killings in the report, three couple-killings were certainly done by GQ, three very likely, and the rest not even close." Roz was in front of a corkboard posted with photos above labels describing locations and names. Kagen looked like George Foreman with hair. As far as that goes, he fit the profile, too.

Even from where Kieffer and I stood, I could see that the sets of photos, one through six, almost looked as though they were of the same couple taken by different photographers. There were variations, but I would've been hard pressed to pick out one from another in a lineup.

Kagen smacked his hand in the center of the board. "The National Center for the Analysis of Violent Crime has sent down the VICAP results. It took so little time because the NCAVC cranked out an almost identical report for Magena Homicide last November after the couple-killing there of Paul Roa and Lena Matos." He pointed at a set of photos and continued.

After the Roa-Matos killings, in great secrecy, the Behavioral Sciences gang at Quantico moved in with the Magena PD. All very hush-hush. No media. Magena had a Funtown problem bigger than Baldwin's. No one wants to spend holiday dollars gambling in a place where the big bet was whether or not you were going to see another sunrise. I looked at Dock. The Magena killings didn't appear to surprise him at all.

I worked my way around the backs of the occupied chairs until I could get a closer look at the corkboard. Kagen went through the chronology, and from the six double murders, one set was in South River, one in Baldwin, one in Magena, and much earlier, two in Philadelphia, and one in Boston.

Kagen went to the slide projector, which jammed. While he fought with the demon of the machine, I studied the head shots. Paul Roa from the Magena killings. The data tics below his picture fit within the general set which included Vince Polizzi and Renzo DeStefano: black & brown, medium height just short of six feet, pale olive complexion, and dressed like a *Godfather II* extra. Roa was a well-to-do Mercedes dealer in Magena, but with a reputation for using his fists. Lena Matos was so close in resemblance to the Salvati sisters, I turned away.

Standing just outside Dockery's office door, wearing a dark wide-brimmed hat that kept all but her mouth in shadows, was the PI, Julia Powers. Instead of her sweats, she was wearing dark blue slacks and a tan jacket over a cream-colored blouse. A much improved look over her gray sweats.

"We have three couple-killings in our area," Kagen continued, "The one in Baldwin a year ago, the one in Magena last November and the one in South River two days ago." He reached out and pointed with his finger at two additional couples. "There were two couple-killings that took place in Philadelphia that have some striking similarities to our killings."

I looked at the photos from the Philadelphia pair of couples. The captions read: Leander Johns and Maria Corvo, and a year later, Brad Pastor and Gina Fusco. The female faces were a dead match.

"That blows my anti-Italian theory," Kieff said quietly.

"What are you talking about?"

"The first of the Philadelphia couples. Leander Johns. The man's black."

I turned to the photos and tried to see them the way Kieffer saw them. It wasn't working. "Johns wasn't black, Kieff, except for his hair. Brown eyes, just under six feet in height, pale olive complexion, and look at that suit and tie. Straight out of *Goodfellas.*"

"He's black."

"What makes him black?"

"Don't start with me. Check out the kinky hair, the nose."

"What about the nose?"

'It's a black nose."

"It's Butterfinger tan. It's narrower than either Vince Polizzi's or Renzo DeStefano's, and it's lighter than mine."

I noticed that the room was very quiet, all eyes aimed in my direction. "Sorry."

Kagen turned back to loading the slide projector and Kieff said in a low voice, "It's a *black* nose."

"Is not."

"Is so."

"Is not."

"Is so."

"It's the name, right?" I asked.

"What?"

I nodded toward Kagen's board. "Leander. You figure he's black because he's got a name like Leander Johns. Would you call that a black nose if his name was Carmine Pazula or Vito Guiccione?"

"Why am I getting these intense cravings for linguini," said Roz, "with *clam* sauce!" As a wave of chuckles worked it's way over the room, the FBI profiler glared down at the turntable and said to the universe at large, "Is there anyone who knows the secret to this damned thing?"

Stan Brooks and Winnie Hewitt got up, and as the three of them investigated the mechanical mysteries, I turned to Kieff. "You're right. It's not an anti-Italian thing. But GQ *is* after that." I pointed at the picture of Leander Johns. "He is after men who look like that, who act like that, however they've been labeled, who love women who look and act like that." I pointed at Maria Corvo, then paused, my gaze fixed on her image. "How did the women act, Kieff? The males were tough guys doing wiseguy impressions, but what about the females?"

"Dancers, strippers, call girls. They all pay for the bacon by stirring testosterone."

"Look at that face." I pointed at the shot of Juna Salvati. "What is that face saying to you, Kieff?"

He grinned. "Man, you know what it says."

"Yeah. You have a chance with me, fella," I said, trying to articulate my feelings. "Try for it. Try for it, and if you grab the brass ring, baby, I'll take you to the stars." I shook my head. "But a TV addict. How could she be so strong, so confident of her own sexual power, to have that expression, to get up on that stage at The Score, and dance—"

And then it was as clear as diamonds in gin. She was a TV addict. She spent her growing years, her adult years, in Hollywood fantasies. The expression in that photo. Not the face, but the expression. I'd seen it before on Susan Hayward, Ava Gardner, Hedy Lamarr, Jane Russell, Sharon Stone. "Jessica Rabbit," I said out loud.

"Say what?"

"Jessica Rabbit. Their manner. Like with the male vics acting like they're connected, the female vics all have a manner based on a role. They're playacting, but they're also not playacting. They really are in love leaving no room for anyone else. Their expression, though, is taken from the movies. If this was Japan instead of the US, they'd be peeking demurely over a fan and giggling."

"In love," Kieff repeated. "All fantasy, but in true love. You think that's his mother's attitude projected onto the female vics?"

"Yes, but only when her face is matched up with Al Pacino Bodda Bingo." I pointed at the photos of the male vics.

"Okay, but what face is GQ carrying when he shows at the door carrying his chopper?" asked Kieffer.

"Good question." I tapped my finger on the photos of the female vics one after another. "That face has everything to do with GQ's issues, though." I did the same with the male vics. "That face, too, has everything to do with GQ's issues." I lowered my hand. "The face GQ carries when he comes calling, though, is coldly calculated to do only with the vics' issues." Kieffer stared at me for a moment, then Winnie clapped her hands together.

"Okay," announced Kagen, "The robot rebellion has been put down." A tension-cracking chuckle erupted from the men and women in the chairs as the first of the crime scene shots in the Magena killings went up on the screen: A front door beneath a bright light with an observation window, no signs of forced entry, partly open revealing a near puddle of blood where Lena Matos had been standing when she opened her door. Next to the puddle of clotted blood were the glints of a group of highly polished brass shell casings.

Stan and Winnie headed for their chairs, and I watched as Winnie Hewitt sat down and pulled out her handheld. She was dressed in a trim brownish pant suit thing with a yellow and orange scarf wrapped around her neck, her long reddish brown hair wrapped into a bun.

I nudged Kieff. "What do you think about Winnie?"

"As a suspect?"

"No, idiot. As a date."

Kieffer's eyebrows went up. "I am married and definitely not in the market for any extra-curricular activities."

"Are there a lot of morons in your family, Kieff? It might be a genetic thing. A date *for me*, detective. A date for *me*."

The corners of his mouth went down as his eyebrows went up.

"What's wrong with Winnie?" I asked him. "Are we policied out in MCU?"

"It's not that. Girlfriend has an agenda, Joe, and where political correctness is concerned, you are out there in absolute elsewhere."

I faced the screen and leaned back against the wall as the shot of Lena Matos's kitchen table seemed to fill the room. Whoever was doing crime scene shots up in Magena had a real gift for composition. Ought to apply for a job with Quentin Tarantino or Freddy Kruger. One of the uniformed officers in back grabbed a wastebasket and held it between his knees as the officers sitting on either side of him edged toward the aisles. A few others averted their eyes from the screen. Winnie Hewitt didn't. She was burning up her handheld with notes. Neither was Ward Staples. His gaze was fixed to the screen, eating it up slide-by-slide, and not taking any notes. Clair Turner wasn't looking at all. She was passed out stone cold in her chair, a package of Dramamine clutched in her numb fingers. Julia Powers was gone.

In the two Philadelphia couple-killings a decade earlier, the faces were the same but the carnage considerably less dramatic. The vics had been taken down with a small-bore handgun—a .22 semiautomatic. Two shots each, both in the heart, polished brass left on the floor, but scattered. There had been no dismemberment, but significant mutilation. With tiny cuts GQ had marked out the amputations he would make years later on subsequent victims.

What was probably the first couple-killing of the series had taken place in Boston. Strictly speaking, it wasn't a couple killing. Boston attorney Angelo Petro had not been murdered along with his lover, bar girl Tommy Sue West. He had died five days later. Roz Kagen made a point: It only had to appear as a couple killing to GQ, not to the Bureau statisticians. Perhaps the Petro-West killings marked the point where GQ made the all important connection between that particular woman's face with that particular man's face. Nevertheless, predating the Boston couple, there might be more single killings of women with that face. Kagen was talking about the Bureau attempting to coordinate with police agencies in the tri-county area to identify, locate, and at least warn women and men carrying those faces that they were at risk.

Capt. Foxworthy, who looked like a skinny Al Gore, rose to let us know that the Magena Police were in the process of baiting the killer. They had intended to keep the operation under wraps, but his pride-fueled jaw couldn't resist a wag or three. Two undercover officers, one playing a prostitute, the other her lover, had already set themselves up in a down neighborhood apartment. He waved a couple of photos in the air, and Staples took them, placed them on the viewing deck of his overhead projector, and flicked it on.

The male was Leo Martini, a thirty year old married detective who looked more like Andy Garcia than Andy Garcia did. Playing Martini's lover, though, was Teresa Morales, a stunningly beautiful uniformed officer in her mid twenties. She had been working the street as a no-delivery prostitute and going home with Martini for the past six days and nights. There were a couple of muffled comments in back, Winnie Hewitt's eyes narrowed at the crudity, and I went back to looking at the face of Teresa Morales.

My opinion was the Magena game was over before it ever started. They could dangle that piece of bait until Teresa Morales was a shaking old crone without getting a nibble. She had that dusky gypsy-like attractiveness all of the female vics had, even the same general features, but she didn't have the spark, the same visceral pull the others had.

No promises in Teresa's face. Perhaps it was just the photo. Cop ID, her hair pinned up, a deadpan expression. But it wasn't the photo. It was something about her bearing—her manner—perhaps her view of herself, her place in the universe. She was all job. Her eyes weren't promising anything except to get through the photo shoot as soon as possible. They weren't promising endless nights of ecstasy the way Juna's photo did. It was a police ID photo, and she was a cop, but I knew if Juna Salvati or any of GQ's other female vics put on the same uniform, pinned up her hair the same way, and stepped in front of that same cop photographer, that hot, testosterone-carbonating look would have come through.

Later Kieffer and I talked it over with Chess Pattengill and his boss, Capt. Foxworthy. Chess had noticed Officer Morales's lack of "the look," as well. Foxworthy thought it unimportant. "You amateur profilers really are full of shit. You read a John Douglas book and figure you got a handle on the whole serial-killer thing." Foxworthy zeroed in on me. "You give this guy too much credit, Torio. He's nothing but a pissed-off mama's boy who's letting his Johnson do his thinking for him. Let me tell you guys something." He grinned and raised his eyebrows, "Officer Morales turns *me* on plenty."

"She must be very proud," remarked Kieffer in a flat voice with a deadpan expression, drawing a momentary blank look from Foxworthy.

Later, as all but the MCU staff personnel said their goodbyes and filed out, our people began to record, review, absorb, and process the additional crime scenes. Mike Ijumaa dropped by to let me know that there might have been foreign DNA on Juna Salvati's left arm at one time, but the arm had been thoroughly scrubbed with bleach before being placed on the back porch. "I don't care what the Bureau thinks," said Mike as he walked away. "We're after a cop."

I looked over at Winnie Hewitt and pondered my assignment to join the human race. Well, as my old ski guru, Aunt Cella, loved to point out: no slope ever got less steep through hesitation. I walked over to Winnie's desk, but before I could open my mouth, she looked up, smiled, and said, "After we get off tonight, Joe, you want to go see a movie?"

". . . Yeah. Great. You mean together?"

"Yes. Have you ever seen *The Whales of August?*"

"No." Excellent, I thought. I loved sea stories. The Gregory Peck version of *Moby Dick* had always been one of my favorites. "I never saw it. Dinner first? Fratiano's?"

She smiled and nodded. "Do you have wheels?" she asked.

"Yeah, but the reviews I've been getting lately have been real hounds."

"I have my car, if that's all right. Besides," she said with a smile, "your car is very recognizable and people are shooting at you."

"True. Okay, but I'm not going to have to arm-wrestle you for the check at dinner, am I?"

She studied me for a second, then shook her head. Right then she looked very pretty. "You can pay for the theater tickets, too."

As I settled in next to Kieffer and pulled out my handheld to sync it with all the new information, Kieffer said, "So, you got a date?"

"It appears so, brother. How would you like to make it a foursome? Dinner at Fratiano's, then an action thriller called *The Whales of August.*"

He smiled, nodded, and reached for a telephone. "Let me see what Miriam says and if we can get a babysitter."

"Thanks, partner. I don't know if I'm ready to solo yet."

As I turned to my computer, I caught a glimpse of Julia Powers leaving Dock's office. She nodded at me once, turned, and headed for the stairwell. No elevator for her. She was probably going to jog back to Glenn Heights.

I picked up a phone, got an outside line, and called to make reservations at Fratiano's.

TANGENTS

I checked with West Beverly Detectives, and they had nothing more on last night's shooting. Just for the heck of it, I called up IAB. They had the ballistics results but were not going to release them for the nonce. I left a note for Dock concerning the necessity for MCU to get those ballistics results.

There was a call for Kieffer while he was down in CSU collecting reports on the Booth Street analysis. I took the call, and it was Miriam Kieffer. She had gotten her husband's message on her voicemail. A babysitter was no problem. In fact, she already had one. The double date was off, though. With restrained heat, she said something about a prior commitment of her husband's involving dinner, a card, some candles, and since he had forgotten their seventh anniversary, it would probably involve a rather expensive piece of jewelry if not a new car. I took a note. As Kieffer arrived and put the forms down on his desk, I grinned, handed him the slip and beat it the hell out of there.

At Fratiano's on 24th, Winnie and I had *pasta alla norma,* a dish my father insisted the chef there learn how to prepare. Candle light cast a warm glow and dinner was delicious. Papa Orsino, who had been warped as a child by a viewing of *Lady and the Tramp,* performed for us complete with apron and black handlebar moustache as he massaged his squeeze box and sang. He was actually pretty good. I relaxed and Winnie Hewitt and I talked murder.

Winnie had noted the difference between the female vics and Officer Morales, as well. "GQ knows his victims," she said. "Even if he never met them. The

222

Magena thing is going nowhere. If even we can see Morales is not one of his targets, you can be certain GQ does."

After dinner, Winnie had white wine and I had another Dr Pepper. She studied me for a moment, made some sort of internal decision, then pulled a photo out of her purse. She handed it to me. "Look at this."

I took the photo, looked at it, and damned near threw a shoe. It was a very well done almost nude portrait of Gina Fusco, the Philadelphia stripper slain by GQ. Her back was toward the camera, and she was looking back over her right shoulder, those smoky eyes promising universes Gina could no longer deliver. In the shot, all she wore were white high-heels and matching panties—those old-fashioned down-off-the hip bikinis that faded out when the crotch-floss high-cut things came in. She had her right thumb hooked in the elastic and had the panties on that side pulled down almost to her knee.

"Okay," I managed to wheeze as I looked up at Winnie.

"I was going to ask you if that turned you on, but judging from the projectile drooling, I surmise it did."

"Hey, sister, you're the one who brought the dirty pictures." I handed it back to her.

She took the photo and studied the image. "I'm trying to understand something about men, Joe—particularly about men like GQ—but men in general." She nodded toward the photo. "What is the turn on?"

"In ten words or less?"

Holding the photo out, she fixed me with an all-business stare. "This is some wood fiber, some photo-sensitive chemicals—hell, it's not even in color. This is nothing but feathers. You never met this woman and hardly know anything about her. Did she get good grades in school, have an athletic career, know another language, was she married, did she have children? Maybe she was an idiot, a bigot, or a secret man-hater. What's her favorite color? Did she ever vote? Which way? There is so much more about her you don't know, yet you're turned on by the feathers."

"Um, yes indeedy. What's even more curious than the things you mentioned, I even know she's dead."

"Well, is it something about the shape, the pose, the expression?"

I leaned back, took a swallow of soda, and put down the glass. She was asking a serious question. It deserved a considered response. "Okay. Yes. All of the above. And more. On some level, I think primitive instinct has something to do with it. You remember in the movie *Quest For Fire,* the scene where the women are bending over the stream and Og, or whatever his name is, sees their bare butts, goes into rutting frenzy, and pokes one of them?"

"Look, Ally Oop, we're a long way from Neanderthal Man."

"Most of us, maybe. In most parts, maybe. The rest, I'm not so sure. It's very confusing being a man nowadays, Winnie. Women don't shave their legs or armpits anymore, but Arnold Schwarzenegger does." She laughed and I leaned across the table, pointed at the photo and traced the lines of Gina Fusco's buttocks with my fingertip. "Way before Euclid they knew that tangent curves were a male turn-on: buttocks, breasts, groin, the back of a knee, the crook of an elbow, beneath the chin, back of a bare neck." I sat back, frowning. I was getting myself not just a little cranked. "I don't know how all men look at it."

"How do you look at it, Joe?"

"Oh, hell, Winnie, when I was a teenager, a couple of loaves of bread cooling together on a rack was enough to crank me up. I still have a thing for cracked wheat."

She laughed and shook her head. "What about the rest of her, Joe? She was more than just a collection of surfaces and curves."

"The feathers are what you see first, Winnie. You don't get to see the rest unless the person chooses to reveal it to you."

"But you react to the feathers."

"So do turkeys. What about you? When the hunks are up on the silver screen or out on the beach, Winnie, doesn't your imagination ever grab a little involuntary playtime for you?"

"Not like men seem to do. We're investigating a number of quite grisly murders. Yet you guys at that briefing reminded me of a bunch of horny little puppies grabbing onto and trying to mount anything and everything warm and vertical."

I laughed out loud. "Yeah. That's more true than is comfortable to admit. As with puppies, though, I think it might be instinctual. And like every instinct, it can be damaged, twisted, misdirected, diminished, intensified." I looked at the picture, upside down from my point-of-view, letting my gaze wander among the curves and tucks, remembering that oil pastel I had drawn for Betty Grable back in therapy. It had been a rear view of a female torso with the lines repeated to the right again and again, each set of lines more distant than the previous set, making an endless field of feminine curves. Betty had asked me what I wanted to do with all those acres of curves. I had stared at the drawing, trying to name my feelings, at last telling her that all I wanted to do was dive right into the middle of them—Dive in and lose myself forever. I noticed Winnie's breasts straining against the orange satin blouse she wore, the way her long neck—

"Joe?"

I looked up at Winnie's face. "Huh?"

"What were you thinking about?"

My face reddened. "Aside from fantasies of the two of us writhing in unbridled passion?"

"Yes," she said with a smile and a momentary blush of her own. "Aside from that."

I shrugged. "Betty Grable once told me in therapy that as a child I hadn't been cuddled enough. It results in an above-average craving for all of those bumps and curves—all of that touch and caress sensation. Maybe that's the root you're looking for."

"What do you think is driving GQ? Lack of sex?"

"No. Too much sex; the wrong kind and with the wrong person."

"Incest?"

"That, physical abuse, and probably more. Despite the groupings and poses, though, the murders aren't sexual, at least not for GQ. For him the feathers—male and female—are prerequisites, like labels on cans of peas. My guess is that it's love and guilt driving our boy. Mother love and mother guilt."

I shifted my attention to Winnie's face, warm and soft in the light from the candle. "Right now, Winnie, I would bet you my piece of blue bottle glass, my new Duncan yo-yo string, and my dried-up piece of John Wilkes Booth's finger that either GQ's mother committed suicide or he killed her. Either way, he blames himself for her death. I think he was kicked out of his mother's bed, did something to get rid of his rival—perhaps more than once—and it eventually led to his mother's death."

"So, what is he doing by posing these body parts to mimic different sexual positions?"

I leaned my elbows on the edge of the table. "Every spot where he's paired up body parts is a place where he saw them making love and damned them for it—hated them for it. What I think he's doing with these murders, in his own mind, is making amends: getting Mom as much of the loving she sought as he possibly can; making up for the loving he cost her."

"He's getting his mom laid six times per murdered couple?"

"Well said."

She stared at me for a full ten seconds, took the photo from the table, and returned it to her purse. Just when I was thinking she was out of there, she looked back at me, her lips parted in a warm smile. "Thank you, Joe, for being honest with me." She nodded her head toward her wristwatch. "We have just about enough time to get over to Roosevelt Notch if we want to catch *The Whales of August.*"

Roosevelt Notch was a triangular section of southeast Vadalia formed by Baines Boulevard on the east, Canal on the south, and Roosevelt Avenue on the west. Back in the early 'Seventies, when everybody's hearts were in the right place but their brains were out to lunch, the Notch was South River's Haight-Ashbury district: head shops, drug drops, dim little bookstores operated by the morally and hygienically challenged, and a theater—The Flik—that wouldn't allow a film in

226

through the doors unless it had subtitles. Back then half the acid heads in town were hallucinating in Swedish. All that was left of the subculture now were the few surviving burn-outs begging from the shadows, and the theater, rehabilitated by a community arts drive from its decade as a porno house. Now, fully restored, it showed films the community arts people wanted to see. It had played *Casablanca* so many times, whole generations referred to the theater as "The Rick." As Winnie and I sat down on the comfortable new seats and shared a bucket of popcorn, our fingers actually touched. The lights dimmed, and I smiled and settled in. The Torio ducks were lining up again.

The Whales of August. I first realized I had a problem with the 1987 production when I found myself fascinated with wiggling my right kneecap back and forth. After fifteen minutes engrossed in dedicated tugging on a rogue ear hair, I explored with my tongue something caught between two upper teeth, dozed twice, and when I couldn't sleep anymore, I began silently urging Lillian Gish to roll Bette Davis off the damned cliff, then switched sides and begged Bette to pull a filleting knife and disembowel Lillian in mid sentence. Anything to get the damned story moving. For the last three or four hours of the performance the only thing that kept me going was guilt about abandoning Winnie at the theater and wanting to hang in there to see the aforementioned whales. As the credits rolled, drawing a smattering of applause from the audience, I muttered, "No whales."

"What?" she asked.

"The Whales of August, and no whales. Not even a stinking minke." I faced Winnie. "Have you ever before prayed so hard to have a revenge-crazed killer grab an AK-47, bus in, and hose down a couple of boring old bags?"

The return look I received cracked the fillings in my teeth, made me instantly impotent, and put off the threat of global warming for the next fifteen years. When she dropped me off at the Tower, she didn't even walk me to the door. It turned out the movie was Winnie's favorite.

She'd seen it eleven times, and taking me to see it had been something of a test. Some brought them home to meet mother. Winnie Hewitt brought them to see *The Whales of August*.

Perhaps she wasn't the one.

At home in the music room, the blinds pulled over the still boarded up window, I was standing next to the wall-mounted rack that held Pop's autographed baseball bat. I was looking up *The Whales of August* in *Leonard Maltin's Movie and Video Guide*. Leonard gave the film three and a half out of four stars. "An exquisitely delicate film," wrote Leonard. I was busy ripping up Leonard and tossing him into the trash can when Pop came in from his den.

"How'd your date go, Joe?"

"Any openings left on death row, Pop?"

He laughed and I walked to the coffee table, grabbed the TV remote, and punched on the set. "Joe," he began, "they got anything on the shooter from last night?"

"Nothing they're willing to share. When's the window getting fixed?"

"Caitlyn was here when the glass man showed up. He had the replacement with him, but he wanted to wait to put it in until you catch the sniper."

"Combat pay for glaziers," I muttered.

"Is he from an old case, Joe?"

"Who? The sniper?"

"Yes. Maybe that Guardian fellow?"

"I don't know. Seems odd that Lt. Roemer got it that way and then a sniper threw a couple of rounds at me."

"You need something to eat?"

I flopped down on the couch. "No, thanks, Pop. I'm up to here in pasta, popcorn, and phantom whale blubber."

The hangman sat down next to me on the couch, picked the *TV Guide* off the coffee table, and pointed where he had marked a movie. It was *All Quiet on the Western Front*. "See, it's the Lew Ayres version."

"It'll be the remake with John Boy, Pop. Ever since I can remember, the *TV Guide* lists the Lew Ayres version but they always play the Richard Thomas remake. Someone ought to write a letter."

Pop began leafing through the magazine to see if there was something else to watch, when I remembered Juna Salvati's tape collection, with the original version of *All Quiet on the Western Front*. I remembered her father, Marco, crying bitterly about children who had been given the keys to the universe but, to his mind, chose to throw their lives away on television, dirty dancing, and unworthy men.

The hangman picked up the remote and changed the channel. "What'd you find?" I asked.

"El Cid."

"You're kidding."

"You wait a couple minutes and see. I get some Dr Pepper."

"And popcorn."

As Pop left to get the refreshments, I settled in once again to watch the great epic starring Charlton Heston and Sophia Loren. I'd owned a pro copy of the tape ever since I was sixteen, but hardly ever watched it, the most recent time with Jane Draper. Every time it was being shown, though, commercials and all, I would watch. There was something about it coming up on TV that seemed to make watching the movie something "we" were doing: the broadcaster and me. At least a kind of human interaction. Watching it on tape seemed like doing it by myself. Visual masturbation. I called Jane to let her know it was on again. She went right to it.

As the uplifting Miklos Rozsa score started, the two-color line drawings came up and the credits began. Pop came in with the drinks. "Popcorn working."

"Thanks."

He stood watching as the smell of the popcorn popping filled the house. Before he returned to the kitchen, I was already lost in this tale of deep passions, great goals, honor, love, and treachery so immense that monuments could be constructed from the dust. Kings, knights, sweeping religious wars, trial by combat, and Sophia Loren.

It was after two, with Pop tucked into the corner of the big leather couch, sleeping quietly, the Cid on his death bed, Sophia's tears falling on his wounded chest, when I remembered a question Betty Grable asked me that one day in therapy. Why does Joe Torio do what he does? As I watched *El Cid*, I realized why I'd always wanted to be a cop. I knew why I wanted to be in MCU and to be after GQ. It was much more than pitting myself against the monster or protecting the citizenry like the knight Jane Draper imagined.

Instead of paint and brushes, murder addicts paint with blood, death, and lightning bolts. That's how they see the universe: Towering crimes and passions, bottomless, endless, pitiless torments—their own and to be inflicted upon others. But more than that, since they are such experts at it and hate it so, they are untiring enemies of sham. That's the killer's thrill in showing up the crime fighters, popping the bubbles of self-righteous do-gooders, and bearding pompous politicians.

Betty was right about one thing, though: the job frightened me. But it was like skiing a heart-stopping double black diamond, even if it pounds the hell out of you. You might enjoy cruising a few blue trails afterward, but there's this little dissatisfaction that never leaves; that knows you are dogging it, letting your fear steer your boots. You want, you need, to get back on the steeps. And you go because if you don't, you aren't reaching for your limit, and reaching for it is the only way to find out where it is.

And there was also the big joke some comedian chiseled above the entrance to the Supreme Court building: Equal justice under the law. That bone was in my body. Every now and then I got to see it happen. Fear and justice: my motto. I looked at Pop as he slept, remembering what he said once when we were watching something on Court TV. A commentator said something about "Justice is blind." Pop shook his head and said, "No. The law is blind. Justice has to peek."

By the time I put Pop to bed, another movie was on. *Manhunter*, the original motion picture adaptation of Thomas Harris's *The Red Dragon,* rather than the sucky remake with Edward Norton. *Manhunter* trapped me as it always did. The music, the images, the killer's vulnerability, the manhunter's terrible mental scars. I was in there somewhere and somewhere in there I fell asleep.

A WORM OF OUR OWN

The next morning it was still dark, the temperature hovering at zero, and my Mazda was doing a great impression of a tectonic plate without all the motion. It groaned twice, ground to a stop, and died. The hangman and his jumper cables were off on a consult so I called Kieffer for a ride. He showed at the door replete with yawns and baggy eyes and drove us to Benny's Waffle Palace on St. George Street near City Hall for breakfast. The TV in the waffle house crackled with the story of GQ, the other patrons silently listening as the blow-dries dragged out the Salvati girls' promotion photos, their parents, the Matos girl's brother, and one young fool from Channel Nine actually managed to shove a mike into Don Francesco Scozarri's face as he was coming out of late night mass. The Don peered at the reporter as though being approached by an alien life form. Tommy Zerilli and another hairy fellow led the reporter away, a suggestion or two about rearranged knee joints should the annoyance persist most likely whispered into the reporter's shell-like. The shooting at Pop's house hardly rated ten seconds and Drusilla Butts got no air time at all.

"You look like hell, Joe," said Kieff. "Up all night? Wink, wink."

"You look all winked up yourself." I laughed and with my fork chased a piece of bacon through the maple syrup on my plate. "Not much sleep."

"Well, well. Kiss and tell," Kieffer demanded as he speared another mouthful of pancake with a bit of sausage.

"Actually, partner, I'm thinking of joining the Papal police force. The Swiss Guard? Don't they have to be celibate anyway?"

"I think you have to be Swiss and unmarried. Being Catholic might help, too."

"I can fake Swiss. I already own the knife."

"You'd look good in striped bloomers, Joe." He swallowed and motioned toward me with his fork. "So, what was it with you and Winnie? Religious differences? Politics? Ethnic incompatibility?"

"Artistic differences. Things all patched up on the anniversary front, you and Miriam?"

He grinned widely. "Very well. We had a nice little party and, well, it was very nice."

"Partial to diamonds, is she?"

He laughed and nodded. "Told you about that, did she?"

"If you want to see a good movie with Miriam sometime, partner, catch *The Whales of August* at The Flik. It'll be there for another week."

"Really good?"

"I couldn't stop talking about it."

"Anything more about your sniper?"

I shook my head. "Mike's trying to get the slug from the Roemer killing for comparison, but IAB won't release it. Dock is twisting arms. You hear anything from Homicide on the Guardian?"

"The word is that they're looking at it as a bunch of cold cases that belong on Cab Nelson's desk, not theirs."

"Just a bunch of coincidences."

"That's the word," Kieff confirmed.

On Channel Four they were running a clip with Gil Franklin interviewing the mother of Renzo DeStefano. She had obviously purchased a new dress and had gotten her hair done for the interview. Made me sad for some reason. Kieffer pushed his half-eaten stack of pancakes away, took a sip of his coffee, sat back, and said, "I sure hope this guy is at the end of his fifteen minutes."

"That's TV journalism for you," I said.

"Don't kid yourself, Joe. Every time there's a gang bang, a disaster or crime scene, you can bet the print reporters are in there working the victims, relatives, and spectators as hard as anyone for wows, icks, and oh-nos. Blood keeps up circulation: Our credo. You ever run into that little maggot from the *Herald*? His name's Cox?"

"No. Don't recall him."

"Short, bug-eyed. He looks like Spike Lee after a reverse enema. One reason I quit was because I was becoming too much like him."

I shook my head and talked around my bacon. "No bells."

"You sure? He was the one, Joe, who got all those angry citizens together—the ones who staged the demonstration after that bum went after you with the Beretta and had all those pictures taken."

"Oh. *That* Harry Cox." I laughed. "Speaking of skiing, what'd you think of the PI?"

"Skiing?"

"I'm cleverly changing the subject."

"Almost missed that turn, partner. What do I think of Powers, you want to know."

"Julia," I said.

He had a slightly troubled look on his face. "I like her, but there're a lot of rumors rumbling around the Tower from back when she did Vice."

"Think we should pay any attention to rumors about her?"

"The thesis of those rumors is that she is a psycho killer herself."

"How would that interfere with her skiing?"

Kieff sipped at his coffee and nodded at me. "Point taken. New subject: Martini and Morales."

"The Magena PD bait is no good," I said. "They're going to blow it."

"Think we could do a better job, homey?"

"What? We put our own worm on the hook?"

"I suggested running out our own bait to Dock a couple of days ago."

"Who?"

"You, for one."

I pointed my fork at him. "What about you?"

"I'm black."

"Partner, you got to get this nonsense out of your head. You're no more black than Tom Hanks or Leander

234

Johns. You already have the brown eyes, the height, you're what, one ninety—"

"One eighty-two, and that is after more celery than I want to think about."

"We can put a Pacino nest on your head, touch up the skin a bit, some cool threads, a little bodda bing—"

"Waitress!" Kieffer called out, turning away. "Check please, and a large Valium for my friend."

When we rolled into the underground parking lot and took the elevator to the fourth floor, Dock was in the bullpen waiting for us. His suit looked like he'd used it for a pillow. His face looked like it hadn't seen a pillow in weeks.

"I guess none of us got any sleep last night," he said looking between Kieff and me. He cocked his head toward his office and we followed him into the glass-walled enclosure, the TV on in the corner tuned to a news program with the sound low. Dockery eased into his chair like his butt was made of glass. His wastebasket runneth over with Duncan Donut cups and boxes. Kieffer and I sat in the two chairs facing his desk.

"Something wrong with your back?" asked Kieff.

"Just about the time you've lived long enough to have something worthwhile to contribute, the body can't lift it and the brain can't remember what it was."

"Been out doing the clubs, Dock?" I inquired.

He suddenly grinned very widely. "As a matter of fact, Slugger, I have. Very educational."

"Did you bring Ellie?"

The grin became wider. "Official police business." He looked from me to Kieffer, and from Kieffer back to me. "Okay," he began, "we are agreed that Officer Morales couldn't draw flies holding a hat full of cow shit on a hot summer day. I want to run real bait down here in South River. Julia Powers is an undercover expert, among other things. I've been talking to her about Kieffer's suggestion—"

I looked at my partner.

"That's Lt. Kieffer, to you, squid."

"Oh, *now* we start pulling rank—"

"You two want to quit clowning around," said Dock. "I'm on empty right now, yet still in a moderately good mood. You'll want to conserve as much of that as possible in the coming hours."

Kieff and I exchanged looks and faced Dock.

"Okay," he continued, "we need to keep this business with Powers deep and dark, understand? Not a word to anyone, not even the rest of the MCU team. Got that?"

"So, you're sure it's a cop?" I said.

"No, I'm not. But I can't afford to take any chances, especially not with this pipeline to the media we appear to have."

"The leak isn't anyone in MCU," said Kieffer.

Dock looked at me. "What do you think, Joe? Are we after a cop?"

"Yes. He's too good to be a cop wannabe."

"What about a crime scene tech?"

I slowly shook my head. "No. I thought about that, but the warnings seemed aimed at the cops." I shrugged and smiled. "He likes us."

Dock frowned for a moment then nodded. "All the stuff from the Boston and Philly PDs is in the house, and we need to boil it down. The Philly investigations came up with a couple of names that are interesting. Work them. From the timing on the killings we are aware of, you might think it looks like we have months to play with, but that's only the killings we know about. There's an expert opinion in the Philly file that says GQ might not be limited to couple killings, using a gun, or on any kind of time schedule." He looked at me. "Joe, in Boston and Philly both they had ice pick head stabbings just like your Guardian's. No connection to you that we can see. All of them were sex offenders, pedophiles. We've also managed to get IAB and Homicide to release the Guardian investigation and the sniper shootings to MCU."

"Great. So, any news on the slugs?" I asked.

"The ones thrown at you match the one that killed Roemer. What do you make of that?"

I let out a breath. "I'm beginning to see Lydia Jenks's side of it."

"Who? The author?"

236

"Yeah. She said you can't sell a mystery if it has too many murders. Too many factors. Too complicated."

Dock leaned back in his chair. "We don't have to worry about selling this mess of murders; we already bought it."

"Are we running GQ, Sniper, and Guardian as separate cases?" I asked.

"We continue as is on GQ. I'm putting a research team together under Clair Turner to sift the Guardian and Sniper information to see if they are related." He looked at Kieff. "I want to recommend her for detective sergeant. Okay with you?"

"About time," Kieff agreed.

Dock gingerly leaned forward in his chair. "Okay, back on GQ. We know the killer is locked into that combination of faces, whether it pops up once or a dozen times a year."

"We can sift current homicides in surrounding jurisdictions," said Kieff, "and see if familiar faces are among the deceased."

"Good," said Dock.

"Do you want me on that, too?" I asked, getting to my feet.

"No, Slugger. I want you to go out to Sixteen Stanton Circle and get yourself fitted out to become the male half of the bait team. Your appointment is at nine. Maybe that'll get you out of the Sniper's line of fire for awhile."

I scratched the back of my head as I thought of something. "Maybe you ought to get a tap on my land line at home, Dock. I got a guy who calls me almost every morning with death threats. He might be all growl and no bite—that's what he sounds like—but I'm not sure."

Dock made a note. When he was finished, he stared at his notepad. He stared at the pad and tapped it with his pencil. "Is it possible that all these killings are connected somehow? GQ, the Sniper, and the Guardian. Throw in what happened at the Rizzo brother's garage, too. We still don't know who called in that tip, or shot Carlo, or put that tourniquet on your shoulder, Joe."

"Or who killed Nicky Batts while I was being grilled by a shooting board."

"Shades," muttered Dock as though issuing a curse.

"They had a corrections officer probie at Books who'd been there less than a week who never showed after the Battaglia murder," said Kieffer. "Their investigation showed he simply moved out of his apartment and vanished. His prints don't match anything anywhere and his ID photo could be almost anybody with some good makeup."

"Our boy is good with makeup," I said, shaking my head. "I can't believe this tar baby of an investigation. Every time we poke at it the body count goes up and the answers more elusive. We still have no idea what the extent of the killing is."

Kieffer said, "There's more than one killer. Perhaps as many as three; perhaps working in concert."

I nodded. "At least two," I said. After another peek at Kieffer, I faced Dock, "Do you know who Powers picked for the female half of the bait team?"

Big grin from our commander. "As a matter of fact, I do."

Since Dock didn't expand on that, it appeared we were done. As we left, I turned and looked at Dockery, stretched out, his arms behind his head, his eyes closed. "So, did the audition for the female part go well?" asked Kieffer.

A big smile spread over Dock's face. "Gold star. Close the door on your way out, fellas. Let me know when the fresh donuts show up."

HAVEN'T FORGOTTEN YOU

I picked up a Dr Pepper from the machine in the coffee room on the way back to our desks in the MCU bullpen. After draining half the can, I looked at Kieffer, already wading through the Philly PD materials. "Kieff, how long ago did you and Dock decide on doing bait?"

He raised an eyebrow at me. "About ten minutes before you got the call to show at Booth Street. We already had a hint about the killings in Magena. After he got a load of what we had at Juna Salvati's house, Dock called Chess Pattengill off the books. Chess confirmed what we had suspected and bait was the obvious next step. You were the obvious pick for the male half."

"Got any more secrets?"

"Crates and crates." He smiled and turned back to the files.

I leaned against the edge of my desk. "You were on the Gray-eye Killer story for the *Herald*, weren't you?"

"I was."

"Did Powers's name come up at all?"

"No. We never had enough corroboration to print anything concerning her. All we knew for certain was that Gerald Soams was dead, he was the Gray-eye Killer, and that he had bled to death as the result of a wound received in the course of an undercover take down in the old governor's mansion out in Fishkill." He turned to his computer terminal and began punching the keyboard. "You better get to that appointment."

"Okay. While you're at it, though, generalissimo, see what you can squeeze out of that machine on Julia Powers."

"Consider it done."

As I headed for the elevator, Kieffer was tapping away. He whistled in astonishment just as the doors were closing. I scrambled to get the doors open again, and as I did so Kieffer rocked back in his chair and laughed.

And they say Vaudeville is dead.

Down in the garage I drew a pool car: yet another unmarked blue-gray Taurus four-door in an endless succession of unmarked blue-gray Taurus four-doors. I pulled out of the garage on the park side and paused at the stop sign before entering the traffic on Pine Street. Seeing a clear stretch in the light traffic, I took my foot off the brake and hit the gas. Just then something went through the windshield and plowed into the back of the bench seat next to my recently-healed shoulder. I actually sat there for a second worrying about being responsible for the damage to the vehicle I'd signed out when the second round came through the driver's side and whizzed by my neck.

I didn't look to see where the shooter was. Instead I made every effort I could to climb beneath the dash, pushing on the gas pedal with my right foot. I could hear a slug hit the engine block and another went through the windshield as the car blindly lurched across Pine Street, jumped the curb, and rammed into a snow bank backed up by a two hundred year old frozen maple with all of the flexibility of Gibraltar.

As the stars subsided, I pushed myself up into a sitting position, noting that snow now completely covered the windshield which now had three bullet holes in it. I also noted that the airbags hadn't deployed, making me wonder what it would take. I heard something to my left and dizzily wobbled my gaze in that direction. There was the shaking open end of a 9mm barrel aimed at my face. A young officer in a blue parka was screaming unintelligibly at me. The electric windows still worked and I pushed the button for the driver's window and said, "What?"

He screamed again. Young Kojak, a uniformed patrol officer out of Central Division, was giving me his very best police presence demeanor which to me resembled a psychotic breakdown in a hissy-fit ward. I could've sworn he was bellowing in a foreign language. At last, he lowered the weapon a bit, and enunciated more clearly, "Put your hands where I can see them!"

I looked and my hands were both gripping the top of the steering wheel. I faced him to say something constructively rude when the airbags blew, smacking my arms aside and giving me a rather substantial punch in the side of my head.

Lots of pretty lights and tinkle sounds, but I felt an overwhelming need to get the hell out of that car. I fumbled for the seatbelt, the door handle, and opened both. Young Blue was breaking down again, his Glock quivering in my face, ordering me back into the car. I pulled my ID and flashed my badge at him. "Det. Sgt. Torio, MCU, you moron. Put your piece away before you hurt someone." As he did, I said, "Give me your squawk." He handed me his radio.

I called it in, since Officer Pelletier seemed unable to figure out how to work his radio without letting go of his weapon. I gathered I had excited him somewhat when the Taurus grazed his butt and bounced him into the street as I raced for the relative protection of the big trees lining the park. I also called it in to MCU and filled Kieffer in on what had happened. After looking at my own shaking hands, I also explained I wouldn't be there when anybody eventually responded. In addition, I was going to miss my appointment with Julia Powers. I needed to get my head screwed on straight.

I handed the squawk back to Officer Pelletier, pulled my cell phone, and told Betty Grable's receptionist, Roscoe, that ready or not, Torio was coming in. Officer Pelletier made noises like I needed to stay, but after awhile it was obvious even to him that I wasn't even able to listen.

Delighted to find I was still able, I walked west on Pine, beneath the maples, trying to see where the shooter had been as I moved quickly from tree-to-tree. The sniper had to have been on the roof of City Hall on the opposite side of the park, easily five football fields away. Something preyed on my mind: Between Central Division and all of the other units and support services located in the Tower, there had to be a hundred or more plain blue-gray Taurus four doors or other nondescripts that exited the garage that morning. Why had the slugs come through the windshield of the crapheap I happened to be driving? I couldn't help but believe that it reflected rather badly upon Det. Stanker's random sniper theory.

At the corner of Fifteenth and Pine, as the light changed, I ran across the street toward the entrance to the Smith Building, my back muscles cringing.

In Betty's waiting room, her receptionist, Roscoe, told me I'd have to wait a few minutes. "Here you go, sergeant," he said as he handed me a bottle of Dr Pepper. Just then Betty's door opened.

"Joe? What's the emergency?"

I looked up at her. She peered back at me through concerned brown eyes. A billowy black, green, and yellow scarf accented her dark green suit. A conservative Tina Turner. "Joe," she said, "you look like somebody spent the night sucking your blood."

"It's this new aftershave I've been injecting." I felt a migraine coming on. I held a hand to my head and ground the heel of my hand into my left eye. "Someone took another shot at me a few minutes ago. Several shots, actually. I think I'm upset."

The cop in her instinctively checked the windows and doors. She nodded at Roscoe and he nodded back and began closing blinds. Betty pointed at her open office door and I went in.

Leaning back in her couch, rested my head against the soft leather. "Betty, I have my very own sniper stalking me. He shot up my father's house night before last. Right outside the Tower next door, he tried again."

"This morning? Right before you came in?"

"Yes."

"So, that's what that was. Like five or six pops—a cracking sound." Her eyebrows went up. "Are you all right? Did you get hit?"

"An airbag punched me, a police officer almost shot me, and I have a couple of glass splinters in my ass.

242

Other than that I'm—well, I'm not okay. I'm rattled to hell."

"Do you think it's an old case?"

I allowed myself a moment to think on that. "I don't know." I thought a bit more. "The Sniper was the same one who iced Lt. Roemer. The slug matches the ones dug out of Pop's couch. I bet the one's in that car's seat matches the others."

"What are you working on right now, Joe?"

"Major Crimes. The GQ killings. Thanks for signing those conditional papers, by the way."

"They are *very* limited, DiMaggio. Don't miss any appointments."

"I won't." I frowned as I thought on it. "The Sniper: You think someone wants me off the team?"

"It worked once before, as I recall." Her eyebrows went up. "The bum with the Beretta?"

A rational thought nudged my panic aside. "You just might be right. Maybe I'm alive not because my sniper isn't that good, but because he *is* that good."

"Trying to scare you off your current investigation?"

"Yeah. You know, Betty, it's funny because the investigation I'm on right now is bogged down worse than the economic stimulus program. Instead of scaring me off, he's providing me with more information. Yeah." I placed my hands on my knees and stood. "Yeah. More information. Thanks, Betty. That just might keep me pasted together for the rest of the day."

"As long as you're here, DiMaggio. Did you make any progress with that other matter I suggested you work on? Remember our last session?"

"Progress— Oh. Something besides the job. Make a friend."

"That's right."

I sat back down. "As a matter of fact, I have made progress. My new partner is great. I had a date last night, too. With a woman. Dinner and a movie."

She smiled widely as her eyebrows went up. "That's terrific, Joe. And?" Her arched eyebrows hovered expectantly.

"Fratiano's makes great pasta, my date is a terrific cop, and *The Whales of August* ought to be shown every

243

day on death row. It'd eliminate the appeals process altogether."

She laughed and I was headed toward the door when something occurred to me. "Did I mention that new connection to Kirby Flagg I discovered?"

"Something that can wait until next session?" she asked.

I grinned in relief. "Sure. No problem."

"In that case, come on back and let's talk about it."

I frowned. "It's not nice to trick me like that," I said on my way to her couch. "I'm a police officer wounded in the line of duty."

She gave me the horse laugh again. "So am I, DiMaggio. Someday we'll compare scars. Right now, though, tell me about Kirby Flagg."

ON LIMIT

Back at four forty-seven, Dock had me answer some questions for Ward and Brooks along with a couple of suits from Central Detectives about the sniper shooting out in front of the Tower. When asked where I had been for the past hour and a half, I told detectives Biggs and Vorda that I had been consulting with a psychologist who had an interest in the case, which was not a total lie. Dock grinned once and went stone faced. I had a hard time concentrating. Vorda had a disturbing resemblance to Geraldo Rivera, with special attention to the huge mustachio. According to him, CSU had found nothing useful on the roof of City Hall. The car I had been driving was being processed.

Alone at last with Dock, he went to his office fridge behind his desk and came back with a Dr Pepper for me and an iced coffee for himself.

I dropped into a chair facing his desk as he pushed the can of soda toward me. "Dr. Grable said she had your permission to talk to me about Kirby Flagg."

"Yeah." I popped the top on the can and took a long swallow.

"He was your father? Are you certain?"

"As certain as I can get without a DNA test."

He raised and lowered his eyebrows, took a pull on his iced coffee, and rested his cup on the top of his belly. "I need you, Joe, but you're no good to me dead."

"I'm still on this side of the dirt, Dock."

"Did we bring you in too early?"

I winced at the question and shrugged at the answer. "I don't know, Dock, and Betty didn't say. She isn't pulling my papers for the moment. What she did say, it doesn't sound like some citizen is working off a case of

245

revenge regarding an old case." I held up my arms. "You notice I don't have any new holes in me. This guy has thrown at least eight shots at me, with a substantial number of very close misses at distances that really impress me. I think that probably makes him a one hell of a good shot."

"You think GQ is trying to chase you off the case?"

"Betty thinks so."

"What about you?"

"He wants me off the case; that much feels right. The guy behind the rifle may or may not be GQ."

"An accomplice," said Dock to himself. Looking at me, he said, "Joe, if GQ wants you off the case, why doesn't he just drill you? Dead would get you off."

I drummed my fingertips on my knee for a couple of seconds, then shrugged. "This is going to sound real stupid, Dock, but whoever is doing this or controlling it I think likes me. He likes cops but me in particular."

"All those lead valentines, right?"

"Warning shots." I rubbed my eyes and lowered my hand. "If it's true, Dock, maybe we can use it to catch him."

"Oh?"

"Right now our path doesn't cross with GQ's until we find victims, and by then his path is cold and swept clean."

Dock's eyes squinted. "Go on."

"Every time he throws lead at me, though, our paths cross, and his is red hot. Maybe it doubles or triples our chances of nailing him."

Swinging his chair around, Dock looked through his window. It overlooked the park and the roof of City Hall. He cocked his head to one side, then the other. "Yeah." He nodded to himself. "It's a bit like looking for a gas leak with a blow torch, but I—" He stared at the window a moment longer, then said, "Jesus Christ!" He jumped up and dropped the blinds, cutting off the view. He turned and looked at me, his eyes wide.

"You okay, Dock?"

"Just had an empathetic moment with a shooting gallery duck." He frowned. "Joe, who knew you were taking out a pool car?"

"Kieffer, you, everybody who was in the bullpen and saw me leave. There was the clerk down in the motor pool, anyone down there who overheard us. SWAT was drawing a vehicle. Two dicks from Central. Whoever monitors the security cameras in the garage." I held up my hands then dropped them to my lap. "There were a couple of uniforms down in the motor pool, a mechanic or two. And there was whoever you talked to out at Sixteen Stanton Circle. None of them had time enough to grab a gun, climb up to the City Hall roof, and wait for me, though. Whoever it was had to have already been in place, waiting."

"Plenty of time to call an accomplice, though," flatly stated Dock. He pursed his lips, closed his eyes, and frowned. "Yeah. Whether it's GQ or not, your sniper has an accomplice. But, anything we do to prepare to nab the sniper would tip off the in-house half of the team." He looked at me. "I was hoping it wasn't, but it really is a cop." Dock shook a hand in the general direction of the door. "I have to think about this. Meanwhile, you need to get over to Julia's. Have Kieffer drive you."

"I'm okay, now."

"You look shaky to me. Anyway, you're going to pick up another set of wheels there. You might want to think about wearing some body armor, especially if we're going use you to lure your sniper into throwing more shots at you."

"If this guy is as good as we think he is, Dock, a Kevlar vest isn't going to keep him from planting one between my horns. Besides, we don't want him to think we're dangling me in front of him to get him to reveal himself. He might decide he needs to show us he's serious and start taking out body parts."

I rode in the passenger seat as Kieff wheeled my second unmarked blue-gray Taurus four-door of the day out of the garage. He took us out the Court Street side. By the time we'd turned from Roosevelt onto Canal going east, the subject of the Sniper's most recent attack was tired and we were on Kieff's tour of the Philly evidence.

"A name kept coming up in the Brad Pastore-Gina Fusco killings: William Riggs. Yale prelaw, white, brown and blue, six feet, early twenties then. According to the notes, Riggs frequented the theater where Gina Fusco danced, talked to her on several occasions, and suddenly became very scarce about a week before Pastore and Fusco were killed. Riggs admitted he knew Fusco, but he was alibied up solid. At the time Pastore and Fusco were being made dead, seven in the morning or thereabouts, Riggs was a hundred and eighty miles away with four other students rehearsing a role-playing demo that they later put on in a one o'clock abnormal psych class." He glanced at me. "Any chance that this is a group effort? That they alibied each other out of it?"

"Five of them? We start off with a lone serial killer, we add a sniper accomplice, and now we're talking about a death squad?"

"It doesn't make a lot of sense, does it," said Kieff. "With a group effort you get the Sharon Tate crime scene. Our boy is controlled, compulsively neat, focused."

"What about back then?" I offered. "Maybe when he was in college he wasn't so focused. People change. Killers evolve. The first death in a series, even for organized killers, is often accidental. Are we checking all of them?"

"As we speak."

"What was that other name?"

"Nathan Sunday. He was Riggs's roommate, as well as part of his alibi. Incidentally, they were both drama students and both on Yale's rifle team."

"Rifle team?"

"Thought that would get your attention."

"Were they any good?" I asked.

"Both were invited to try out for the Olympic biathlon team. They declined."

"Shooting and skiing; what a sport." I looked at Kieffer. "But they alibi each other. It doesn't go anywhere."

"That's what Philadelphia thought."

"You find something?"

He smiled. "Out of all the possible places in this world where Nathan Sunday could call home, guess from whence he hailed."

I felt my eyebrows ascend. "South River?"

"Two fifty-one Oak, in St. George, City and County of South River. He sold the house some years ago, but Clair Turner is on his trail. Did you sync up before we left?"

"Yes."

"Then you have what we have on Riggs and Sunday. I have a strong feeling that they are our pair."

I looked in my handheld, called up the Philly file, and poked around in it for a few minutes. When I looked up, we were stopped at the Fortieth Street light facing the oppressive gray complex of Books prison. The light changed, we made the left at the Heights Road intersection, crossed to the other side of the canal, and headed northeast. In minutes we were past the foot of Breadloaf Mountain and into Glenn Heights. Although there were other areas of the city that sported the name "Heights," Glenn Heights was the one they called "The Heights." It was divided into five circles. Four of the circles—Vail, Temple, Randolph, and Marygrove—were double, with estates on both an inner and outer circle drive. Homes there began at two mill, and the mansions on the new-money circles were shacks compared to the palaces on Stanton Circle.

Stanton Circle had a single circular drive, the estates on it few, far between, and hidden behind high walls and modern security systems. The center of the circle was a private park enclosing gardens and a rather large pond. The home at One Stanton Circle came into view. High on a treeless rise, it was literally a castle purchased by the founder of Reston Steel and floated over stone-by-stone from Ireland in the late Nineteenth century. I had been inside the castle only once, on police business.

All we could see as the car passed by the gate to Five Stanton Circle was a concrete drive disappearing into the trees. Coco Torrance's crime scene back there in that modernistic palace that Frank Lloyd Wright must have dreamed up during a college blow party. The image of Coco—

I was stacking up old crime scenes. Betty said that was a no-no. I shook it out of my head and asked Kieffer, "Did you run Julia Powers?"

"I did. You know, she owns Hood Semiconductor."

"Yes."

"Hood Semiconductor, some computer company, hospitals, EMS services, construction companies, Belcamp Industrial Electronics, she owns a school outside of Nelson, too."

"Rich, huh?"

"Look where we are, homey, and tell me what your guess is."

"What else?"

"She graduated from Lanford Academy and Breadloaf University with a degree in psych," Kieffer continued, "The Police Academy after college then she resigned from the force two years later after the Gray-eye Killer take down. She went to work for the Goodman Agency, private investigators, then bought Goodman out a year later, formed her own PI agency, and moved it to Sixteen Stanton circle. She has black belts in judo, karate, and something I can't even pronounce."

"Faster than a speeding bullet!" I announced.

"More powerful than a locomotive!" Kieffer joined in.

"Able to leap tall buildings at a single bound!" we voiced together.

"Think she's the one, Joe?"

"Oh. Right, Kieff. Yeah. I'm just what Julia Powers has been waiting for all this time."

"Serendipity, partner. Fate draws you together—"

"I thought it was a serial killer."

"—Fate draws you together and love blooms. She could be the one." He gave me a stern look. "Don't forget to ask her about *The Whales of August.*"

"You talked to Winnie."

"Yes. And thanks for the movie recommendation, partner, pal, chum, buddy of mine."

"Any time."

"You going to ask Julia for a date?"

"Actually, I think I have a better chance trying Winnie again."

A gleaming maroon cruiser, one of the Molson Security units, came slowly from the opposite direction. The two gray-clad shopcops studied Kieffer and me like we were wearing ski masks and packing Kalashnikovs.

The one riding shotgun picked up the unit's hand mike and called in the suspicious vehicle in the area.

"If they take us down," said Kieff, "I'll roll on you in a second, white boy. I can't do no time. You hear me?"

"No sweat, homey. Repeat after me: You ain't got nuttin' on me, coppah."

"You-u-u dirty rat."

"Top of the world, Ma!"

"Could this be the end of Rico!"

We traded old James Cagney lines until we turned in at the imposing wrought iron and natural stone gate at Sixteen Stanton Circle. Kieff pulled up before it and rolled down the window as a man in casual civilian clothes topped with a buff-colored parka came out of a stone gatehouse large enough to be a mansion in most neighborhoods. He was a chunky man, athletic-looking, with salt-and-pepper hair and a face that was modeled after a cinder block. As he bent over and looked in the window at Kieffer and me, I noticed a suspicious bulge in the parka beneath his left arm. "You must be Julia's nine o'clock," he said with a grin to both of us. "I could smell a department crapheap like this at a skunk day squirt-off. Blue-Gray, underpowered, and no AC," he said, patting the top of the car. "Excellent selection, sir."

Something familiar about him. "Weren't you out of Sherman Park detectives a lot of years ago?" I asked.

He stuck his hand in Kieffer's window and held it out. "Bill French, Joe. We met back when you were still in uniform. The Charlie Matthews thing?" I shook hands with the former detective across Kieff's lap. He did a verbal greeting with Kieffer, turned, coded the electronic lock on the gate, and opened it.

As we drove through, Kieffer poked my arm. "Check it out."

I looked where he was gesturing with his head and noticed that behind the gate house wisps of steam were rising from a heated outdoor swimming pool. "The private security sector is looking up."

The twisting driveway was paved with yellow brick and crowded on both sides with large evergreens. More trees surrounded the chocolate-stone mansion at the top of the gentle rise, almost hiding it from view. When we

251

reached the portico and I got out of the car, I noted at least two remote cameras following my movements.

Kieffer looked past me at the cameras and imposing doors. "Want me to come in with you?"

"You and Clair need to get on those names out of the Philly and Boston cases and see where they lead." I heard the door open behind me and turned to look. A Shaquille O'Neal clone in an olive suit who looked as though he spent the better part of each day bench pressing a Buick took a step through the door. I bent over and looked through the passenger window at Kieffer.

"If you don't hear from me in an hour, I leave everything to knee replacement research."

Kieffer waved a hand, and the car pulled away. I turned and climbed the five stairs until I was standing in front of the man. "I'm Det. Sgt. Torio."

"Mohammad Ali MacGregor," he answered standing to one side. "Come on in. Julia and Monica are tossing meat." Big grin. No elucidation.

MacGregor was wearing an impeccably tailored double-breasted, with dark olive shirt and tan-and-wine striped tie. His ensemble was complete with a slight bulge beneath his left arm. Inside he took my topcoat, placed it on a chair, then led me past some deserted offices through a spacious oak-paneled foyer into an elevator.

The ride was smooth, seeming not to move at all. I looked at MacGregor. "Retired from the job?"

"Yes." He held out a hand the size of a dinner plate and we shook hands. "East Branch and Central detectives, and SCU."

Special Crimes. Anti sex-crimes squad disbanded six years before for rewriting, with extreme prejudice, the meaning of due process. The rewrites resulted in the alleged premature deaths of a number of rape and child abuse suspects and the early retirement of a number of detectives. As the blood came back into my fingers, the elevator stopped, the doors opened, and MacGregor nodded his massive head toward the passageway beyond. "End of the hall on the left."

"Thanks."

I stepped out, the doors closed, and I was alone in the red carpeted hallway. Moving toward the opposite end of the hall, my gaze brushed over the paintings hanging on the walls. Julia Powers's tastes appeared to run toward abstract and expressionistic pieces. A strange mixture of heavy and light, beautiful and ugly. I stopped three times to check names on paintings. The first two I never heard of, the third I couldn't make out. After passing the open door of a guest bedroom bigger than the MCU bullpen, my gaze rested upon a painting done by an artist whose name I did recognize. I knew the painting, as well. The abstract, a somber study in browns, blacks, and creams titled "On Limit," was a Kirsten. It was at the big show at the River Song Gallery last November.

I remembered it because it matched my own mood at the moment. The tans and pale browns building upon ever-darkening solids toward jagged black against bone white. It was saying, "Just one more thing. Just one more thing, creep, then watch out!"

I wondered what the Kirsten said to Julia Powers. There hadn't been anything in the show going for less than thirty grand. What must it be like to be able to afford any price to buy artistic authentication of a mood.

"Maybe she is the one," I whispered to myself. Why not? That's what all the mob connected multi millionaires are going for nowadays: your basic retreaded Homicide dick on probation driving a twenty year-old kennel-on-wheels, still living at home with his father. I turned and faced the end of the hall, the deep red carpeting glowing warmly beneath a row of crystal chandeliers. "Careful, Icarus. That sun is hot."

The room at the end of the hall was a small gym, fifty feet on a side, hardwood floors partially covered with shiny blue wrestling mats. Away from the mats were treadmills, climbing, rowing, pushing, thumping, breaking, smacking, and cracking machines. I was ushered inside by Sixteen Stanton Circle's number two, a sweats-clad Dolores Del Rio on steroids named Monica Rojas. As she closed the door, she laughed and said, "Your partner's a dead man."

I didn't even pretend my jaw didn't drop. *"What?"*

"Don't you watch TV?" She pointed up at a monitor mounted to the right of the door. The current view was of the front entrance where Kieffer had let me off.

"Black cop, white cop. The black cop always has to die so the white cop can emote, possibly give mouth-to-mouth, thereby demonstrating that love and devotion overcome all racial prejudice. It's in the movies all the time."

A joke. Once I got my heart started again, I had to grin. "That doesn't apply to us, Monica. We don't believe in black or white people, so if anybody drops, it'll probably be me again."

The sound of a door closing, then through an open hallway in the back of the gym, there was Julia. Her blond hair looked like a sack of hay twisted into a ratty topknot. Red-faced and sweat-soaked, her baggy gray sweats had the sleeves cut off the shirt. Centered on the shirt, the Greek letter *pi* was silk screened in blue.

She was breathing hard, and with Monica observing from the doorway, she walked around me checking me out like a chunk of pot roast. In the midst of her examination, she said, "Where'd you get that bruise on your right cheek?"

"Belated airbag release."

"Someone chase you off the road?"

"You could say that."

She nodded. "It helps your face. Kieffer was right. You'll do, Joe."

Monica nodded, as well, her face deadpan as she moved up next to Julia and studied me. "Very cute. A haircut, some teasing, a little lightening on the sides of his nose."

"Oil in his hair," Julia chimed in. "A nice shiny suit, make him look like he likes himself, and he'll be perfect."

I glared at her as I felt my face getting red. "Am I a-gonna have to make-a da ice-a cream or buy-a da monkey?"

Her gaze leveled on me. "We're after a killer who thinks, acts, and kills in terms of symbols, Joe. One of the symbols he is fixated on is any heterosexual couple with certain physical traits and behavioral mannerisms who find a bit of sleazy excitement with each other in bedrooms, hotel rooms, and gentleman's clubs. The closer the individuals are to meeting the image the killer has in his mind, the more likely they are to get killed. That is what we're trying to do: Get this guy to try and kill us. So, if putting you out on the sidewalk with a monkey grinding an organ and singing 'Volare' draws out the killer, that's what we do."

"Who's supposed to be my date?" I asked. I held my thumb out toward Monica Rojas. "Her?"

Monica stepped forward, lifted a hand, and pinched my left cheek. "To dance for you, Joe Torio, that will be my dream for tonight. You are *so cute*."

My face was getting hot and I knew it showed.

"I'll be your date," answered Julia, "as Margarita Azzurro, a fairly new dancer at The Score. I've already taken her place and her face. You're going to be Margarita's new boyfriend. We'll both be in disguise. Monica, go call Benny. He's going to have to get to work right away if young Santino here is going to have his hunting threads in time for tomorrow night." Monica went to a wall phone.

"Santino?" I asked Julia.

"Santino Mirabella. If you want another name, let's have it. We have enough time to work up new ID."

I held out my hands and shrugged. "Santino is fine. But what do you mean about making me look as though I like myself?"

"Do you?"

"I don't put a lip lock on myself in the shower, but I don't hide under the covers cutting myself with razors."

"Santino is into the self-administered lip locks. When Benny's finished measuring you, I want to see you shoot. Any questions?"

"Yeah. Can I get a look at your contract with the city?"

"Maybe you should call Lt. Dockery and find out what page of it you're supposed to be on. Meanwhile . . ." she nodded toward the door. I followed her gaze and saw a diminutive man of about seventy. He wore well tailored dark slacks and a white dress shirt with the sleeves rolled above his elbows. There was a cloth measuring tape hanging from his neck. "Benny will take your measurements. Benny, as soon as you're done with him, tell Monica."

"My pleasure," answered the old man, his voice surprisingly deep and strong. He looked me up and down, then glanced at Julia. "Black shirt and slacks, gold silk coat, no tie." He looked back at me, his gaze wandering down to my feet. "Young man, do you have any yellow dancing shoes or black ones with gold buckles or chains?"

"Not since I left the circus."

"What size are your feet?"

"Ten wides."

"Maybe I can fix you up with something that won't pinch too badly." He faced Julia. "We'll finish him off with a medium length black topcoat, matching hat, and gold scarf."

"Good."

Julia and Monica went to a back mat and resumed tossing meat, that is, each other. I faced the tailor. "Well, sir, I guess you better get started doing whatever it is that you do. What's your last name?"

"Goodman."

"Goodman?"

The old man took the tape from around his neck. "That's right."

"Benny Goodman?"

"English isn't your first language, is it, detective?"

"It's not a joke?"

The old man turned me around and held the tape to the nape of my neck. "I have no sense of humor whatever, detective. Life for me is simply one long, brooding interlude."

As he continued taking measurements, Benny Goodman began whistling "Stomping at the Savoy."

THE AUDITION

In the basement of the mansion, among other facilities, was a fully equipped shooting range. I had my 669 back and I fired several times at the designated targets using filled magazines provided by the management. When I was finished, motor-driven cables ran the final target back to the firing line. Tight group.

While Julia, still clad in her gray sweats, examined the final target, I went to the cleaning table and began field stripping my weapon. "I suppose now you whip out a piece and at a hundred yards put twenty rounds into a gnat's eye, blindfolded and standing on your head."

She finished studying the target, then tossed it into a trash can. She leaned a hip against the firing line fence and frowned. "You may have a self-esteem problem, Joe. I could recommend a good therapist. A man, if that makes a difference." When I didn't respond but continued cleaning Fido, Julia walked over and came to a stop on the other side of the table.

"I know you but I don't know you, Joe. From what I've read and have been told, you are anything from Super Cop to Daffy Duck with the intuition of either Einstein or Daffy Duck." She nodded downrange. "I wanted to see if your shoulder had healed well enough to shoot straight, and it appears it has." She nodded toward my shoulder. "How is it?"

"Almost a hundred percent." The assembly of my weapon complete, I drove my own magazine into the grip and holstered it. I did a one ham sit down on the edge of the cleaning table. "I have a question, Julia."

She gave me a wry smile. "Okay."

"Do you think GQ is a cop?"

She thought for a moment. "Cops have been serial killers before. It would be a way to get in the door. GQ knows how to leave very little evidence behind. It's likely. What do you think?"

"A uniform might have gotten GQ through the door with the pair in Baldwin and the pair in Magena, but I don't see Vince Polizzi falling for it. If it had been a cop in uniform or with ID, Vince would have been covering him from the top of the stairs with one hand and calling his boys with the other."

She grinned. "Mob racial memory about Valentine's Day?"

"Exactly. Maybe GQ is a cop, but he sure doesn't look like one when he comes calling."

"Do you think GQ is a cop?"

"I do, but I hope not. If GQ is a cop and out of South River, or hooked up with any of the departments represented in MCU, he might already know about Dock's bait game: Margarita and Santino. What if he just skips us?"

She studied me for a moment. "You're the one peeking into his head, Joe."

I thought for a moment. "Okay. GQ lives in a different universe and that universe operates by a different set of rules. For us, the rules have to do with living, loving, making a buck, getting caught and getting away. With GQ, getting caught is only a problem if it impedes his mission."

She raised her eyebrows. "Which is?"

"It appears to be getting Mom laid. There might be a wrinkle, though. There's a reluctance about the Polizzi-Salvati scene. It's just a feeling."

"Do you think GQ wants off the ride?" she asked.

"Maybe. But I'm dead sure he wants me off the ride. Did you hear about what happened when I tried to arrive at this appointment on time?"

She glanced down. "Kieff called me. He said you almost got your head blown off."

"The key word there is *almost*. Here's my question: A trigger is a trigger, whether the bomb wants to go off or not, right? If this guy is hard wired enough, even if GQ knows all about our scam, if we really do a good enough job to pull his trigger, he's got to react. Right?"

She frowned, glanced at the floor, then back at me. "To do that, Joe, we would need to convince GQ that we are genuinely and passionately in love with each other."

I grinned. "Like Vince Polizzi: 'Prisoner of love.'"

She nodded. "He was silly in love, wasn't he?"

"Mouse ears and magic."

"The trigger isn't just visual, Joe. It's also emotional. Especially if he's onto us, you and I have to convince GQ that we are the same kind of silly in love. That's the real bait." Julia sat on the edge of the cleaning table, turned something over in her mind, then glanced at me. "The costume Benny is cooking up, take it home with you. I'll supply you with the car you'll be driving. Before you leave I'll show you how to work the makeup to make yourself look like Margarita's new lover and cover up that bruise."

Julia handed me a small red terrycloth towel. I took it, began wiping my hands, and decided to take that empty-handed leap into the void. "Julia, how would you like to go watch a movie sometime or some TV? Dinner? Together with me."

"As in a date?"

"Just like in a date."

Her right eyebrow arched. "Do I have to ride in that Mazda?"

"Not in the back. I can even hit the upholstery with a couple shots of Febreze. Maybe put in a throw rug. Rent a limo? Buy a new car?" I raised my eyebrows. "You can drive."

She laughed and nodded. "It's a possibility."

A possibility. That could be interpreted as a positive response, I reflected. Now all I had to do was figure out a way to go on a date without either of us getting shot by my little sniper friend or burgered by his buddy, GQ. "Do we go to The Score together tonight?"

"No. We have to increase the chances of GQ seeing me as being alone. We might be cutting it too thin with only two nights without Bruno, the real Margarita's current boyfriend." She held out a hand. "Actually, it might not even matter. If the boyfriend isn't that certain someone, GQ might already consider Margarita alone."

"And he might already know we're bait," I added.

She looked me in the eyes. "We have to keep open the possibility that he isn't a cop, Joe, and that he doesn't know anything about us. We'll start tomorrow night. I'll dance and your job is to drool on the stage. You need to radiate absolute infatuation; like the Easter Bunny hit you with a bucket of lust dust. Can you do horny?"

I burst out with a laugh. "That I can do."

"After the club, we go to Margarita Azzurro's place, steam GQ's goggles, and hope he strikes the next morning." She smiled. More and more I was getting hooked on that smile. "Look, Joe, we are in love. Head-over-heels, can't-think-about-nothin'-else, rutting like a bull moose, in love. Remember Vince, big-time wiseguy enforcer, in the mouse ears. Get in that mind set. Before you pick me up tomorrow night, you need to believe it. You need to make me believe it. Most important, you need to make GQ believe it. If we're right, if he believes we're in love, it might not matter if he knows we're bait."

I let my gaze wander from her face to her stained sweats down to her ancient joggers, and back up to her face. I sang, "M-I-C-K-E-Y—"

"I plan to primp myself up a bit."

"I'm encouraged."

"After we put on our act at The Score, we go back to Randall Street and wait. We give GQ every opportunity to peek in the windows and see us having a great time." She stared off and talked more to herself than to me. "GQ hits first thing in the morning."

"Seven."

"Right." She fixed me with that look again. "What's your feeling about backup?"

"I think Vince Polizzi's bodyguards are missing because they're deader than Elvis."

"I agree. We go in naked. Shall we move on to beauty school?" I didn't move and her eyebrows went up. "Something else?"

I looked down range then back at her. "Yeah. I'd like to see you blind that gnat."

She held out her hand and I handed over Fido, butt first. She didn't stand on her head or do it blindfolded, but after jacking in a round, in under five seconds she put eight rounds through the ten spot in a group that could be covered by a half-dollar.

SHADOW BLUE

Pop had gotten the auto club to resurrect the MX3, which meant a new battery. After dropping Julia's gold and black Cadillac pimpmobile and my costume off at Pop's, I took the MX3 back to the Tower, the contrast between the Caddy's ride and the MX3's causing me to reconsider new shocks. At MCU Kieffer aimed me at my computer to bring me up to speed. I was wading through Nathan Sunday's college transcripts at Yale, his grade point average doing nothing for my self-esteem, when Ward Staples dropped by and renewed an acquaintance that I really couldn't remember.

"I heard a rumor we're running bait on GQ: you and Julia Powers."

That hadn't taken long. "I'm pleased to be able to put that rumor to rest, Ward."

"It's not true?"

"No. It is true, but now it's no longer a rumor. Where did you hear it?"

"Around."

"Is that A. Round, like in Archibald Round, or a-round like in you refuse to say?"

His eyebrows went up. "I overhead something in the locker room. One of the uniforms. Norris, I think. He was kicking it around with Pendleton, Cruz, and some others."

"Jesus," muttered Kieffer.

Ward Staples frowned at Kieff's outburst, then looked at me, a modicum of concern on his face. "Joe, you know I was a PI before I became a cop."

"I heard."

"I wanted to give you a heads up about Powers. A couple of times I came into contact with her professionally."

"And?" I prompted.

"I just thought you'd want to know, man: All her bulbs aren't screwed in. Give her half a chance, buddy, and she'll boil your bunny. Know what I mean?" He made a gun with his fingers, aimed it between my eyes, and fired. "Word to the wise."

Staples turned and headed toward his desk. I looked at Kieffer, and he was frowning back. "Is Staples a flake?" I asked.

Kieff shrugged. "According to you, everybody's a flake. What's concerning me right now is everyone in the department except maybe the cleaning staff, apparently knows about the operation."

"I discussed it with Julia. She thinks we'll be so good that GQ will go for it anyway."

Kieffer paused and frowned. "Really."

"The key is love, partner. If we push the right buttons, he'll go for it. That's the theory anyway."

Kieff grinned skeptically. "I wish I could be as sanguine about it as she seems to be." He looked at me with a sly expression. "So, did you ask her for a date?"

"As a matter of fact, I did."

"And?"

"She said it was a distinct possibility. That's almost a yes."

"You like her?" he asked.

"You know, I believe I do. A lot."

Kieffer frowned and reached for his telephone. "Maybe it's worth finding out what Ward was talking about, boiled bunnywise."

I thought about that for a minute or two, then reached for my phone and punched in the number for SWAT.

"Powers was recruited by Vice fresh out of the Academy to go undercover," said Lt. Carlton. He was number one at SWAT, a big man, steel gray hair cut into a burr, blue eyes, a man of action uncomfortable in a necktie. The man's voice was nasal with a suggestion of

West Virginia. I leaned against the counter in the third-floor coffee room, off the Homicide bullpen.

"She was good at it, Torio. I've seen her made up like a little boy, a sixty year old street junky, and a Chinese whore, and didn't know it was anything other than a little boy, an old street junky, or a Chinese whore. Over about twenty months, many, many collars." Dave Carlton fell silent.

"Sounds like a career-maker," I prompted.

"Yeah. For both of us." He cocked his head toward the bullpen. "It was anyway until Homicide heard about us. They had a case they were working in conjunction with LA and Vegas. Leland Eckhart. Remember, he had the bodies of all those whores buried under his house?"

"I remember Eckhart. I don't remember Powers having anything to do with the case."

"We never let the media have her name or mine. Homicide used her for bait and I covered her. Campbell and Lee took credit for the collar. There were some questions, but the case was cleared. Then came Gerald Soams and all his damned gray eyeballs. After the Gray-eye thing, there were lots more questions. The brass got scared and Powers wouldn't defend herself. Anyway," the lieutenant continued, "she turned in her badge and runs her own agency now. The department even contracts with her. Remember Henry Dyne?"

"The Black Bag Rapist." Henry Dyne hadn't made it into court alive, either. I took a swallow of my Dr Pepper thinking that I wasn't getting the information I needed. "Too bad the department let a cop like that get away just because the brass got a knot in its thong."

"I said she turned in her badge."

"With 9mm bore marks in her ear, I bet."

Carlton flushed red and chuckled. "Yeah, I guess you could say that."

"I just did say that."

He raised an eyebrow. "Remember Dion Orgoglio?"

"One of Don Scozarri's button boys. Went out of control and was found drowned two years ago. Is that on Powers?"

"If we could prove it, she'd be in Books right now writing her memoirs." There was a moment of silence, then, as he looked down, Carlton said, "Look, Torio, I'll be honest with you. I was the one who ratted her out to IAB."

"Her partner?"

The lieutenant faced me. "No. I was a police officer in the business of bringing in perps and clearing cases. You know what I think she is?"

"What?"

"Julia Powers is a serial killer who's figured out how to do it legally."

"That's what the media is always suggesting I am."

Carlton was quiet for a moment, trying to make a decision. "Look, after she dropped the Gray-eye Killer, when I arrived on the scene I found Soams bleeding to death. He was pumping out from a severed carotid artery, she was naked, covered with Soams's blood, cuddling his head in her lap, and crying like a baby. She hadn't even cleared him. He had a knife in one hand and a gun in the other. I mean, what kind of cop leaves a gun in a perp's hand?"

"A question asked more often than one might think," I answered quietly. "What happened then?"

"After that she went numb, like a rag doll. I had to send her to Riverside General in an ambulance. The doctor said there was nothing physically wrong with her." He tapped the side of his head.

"So, lieutenant, you're saying her wiring isn't up to code?"

Carlton poured himself some more coffee and faced me. "You gotta ask yourself, Torio: is that who you want to go through the door with? The way I hear it, GQ doesn't leave a whole lot of margin for error. It could be the Rizzos all over again. Know what I mean?"

"Yeah. Thanks for coming over, lieutenant."

"Just trying to save a life: yours." He took his coffee and left the coffee room.

No cop had all his Chiclets in the box. There's useful crazy, of course, and not so useful crazy. Lt. Carlton ran SWAT and those boys weren't shy at all about adding to the body count. Yet Carlton sounded afraid of Julia

Powers. Afraid of who she was; what she might do. My cell phone rang and I opened it. "Yeah?"

"Clair Turner, Joe."

"What's up?"

"Doc Kratzer's got Vince Polizzi's bodyguards down in the morgue. Couple of naked stiffs they found beneath the Seventh Street Bridge. They thought they were just a couple of homeless men until Kratzer ID'd them."

"How'd they catch it?"

"Two in the hat, each with a .22."

"I'll be right up."

By the time I returned to MCU, Lt. Dockery and Kieffer had their coats on and were heading for the morgue. As Kieffer buttoned up his overcoat, he glanced at me. "While you were downstairs I heard from Powers. She said you two will be going in without backup? You think that's a good idea?"

"While you're down at the morgue, Kieff, ask Pitone and Casale how that backup thing worked out for them."

Kieffer glanced at Dock and Dock looked at me. "Okay, Joe, go home. Practice whatever you need to practice to do your best when you and Powers go undercover tomorrow night."

"It's only three."

"Go home," said Dock. "Get some sleep. It's been a busy day, you've had a jolt or two, and you could use a rest."

"Okay. As soon as I take care of something," I said.

"I kind of like Julia," said Kieffer. He stood there silently for a moment, his eyes focused on something in space. "I have this picture in mind, Joe, of Miriam and me, you and Julia, up on the top of Breadloaf skiing down Helldiver, then in the lodge warming our toes, sucking down hot chocolate, getting ready for our next run." He grinned and looked at me. "Tough to hold in that hot choc when you're full of bullet holes."

"Chocolate is the penicillin of the soul. I'll be careful."

Later, after they left, I synced my handheld and waited for the computer to compare, update, and otherwise nibble it's bytes. While that was going on, I pushed the Sniper and Lt. Carlton out of my head and pondered the problem of becoming Sonny Mirabella.

Julia seemed to have no doubts on how to become Margarita Azzurro, but I was at a loss with Santino Mirabella. As a rare ray of sunshine fought its way through my mental overcast, I smiled. Sonny Mirabella was only a name. My job was to become Vince Polizzi, and the key to that was back at my old seat on the Cold Cases Desk. I pulled my handheld from its cradle, grabbed my coat, and headed for the elevator.

Cab looked around at me. "Well, you still alive? There's hope for every corpse in South River."

"When you're born to hang, Cab, you don't have to worry about knives and guns."

Cab shrugged. "So, you on GQ?"

"I am."

"Ah, yes. The fellow who shoots and chops up young lovers." His bushy eyebrows went up. "Your love life still a disaster?"

"It's on the upswing, you unromantic old fart. At this very moment there is a woman of means who has admitted that dating me is a possibility."

One of his eyebrows arose skeptically. "Saber-toothed crotch crickets from outer space are a possibility, Joe."

"Indeed, and I have seen more than my share."

"What about that Sniper business out front? Any leads?"

I shook my head. "Only guesses. Cab, I need an interrogation video from records."

"What, too cheap to go to Blockbuster?" He nodded toward the other terminal. "You know how to get it."

"Thanks."

I settled in at the other terminal, ran Vince Polizzi's name, and came up with a very long list of suspicions, detentions, and even a couple of arrests, none of which led to anything. Since 'Ninety-two, however, state law required all police interrogations to be video taped, and three of those arrests and subsequent interrogations had been after 'Ninety-two.

I took down the file numbers for the three tapes, went to the stacks, and looked them up. I played parts of all three, picked the one I wanted, and began making a high speed copy. As I stood to leave, my cell phone squeaked at me. I punched it on and Mike Ijumaa was on the other end with some interesting information on the recovered slugs that had been thrown at me from the roof of City Hall: They were different than the ones Mike had dug out of Pop's couch.

"Good news?" asked Cab facetiously as I punched off.

"Well, let's see: Either the Sniper goes to work with a variety of weapons or I've got a minimum of two of the bastards after me."

"And they say it's hard to start a trend."

SLOPE THERAPY

David Berkowitz's dog was starting to talk to me. My hands already had the geezer shakes. Before I started dribbling oatmeal down my bib, I needed to get out of my head. My preferred way to leave the job at the office was to eat a glacier and squirt it out my ears. Gravity plus an inclined plane plus some white stuff and a low friction coefficient equals a head trip away from the snake pit. It was starting to get dark, but they had night skiing at Breadloaf. Instead of going home to get my gear, thereby increasing my chances of picking up a tail, I took the MX3 out of the garage on the Court Street side, made certain I wasn't being tailed, then went up to Oak and headed straight east out of the city, up the mountain to Lodge Road, parked the car at the lodge and headed for the rental shop as the sun dipped behind West Bluff and the river. The kid in the rental shop talked me into trying a pair of Atomic Nomad Premiums. They were a lot shorter than my old Dynastars, but if I didn't love them he said he'd pay the rental himself. BS probably, but a good pitch. I got boots and poles, too.

After depositing the skis and poles at the outside racks on the trail takeoff deck, I returned to the main lodge and went to the shop off the main changing area. After poking around in the bargain bin, I came out with a pair of black ski gloves, a red fleece cap, a half-decent pair of clear goggles, and a red shell to wear over my sweater. I left my overcoat, jacket, tie, cell phone, and gun in a locker, put on my bargain bin ensemble, and headed for the slopes.

The happy place. I loved it all: the Darth Vader ski-boot walk, the bite of the wind at the edges of my shell, the first bit of gravity-induced slide as I rode the skis down from the takeoff deck onto the lower end of the North Mountain X-Cut beneath the chair lift. Rather than jam myself into the tram with six dozen other skiers, I aimed my points at the double chair lift.

Three teen snowboarders cut past me, and I watched one of them carve turns weaving in and out of the chair lift pylons. By the time I and another skier reached the lift and I felt the familiar slam of the seat edge behind my calves, I was out of the case, out of the Sniper's scope, and out of GQ's head. The other occupant of the chair was a middle-aged woman, a secretary at Jansen Brass. I said I was a rope salesman. She was pleasant enough. It was just that I wasn't looking to team up with anyone, especially since she was strictly a green-trailer. I juggled my poles until the handles were beneath my left leg, opened the large chest pocket on the shell, pulled out my Mini Maglite, and looked at the trail map. I wanted to get into the steeps and I decided to take the mid-lift bailout at the bottom of Rounder and take the Super-Quad to the top of the mountain.

As I put the trail map and light back into the chest pocket, zipping it shut, the chair passed the end of the takeoff landing revealing the glaring wonderland of the Breadloaf Sports Club below. Five enormous bubbling illuminated sunken hot tubs spaced evenly along the length of the deck, bikini-clad lunatics running from the hot water to the snow banks, and back to the tubs, columns of steam rising in the icy air. At the Super-quad bailout on Lower Rounder, I bid the woman good-bye, left the chair, skied down the exit ramp, carved to the left, and traveled the short trail to the Quad.

There wasn't much of a line and I slid into the center-right gate. The detachable seats slowed, allowing four skiers at a time to sit slowly like ladies and gentlemen before it reattached itself and began racing up the mountain. A snowboarder pulled up in the far-left just before the gates opened. We both got on the chair and struck up a conversation. He was around twenty and had been at it all day. He reported that the good smooth snow was on Helldiver and Cruiser, trails on the southernmost side.

The nasty snow was beneath us and that was where the boarder was headed. The trail under the quad was a black diamond bump garden that I had been down once before just to say I had done it. Straight, lumpy, ungroomed, and narrow, it was basically a good way to wear yourself out early. To my right I could see Rounder gently snaking its way down to the bottom of the quad, the hiss of the snow guns below us making flake on a darkened trail placing us momentarily in a small whiteout. Beyond Rounder I could catch only an occasional glimpse of Helldiver.

The upper part of Helldiver was a black diamond, the lower part a double black diamond. I had only been all the way down Helldiver once. Usually I'd take Chicken Switch at the top of Lower Helldiver and finish the run over on Rounder. The double diamond stretch of Helldiver was wide, steep, a hunk of mandatory moguls, and three places where you either had to jump down a small cliff or pitch a tent and camp for the night. The jumps weren't record-setters, ranging from three to thirty feet, with the landings on anywhere from forty to fifty-five degree slopes. By the time you touched down, though, if you were still upright, you were burning rockets. It was more than what I usually wanted to take on. By the time I reached the top, however, I went for it. If Helldiver couldn't shake snipers and such out of my head, nothing could.

After unloading at the top, I worked the gentle turns until I reached the head of Helldiver, the steep groomed surface in the artificial light seeming to twist down into the illuminated bowels of the earth.

I didn't pause. Hesitation never decreased the pitch of any slope. Straight into it, the fronts of my shins into the boots, my upper body facing down slope as I cut into the first turn then shifted back into gentle ess curves, the Chopper stretching before me. The skis the kid talked me into were great; Easier turns, more control. I aimed toward the little cliff. Chopper was the only optional cliff on the run, the groomed slope going down a kinder, gentler route to the left. I caught my breath and aimed for the center of the drop, my legs jumping against the skis only slightly as I reached the edge. A ten-foot drop,

I landed clean, went into a wide turn to the left, got on a groomed ridge for the boarders, and cut the top back and forth, sailing down at the end into the wide expanse above the island they called Poacher's Glade.

My head was clear. The rush, the challenge, hitting the right flake at the right time at the right speed and angle —I was high, the killers and those who made them far, far away. I streaked by Chicken Switch, slowed, carved my way down to the right of the first mogul, then cut in a sharp left turn into the fall line, right, left, almost into a rhythm, then I caught an edge, inverted and began bouncing from the top of one mogul to the next, the lights spinning, then landed on my back, bounced to the next mogul on my face, twisted around, and plowed to a halt.

I started laughing and couldn't answer a woman who had been following me through the mogul field. She wanted to know if I was all right. All I could do was laugh and nod.

I fell twice more in the mogul field, then free of it, I opened up and streaked down to the next jump, Split Cliff, named that for the tree-filled notch right in its center. I flew over the edge, felt my heart rise in my chest, and hit, my knees buckled, and I pitched back, rolled forward and somehow wound up on my feet. I checked and saw there was still a ski attached to each boot, and I took the snow straight down, speed increasing, until the edge of caution forced me to turn.

I slowed a bit, then saw a warning sign about the approaching Helldiver Cliff.

YOU NEED ALL THE SPEED YOU CAN GET.

The drop was only twenty to thirty feet, depending on the end picked, but Helldiver wasn't anything you could creep up on and take slow. Helldiver didn't go straight down. It had a bit of a slope to it. Not enough to hold much snow, but enough to catch timid skiers in the rocks at the bottom. Not a cautious jump. Time for commitment.

I had done it once before and had almost bought it in the rocks, then bounced, then had a yard sale. I straightened my fall line and streaked for the center. At the edge, I jumped up into it, felt myself beginning a forward rotation, straightened up, and held out my arms to catch some wind.

Down, landing on the steep incline beneath the cliff, I hardly felt it when my planks touched the snow. I sang out a war whoop and took the fifteen-foot Dumper that followed a scant fifty yards beyond Helldiver, where I wiped out.

I did Rounder Trail next, eating the long shallow turns, then Lazy Susan, a green trail, wide and smooth. I did the mountain until my thighs burned, then took the Tram up to South Peak to finish the night going down Cruiser, steep, fast, and smooth.

Standing in the car packed sardine-like with sixty other skiers, I quickly scanned the other occupants, backs of heads mostly. No one in the car appeared to be thinking of murder. Smiling, I looked through a clear spot in the window down at Cruiser. The trail was a long, stretched-out question mark with an island in the wide middle half way down. I could see that much of the grooming on the south edge still remained. If I stuck to the edge, the ride would be fast, smooth, a great finish.

The tram docked and I exited with the others below the restaurant. I carried my skis just outside the door, snapped my boots into the bindings, and waited for the other skiers to push off. While I waited for the traffic to clear, I did some quickie stretching exercises to loosen my leg muscles. I turned, stretching my neck and back, until I was facing the tram exit. Just then I head a loud crack and saw the carved oak lintel of the tram exit splinter.

I stared dumbly at the splintered wood for a second, then turned my head. Just past the light that marked the head of Cruiser, beyond an orange out-of-boundaries rope, there was a tall, heavily muscled skier in a black snowsuit, who was holding something strange in his arms. It looked like a severely bent ski pole and he was aiming it at me! I jumped to my right as he fired and I landed on my right side in the snow.

The shooter slung the rifle across his back, snow skating away from the lights down the darkness of South

Ridge, a black diamond trail, closed to the public, no lights.

"You sonofabitch!" I yelled.

I scrambled to my skis, pushed off, and snow skated to the head of the trail, squatted as I slid beneath the boundary rope and streaked into the steep dark beyond.

South Ridge Trail was easy enough in the daylight, but in the dark I couldn't read the snow. I could see the shooter far ahead, black against the whiteness, but I couldn't make out the contours of the surface. I went into a tuck, accelerated, and held it as long as I could, the speed, the steep, and the dark pulling my fear of heights back into my current terror column.

The shadow disappeared around a turn, and I cut the corner by going off trail through a clear place between the trees, a bit of air on the way out, and a near wipeout as I landed in a patch of deep snow. Then I caught some unintentional air, screamed in surprise, then hit the ungroomed crud, my arms windmilling down the slope, the shadow a little closer.

As I landed on one leg and recovered, twenty yards ahead the shadow turned into another trail and I simply followed, not knowing which trail was which in the darkness.

At one turn I came out of the trees and saw the city spread below me on my right, headlights coming at me from that direction. I screamed as the car went beneath me, and I realized I was on one of the trail bridges that went over South Alpine Drive. We were heading south toward Idiot's Drop.

There was dim shouting in my ears and I didn't know if it was the shooter's cries or my own. All I knew was I had to catch the Sniper before he reached South Breadloaf Circle and the Drop. It was permanently out of bounds mainly because of all the skiers who managed to get themselves killed there. I could just barely do the Drop in the daytime. If I went in the dark they'd be squeegeeing me off the trees for weeks.

A tighter tuck, my hands together in front of me forming the apex of the windbreak just like the heroes do on the Warren Miller films. No slowing turns, cutting the corners close, at one point going off trail at a spot I came out just above the shooter as the shadow went into his own tuck and seemed to rocket away. I cut one more corner, felt my right ski catch an edge, and I launched up into the night.

I bounced once on my butt, flew back into the sky, then slammed into something flat and unyielding with my back, fell down, and came to rest on my face.

Sounds. Skis.

I pulled my face out of the snow and looked around. Two dark shapes on skis were racing toward me. My heart went into my throat until I dimly made out the white crosses on their shells. Ski Patrol.

They pulled up next to me, popped their bindings, and were at my side on foot in a matter of seconds. "Hey, rocket man," said the first. "You all right?"

"I look all right?"

"I'm Hal and that's Tom." Hal squatted next to me. "How about we check you out?"

I got to my knees. "Did either of you see what happened to the guy I was chasing?"

"Long gone," said the shadow called Tom. "So much for the buddy system. You know, pal, going out of bounds can cost you your lift ticket."

Tom had my poles, Hal had my skis. I had nothing to throw. "I bet during the summer you clowns do Smoky Bear impressions. I'm a police officer. Det. Sgt. Torio. The person I was chasing took a couple of shots at me at the tram. You want to get on your little squawk box and notify mountain security to get in touch with the SRPD? Think you can handle that, Spunky?"

Hal nodded at his partner who called to base and reached security. Tom handed the unit to me. I described the shooter to security, gave our location, made arrangements to meet with them down at the lodge, and handed the radio back to Tom.

"How are you doing, detective?" asked Hal. "We could get a sled for you down here in ten minutes."

"How're my skis?"

Tom held them out. I took out my Maglite and gave them the once over. They weren't broken. I reset the bindings, dropped the skis on the snow, and stepped into them. Out of curiosity I turned and played the light on the hard flat surface that had interrupted my flight. It was a sign. It said: WHY NOT TAKE A LESSON?

"Words to live by," offered Hal.

WISEGUY SCHOOL

After a thoroughly useless hour of debate with Breadloaf Mountain Security and a detective from Breadloaf/North Valley Division, I went home. A snack, a shower, and a half-hour nap from which I awakened screaming, then I settled in the music room with the copy of the Polizzi interrogation tape.

Someone was dead. As a matter of fact, it was old Goggles, found drowned in Canal Park. Dion Orgoglio, the Scozarri hitter, had gone berserk and began slaying for the sheer fun of it: His garbage man, his pharmacist, someone on the street, Nicky Batts's dog groomer. When he was found drowned, although the department was grateful, there was still the small matter of whether Goggles had died by the numbers. Since Vince Polizzi was suspected of being in charge of such housekeeping chores for the family, it was logical to bring him in for questioning. What was illogical was to expect to get any answers, and the cops on this one didn't. Everyone was phoning it in.

Polizzi had been pulled out of a nightclub. The image on the screen showed Vince Polizzi leaning back in a chair, his white silk shirt open at the neck revealing a smooth gold necklace above curls of black chest hair. Pop came in dressed in his pajamas and robe and sat down next to me on the couch. He handed me a Dr Pepper in a can and took a sip off his own. "That the Polizzi boy."

"Yeah. This is who I have to become before tomorrow night."

As the hangman settled in, studied the clothes, the image, the body language of the mobbed up thug, he

277

nodded. "You remember the old war movies? The war in Italy?"

"Yeah."

The hangman waved his hand at the screen. "He remind you of somebody? You got any sound on the Polizzi boy? Where he's talking?"

I ran the tape ahead, stopped where one of the interrogators got up, left the room, and came back in again with coffee for Vince. "Here." I hit the mute.

Vince's voice, confident only as a made man can be confident, was trying to make the detectives feel at ease. *"Hey, I know you boys are just doing your job. Reporters all over the place,"* he smiled and waved his hand expansively, *"and you have to dance a little for 'em once in awhile, right?"* He stuck his prominent chin out with a big manly we-guys-are-all-in-this-together grin. *"Hey, am I right?"* He fixed them with a clear open-eyed look that allowed no disagreement.

The two detectives mumbled their concurrence. I didn't recognize either of them. Bottom rungers from the OCTF. Vince waved his hand in a depreciating gesture.

"Hey, everybody does it: the mayor, the President, the Pope, even Frank Scozarri." He looked around the room, frowning, as though something was missing. *"No babes, no band, no beer."* Almost as though a light bulb illuminated above his head, his face erupted into a eureka expression as he snapped his fingers. *"Hey, you guys! How about a pizza and some real coffee in here? On me. Guidici's Pizzeria on Canal. They deliver. You know me. Always the best for the Vince."*

The Vince.

The cops laughed and as one reached out to shut down the tape, I thought about it. Would it be possible to act as though nothing could touch me? Vince oozed magnanimity, invulnerability, almost immortality. He could afford to be broad-minded about police investigations that were guaranteed to go nowhere. Vince was under the protection of Frank Scozarri. No one—cop, DA, judge, crook, or hitter—would be crazy enough to muss even a hair. Nothing could touch him— Nothing but a killer to whom the normal rules and cautions had no meaning.

Suddenly the hangman pointed at the screen and snapped his fingers, "Ah-hah!" He looked at me, his finger still pointed at the screen. "Benito Mussolini!"

"He doesn't look anything like Mussolini. He looks more like that old singer—Dean Martin."

"No, Joe. Not his face. How he act. *Arroganza*."

The hangman ran the tape back as I tried to recall those old news clips from the thirties and forties. Benito Mussolini. That chunky, clownish, self-centered arrogant thug—

Vince started talking and I closed my eyes, trying to see that fat, bald, strutting rooster on that balcony. "*— Everybody does it: the mayor, the President, the Pope, even Frank Scozarri.*" A silence, imagining that smirk, that protruding lower lip, that down the nose look at the cheering multitude. "*No babes, no music, no beer.*" A beat. "*Hey, you guys! How about a pizza . . . Always the best for the Vince.*"

The Vince. *Arroganza*, indeed.

I opened my eyes. "That could almost be Benito Mussolini trying to do Al Pacino. He reminds me of someone else, though."

"I know what you mean." The hangman punched the pause, stood, placed his fists on his hips, and thrust out his lower lip as he held back his head and swaggered around the room. It was a caricature of Mussolini. A good one. The hangman stopped, looked down at the floor, his face like stone, his eyes glistening. I got up.

"What is it, Pop?"

He shook his head. "Nothing." He gestured with his hand, dismissing the image of Polizzi on the screen. "I know people like that my whole life. In Sicily one of them, he took the man," and his voice trailed off. "The man I think of as my father. One of these *gavones* killed him." He waved a hand at me. "Long time ago. Nineteen forty-three." He nodded once to himself. "Salvatore Piranio, like the fish. He would make you a good Vince Polizzi."

The hangman nodded, shook the memory out of his head, and pointed upstairs. "Get to your room and try on those clothes, see how they look on you." As I was half way up the circular staircase, the hangman shouted from

279

the music room, "Find that gold chain the Vitamante girl give you on your birthday. The one you hate? Wear that. *Perfetto*."

In my room, I looked at Santino Mirabella in the mirror. That gold silk jacket wasn't just shiny. It practically glowed in the dark. Placed against the black shirt and slacks, it looked kind of sharp. In the inside breast pocket of the jacket was a wallet with complete ID for Santino Mirabella, and even a couple of family photos and a carry permit. I was in the real estate business the way Al Capone had been in antiques. There were also two thousand dollars in hundreds and fifties, several credit cards, and a phony driver's license. In a box on top of the dresser were a black snap-brim hat, a pair of gleaming black dancing shoes with brass-tipped tassels, a black leather shoulder holster with elastic back band, and a nickel-plated S&W Model 29 hog leg .44 revolver loaded with hollow points.

I checked the makeup on my face. I had reproduced it almost as well as Julia's effort. I was a different person, at least on the outside. I had an urge to go down to Beverly Street and lean on a few merchants for protection. I remembered to put on the gold chain. As I was putting on the jacket and adjusting the hat on my head, I heard the hangman shouting. Rushing to the door, I ran out into the hall and toward the circular staircase. "Pop?"

"I got it! Joe! I found Santino! I got you, you goomba sonabitch!"

By the time I got into the music room, the hangman bowed and held out his hand toward the TV. Captured in a freeze frame was an image of the *bella figura* himself: Joe Mantegna as the stylish middle-management Mafioso, Joey Zasa from *Godfather III*.

We worked on the character for about an hour. The fourth time we ran the Joe Mantegna parts of *Godfather III,* we kept watching the movie until the end.

In bed, as I was just starting to fall asleep, I remembered who the picture of Nathan Sunday looked like. I'd just seen him on TV with the mayor. Nathan

Sunday looked like a young version of Anderson, the Police Academy chaplain.

That buzzed my head so thoroughly I couldn't sleep. I had to take my handheld and work my way back to sleep by going through the evidence inventories from the crime scenes in South River, Magena, and Baldwin. I compared junk mail found at the three crime scenes until, from sheer boredom, I dropped off to sleep.

WILD CARD

I jerked awake from my dream: rocketing down the steeps in the dark, chasing after the Sniper, suddenly running out of snow, twisting and bouncing from boulder to boulder, splashing blood on the rocks. My hand was grabbing beneath my pillow for Fido as my cell phone on the nightstand rang.

I collapsed on my pillow and waited for a breath. Lifting my head, I glanced at the clock. Five fifty. Every muscle I had ached.

The phone rang again. I grabbed it and punched it on. "Yeah."

"Death, Torio. I'm going to kill you the same way you killed the Rizzo brothers—"

"Thank you," I interrupted. "You have reached the number for Assholes Anonymous. Congratulations on this your first step in getting honest with yourself. At the tone leave your name, address, and asshole size, and we'll be happy to send a truck by as soon as a vehicle large enough becomes available. *Beeeep!"*

I listened for a moment, but the only sound appeared to be something gurgling or gasping for air. No message. I punched off the phone. "I guess he isn't ready yet."

The smell of pancakes cooking downstairs pushed my maunderings aside. I moved over to the tank next to my desk near the double windows and put some fish food in for Jaws, the goldfish Dock had gotten me while I was in the hospital. The fish wouldn't eat with me watching. I could turn my back for thirty seconds, look again, and all the food would be gone. But not with me watching.

"What is it with you?"

282

The fish just looked at me out of the side of the tank, moving its fins and tail just enough to hover and keep an eye on me, its mouth opening and closing. I turned away, held it for a count of five and turned back. The fish hadn't moved.

"I see a light breading, some parsley, and a squirt of lemon juice in your future."

I left the blinds pulled and went downstairs for another early breakfast. Before I left for the Tower I checked in with Breadloaf/North Valley Detectives. The slug dug out of the tram sign didn't match either the Roemer hit or any of the attempts on me. Either two citizens had been simultaneously moved to launch careers as spree snipers, using Lt. Roemer for their season opener, or the shooter was going through high powered rifles at the rate of one per day. Whether he was buying them, borrowing them, or stealing them, that was conspicuous consumption.

One more thing. I had told no one that I had decided to go skiing. I went on the spur of the moment. The first person who knew I'd gone skiing was the woman at the lodge who sold me the lift ticket. I was being tailed and by someone who really knew what he was doing. He either traveled with skis and an armory or he notified someone who did. It could be either Riggs or Sunday, I decided. They were both biathlon stars. Remembering Aunt Cella advising me to always ski with those who were better at it than I was, I had to laugh. That I had done.

Kieffer had a dental appointment first thing, so I drove in alone. On Eighteenth, the Mazda's right front dropped into a cosmic pothole, throwing a hubcap and slapping whatever was loose in the MX3's radio over to the other side, the radio working for the first time in over a week. After collecting my hubcap, Delbert McClinton sang about a girl named Rita who, when she bailed on him, stole his ragtop, left it in the middle of a desert, and burned it down to the axels. It made me think. At least Cherie hadn't burned my MX3. Instead, she'd had her Rottweiler eat it. Which led to thinking about women, Winnie Hewitt, whales in August, and Annie Oakley out on Stanton Circle who was going to boil my bunny. That night we were going to begin fishing for GQ, the Sniper still a big question. I believed GQ and the Guardian were one in the same, the Sniper a different person. If GQ wanted to kill me and the Guardian wanted to protect me, I wondered who would win? I had a sudden itch to upgrade my life insurance.

I got Clair Turner to try and connect up the Sniper to rifle thefts and sales in the state, and asked her to do a discrete overview of such weapons in police and evidence room inventories in local jurisdictions. Already done, she said. All weapons matching those used by the Sniper sold in the tri-state area during the past year, 2,721 of them, were in the process of being accounted for. Admirable efficiency, but a big old goose egg all the same. I turned to my desk. The mail inventories I'd gone through the night before as a sleeping exercise began itching at me. I couldn't think of any good reason for the itch, but couldn't think of any good reason to ignore it. I went down to the evidence room and checked out the mail inventories for the Booth Street scene and the material we had grabbed up from Chief Poleman's evidence room in Baldwin.

Juna Salvati's mail and Lacy Salvati's mail had things in common: both had bills from Big Ed, their respective water departments, occupant flyers from Sears and Price-Rite, catalogs from Bloomies, Sundown, Pottery Works, Lamp Heaven, and Victoria's Secret. Both the vics had made the guaranteed gozillion dollar super prize cut from Publishing Clearing House's Board of Judges: You are already a guaranteed winner, blah, blah, blah.

I picked up one of the Victoria's Secret catalogs and leafed through it, bemoaning once again the ascendance of crotch floss panties. Someone must've thought the high cut things looked sexy, but they just looked like forever wedgies. Uncomfortable and hardly anyone looked good in them. On women, I much preferred the off-the-hip low-cut panties from back in the 'Seventies, like the ones Gina Fusco had been almost wearing in the shot Winnie Hewitt had flashed at me on our lone night out.

The order form was missing from Juna Salvati's copy of the catalog. Going to Lacy's Victoria's Secret catalog, her order form was also missing. The inventories in the data base from Magena, Philadelphia, and Boston weren't that detailed, so I burned up three hours on the phone going through the mail inventories with truculent evidence clerks and police assistants in all three jurisdictions. When I was finished, I wasn't certain what I had.

All of the female vics received the Victoria's Secret catalog. The order forms were missing from all of them. Although one or more order forms were missing from each set of the other catalogs, only the Victoria's Secret catalogs all had their order forms missing.

After making a note in my handheld, I sat back and mulled it over. UPS? Beware of Big Brown? Federal Express? None of the delivery services delivered on Sundays, but if UPS knocked on the door on a Sunday morning, would the typical person be suspicious or sleepily figure he got the day wrong?

Perhaps it was someone from Victoria's Secret itself. Some pervert working in their catalog delivery warehouse who finally went ditzy after twenty years fondling millions of ladies undergarments. Hubert McDrool, four hundred and seventy pounds, greasy tee-shirt, and a fuchsia tattoo of Bill Clinton on his butt. But, if I was Juna Salvati, naked save for a bathrobe, would I open my door to let in Hubert McDrool, especially if he was aiming a peek-a-boo teddy at me?

But what if it was some incredibly stunning model wearing Victoria's latest breast-plump and crotch-pinch? Would I open the door? "Yeah, if only to find out what she was doing standing in the snow in her underwear holding a submachine gun."

This was going nowhere.

On my desk was the report Clair had put together on Nathan Sunday, graduate of Yale, roommate of William Riggs. As soon as I saw the picture of Sunday's mother, Angela, I sat forward, every nerve trembling on the surface. The doubts were gone. I didn't care if all nine justices of the U.S. Supreme Court were the ones supplying Sunday's alibi, Nathan Sunday was GQ.

Dock came in and sat on the edge of my desk. "I smell wood burning. What you thinking on, Joe?"

"That is our boy."

"GQ?" Dock looked at the picture. "What makes you think so?"

"Look at the photo of his mother." I tapped my finger on it.

Dock took the photo from my desk and stood up to examine it. "Hello, Juna. Hello, Lacy. I'll be damned. I think you're right."

"That is our boy, Dock. I can't prove it, I can't crack his alibi for the Pastore-Fusco killings, I don't know where he is, I don't know who he is now, and I don't know how he looks when he comes calling. But he is GQ."

"That's a lot of gaps."

"Yeah. Has anyone tracked down William Riggs yet?"

"Clair's on that. He's a sometime lobbyist in D.C. for the trial lawyers, but as far as anyone there knows, he's out at Heavenly skiing. The South Lake Tahoe PD is trying to track him down."

"Skiing?"

"That lit you up."

"You heard about that little thing that happened to me up on Breadloaf last night?"

He nodded. "That's why I never took up Alpine skiing. You people are much too fussy about who gets to ski."

"Okay. Riggs is out on the top of City Hall waiting for Sunday's tip-off that I'm leaving the garage. Pow."

"So?" urged Dock. "Who knew you were going to go skiing last night?"

"No one. I didn't even know until I went."

"Make any calls? Radio? Cell phone?"

I shook my head. "Nope. I just went. The Sniper's tailing me, Dock. Either he or an accomplice. He's tailing me and I can't see him. Awful hard to miss a tail if you're looking for one."

"What about getting you out of the line of fire, DiMaggio?"

"No point."

"Keeping you alive would be one point. You got to admit, between GQ and the sniper, everyone seems to be ahead of us at every turn."

"Either the guy isn't trying to chase me off the GQ case or he is. If he isn't, we aren't doing anything but making me a better target by putting me on something else. If he is trying to chase me off the GQ case, then having him throwing shots at me every so often makes him more vulnerable, right?" I nodded toward my screen. "Dock, I was running through the mail inventories earlier and did you know that all of the vics we know about were getting Victoria's Secret catalogs?"

"It's not exactly an exclusive mailing, Slugger."

"All of those Victoria Secret catalogs have their order forms missing," I added. "Not something I can say for any of the other catalogs they had in common."

Dock stuck out his lower lip. "That sounds almost like a clue. You think GQ delivers digestible panties?"

"Still working on that." I pushed aside the school photo of the very young Nathan Sunday from Nat Turner Elementary in East Branch and reached for his Yale yearbook head shot and faced it toward Dock. "Age this face fifteen or twenty years and who do you have?"

Dockery studied the image, frowned, then cracked a smile. "Perry Como." He frowned again. "Jesus. Chuck Anderson, the Police Academy chaplain."

"That's how it struck me, too."

Dock studied the picture again. "I don't know, DiMaggio. Chuck Anderson? He's a minister. Besides, he's a lot darker than this and he's got straight hair."

"A little makeup and a do? What about a minister coming to your door Sunday morning? Would you let him in?"

"What? Aiming a 9mm fully automatic bible at me?"

I tossed the photo back on top of the file. "I asked Clair to run the chaplain anyway." Dock picked up the photo and studied it some more while I continued. "Everything I can dream up in my head eventually falls apart when it comes to opening that front door. These killings don't take place in West Bluff or Glenn Heights. There you could wear blue jeans, hang a piece of aluminum foil out of your pocket, tell 'em you're a cop, and they'd buy it and welcome you in. These killings, though, take place in rough neighborhoods where the residents are a little more than just street smart. Yet every time the doorbell rings they simply open the door and say 'Hi. Come on in. Welcome. Glad to see you. Happy you could drop by.'"

A shot of Vince Polizzi's right hand was up on the screen. I pointed at the nickel-plated .44. in his hand. "Did CSU find anything on the gun?"

"No blood. Not a trace. It's brand new. He'd only had it four days when he died."

"So, he didn't have his gun with him when he dropped. Who could be at the door that Vince would come downstairs without calling his boys and without bringing his insurance?"

Dockery pointed at the telephone. "Why don't you call his papa and find out? And remember, you're on the air."

As Dock wandered in the direction of Ward Staples and Clair Turner, I thought calling Scozarri sounded almost like a good idea. I checked the data base, found Don Scozarri's number, and punched it in. A strange voice answered, *"Yeah?"*

"My good man, Det. Sgt. Joe Torio here, South River Major Crimes. Could you put your boss on the line?"

"Joey D! Hey, DiMaggio! This is Tommy Zerilli. You heard-a me?"

"Why, yes. I read the mug books once in awhile."

Zerilli burst forth with an evil chuckle. *"Yeah. Ain't exactly art studies, though, huh? Joe, I just want to say, good job on the Rizzo brothers. Clean. Too bad about the shoulder. Hang a sec—so to speak."*

Without waiting for a response, the receiver was placed on a hard surface as the sounds of footsteps faded in the distance along with the button man's laughter. Thomas Zerilli, a.k.a. Tommy Zee, a.k.a. Tommy Zap, soldier for the Scozarri family, suspect in a pile of his own killings. His method depended on the moment. He had been linked in the past to killings involving piano wire garrotes, hand guns, automatic weapons, and his sentimental favorite, the old-fashioned ice pick. I had gotten from the man the highest compliment one professional hitter can give another on his or her work: *Clean.* Target zeroed out, no legal complications, collect the payoff, and home free.

"Just the kind of thing to perk up the old résumé," I muttered, suddenly recalling Dockery's warning about the don's line being tapped. Tommy Zerilli was quite accomplished. He was good with any weapon and he could follow a rabbit on amphetamines over a floor covered with cornflakes and not be detected. Vince Polizzi being gone would mean a promotion for Tommy and he was the first to report Vince's death. Would he go to all the trouble of copying GQ's pattern? He could get the information.

There was still GQ opening that door. I'd seen Tommy Zee before and I couldn't see Juna Salvati or anyone else opening her door to that face under any circumstances, particularly not if he was toting an Uzi. Another phone was picked up while the original receiver was hung in its cradle.

"Joe DiMaggio Torio," began a rich voice edged with decades. *"That little visit you took to the Rizzo brothers all by yourself. You know, if you weren't so blue, you could be a friend of ours."*

Friend of ours. A heavy euphemism for that old gang of mine. "Don Scozarri—"

"What can I do for you, detective—Joe, if I may?"

"That'll be fine, Frank. I'm calling about your son, Vincente." A long silence.

"Okay. First, tell me something, Joe."

"If I can."

"This police investigation into the death of my son, is it serious?"

"All investigations are serious."

"That lump on my head isn't because I just fell off the turnip truck."

"I'm after a killer, Frank, and this killer has taken out a lot of human beings besides your son. This investigation is as serious as it gets, and you might be able to help. That's why I'm calling."

"What do you need? I heard you found Vince's two boys dead."

"Yes."

"Their families will be taken care of." There was a long silence, then a puzzled tooth sucking sound. *"I hear you and my PI are going on the hook to bait this guy."*

"You know an awful lot more than you're supposed to know, Frank."

There was a sad chuckle followed by a silence. *"A little something for all the taxes I pay. Man-to-man, Joe, what are the odds of you and the Powers girl getting this guy?"*

"I don't know."

"Ah. A man who can say he doesn't know."

"It's not much of an accomplishment."

"You would be surprised at how few know how to keep their tongues from speaking more clearly than their brains are thinking. Even so, a wild guess would be better than nothing."

I changed the receiver from my right ear to my left. "It's not like going after a button, or somebody doing it for money or revenge. The guy we want is after something different, something in his head and heart, something we can only guess at right now. That makes catching him a bigger question."

"I thought the Feds know how to crack these guys. You know, Joe, those suits you used to see on the tube all the time. Ressler and that other guy, Douglas."

"Profilers."

"Yeah. They can even tell you what kind of hat the guy will have on when you catch him."

"That's how it works some of the time. The Bureau has a profiler working with the Magena PD and another working with us, Roz Kagen. Julia Powers and I are profiling the victims, though, and we know a lot about the victims."

"Yeah, bait. You paint a big bull's-eye on your backside and wait for someone to stick it to you."

"It doesn't sound real smart when you put it like that, Don Francesco."

"Joe, I want to tell you something about Vince." The don's voice was very serious. *"I'm not being disrespectful to his memory, God rest his soul. About Vince. He was on, charged up, ready to go all the time. Never far from his piece. Understand?"*

"I understand."

"I wouldn't want to say anything against him, you know, but Vince was not bashful about letting it fly. He was a little too quick, if you know what I mean. Got in plenty of trouble with some people I know."

"This isn't necessary, Frank. I already know GQ is dangerous."

"I want you to understand how dangerous. Vince is dead, which makes GQ more dangerous than Vince, and there's no one more dangerous than Vince—than Vince was. I don't know what it is, but this killer has one hell of a big edge. He has that chopper already out, cocked, aimed, ready to fire. His finger is on the trigger. That's the only way he could've taken Vince."

"That's why I called, Frank. As near as we can determine, Vince was downstairs and didn't have his gun with him when he was cut down."

"Impossible."

"Well, I guess that answers my question."

"What question?"

"Who would Vince answer the door to wearing only pajama bottoms, leaving his gun upstairs?"

"Demi Moore," the don answered automatically. In a second he laughed a little at his own answer. *"Demi Moore, Andie McDowell, Sophia Loren. What were some of the others?"*

"Movie stars?"

"Vince spent all his time in the movies when he was a kid. Movies and the TV. Al Pacino. He'd stand on burning coals with his hands tied behind him to meet Al Pacino. Steve Martin. Tom Hanks. Jeanne Triplehorn." The don chuckled and I listened as the old man touched a memory. *"Even if she was wheeling up a Gatling gun in full view, he'd open the door to Jeanne Triplehorn."*

"Something else, Frank. Vince's bodyguards, how would Pitone and Casale have covered Vince?"

"Usual way, outside. One in the car out front in full view to let them know Vince was covered, one in the shadows as a wild card."

"We haven't found the car."

A muttered curse bordering on grudging admiration came from the don. *"This guy is a ghost."* There was a long pause. *"Joe, maybe you can help me understand. Vince had enemies. Who doesn't? But, cut him to pieces? I had to tell his mother before it went out all over the news. She just stares at the walls now. And that girl, Juna. Such a sweetheart. Vince brought her to dinner here. What a lovely girl. Why does this monster do such things? What does it do for him?"*

"Frank, have you ever hated someone so much you wanted to wipe them out of existence? The person, his family, everything he's ever accomplished, even everyone's memories of him?"

"Yes." Don Scozarri paused, but did not identify the object of his hatred, presumably perforated and filed. *"But we had history. What you people been telling me, GQ probably didn't even know Vince. Never even met him."*

"The killer knows himself, though. What GQ does, Frank, that's how much he hates himself."

Don Scozarri's voice filled with that famous temper. *"If he hates himself so damned bad, why don't he eat a gun?"*

"Because he doesn't think it's his fault."

"What? Fault? That doesn't make any sense!"

"You've put your finger on it, Frank."

"He's crazy?"

"A special kind of crazy."

"That means he gets off?"

"No. If we get him alive, he won't be found legally crazy, even if he is. If we get him, he won't get off."

"That's good."

"No. That's not good, but that's the way it is." I tapped my finger on the edge of the desk. There was one last thing. "Don Francesco, when Tony Rizzo stuck that knife in my back, he said to me, 'Dago Frank says, "Hi."' What did he mean?"

The Don thought about that for awhile. *"It's smoke,"* he said at last. *"Lot of heat on the Rizzos since Nicky Batts caught it. Maybe the Rizzos tried to push some of that heat in my direction and things got out of hand. I want to send a message, Joe, I don't use Tony Rizzo for a messenger. Trust me on this."*

"Would you know who tipped us off that the Rizzo brothers would be in their place that night?"

"I asked around. I was kind of curious myself. It wasn't any of my people."

It sounded right. "Okay. Thanks. That's all I have."

Long silence. At last, he said, *"This job you and Julia are doing. To do this you got to have 'em like grapefruits. Too bad you carry that badge. You would've made a good soldier."*

"I would've made a terrible soldier, Frank. The first time I got an order I thought was wrong, I would disobey it."

"That happens in the cops?"

I laughed at that. "As a matter of fact, it does. In some circles I'm not considered a very good cop. Got in plenty of trouble with some people I know."

The don chuckled at that. He knew we had a listening audience. *"You wouldn't sell your loyalty, Joe. That's what I mean. It's not like it was."*

"Nothing is, Don Francesco. I'll let you know if anything breaks."

Touched, perhaps, by the use of the title of respect, he simply said quietly *"God keep you."*

I hung up and looked at the receiver for a moment.

"Lot of smoke coming off the top of that head." I turned around and Dockery was grinning down at me.

"I guess my 'mobster' label is having a tough time covering the conversation I just had."

"Tags are useful things, Joe—on toes down in the morgue."

"I wonder what it's like to be a parent and have your child die before you do. And to die that way." I looked up at him. "Dock, Don Scozarri knows just about everything there is to know about the case, including our little bait job."

"He has very long, very well-paid ears."

"Ward Staples, all the locker room uniforms, and Don Scozarri—I wouldn't be surprised if the pancake flipper at Benny's Waffle Palace knows Julia and I are climbing out on that hook."

"Julia thinks GQ will try for it, even so," said Dock. "I just talked with her."

I nodded. "I get the feeling we're being drawn into something." I tried to push it with my mind. "Dock, if he just wants to show up the police—prove that he's cleverer, faster, a step ahead, he's already done that. He might not show at all."

"Or he might come and kill everybody," said Dock. "That'd sure show us up."

"What if what he wants is to die himself?"

"Suicide by cop?" said Dock. "Is that how it feels to you?"

"The only feeling I have is that Sunday wants to be understood." That was the first time I'd put that in words, even to myself. "Yeah. He wants us to know him. It's like he's preparing us for something—maybe his own execution. But, before he goes, he wants us to understand him."

Dock rubbed his chin, glowered at a pencil in his hand, and gave a three hundred pound shrug. "Joe, have you gone through the stuff Clair's collected on Nathan Sunday yet?"

I leaned back in my chair. "Some of it. I looked at his college grades. My Aunt Cella would've loved him."

Dock folded his arms across his chest and dropped one of his massive hams on the edge of my desk. "The no backup aspect of your plan is not sitting well in either Finn's office or the Chief's. Capt. Finn is toying with sneaking in some backup without you and Powers knowing about it."

"He'll kill us all, Dock." I looked up at him. "Look at the score. Including the backup, fourteen bodies that we're sure of. Three of them, Vince and his bodyguards, weren't amateurs. Do we really need to run that experiment again? We go in naked or we don't go in. I expect you to warn us if there's anybody out there so Julia and I can take the night off and go see a movie. Hear me? I expect the warning to come right from you."

"I'll see what I can do."

"I mean it, Dock. You've got to keep Finn out of it, and Kieffer, too. Put backup in there and we're all dead."

Kieffer stumbled into the bullpen and took his seat, his lower lip hanging dead from Novocain. He looked dead, too. "What'd you do, Kieff," asked Dock, "get a root canal through the top of your head?"

The answer sounded something like "Whap fwouba rooda gu."

"One other thing, Joe," said Dock. "Mike Ijumaa's made a mess out of CSU attempting to duplicate the dining room spatters. He did it, though. He couldn't duplicate how far they came down the wall when he's facing the table doing actual back swings, but he can when he faces the wall and uses a one-inch brush to do cast-off. What do you make of that?"

I sat there thinking as Kieffer asked, "Whuv ziz aw 'boot blut 'n' black sing tails?" While Dockery updated Kieffer, I drifted into where I hoped GQ's head was. It wasn't that we should believe that the killer had done all this in the heat of passion. It wasn't a warning. It wasn't a message to us at all. That spatter across the ceiling was a message, a reminder, to himself to die and, perhaps, take the universe with him. There was something I wasn't seeing. I had the feeling there was something GQ wasn't seeing, as well. I was confused. I just hoped that GQ was at least as confused. In fact, I was counting on it.

THE SUNDAY PAPERS

I found in the middle of Nathan Sunday's file a posed B&W photo of a young man wearing Army summer officer's dress. Sharply tailored uniform, smooth tie with an even knot, polished brass. He had a face that looked almost like a young Perry Como, but without the smile. Crossed flintlock pistols insignia on his uniform: Military Police.

Another photo taken with his roommate at Yale, William Riggs. Riggs looked kind of like Capt. Finn, mainly because of the prematurely thinning hair. Other than that, he could have been Sunday's brother. A senior class photo of Sunday from the St. George High School *Dragon*. Good-looking kid.

The next was a photo of teen Sunday standing next to his mother: Angela Domenica, South River prostitute and drug addict, three arrests in East Branch, no time served. I closed my eyes and let her image play with the images of all of the other female vics.

Angela hadn't known who her son's father was. Between beatings and worse from her boyfriends, dealers, and tricks, her son made it into school: Turner Elementary in East Branch on Seventh. When young Nathan was in the seventh grade, he was arrested and charged with sexual assault by a 12 year old classmate. The charge was later dismissed when the girl, Cassie Rubino, confessed to teasing the boy by pretending to seduce him. He punched out her lights and she cried rape. See pictures.

Cassie Rubino, before and after. The after shot looked like she'd gotten a facial with a bucket loader. The before shot was the young-girl take on that face the killer and I both loved. Billows of wavy black hair, those dark smoky eyes.

What a heartbreaker, at least until she decided to break the wrong heart. Cassie simply had no idea just how much fun she was making of the boy when she made her play-pretend pass at him. What a mountain of humiliation.

Picture of the eleven year old Nate. Handsome kid. Long straight nose, flared nostrils, black hair so tightly curled it was almost kinky, deep brown eyes, high cheekbones, and pale skin.

All of those heavy tribal labels were issued and picked up in grade school, and there was something wrong with Nataniele Domenica's set: Black/white; lover/son; punching bag/human being; gifted student/geek; welcome mat/killer. It left him lost—feeling betrayed. Angry. Mad at the system—at a lot of systems: Family, social order, education, law, church, universe, the gods.

Disposition of the Cassie Rubino case: a recommendation by the court that Cassie Rubino and Nataniele Domenica both enter counseling—different counselors. No record of compliance by either. Instead, Nate and his mother were moved uptown to a single family ranch in St. George by her current honey, one Harry Douglas. There was a copy of a clipping from the *Herald* concerning the opening of the new Gold Medal Mart in South River way back when. And there, in the center of a ribbon-cutting ceremony, was Harry Douglas, grinning from ear to ear with all of his chins. Next to him was a very trim woman in a very smart suit, carrying that beautiful face, wide with smiles. There was a boy there, as well, who held his face as an expressionless mask.

Douglas had been well-to-do, dynamic, generous, and a man with plans. According to the article, that was his fifth super mart, including the ones in Baldwin and Nelson. He had site bids in for West Shore, Exeter, and Magena. I had shopped in Gold Medal Marts my whole life. Stereos, toothpaste, blue jeans, power tools, groceries, CDs. If you didn't need frills and wanted to save money, it was the place to go.

Douglas's first wife had died of cancer some years earlier, his children had all graduated from college and moved away. And Harry was rich, lonely and in love with a stunningly beautiful whore.

God, what a rescue fantasy for a generous, trusting old fart. He looked like Dick Cheney and believed that every problem had a solution if you threw enough effort, love, and brains at it. The money didn't hurt, either. In exchange for stroking his fantasy, he decided to save Angela Domenica and her unhappy son, Nathan.

St. George was upper middle, big lawns, new houses, the largest and most beautiful park in the city, St. George's Cathedral, and St. George High School, academically one of the best high schools in the city, public or private. To help put the Turner Elementary experience behind them, Harry Douglas had Angela and Nate change their names from Domenica to Sunday. He put Angela into Riverside General Rehab again, this time for the full two months. After that, he installed her in his new house and gave her nothing to do but be happy and go to A.A. meetings. Nathan Sunday was given his own room, made to stay out of his mother's bed, and enrolled in Covington Junior High School across First Street from the Police Academy campus.

A man who can build a fortune out of ideas and hard work was not afraid of problems. Harry Douglas mistrusted "head workers" and believed that the best therapy in the world was hard work. Angela developed an interest in painting, gardening, and the PTA. Nate excelled academically and athletically, did high school at St. George, gold-star grades, letters in football and track, member of the weight-lifting club, rifle team, and drama club. Harry made piles of money and set up a carpentry shop in the garage where he indulged his desire to work with his hands.

Fully funded trusts were set up for Angela and for Nate, and, in the fall of Nate's senior year, there was even a petition of adoption filed with Nathan Sunday's name on it. Harry Douglas had decided to make Nathan Sunday his son, officially, which involved a new will, as well. Nate would inherit an equal share of the Gold Medal millions along with the other Douglas children.

Nate was to be class valedictorian, Angela had been elected secretary to her A.A. home group, and Harry installed a new radial arm saw, drill press, and wood lathe in his woodworking shop toward his plan to design and build his own furniture. Everyone was looking at happy endings.

One day soon after, Harry, not just old but old fashioned, proposed marriage to the beautiful Angela Sunday. She said yes and passed on the happy news to her son. The next day some unknown assailant beat Harry Douglas like a rented mule. Although hospitalized, Harry would not file charges. While in the hospital, however, Harry was beaten again. Again he refused to file charges, although he did hire a couple of bodyguards to watch his room until he healed and was discharged. After Harry Douglas was released from the hospital, he vanished at something approaching the speed of light. Petition of adoption withdrawn, old will back in effect, Harry moved to Magena, unlisted number, big high fence, goons on the gate, nothing left of him in South River but an echo. Plenty of money left behind and the house. Within days, though, Angela was back into drugs. There was one final boyfriend who moved into her bed, Battaglia family leg-breaker Bobby Naples, see picture.

I looked at the image of Bobby Naples. Taken at a party, the picture showed a man with his fists on his hips, his head thrown back, his lower lip thrust out. Al Pacino doing John Gotti doing Benito Mussolini. The Vince Polizzi, Renzo DeStefano, Paul Roa prototype. "Hello, Sonny Mirabella."

I pulled up the Naples file on my terminal and printed out a shot of him in formal dress at the wedding of Nicky Batts's daughter where he was doing security. Another shot of him at the reception. An autopsy photo, his face relaxed, eyes closed.

Police reports suggested that Bobby Naples died as the result of a mob hit. He had gotten two in the hat with a .22 and had been found on the east river shore next to the tank farm below the confluence of the South and East Branch rivers. Three days later, in front of a neighbor and fellow A.A. who had dropped by because she hadn't seen Angela at meetings for awhile, Angela Sunday took the guard off Harry Douglas's brand new radial arm saw, rotated the blade for ripping, locked it in place, turned it on, clasped her hands together, and pulled her wrists slowly through the blade, cutting off both hands. The neighbor freaked and fainted, and when she came to, the saw was still running, and Angela was dead. See picture.

Across the garage ceiling and down the one wall were spatters of Angela Sunday's blood cast there by the still rotating blade of Harry's saw. There was a break in the spatter directly above the saw, made by the mounting arm blocking the spatter. The spatter also didn't come down the wall much lower than the edge of the table. The spatters were much fainter than the picture Nathan Sunday painted across the dining room ceilings of his victims. Sunday, though, was painting it the way he saw it when he came home from school that day.

Graduation from St. George, a possible return visit to South River between his junior and senior years at Yale, college graduation, a momentary appearance in the Army, and then he fell off the face of the planet.

When I closed the file and threw it on my desk, Kieffer was looking at me. "How's the tooth?" I asked him.

"Novocain wore off." He nodded toward the file. "Dock says you like Sunday?"

"You get a look at his mother?" I tapped on the file. "We need to get that Army head shot of Sunday's computerized, and aged." I thought for a moment. "Yeah. Then we can put it on the net and tell everyone that the one person in the world Nathan Sunday won't look like is that."

"Don't you think he has to come up for air once in awhile?"

"He knows what's in that file—every page of it—and he knows we have it. Is Harry Douglas still alive?"

Kieffer shook his head. "Heart attack in 'oh-one. Never recovered."

"I guess that would've been too easy." I got to my feet.

"Where're you going?" he asked.

"A couple errands, then I pick up Julia and spend the evening at The Score sweating over a bevy of hot nudes."

"A dirty job."

"If you do it right."

"Joe."

"What?"

Kieffer's gaze was fixed on me. "If you do everything right, GQ visits seven tomorrow morning. Still going in naked?"

"Yeah."

"And you still have that sniper dogging you."

"Unh huh."

"Are you at least going to pack some firepower with you?"

"Like what? Rocket propelled grenades?"

"Look, Joe, I can do a po' ol' homeless junky that has gotten Golden Globe awards."

I looked into those big browns. He really was worried. "No backup, Kieff. Didn't Pitone and Casale's corpses say anything to you?"

His eyebrows went up in mock injured pride. "They were mere hoods. I am a law enforcement professional."

"Getting cold feet, Kieff?"

He frowned. "Aren't you?"

"I could flash-freeze chicken nuggets between my toes."

"I wish you'd reconsider the backup. We can figure out something."

"No backup, Kieff. Take your tooth home and have Miriam fill you with warm milk and tuck your tootsies into bed. No volunteers out there lurking in the shadows, please, and I don't care if they do a fantastic slippery elm. They'll get us all killed."

DREAMS

When I left the Tower just after noon, I took enough tail revealing turns to open my own pretzel factory, damn near causing an accident on Oak as I made a traffic-light scraper coming off Eleventh. Nevertheless, I kept trying to look in four directions all at once as I worked my way out to the west end of St. George Division. The Police Academy was located on the old City College campus which spread out over the four blocks bounded by Vogel on the north, Alexander on the south, and Orchard and First. I parked on First and got out of the car, nervously scanning the rooftops.

Not much traffic at that hour and no one visible on the rooftops except a Direct TV guy putting in a dish. The street there was wide and lined on both sides with craggy old maples, the new snow still on the branches. Wide sidewalks, the edges piled high with snow, fine old homes with the smell of wood smoke thick in the air. The Police Academy still looked like a college campus. No fences, no security worth the name.

Across First Street, in the middle of the block between Pine and Alexander, was Covington Junior High, where Nathan Sunday did his first academic years in St. George. Compared to Turner Elementary, Covington was plush: well-tended athletic fields, field houses, ivy-covered classroom buildings, paths, lawns, shrubs, and a strictly enforced dress code. When I was in the eighth grade and on my school's junior rifle team, we'd done a couple of matches at Covington. Next to their students we had looked like bums.

Two blocks north and east, I pulled up in front of two fifty-one Oak. There stood the home purchased for the Sundays by Gold Medal Harry. Melissa Vebles, the sixtyish mother of the bride to the current owners, Brian and Carlotta Newton, was home. Once I flashed my ID and said I was with Major Crimes, Melissa Vebles immediately connected me with the GQ investigation and guessed as well that GQ had once lived in her daughter's and son-in-law's home. In seconds I was filled with tea and brownies and covered with questions. Melissa was practically having an orgasm. She was ready to marry me when I told her I had once met Lydia Jenks. A real true crime fan.

When I could eat no more brownies, she showed me whatever I wanted to see. I took the complete tour. The ranch was laid out in a sprawling horseshoe around a fair-sized backyard swimming pool, covered for the season. Five bedrooms, huge living room, TV room. Three car garage, Sunday's nightmare all cleaned and painted away years before. I wondered what I was doing there, and the simple truth was that I was following a feeling that appeared to be leading me nowhere.

After pulling out of there, I turned south on Sixth. The expanses of the park to the left, St. George High School on the right, it's main building constructed from black granite. Athletic field to the right. I tried to remember the fight that had happened there, but couldn't bring it back. I vaguely recalled an unpleasantness I had at the Covington School, too: Sharp words that didn't amount to much more than shoving and a couple of bloody noses. I did seem to get into a lot of fights. It was always between me and the bullies, though. Jane Draper's imagined knighthood notwithstanding, I wasn't protecting the helpless from the bullies as much as I was wreaking vengeance on them for the beatings I'd suffered myself.

At St. George Street, I took a left, then a right onto Seventh. As I approached the Seventh Street Bridge, I caught a red light at the East Branch River Road. While I waited, I looked at the bridge across the East Branch River, a plain concrete roadbed with green-painted steel pedestrian railings. The river itself there was maybe a hundred feet wide. Crime scene tape stretched from the abutments to the scrubby trees on both sides, crossing the paths that led down to the banks below. Across the bridge rose the bleak red brick walls of Nat Turner Elementary School. It sat there looking like a factory hiding an enigma. In my gut I knew that on some level, this was where Nathan Sunday found his beginnings.

The light changed and I crossed the bridge beneath which Vince Polizzi's dead bodyguards had been found. At the other end, I turned right, found a parking place in the crowded school parking lot, and turned off the ignition. I watched the traffic in my rear-view window for five full minutes, then got out and entered Nathan Sunday's alma mater.

Inside the main entrance, the familiar odors of chalk dust, cafeteria slop, boredom, and desperation instantly yanked me back to King Elementary in West Beverly, with all the anxiety that went with it. I worked my way through the students heading toward their busses. One student, the only one who didn't appear to have rivets in his head, pointed the way to the school office: "On the left, halfway down," he said.

My thanks hung in the air as the boy turned and rushed for the main door, disappearing into the river of shouting kids. The din eased as the high-ceilinged hallway emptied. By the time I was in front of the school office, the hall was almost deserted, the distant shouting from outside rapidly fading. As I put my hand on the doorknob, I glanced down the hall. On the wall at the far end was a mural in the center of which was an image of a raggedly-dressed dark-skinned man who bore a startling resemblance to Wesley Snipes. As I came closer the inscription beneath the mural became clear: Nat Turner. It was dated Nineteen Sixty-four and signed LH.

As I came even closer, I could see the image was flanked by framed pieces of poetry written by students from Turner, one poem for each year since Nat was put up on the wall. Most of the pieces were the usual adolescent paeans to school, world peace, green stuff, football, and horses. One selection, though, caught my attention. It was a free verse composition titled "Dreams."

I have no control in dreams,
No judgment no sense
Of what is right wrong or possible.

Lucid dreams are when in a dream
You know you are in a dream
And in a dream that is lucid you are in control
And can do anything you want.

I tried many times to lucid dream,
But I only did it once.
I did not kill anything or heal anything
Make or take a life or do any of the things
They or I would call my obsessions.

Instead I stretched out my arms, looked up and flew
High into the sky, through the clouds, into the light.

It was attributed to ND. I pulled out my handheld and began copying it, goose bumps on my skin because I was plagued by the feeling there was something wrong with the words.

"Excuse me. I'm Mrs. Powell. Can I help you?"

I turned to see a fiftyish woman, steel gray hair streaked with white. Tall, sharply dressed in a foam green suit. For some odd reason she reminded me of Cher. I pulled my badge and showed it to her. "Det. Sgt. Torio. South River MCU."

"Major Crimes?" Her carefully lined eyebrows arched. "Det. Sgt. Torio—Aren't you the detective who was involved with the Rizzo brothers?"

"Only for one evening."

"Quite an evening," she said with a bit of a wry smile.

"I'm in MCU now. How long have you been employed here?"

The eyebrows went up even further. "Am I a suspect in that couple killing that's all over the news?" She grinned. "If you take me out of here in cuffs, detective, you will completely rejuvenate my standing among the students."

I smiled back. "Perhaps we can work something out. How long?"

"I have taught English here at Turner since September of 'Seventy-two."

I nodded toward the end of the hall. "ND was a student of yours? Nataniele Domenica?"

"Yes, although he called himself Nathan." Significant silence. "Is he dead?"

"Why would you ask that?"

"Victim or killer. With Nathan there were never any middles. Frustrating child in a frustrating situation."

"As far as we know, he isn't dead."

"A suspect, then?"

"How about letting me ask a couple questions."

She grinned. "I apologize. Being a teacher is like reading only the opening chapters to thousands of novels. There are a number of those stories I'd really like to finish. I suppose you know about the Cassie Rubino fiasco."

"The false rape charge."

"That poem you were admiring was written two years before that. God knows what additional twist the Cassie episode put on Nathan's rather unique worldview. He was the best student I ever had, detective, and I couldn't wait for him to leave." She studied me carefully then pointed at the writing on the wall. "See anything wrong with that?"

"It doesn't seem arranged right and something's missing, isn't it?"

She studied me then gave me a nod of approval. "Wait here." She turned and went into one of the classrooms. When she returned a minute later, she was carrying a thick manila nine-by-twelve envelope. She tapped it and said, "Follow me."

I followed her to the other side of the school office. There she pushed open a door that had TEACHERS LOUNGE stenciled on it in yellow. On the other side of the door was a moderately large room painted in institutional green and illuminated by indirect neon. The usual ignored employment, safety, and NEA posters on the walls, a big erasable school calendar with games, assemblies, and exams marked out in multiple colors, kitchen facilities, eight tables with folding chairs, and a threadbare couch with a scattering of upholstered chairs completed the decor. She offered me coffee that had been boiling for the better part of the school year and a seat on the couch.

Seating herself beside me, she opened the clasp on the envelope and pulled a wad of lined papers onto her lap. She leafed through them, pulled one from the wad, and handed it to me. It was the original of the poem on the Nat Turner wall:

dreams
i have no control
in dreams
no judgment no sense
of what is right wrong
or possible

mother is in my dreams
faces and faces
dark eyes
shadow moments

there is always blood
unrealistic amounts
all from unlikely sources
the things i want
the things i need
never fulfilled

lucid dreams are when
in a dream
you know you are
in a dream
and
in a dream
that is lucid you are in control
and can do anything you want

i tried many times
to lucid dream

                                    but only did it once

                                 i did not kill anything
                                      or heal anything
                                     make or take a life
                                  or do any of the things
                                             they or i
                              would call my obsessions

                                         instead i flew
                                       up into the sky
                                     through the clouds
                                         into the light

"No upper case. All the lines on the wall start with caps, are justified to the left, and are combined out of a couple of the original lines."

"No punctuation, either. You see, detective, the English Department runs the poem-of-the-year contest."

"And English teachers are English teachers?"

"Everheart certainly was. The head of the department then, Wilfred Everheart, insisted on dropping those verses, punctuating it, combining the lines to fatten them up, and finally started each line with an upper case letter because it would be on the wall and, hence, a model to which the other students might aspire."

"Is that a quote?"

"My, yes," she answered with a wry smile. Looking down at the paper, she slowly shook her head. "Everheart. What a fucking drone. Once it was put on the wall, Nathan never looked at it or acknowledged that it was his, and would, in fact, deny it when asked."

I pointed at the envelope. "Are those submissions for the poem-of-the-year wall?"

"Only one student's work. These are Nathan's writings from the fifth, sixth, and seventh grades." She put "dreams" back on the stack and held it on her lap with both hands. "Detective, there is some stuff in here that's going to make you wonder why I didn't do anything about Nathan Domenica."

Unconsciously patting the envelope, she nervously bit the inside of her lower lip then said, "Calls for help. English teachers get them all the time. 'Daddy drinks and beats Mommy,' 'My brother is in my pants and wants me to help him deal drugs,' 'I'm being destroyed out here, teacher. What do I do?'" She fixed on a loose thread on her sleeve, as her eyes misted over.

"After talking Nathan into it, I personally took him to our school counselor, Wally Breck. Nathan continued to see Wally the rest of the time he was here, although Nathan's writings became even darker." She faced me, her expression suspended between anger and sadness. "Eleven years ago we learned that Wally had been soliciting sex from the boys. In some cases in exchange for money or drugs, in other cases represented as parts of therapy." She handed the envelope to me. "I hope you can take Nathan alive, Det. Torio."

"Whatever happened to Wally Breck?"

"Over thirty boys were ready to testify against him. He copped a plea, got eighteen months, and served three. Then he found Jesus and a job at a summer camp counseling young boys. Before he could be prosecuted for his camp rapes, he disappeared one night and was later found in the river below the Interstate bridge. It was ruled a suicide."

"Do you think it was a suicide, Mrs. Powell?"

Her gaze leveled on me as she issued a grin devoid of all mirth. "Gee, I certainly hope it wasn't, detective. Don't you?"

Outside, as I was about to get into my car, I looked over the roof and saw a footpath made by the snow being packed down on the edge of the scrubby little soccer field next to the main building. The path led toward the bridge. I tossed the envelope into the car, locked it up, and began walking the icy uneven path. By the time I followed the trail through the trees and down to the bank next to the bridge, my shoes were filled with snow. Crime scene tape was stretched all over the place, essentially attempting to mark out the area beneath the bridge. No blood that I could see, but it didn't take much to figure out that Pitone and Casale had been killed elsewhere and then dumped here.

Despite the dusting of blown snow beneath the bridge, I could see used condoms, syringes, a busted crack pipe, cigarette butts, a few pieces of flotsam left on the concrete during higher waters. As the trucks and cars crossed above, I could hear the tires whining and an expansion joint slamming bam-bam-bam-bam-bam five times in quick succession every time a heavy vehicle left the southbound lane.

Here was where that certain element at Turner Elementary came to smoke their recess joints, earn a little drug money selling sex to budget-conscious pedophiles, marking time until the system moved them up to junior high. The water in the river was mostly open, but Pitone and Casale had been left beneath the bridge to be found. Like Vince's Rolex. Like Vince's gun. More messages: *Don't tread on me.*

I pulled out my cell phone and called Cab Nelson. He answered on the first ring.

"Nelson."

"Cab. Do me a favor, will you?"

"We also wait who only sit and serve. Let me have it, Joe."

"I need a search on every crime in the records that took place on, beneath, or near the Seventh Street Bridge from about 'Seventy-one until 'Seventy-seven. Include anything that might have been washed out of East Branch and found on the banks or south of the confluence of the East Branch and the big river."

"'Seventy-two was when Charlie Bonner was killed under the Seventh Street Bridge. My case."

"Who was Charlie Bonner?"

"A bum. Knife stuck in the back of his head, clothing stolen. When we ran his records we found that Charlie had been in the Navy. Corpsman in Nam. Got wounded saving a bunch of Marines and was discharged with the Navy Cross, a disability pension, and an addiction to morphine. Case is still open. You got something?"

"Maybe. When you have that information, I'll be at my pop's place in a couple of hours."

I folded up my phone as another truck rumbled overhead, that expansion joint going bam-bam-bam-bam-bam!

Back in my car, I turned at West Five Corners and took the broken end of Beverly down into the Zone. I didn't know what Charlie Bonner did to earn that knife in the head, but sincere altruists among addicts, as elsewhere, were scarce. The one thing the boy could not abide was a hypocrite. If Nathan Sunday, indeed, had been the one who had killed Charlie Bonner, he would have been only seven or eight years old. But, as we know, eight-year-olds can and do commit murder.

I took a right on Frank Street and stopped at number 270. There wasn't enough left of Nathan's first home even to hold up the numbers. It was a hole in the ground. Fire. Not recent, judging by the amount of garbage. When I looked into the fenced off cellar hole, amidst the burned timbers and snow covered piles of ash, bags of garbage, and weeds, I could see the top of an old forced hot-air furnace. On the remains of the furnace, one of the upper duct connections had a length of dirty blue ribbon tied around it, with six or eight additional inches hanging loose.

Ducts, ears, and ribbons. Something borrowed, something blue.

I did a quick scan of the street, then went through one of several gaping holes in the fence and climbed down into the burned wreckage, paralleling what looked like snowed-in tracks. I reached the furnace. Moving around it and stepping up on the remains of a fire-blackened beam, I looked down into the duct opening tied with the blue ribbon. Inside, resting side-by-side on a bed of frozen charcoal were two Glock 17s, the preferred concealable sidearm of the Scozarri family. I called it in, and while I waited, I pulled off the serial numbers and called them in. The guns belonged to Vince Polizzi's bodyguards, Ed Pitone and Paul Casale, both of whom had South River carry permits.

Well, you can't just leave firepower like that lying around in the street. We in the blue fellowship wouldn't want such weapons to fall into the wrong hands. Some punks might take them, cause a lot of damage, maybe kill a couple of cops. Officer Sunday could not allow that. Sunday was practically shouting that he was a police officer, yet he was never what he appeared to be. It was like that bonehead freshman logic joke in college. True or false: Everything I say is a lie. It was beginning to make sense, too.

THUNDERBOLT

Pop, Caitlyn, and I were sitting in the music room on the big sofa, eating popcorn, a gentle rain falling outside, watching a video tape of *Fargo,* usually one of my favorites. In the movie, the kidnappers were pulled over in Brainerd by the state trooper, Pop looked at me and pointed toward the ceiling with his thumb. "You got your homework done?"

"As much as I can."

"What about tomorrow, Joe?"

"The quiz could be a bear." One of the bad guys in the movie put a bullet in the trooper's head and the cop pitched flat out on the pavement. Caitlyn put the movie on pause.

"If you two are going to talk, I'm going to make more popcorn."

We both mumbled something between a "What?" and a "Thanks."

I nodded and faced the hangman. "If things break the way we want, Pop, we get him tomorrow morning. If not, I'll have to work tomorrow night, too."

"Joe, are the Sniper and GQ connected?"

"Maybe. I think so." I looked at Pop. "I think the Sniper is a guy named Riggs and he's trying to scare me off. Maybe he wants all cops off the case, but I'm certain he wants me off."

"Joe, no jokes. How dangerous is this thing tonight?"

"GQ is a morning man. The main danger tonight is being bored to death. I'm going to spend the evening in this sleaze pit called The Score watching some bad dancing to bad music followed by a dull night in a fleabag waiting for morning."

"If he shows?"

My eyebrows went up. "Well, in that case, tomorrow morning might get a little hairy." The hangman raised a single eyebrow at me. "Okay, it'll have whiskers on it a yard long," I said as I stood. "It's time to get dressed."

He reached out a hand and placed it on my arm. "I guess telling you to be careful would be stupid."

"Actually, it sounds like a pretty good idea." I placed my hand on his. "I'll say good night on my way out, Pop."

In my room, with the themes from *Fargo* playing quietly downstairs, something began nagging at me. On my handheld I paged to an image of the master bedroom upstairs, the one with a shot of the lunch on the floor. "Yeah." Punching in the MCU number, I caught Kieffer in. "Kieff. You remember the barf on the bedroom carpet at Juna Salvati's?"

"Yeah, the burglar's."

"It isn't the burglar's. I think it's GQ's."

A beat of silence. *"How do you figure?"*

"Did you ever step in your own puke?"

A long, introspective silence. *"Can't say I ever did."*

"The burglar stepped in it but the lunch belongs to GQ."

"The lab report might be in. Maybe we can find out where the chunkee eats. —Oh, before I forget, Stan Brooks tracked down Sunday's high school shooting coach at St. George. Monte Sullivan."

I leaned forward in anticipation. "And?"

"I checked him out. Mr. Sullivan is a resident of the Riverview Living Center in West Shore. He's not exactly doing dimensions, but he is dribbling his oatmeal. According to the coach, Nathan Sunday was one hell of a shot, looked like Perry Como, and was gay."

"Gay?"

"That's not the exact word he used. Something about a three dollar bill, I believe. Sullivan says that Nathan Sunday never dated any girls, took drama, wrote poetry, and he made the logical assumption."

"I don't suppose assuming he was sleeping with his mother would've been logical. Was Sunday on the junior rifle team at Covington?"

"Why?"

314

"I got in a shoving match there once. I might have met Sunday."

"I'll check. Remember what the shoving match was about?"

I shrugged to myself "It's a little vague. It was over a girl, I think. Some older girls were giving this fat kid a hard time and I had some words with them. One of those girls tattled to her boyfriend and after the shooting match he and two of his friends, and their girlfriends, were waiting for me." I thought on it, remembering the back of the athletic building that had the rifle range in its attic. Giggles from the girls, sneers and rather rude remarks from the three boys. A few other students watching. It'd turned into a bit more than a shoving match. After I broke the second boy's nose, the third begged off. *"None of my business,"* as he put it.

One of the boys watching the conflict called me "Percy Blakeney," laughed, and walked off. I thought it was a slam and ignored it. Years later from the movie I found out that Percy Blakeney was The Scarlet Pimpernel. I tried to remember that boy's face, but there was nothing there. "Hear anything new about Riggs?"

"Still missing."

"Did you read those poems?"

"About half of them."

"What do you think?"

"Joe, I think you are about to come in second in a contest that has no second place. Ease off the feeling thing, okay?"

"Let me know if you get anything we can use out of those poems."

Punching off, I glanced once more at the mirror, draped the scarf around my neck, put on Santino's topcoat, checked the .44, holstered it, and looked around at the room where I had spent most of my childhood. All the time growing up, I couldn't wait to get out of that room. Now I wondered what my chances were of returning.

For once, Jaws was happily swimming around in his tank, feeding. He would eat for Santino the mobster but not Joe the cop. "Think fish chowder," I said, turning out the light. I left the door open behind me.

□

The night was windless, and overcast, the streets black and cold. I pulled the pimpmobile up in front of Margarita Azzurro's place on Randall, just north of the Egypt Hotel. It was a two story structure separate from the neighboring houses, in need of a couple of coats of paint, but in better shape than most of the other places on the street. I turned off the ignition and climbed out of the car.

The once white panels on the front door were cracked and peeling. It was no cartel hatch. You could poke through it easily with a .22. It had a peephole. No stairs. There was only a granite stoop, damp from rock salt melting the ice. As I stood beneath the light, I pushed the doorbell. The door opened almost immediately. I opened my mouth to do my hey baby, Santino-is-on-deck bit, but before I could utter a syllable, I was struck dumb.

Before me was a ravishing raven-haired beauty clad in a cloud of blood-red chiffon. Standing inside the open door was dancer Margarita Azzurro, olive-skinned, eyes smoky with mischief, ruby lips all framed with clouds of black curls. At the center of the red chiffon she wore a red sheath that glittered with the occasional rhinestone, or diamond for all I could tell. Every sight that stroked my retinas had me thinking about moths, volcanoes, vats of pheromone, feathers, and tangent curves. All I wanted to do was dive into those lips.

"That's good," she whispered.

"Whuh?"

"The struck dumb with lust impersonation. That's exactly the right note."

"Note," I repeated automatically. My chest actually hurt. I felt lightheaded and almost forgot to breathe. What filled my eyes was what I had been searching for my entire life. She reached out a delicate hand and placed it on my arm. Electric currents ran from her fingertips throughout my entire body. In a thick Georgia accent she said, "Why, ah declare, Mr. Mirabella. I do believe you are smitten."

Smitten. Yeah. Burned by the thunderbolt, and it's a god damned wig.

She nodded toward her coat. "Come on, it's chilly."

After a moment I regained motor control of my limbs sufficiently to grab the coat; a silky black thing that did little either to keep her warm or conceal her figure. As I helped her on with the wrap, inhaling her scent, I could feel my heart moving into v-tach.

"Hey. Hey, Santino?"

"Uh?"

She looked up into my face. "Are you all right?"

"All right."

"Don't overdo it, okay? You're supposed to be in love, not brain-damaged." She leaned back her head, gave me a kiss on my lips, then looked into my eyes. "I go on in a few minutes, darlin'. Come on or I'll be late. You look real good."

She turned and walked out the door. I stared after her, the raspberry taste of her still on my lips, until I realized that the door was open and we had just completed act one of our production for the benefit of the street. I followed her, numbly pulling the door shut behind me.

ADAGIO

The Score was a low, white-stucco building without feature save an entrance and a sign carrying the name in bold black script high to the left of the door and back lighted with indirect deep-purple neon. Even with the chill, there was a considerable line in front of the door. The men and women were well-dressed and apparently well-heeled.

"Drive by the line slowly," she said as she looked toward it, her face close to the side window. She waved. A number of hands waved back. "Pull into the lot around back and park." In the rear of the club I pulled into an empty parking space and turned off the ignition. "We go in, happy, arm-in-arm," said Julia. "Once inside, we kiss, and you get busy with your hands."

"My hands?"

She studied me for a second. "Hands? Remember? Back seat of the car? High school?"

"You want me to feel you up?"

"Jesus, has your Cub Scout troop reported you AWOL, yet?" She examined my face. "Look, Santino, if you can't handle a little T&A tickle in front of a few stage hands, you're in for a real treat when I lay that lap dance on you."

"What are you talking about? The customer isn't supposed to touch the dancer. No physical contact. It's the law."

She was silent for a long time. At last she fixed that dark, smoky gaze on me and placed a hand on my cheek. "He can be watching us at any moment. Right now, in the audience, backstage, remote security observer, anywhere and everywhere. And we don't push his buttons unless we are lust wagons: passionately in love.

318

We don't just love each other. We are passionately in *lust*. That's why you make like an octopus from the second we leave this car and every second we're together afterward. I can't get enough of you and you can't get enough of me."

"I got to admit the job description appears to be the fulfillment of every fantasy I ever had when I was fourteen—except for the performing in front of an audience and the guy shooting at us—"

With her left hand she reached, placed a hand on the inside of my right thigh, and slid her fingers up to my crotch. Something cardiac blew a gasket. "Come on, Santino. Get out and open the door for me."

I got out, rearranged a few things, stopped by Julia's door, pulled it open, and held out my hand. "C'mon. You'll be late." She took my hand, stood up, and moved a step away to allow me to close the door. Once the door was shut, she looked up and touched my cheek. I took her in my arms, kissed her on her mouth, and grabbed two handfuls of buttocks. We pulled back our heads for a moment and she frowned slightly. "You're messing up my lipstick."

I cocked my head toward the stage entrance to the club. "Then fix it, Rita."

"Margarita," she corrected.

"I like Rita."

"Okay, Sonny. Anything you say."

"You got that right."

We walked toward the door, my right hand firmly planted on her right buttock, my fingertips noting the firm heat beneath each digit. She placed her right hang on top of mine. Once inside the door, the driving sounds of "Night Train" vibrating the walls, I removed her coat and we kissed. Grope, pet, and caress. As I was again finding it difficult to breathe and stand straight, she whispered in my ear, "The gold necklace is a nice touch."

"It was given to me by a woman who had my car eaten by a dog," I whispered back.

She let her head fall back slightly as she laughed out loud and looked so beautiful I could have gobbled her up on the spot.

When we parted she took her coat and ran to the dressing rooms. I watched her receding form until she was out of sight, turned, and waited for the blood to reach my brain and feet simultaneously. Slightly recovered, I went through a side door that came out in the bar.

Two women were on stage occupying the center of a spotlight, a very healthy and respectably endowed pair with short hair, small waists, and big everything else. They might have been wearing some kind of patch here and there—the law required them—but I couldn't make them out through the haze of smoke. I pulled off my overcoat and draped it over the first hostess I saw, a red-haired maiden favorably decked out in The Score's uniform: black shorts, French knit hose, garter belt, and four-inch heels. From the waist up, imagination be damned.

She smiled at my unabashed stare. "They can make grown men weep."

"You'd be amazed at the little things that make me cry."

She grinned widely. "You need to upgrade, sugar. My name's Bonnie."

"I'm Sonny. Hey, Bonnie." I nodded toward the coat and hat. "Check these in like a doll, okay?" I held out a fifty, saw her face light up, and forced myself not to ask for change as I turned and went to the bar. Fifty dollars to hang up a coat and stow a hat. Santino lived in a different world.

I found an empty stool at the bar, sat on it, and placed a couple of C-notes in front of me. The bartender, a beefy completely bald ex-prize fighter whose combat pictures from his younger days adorned the wall behind the bar, came over and said, "I'm Max Bender and this is my place."

"Hi, Max." I held out my hand. "Sonny Mirabella." We shook hands.

"What can I get you, Sonny?"

I looked the man straight in the eye and said, "Gimme a Dr Pepper."

"Dr Pepper? What, you mean like Forest Gump?" One of Max's hairless eyebrows went up. "Promise you won't get mean?"

I leaned forward on the bar allowing the bartender a peek at Sonny Mirabella's artillery. "My mama always said that life is like a box of forty-fours. You never know who you're goin' t' hit."

While Max went to get my drink, I spent a guilt-ridden moment feeling ashamed. Not about being Sonny Mirabella. About enjoying being Sonny Mirabella. Not loud, but obvious. Brassy, self-centered, arrogant, flashing money, unabashedly wallowing in his appetites, and so in love he could wear mouse ears.

I took a table next to the runway, mere feet away from the dancers. I knew how Sonny Mirabella would act. No out-and-out wolf howls and paw pounding, but he would leer, nod, wince, and moisten his lips at particularly stimulating moments. A constant smile. Sonny was a smiler.

The one on stage was announced as Dandy Bernal. Dark, flashing eyes, incredibly white teeth. Perhaps it was only work to her. Nevertheless, she gave the appearance of industrial-grade estrogen fighting to break free. I didn't recognize the piece she was dancing to. Some New Age tinkle-whistle thing, which didn't matter anyway. Sonny Mirabella wasn't there to listen to the music. Dandy was a doll: compact, the muscles of her legs defined just short of hardness. She was wrapped in a white feather boa that snaked about her head, between her legs, and around her body with an agility that made it seem alive. I lost myself for a moment, aching to become that feather boa, when I remembered that Sonny Mirabella wasn't there to see the girls. He was there to see one particular woman. Tearing my gaze away, I sipped my Dr Pepper and glanced over the patrons sitting at the nearby tables.

Blond guy looking away from me, tapping on his table top with manicured fingernails. Dark, quiet guy with heavy dark-rimmed glasses, his teeth fluorescing in the black light. Old guy, sharp dresser, Daddy Warbucks with a honey at each elbow, wringing every last drop of testosterone out of life. Another quiet one, a wrinkled refugee from the financial district, his eyes glittering as he peered out of the shadows. The professional woman sitting next to him was taking all the advantage she could from the dim lighting. The cheap quality of the fur coat she had around her shoulders was why they called it putting on the dog.

The music came to an end, I faced the stage and saw Dandy Bernal standing, head back, arms outstretched, her feet on some kind of turntable set into the stage. As her compact beauty twisted slowly around, the applause filled the hall and the lights faded to black. Before I could attach meaning to the memory, a familiar piece of music began. After only a few melancholy notes, I recognized the piece. Albinoni. *Adagio* in something or other. A sad, dreamy, steady rhythm. It hushed the crowd and as a single spot slowly came up and picked Margarita Azzurro out of the darkness, I felt something inside my ribcage crack.

Her left side. She was wrapped into a ball that slowly loosened, petal by graceful petal, rising to become a beautiful, glittering, writhing, sensuous blossom.

"Drool on the stage," I whispered to myself. "I can do that." The image of her up there, every curve, every shade, every motion, every expression— I ached to put my hands on her, to bury my face in her, to take her like a drug and rut my way to oblivion.

Somewhere I knew it was all illusion. Feathers. *Great* feathers. A wig, some contacts and paint, a little practice—a lot of practice. She had become what GQ hated and loved the most in the universe. She was what GQ needed to bring the love to in his special way. To me, holding a boiling glass of Dr Pepper in a paralyzed hand, it felt like the vital missing part to a barren existence.

As I watched the divine blossom on the runway open, flow, writhe, and caress itself, the memory of the state's silly no-touch law evaporated like a spring mist in the Sahara. What did a bunch of mossbacks and soccer moms in the legislature know about what was going on in the center of that stage? I didn't care if it was only a disguise, a lure cooked up to trap a psycho. The universe became very small, very clear: there was nothing left for me but to possess, fondle, encompass, and devour the dancer.

Not a sound from the audience. I could feel a silent wave of super-heated lust coming from behind me. Winnie Hewitt's quest to understand male desire drifted by in the shadows. A few photons strike a room full of retinas, a few low-frequency sound waves vibrate a few hundred ears, and trillions of neurons take it from there, drawing each man, and probably more than a few women, down imaginary corridors into fantasy-stoked imaginings.

I watched the curve of her hip beneath the almost invisible thread of her g-string, how each line of her torso drew my gaze deeper into her groin. Halfway through the *Adagio*, the vision danced slowly down the center stairs, the spotlight stalking her like a hungry wolf. She moved through the audience, the patrons still as tombstones, glistening eyes devouring her as she drifted by. A barely noticed couple of bare-chested ghosts vanished with my table and drink, and then she was bending over me, straddling me, her hands on my shoulders, the tips of her bare breasts brushing my lips as her hips twisted and turned above my lap.

It was as if we were the only two beings left in a universe of sound, light, and touch, my hands on the outsides of her calves, an inferno beneath each palm, I slid my hands slowly up her legs, to her knees, her hips, her waist, her breasts where I cupped them and kissed each in turn, then let my hands trail back to her waist, then to her buttocks, around her thigh with my right hand until it was between her legs, and then, as the *Adagio* died and the room faded to black, a roar of applause filled the room as she said into my burning ear, "Good." For a split second we broke contact, and when the lights came up, she was gone.

"Attaboy!" bellowed someone nearby. I turned and saw an overweight man sitting with two other men at the next table. They were still applauding and I realized I was still standing. With a wave at my fellow lust addicts, I forced a grin, and resumed my seat. As the applause subsided and grew again to welcome the next dancer, I was grateful that as a child the hangman had bought briefs for me instead of boxers. If I'd been wearing boxers, the entire club would have been treated to a sight that could have threatened small villages.

The next dancer, a slender thing in crotch floss moving jerkily to "Susie-Q," didn't have my attention at all. Two more shadows moved by, leaving me a table and a fresh Dr Pepper. Somehow I tipped them. Hundreds each, probably. I didn't give a damn.

Margarita's whispered "Good" in my ear was an undeserved compliment to my non-existent acting ability. When we moved together, there had been no thought, no volition. There had been only the vision, the feeling, the living fantasy. Every time I closed my eyes, the vision of her came back, the smooth gliding moves, the feel of her, her touch, her scent—

Julia.

Actually, Margarita. It was, after all, a part she was playing. The next step of the plan called for sitting in a booth and groping for an hour before we left for the house. Before then I was certain my aneurysm would have a blowout. I sipped at the Dr Pepper thinking that seeing her, dancing with her, was like the night Pop hanged Kirby Flagg. From that moment on I knew the world would never be the same.

The Adagio. Something about that piece of music. It ate at me for a moment, then my imagination drifted back to that face, the mischievous eyes, a scent like hot musk, her waist moving without flaw into those hips beneath my fingertips—

"Sonny?" I opened my eyes. Margarita Azzurro, back in her red sheath and chiffon, was looking back. "Are you all right, Sonny?"

I stood, took her in my arms, looked deeply into her eyes, and said, "I think I have kinks in my hemorrhoids."

"What?"

"Let's get out of here."

Her slightly confused expression melted into absolute infinite bedroom. As she moved in and kissed me, her hand stole between my legs and gave me a little stroke. "Something for the tiger?" she asked in a stage whisper.

A few chuckles came from the nearby tables. It was all for the benefit of a possible member of the audience, but I was having vapor lock. I held her at arm's length. "Let's go. I don't want to miss Santa. I'm expecting a bottle of little red wagon polish."

"Isn't it a little early for Santa?"

"Believe me, baby, everything is moving up."

After a pause, she nodded her assent, and with my arm around her, I led her to the hat check window. After a fist full of bills to the topless hat-check girl and more for the doorman and the attendant who brought the car from the back lot, we drove away.

"Okay, steamboat, what gives?" she demanded as I turned the pimpmobile onto Wilson, missing the left turn onto Houlihan.

"I don't know if I can do this."

"What are you talking about? You are Sonny Mirabella—"

"That's right!" I interrupted. "I *am* Sonny Mirabella! From my heart attack right down to my cramped shorts. Look, I'd tell you what all this is doing to me, but I'm not all that eager to be laughed at. This—"

I cut it off as a new issue jabbed suddenly into my awareness. I nodded toward her and motioned for her to move closer. As I turned the radio on, the heavy metal middle of "Starbust'" by Dragonfruit filled the car. I parked the pimpmobile in front of an adult video and strip arcade called Twin Peeks, leaned over, put my arms around her, and placed my lips next to her ear. "Bugs," I whispered.

"Huh?"

"Bugs. In the car. In our clothes. Possible?" After a moment, I felt her nod her head. "Baby, I don't know what's going on," I said out loud. "You know what it's like. Things on my mind."

"Sure, Sonny," she said out loud.

"I just want to get back to the pad." I laughed loudly. "Honey, you have me turned on so hot right now I'm getting blisters."

"It's okay, Sonny. Let's go get something to eat then go home and see if we can find something interesting to put on those blisters."

As I pulled into traffic and made the light for the left down Frank Street, Margarita took a cell phone out of her tiny handbag, punched in a number, and talked in such a low voice I couldn't hear. When she was finished, she put the phone back in her bag and cuddled up to me. "I called Mom to wish her a happy birthday. She says 'Hi.'"

SMALL DREAMS

After veal at Pella's on Randall, it was well after midnight by the time we pulled up the car at Margarita's place. The house was all lit up. A tubby man with bad clothes and a six-pack was on the stoop waving his hand. Just as I was about to make a comment, Margarita put her hand on my arm and said, "My god, it's Mr. French, the landlord. I wonder what he wants."

French. The ex-cop on Julia's gate. Good makeup. I nodded in his direction. "See if you can get rid of him, okay, baby? Our plans don't involve sitting up all night sucking down cheap brew with your landlord."

"I wanted him to fix something. Maybe he finally got around to it."

"Now? In the middle of the night?"

"Be nice." She pushed open the passenger door and slid out. "Mr. French!"

Bill French was playing an inebriated landlord with a bad body and avuncular feelings toward his pretty young tenant. As I climbed out of the Cadillac and closed the door, French slurred his way through an imaginary list of things he had fixed. Julia invited him in for just one beer.

Inside the cramped vestibule, the door closed behind us, French kept up his act as he dropped the six-pack on the chair next to the hall telephone stand and pulled out of his overcoat an elongated silver loop. He went over both of us, concentrating on the clothing I had checked at the club and the handbag and clothing Margarita had left in her dressing room backstage. As he worked, his wand moving a silent instrument needle rather than beeping, I looked around.

It was a one-story existence inside Margarita Azzurro's house, the second floor being a separate residence with its own entrance on the side of the building. Living room, big screen TV, lots of tapes. Behind it, a bedroom and bath. On the opposite side of the house, a combination dining room and kitchen, another bathroom, and two small bedrooms, one of them being used for a home office. I glanced at the telephone table and pushed around the several pieces of unopened mail, doing a quick-and-dirty inventory.

There were the usual opened bills, unopened prize promises, catalogs—one of them Victoria's Secret. I checked: order blank missing. Burpee catalog. My eyebrows went up at the startling cover of the Harsh Mistress Leather and Chain Catalog. It appeared to be a photograph of a superhumanly endowed lass dressed in a shoelace and a full set of skidder chains. Amazing what can be done with a couple of gallon-bladders of silicon.

"Mammaries are made of this," I sang, not entirely beneath my breath.

"Keeping abreast of things?" asked Margarita. Those eyes were looking at me, a wry smile on her face.

I laughed and put down the catalog. "Simply tat for t—"

"Turn around," said Bill to Margarita, stepping on my line. After a brief funeral, I turned to the next item.

Bank statement, also opened. Menu from the House of Chung with a coupon for almond boneless chicken. What about someone delivering take-out? A Micro-Uzi in a big bag full of Hunan chicken. Wouldn't work. Not even Vincente Polizzi could ingest MSG at seven in the morning. I dropped it and went through the rest of the mail.

A bill from the Hair Restoration Institute. The envelope was addressed to one Bruno Fortier, the boyfriend. I checked the wastebasket. Half filled with junk mail. Before I could get to it, Bill French dropped the wand on the stand. No bugs.

"I went over the place, princess," he said to Margarita. "It's clean, at least electronically speaking. Mo is snoozing in doorways nearby. He's seeing if he can spot any passive equipment or lurkers. We can't guarantee we'll catch everything, but you'll be okay inside if you keep your voices down. I'll stay close."

"No, Bill," said Margarita after glancing at me. "You go home to your family. Santino and I can hold down the fort."

"Whatever you say."

She placed a firm hand on Bill French's hefty shoulder. "I am not kidding. If you spend the night skulking out there in the shadows, you or one of your men are liable to either spook our boy or get killed. Neither one is acceptable."

"Julia, it will be no end of trouble if something happens to you."

"You don't catch fish by chasing them away from the worm, Bill. C'mon. We've done this before."

"Not with anyone like this."

"Go home, Bill. Thanks, but go home. Take MacGregor and whoever else you have out there with you." She glanced at me for a moment and added, "And if you see a police officer out there pretending to be a garbage can or a juniper bush, tell him to go home, too."

French studied her, his face deadpan, then he closed his eyes and shrugged. "I'm gone." He glanced at me. "I'll check the Caddy for bugs tomorrow at your place." He took the six-pack from the chair, handed it to me, and left, closing the outside door behind him.

I looked down at the six-pack. Cold Dr Pepper. Julia walked up and stood close to me, her Margarita coming back in full form. She held me close, her hands on my buttocks, and nodded toward the back. "Go take a shower, Sonny," she whispered.

A cold shower right then was the best advice I'd gotten all day. There was a robe in the bedroom. While Margarita made some tea, I stripped, put on the robe, and headed for the shower.

The window in the bathroom was opposite the clear glass sliding doors enclosing the tub and shower. The door unit looked as though it had been recently installed. Not a speck of soap scum on the glass. No shades on the window, no frosted glass. Through the window, over the tops of the tenements beyond, I could see the distant bright windows of a passenger train slowly heading south, the warning lights on the Cross-town flashing red. Except for a can of black bald-spot hair-in-a-can spray for men on the sill, the outside had a clear field of view inside the shower. The bathroom had been made into a theater.

Interesting problem: Even if they weren't the same person, both GQ and the Sniper, were peepers. Getting shot taking a shower might frighten my rubber ducky.

I stepped into the tub, slid shut the unusually heavy glass door, turned the cold water on full force, the thunder of the water rumbling on the thin fiberglass of the tub and stall. I stepped forward into the spray and gasped as the frigid water drenched my legs, my groin and my chest. As passion numbed, the pressure on the back of my neck seemed to ease.

There was a rumbling sound as though a powerful fan had just kicked in. A moment later a hand reached around me, hot breasts pressed against my back. "God, Santino, you're like an icicle!"

Her hand turned up the heat, as well as the water temperature. I shook my head as things went on the rise again. "Julia—"

"Margarita."

"Yeah. Margarita. I can't do this. It was near impossible when we—or at least, I—had clothes on. Now, this—"

"It's a dirty job, Santino, but somebody's got to do it."

"Yeah. Great. What if Sniper Sam decides to sling a shot at us in mid pantomime?"

She rapped on one of the glass panels of the shower doors with her knuckle making a dull thump. "Bulletproof. They were installed this morning."

I was about to make a remark about thoroughness and efficiency but she reached around me with soapy hands, and began rubbing my chest, my stomach, and finally that scrap of tortured flesh that seemed to have ruled my life for the past few hours. Lights exploded behind my eyelids as all perception became concentrated down south.

Feeling lightheaded, I turned and looked down at her. Margarita's hair—her wig—was in a black plastic shower cap. She looked at me, that veiled smoky look in her eyes. "Hold out your hands," she ordered softly. Like an automation I held out my hands, palms up. She picked up a blue plastic squeeze bottle of body shampoo and covered both of my palms. Putting down the container, she turned around and leaned her back against my chest. "Wash me."

"You don't understand. Stuff like this never happens to me."

She laughed a beautifully musical laugh.

As an odor of spicy flowers filled my sinuses, I slid my hands across her back, down to her hips, down her legs to her ankles. As I came back up, I slid my palms up the front of her body pausing as I placed a hand on each breast and felt the nipples, the flawless skin slip beneath my fingers. My hands developed lives of their own, moving as though the touch of her was a drug. There was soft laughter and she reached back, took that throbbing scrap of flesh, and placed it between her legs. "You're like a teenager," she whispered.

Bending forward slightly, she reached between her own legs with a soapy hand and stroked me. A fleeting thought: What was it I had said to the hangman about watching some bad dancing and spending a boring night in some fleabag?

I kissed the base of her neck, her ear, between her shoulder blades, the small of her back, as my hands slid down and around her hips. In a haze, as I turned my head, I glanced through the glass doors and the bathroom window. The train had gone. There was a steady light, possibly a reflection off a glass pane. Some building on Dixon. There were countless vantage points from which a peeper could be watching. If someone was watching, I thought, he must be eating off his own foot by now.

Steam. The water was hot enough to burn, but there was no steam on the window glass. The shower doors weren't fogged at all, not even water beaded on the panes. I looked to the ceiling and saw the source of the rumble: a powerful brand-new exhaust fan. Anti-fog on the glass. Bulletproof. Thorough. Julia Powers is thorough. Every move had been carefully scripted in advance, the bathroom theater rebuilt and equipped for just this performance. For a moment I tried to flog it into a resentment, but let it go. I was caught by something much more powerful than low self-esteem.

She changed places with me and rinsed. Bending forward, with one hand she grasped the water temperature control. With the other she guided me deep within her. I held her by her hips, plunged in, and the world flew into dimensions of electric touch and exploding color. All quandaries became as shadows.

Later, in bed, she was curled in the crook of my right arm while I mentally flogged myself with the she-loves-me, she-loves-me-not thing. What happened in the shower could have been faked, but we hadn't faked it. Not even a little.

Why?

Playing with the answer was a head trip. My arrogance would strut around the chicken yard, stick its thumbs behind its suspenders, and begin crowing only to have this enormous hatchet come down and chase it around the yard.

Yeah, see, I got this incredibly smart, fantastically beautiful, astoundingly talented and sexy multi-millionaire hot for Joe Torio—

Was that Hell I just heard freeze over?

The bedroom television was on, half an hour into Margarita Azzurro's tape of *Psycho*. Anthony Perkins was explaining taxidermy as a hobby to Janet Leigh. I wasn't paying any attention to the old favorite. Instead there was the enigma of Julia Powers stalking my mind. The cop in me pointed out that it was all part of the act. Serial-killer cinema. And there had been Ward Staples's caution about boiling my bunny, and right then my poor little bunny felt like it had been skinned, diced, and stir-fried. Absent-mindedly I lifted my left arm, reached above her head, and rubbed the scar on the front of my right shoulder.

"Don't pick at it or it'll never get any better," she said.

"My shoulder's all healed."

"I wasn't talking about your shoulder." She turned her head to the left and looked up at me. "You've been grinding gears for half an hour. Do you know when you're thinking like that you mutter?"

"I do not."

"I couldn't make out what you were saying, but you were definitely muttering."

"Talking to myself. Well, if I was, I'm not surprised," I answered. On the TV Anthony Perkins was taking down a picture in his room revealing the peep hole through which he had a forbidden view of unit number one and its occupant. I looked down at the living image of Margarita Azzurro. "Why are we watching this? Isn't this a Halloween movie? What time is it?"

"After one."

"Jul— Margarita, what was going on in that shower?"

She held her head back, the right corner of her mouth pulled back in an amused little smile. "Didn't that father of yours ever sit you down and give you a talk?"

"Yeah, great. All right. I can almost accept what went on at The Score. That was the job. That was for GQ, and you must've done a pretty good job of cranking him up, if my own reaction is any indication. But what happened back there in the shower was different. I mean, we weren't exactly miming our way through a love scene."

"No." She nodded, her expression vague. "We didn't."

"Well? Was it just an act? Maybe I'm old-fashioned, but I usually don't engage in gasket-exploding shower sex until the second date, on those rare occasions I make it to a second date."

Draping a lock of her black wig above her upper lip, she worked her eyebrows, crossed her eyes, and adopted a phony Austrian accent . "Zo, you findink it unpleazant, perhaps?"

I laughed, then forced myself to be serious. "You know I didn't. I just don't know what it meant."

"What it meant?" She wiggled her eyebrows. "It zort of eggzplained itzelf as it vas happenink, *jah*?"

It was like repeatedly pinching myself with a pair of Vise Grips to see if I was dreaming. Still, sometimes it's important to know the difference between fantasy and reality. "I want to know what I mean to you."

She pulled back her head and studied my eyes for a long moment, then she nuzzled her face into my neck. "Okay, Joe. I admit, things didn't exactly follow plan A — or plan B or C, for all that matters. See," she said, hesitating a beat, "this kind of stuff never happens to me, either." A long heavy silence. "I'm not sure what's going on with us." She looked at me, and as I teetered on the edge of those eyes, she said, "That dance tonight, Joe. That was our dance."

"Our dance?"

An eyebrow went up. "You don't recall standing, moving with me, touching me, kissing me? Should I fume my nipples for lip prints?"

My face got suddenly warm. "Yeah. Of course I remember. I don't remember what planet I was on at the time, but I do remember the dance. Every moment is burned into my brain for eternity. I think it crisped out some valuable stuff, like my telephone number and how to tie my shoes."

As I drew my left hand up her thigh to her waist, she reached up, and placed a hand alongside my cheek. "Do you believe in coincidences?"

"I'm a detective."

She nodded again, her lower lip pushed out. "Okay, then, what do you make of us?"

"Mystical forces? Pod people? Peyote? At midnight you turn into a pumpkin?" I closed my eyes, pulled her close, and nodded, the incredible feel of her down the length of my body as I whispered into her ear. "Okay. I don't know if it's me, or because I'm too far inside GQ's head, or what. But, right now, wig, contacts, and all, you are so close to my dearest fantasy it's creeping me out just a little."

She pulled back and looked at me, then snuggled back in. "Exactly," she said.

"Exactly? What, exactly? What do you mean, exactly?"

"I mean, exactly."

"Are you saying I'm the fulfillment of *your* big dream?"

She studied my eyes for a moment. "Is that so hard to believe?"

"You've seen my scars and my car, lady. You have no need to dream so small."

She propped herself up on her left elbow . "Listen to me with both ears, Joe DiMaggio Torio with the Rottweiler-broke car. I *never* dream small. You got that?" She jabbed a karate-straightened finger tip into my ribcage._*"Never."*

"Ow! Okay."

Janet Leigh was in the shower and the outline of Norman Bates in drag could be seen through the shower curtain. The Hitchcock violins were shrieking, the butcher knife was raised, and Margarita's hand slipped beneath the covers and began checking Santino's dipstick to see if there was any gas left in the tank. There appeared to be.

ALIBIS

I opened my eyes a step ahead of the Rizzo brothers, my heart thumping. The heat from Julia's back, her form visible in the dim red light from the clock, the sounds of her gentle breathing anchoring me to the moment. I studied the form beneath the covers on my right, her bare back and bottom snuggled against my side, the back of my right hand touching her skin.

"I can smell the wood burning all the way over here," she said.

"Sorry. Didn't mean to wake you."

"What are you thinking about?" she asked.

"You, of course. Are you thinking about something besides me?"

"No." She rolled over onto her left side, snuggled against me, her right knee moving up and across the fronts of my thighs, her left cheek resting on my shoulder. "Why did you call me Rita?"

"Who?"

"Back at The Score you called me Rita. Who's Rita?"

Confession time. "Rita Kwan. A girl I dated once back in high school, a cheerleader from Vadalia High." I told her about my prom and the famous ten-minute date with the most beautiful girl in the world. "I was so obsessed by her beauty, I would've become a stalker if I'd had the patience. I had one dance with her, then it was show-and-tell in the girl's rest room as a few of my lovely classmates filled in Rita on my father's occupation. Rita walked out, called her parents, and went home."

"True love?" she asked.

"My shrink says it's normal to have a fantasy ideal of true love in mind—or maybe she said it's normal for me. Anyway, Rita Kwan was mine until . . ." The thought faded into a morass of images: Juna and Lacy Salvati, Gina Fusco, Sophia Giarusso, Angela Sunday. "She was my ideal until this case. Until you—or Margarita Azzurro. I'm not sure which. I don't suppose you'd agree to stay made up like that for the rest of your life."

She sat up, turned, and placed her head in my lap, her knees beneath my right arm. I put my hand on her thigh and drew it softly across her bottom to her waist. "I'm guessing we're both going at this a little fast," she said. "And there are other considerations."

"Like what?"

"Like our visitor?" She nodded toward the window. "It's getting light."

I slid my hand down to her hip and across her bottom again, thrilling once more at the incredible feel of her skin. My hand froze. "I think I see a problem."

"What?"

"What if we can only get it on if there's a killer outside the door?"

"We may have to travel," she whispered with a grin. I sat up, bent over her, kissed her on the neck and then on her lips as my arms encircled her. I pulled back for a moment. "We have a couple of hours," she said.

"Oh, it isn't going to take that long."

Afterward, guns close by, we waited in bed for our caller. The sky grew light and seven o'clock came and went. We showered, got dressed, and I headed for the Tower.

"You call that plain clothes?" said Dock from his door as I entered MCU's bullpen. The comic reviews from Kieffer, Staples, Brooks, Hewitt, and Dock concerning my attire at last exhausted, I settled at my desk, synced up my handheld, and checked for updates.

Kieffer had scanned and posted the Nathan Sunday pieces supplied by the English teacher at Turner Elementary. Clair had tracked down Nathan Sunday's English teachers at Covington and St. George, and each one had saved a few pieces from their best and least favorite student. There was one thing he wrote, possibly an early reach for help:

□

bless me father
for i have sinned
it has been
four and a half billion years
since my last confession

i cannot confess

if i told you
what i have done
i would have to kill you

no
i dont believe you would
break your vow
of silence

but see if i tell you my sins
you could not bear the pain
and i would have to put you
out of your misery

you can pray for me
that is as much as you can do

certainly i trust you
who wouldn't trust a man
who prays to god
wearing a dress
with a jug of wine in one hand
and a cracker in the other

Teaching Nathan Sunday must have been the educational system's answer to a double black diamond ski trail. You want a challenge, Mr. Chips? Do I ever have a student for you. With every writing, Nathan Sunday supplied one or two additional atoms of himself: enough to tease, enough to want to know more, but not enough to know the key to the machine.

"Kieff, you heard back from the Army yet?"

338

Kieffer leaned forward and pushed around some papers on his desk, at last finding one. "There was a record of one 2nd Lt. Nathan Sunday reporting to Camp Gordon, Georgia shortly after our Nathan Sunday graduated from Yale. As far as anyone can tell, though, he either deserted or was abducted by aliens the same day. No pay vouchers issued, no quarters assignment made, no company records."

"You think he just found something more interesting to do?"

Kieffer shrugged. "You're the one who wants to get in his head. Oh. This just in." He picked up another sheet. "Way back when there was this controversial student identification program that finger printed all first and second graders. You ever hear of it?"

"I remember. I was in kindergarten."

"Sunday was in first grade and Child Services still has the prints. One of the sets of prints Mike got off those poems matched the ID prints they took of Nataniele Domenica, student of Nat Turner Elementary School, son of Angela Domenica, 270 Frank St., East Branch."

"We already knew that."

"Here's something we didn't know. Those prints don't match the prints supplied to us by the Army."

"Love it when those clues poke you right in the eye. Do we know who belongs to those prints?"

"Working. My money is on Riggs, though. He's from out of state—Pennsylvania. So, we don't have any prints yet."

I returned to the poetry of Nathan Sunday. He had one about philosophy, shut-ins, fantasy, and reality. What he got out of college philosophy was what I got out of college philosophy: reality is real, but every perception we have of it is symbolic, not real. Play with the symbols and you can make reality anything you want, for yourself or for anyone else.

Symbols. A bold enterprising kid who lived across the street from the Police Academy, who had full access to the Police Academy Book Store as well as the Academy Library, would know of at least half a dozen effective ways to supply the Army with a bogus set of prints.

Unless he sent someone to stand in for him—perhaps a law student not so familiar with lifts who eventually blew the stunt, making it necessary for Lt. Sunday to vanish.

Kieffer hung up his phone and whistled to himself.

"What?" I asked. "Did they finally flush Sunday's Yale roommate out of Heavenly?"

"He's been flushed somewhere. William Riggs's attorney has been having difficulty reaching his client, he says, but he is confident that Mr. Riggs will make an appearance at the appropriate time."

"In other words, Billy Riggs is in the wind."

"Bingo." Kieffer gave me the big grin. "I got a call from Latents. Guess whose prints supplied by the Capitol police match Lt. Sunday's supplied by the Army?"

"Riggs." I rubbed my eyes, let my hand drop to my lap, and looked at Kieffer. "One burgers young lovers, the other is a sniper. There's no evidence that the Sniper got his feet bloody at any of the killings, and there wasn't any sniping until after Vince Polizzi and Juna Salvati got killed."

"Then what?"

"For reasons I don't really understand yet, Kieff, I think GQ wanted me on the case."

"He *wanted* you."

"Yeah. But now he wants me *off* the case. Riggs was called in to do the chasing."

"Third Eye?" he asked.

"Wild guess," I answered. Nibbling on the inside of my lower lip, I tried to get a feeling for William Riggs. We knew a few things about him: Attorney. Lobbyist. D.C. insider. Came from Philly. Husband and father of three. Never had been in any of the services.

"What about Nathan and his roomie out doing the rifle ranges between sis-boom-bah sessions at Yale?" I suggested. "Do you think it would be worthwhile checking the firing ranges around New Haven?"

"Think about it," said Kieff. "Long distance sniping: the kind of shooting involved would have drawn too much of the wrong kind of notice."

"You mean like going to 747 flight school and not being particularly interested in takeoffs and landings?"

"Yeah. Like that."

"We got that update yet on the mystery barf?"

"The report is up."

I turned back to my screen and called up the report on the puddle of puke. The latest on the breakfast: Ham, plain pancakes, boysenberry-flavored corn syrup, spoiled OJ, and coffee with half & half. "Kieff!"

He jumped about three inches out of his chair. "What?"

"Boysenberry-flavored corn syrup. There's only one all-night breakfast place I can think of with the stones to call that rat pee syrup."

"Jolly's 24 Hour Drive-In," he said, his eyebrows up.

"Ninth and Stanley, six blocks north of Juna Salvati's place."

"But, Joe, it was closed when we—right. When was it closed?" He reached for his phone and rang up the City Health Department while I went back to the report.

The orange juice had been contaminated, said the lab. Most likely it had been mixed from concentrate and stored for too long in an unsuitable metal container, turning the juice into a rather effective emetic. Nathan Sunday ate his breakfast in preparation for a hard morning's carving, got sick, and ralphed his griddle cakes right in the middle of the crime scene. Next page, blood type, A positive, same as Nathan Sunday, and only one person's. GQ hadn't been drinking any blood, at least not before he deposited his giblets on the floor. DNA working.

"Two in the afternoon on the day Vince Polizzi and Juna Salvati caught it."

I looked up at Kieff. "Huh?"

"When the Health Department closed down Jolly's. It was seven hours after GQ rang the doorbell." Big grin. "Guess what else I found."

"What?"

"The Health Department records its incoming calls just like we do. Someone else didn't like the orange juice, either. We got someone who ate breakfast in the same place that same morning, along with his name, address, and telephone number. Think he might remember who he ate breakfast with?"

"Could be."

Kieffer ran off with his bone to gnaw on it, I rubbed my eyes and began shutting down. Sleep. I needed to get home, shower, and get some sleep. I also needed to get the car home so Bill French could sweep it for bugs. Ward Staples was stretching his arms above his head, his feet up on his desk, still going through the surveillance tapes from the G-clubs.

Former private investigator, surveillance expert, Ward looked to be about the right age. He didn't look like Perry Como. He looked like a well-tanned but young Neil Diamond. Suddenly he was grinning widely, the whiteness of his teeth standing out against his toasted nut complexion. He had seen me staring at him. Picking up an envelope, he got up from his chair, walked around Winnie Hewitt's desk and the broken copier, and came to a stop facing me. "Did you want to charge me with something or ask me for a date?"

"Sorry. Just mentally fitting you for something."

"How did I fit?"

"I don't know. Have you ever heard me talk about the advantages of selling Amway products door-to-door?"

His jaw dropped. "You're kidding."

"Yes, I am." I sat up. "About the boiled bunny?"

He frowned for an instant, then his eyebrows went up. "Julia Powers."

"Yeah, Ward. I took your reference to the movie *Fatal Attraction* as suggesting I might have some kind of problem with Julia. Did I misread that?"

He glanced around, pulled an unoccupied chair from another desk, rolled it around facing me, and sat in it. "Okay. For about five years I worked for Blue Link, setting up security systems and conducting electronic surveillance. One time Blue Link loaned me and my partner Lonnie Steegins to Sixteen Stanton Circle to do surveillance out at Pauling's Christian, that private school out on the Old Baldwin Road?"

"I know it."

"Well, we were set up down in the basement of this building watching monitors—we were trying to get tape on a perv teacher. Anyway, I went outside for a smoke. I didn't even get a chance to light up when I heard a lot of racket coming from the basement then Lonnie screamed. I got down there, your Julia was at the monitors taking notes, and Lonnie Steegins was curled up in the corner, his face covered with blood, holding onto his nuts with both hands, and crying for his mama. She says to me, 'Take your partner to Riverside General then come back.'"

"What happened?" I asked Staples.

"I drove Lonnie in and stuck around in the hospital long enough to find out that he had a broken nose, a fractured jaw, two cracked ribs, a sprained back, and a couple of badly vibrating testicles. I asked him what happened and he machoed me around a bit. What it came down to was that Lonnie had a problem working for women."

"I surmised that from the screaming and all the broken bones," I said. "Did Lonnie ever come clean about what happened?"

"Yeah, he finally admitted that he made some wisecrack about one of the kids, a well-built girl in the class we were observing. Julia told him to button it up, he told her what she could do with her request. He really liked using the B-word. At the time her back was toward him so Lonnie took advantage of the opportunity and patted her bottom. She turned and decked him. After getting off the floor, he attempted to hit her, and then she—"

"And then she fed him his own ass with a backhoe," I completed.

"Yeah. That pretty much describes it."

"Is that it, Ward? An asshole tries to cop a feel off a double black belt and gets a few well-earned lumps? She might tenderize my bunny, pal, but I don't see her boiling it unless I'm an asshole, too."

Ward shrugged. "Working next to someone like that would make me a little nervous."

"Okay, Ward, the next time you see Winnie, pat her ass and see what happens."

"Hey, man. She's MCU. Not funny."

"Wasn't trying to be funny. Where is Clair, anyway?

He nodded toward the papers on my desk. "After she read through those poems young Sunday wrote, she said she had an idea, grabbed her hat and coat, and took off."

"Where to?"

"She didn't say."

"Did you find anything in those surveillance tapes from the gentlemen's clubs?

"Some interesting faces, should MCU ever decide to explore the budgetary possibilities to be had in blackmail. For what we want, though, I don't think it's going anywhere. The setups in most of the clubs have too many dark corners and blind spots for the quality of video equipment being used. If our boy is smart, he knows where to sit, and I think we're all agreed he's smart."

"Who were the interesting faces?"

Ward grinned conspiratorially and lowered his voice. "How about James Fitzgerald McCann?"

"You're kidding! The governor? I thought he spent all his time watching CNN, sipping Starbucks, and masturbating to *The New York Times*."

"Three times in the past two weeks at The Scarlet Letter."

"You alibi him yet?"

"Yeah. Too bad. Guy I know who works for the *Herald* was covering McCann that day. Twenty minutes after Vince Polizzi and Juna Salvati were made dead, the governor was in Grove City at a tree hugger fundraiser getting ready to talk global warming."

There was no way to get from South River to Grove City in under two hours without a jet fighter, and Grove City had no airport. "Who else?"

Ward showed me where the G-club repeaters were in the files. Before I got into them, I glanced up at Ward. "Just for the hell of it, where were you seven o'clock the morning Vince and Juna caught it?"

Ward grinned. "I was in Dock's office with Capt. Finn going over some equipment requisitions preparing for the budget meeting. How's that for an alibi?"

"Seems a little overdone."

"Where were you?"

"In bed by myself having a nightmare."

"Kind of lame, Joe." After Ward laughed and left, I called up Staples's gentlemen's club repeaters list and laughed out loud. Right at the top of the list was Stan Brooks. Alibied out of the Magena killings, he was in South Amboy, New Jersey visiting his grandmother. When Juna and Vince bought it, Stan was on a sleepover with a friend named Dandy Bernal, dancer at The Score, she of the heavenly white feather boa. "My, my, Stanley," I muttered

Next was Harry Cox, reporter at the *Herald*. He was the one who had alibied Gov. McCann. They were both in Grove City. Cox didn't have an alibi for the Magena killings. I punched up the picture, and Cox did look sort of like a swollen Spike Lee. I leaned back and closed my eyes, trying to bring Cox's image up before my mind's eye. A little bastard, perhaps five-five or five six, assertive as hell, but way too slight. Cox wouldn't have been able to lift Vince's body onto that table.

But I knew someone who could. I pushed back my chair and headed straight for Dock's office.

As I closed his door, Dock put a sheet of paper on top of a stack of files and looked over the tops of his glasses at me. "Can I help you?"

I dropped into the chair facing his desk and held onto the armrests with both hands. "What about Kieffer? What are his alibis?"

His eyes went wide. "What put *this* hair up your ass?"

"He writes. He's a cop. He's a forensic encyclopedia. He's smart. He's strong."

"And he likes you."

"Yes. That too."

"Except for liking you, Slugger, you just described yourself." Dock leaned back in his chair, rubbed his hands together and shrugged. "Okay, when the Booth Street mess went down, Kieffer was eating breakfast with Miriam and Mona. Afterward, he drove Mona to school before coming into the Tower. When the Magena killings went down, Kieffer was in Quantico taking the Bureau's Bundy, Berkowitz, and baying at the moon course."

"What about during the killings in Baldwin?"

"No one has an alibi for that. Where were you?"

"I don't know. That was over a year ago."

"My point," he said, tapping a finger on his pile of files. "I do have some work to finish."

"Sorry."

"There are still a lot of cops who aren't in MCU we haven't finished checking yet, as well as a bunch of ex-cops. Lt. Trask lent us a couple of bodies from IAB to help Clair with the screening. They're on that now."

I rubbed my eyes, the lack of sleep making me woozy. I stood. "As long as you were checking anyway, what about Mike Ijumaa?"

"Do you know him well?"

"I dated his sister once."

"Only once? That's troubling. What was it that time?"

"Racial differences. She thought hers was different from mine."

"They never learn, do they?"

"Where was Mike?"

"Both sets of murders happened when he was off duty, DiMaggio. When the Roa-Matos killings went down, Mike says he was kayaking the whitewater east of Nelson. All we can establish for certain is that there is, indeed, whitewater east of Nelson, and that he bought gas there in the city on that date. When the Polizzi-Salvati killings happened, he said he was snowshoeing up on Silver Mountain. We can't find anyone who saw him there."

"Not exactly air tight. What about Julia Powers and the people out at Sixteen Stanton Circle? A heap of retired cops out there."

"We're working on that. Anything else?"

"She doesn't have alibis?"

"Julia? She might very well have alibis. We just don't know what they are yet." He tapped his paperwork once again. "Anything else?"

I could feel the wind leaking out of my panic attack. "So what about you, Dock? What's your alibi?" I joked.

"I thought you would never ask. Let me tell you about my back." And before I could extricate myself from his office, he gave me the history of his crushed disk, the referred pain in his coccyx, testicles, and buttocks, a description of the operation he was scheduled for next month, the process of recovery, and the names, addresses, and phone numbers of his physician, his orthopedist, and the neurosurgeon at West Shore Spine Associates, the upshot of which was that lifting more than ten or twenty pounds on the dates in question would have caused Dock excruciating pain, hence tossing around two hundred pounds of Vince Polizzi was not very likely, and before he began expanding upon the details, I fled back to my desk where I learned that Mr. Skip Phillips was in the house and on his way up to MCU.

"Who?" I asked Kieff.

"The guy who called in the complaint on Jolly's."

THE BREAKFAST CLUB

"Well, sure, that's Chuck Anderson. The police chaplain?" Skip Phillips tapped the aged Army photo of William Riggs made up to look like Nathan Sunday on the table. "Never knew he was Army. I go to the First Meth up in Avon and he's assistant pastor there. He knows me. Sure. He eats breakfast at Jolly's weekdays because it's on his way to the Police Academy. The day starts early there, but I don't have to tell you guys. Sometimes, though, if the chaplain don't have anyone with him, we eat breakfast together."

I sat back in the chair and looked across the scarred wooden table at Phillips. He was in his forties, under six feet, brown and blue, tending toward overweight, wearing jeans and a tan windbreaker sporting the city water department's leaky spigot logo. Kieffer sat to Phillips's left. More in service to his sore butt than to any kind of interrogation effect, Dockery stood leaning against the wall next to the door facing Phillips.

"Did he usually have someone with him at breakfast?" asked Kieffer.

"Sure. He carpools with a couple of the instructors up at the Academy."

"Do you know their names?" I asked.

Phillips frowned and sipped at his coffee. "Yeah. The one guy, Abe. I don't recall his last name. He teaches all that karate stuff at the Academy."

"Farah," interrupted Dockery. "Sgt. Ibrahim Farah."

"That's the name," Phillips said, nodding.

"He teaches hand-to-hand," Dockery added, glancing at me, his eyebrows arched for emphasis. "Big guy. Strong."

"Anyone else?" asked Kieffer.

"Yeah. Dave. Lt. Dave Carlton? Head of the SWAT team? He teaches shooting and puts on those shooting demos out at the Academy. I saw him at that Police Field Day last summer. Man, can he ever shoot."

Anderson, plus Carlton, plus Farah, plus all of them being cops, plus all of them frequenting Jolly's equaled what? On the morning Vince Polizzi and Juna Salvati died, it turned out, Chaplain Anderson was at Jolly's alone, and, according to Skip Phillips, was acting "kinda strange." That morning the chaplain didn't want Skip to eat with him, mentioning something about the flu as a reason; not wanting to spread it. "Flu or no flu," said Skip, "Chaplain Anderson wolfed down those wheat cakes and syrup like someone was going to take 'em away from him. Big glass of OJ, too. Me, when I get the flu, packing my face isn't my big thing."

Charles Anderson, Police Academy chaplain, was originally from Trenton, New Jersey, mere moments from Philadelphia with its pair of couple killings, and a few hours from Boston, where Angelo Petro and Tommy Sue West caught those .22s in their hearts. It was enough to bring in Farah, Carlton, and Anderson for questioning. As the calls went out and Brooks took a half dozen uniforms out of Central to track them down, Dock had Kieffer and me get together in his office to pinch the dream.

"Possible?" asked Dock.

Kieffer nodded and I shrugged. Dock looked at me. "We know why Kieff thinks it's possible. Why don't you?"

"It just doesn't feel right."

"*Feel* right."

"That's the only reason you two took me on, right?"

"We wanted to use you for bait."

I shook my head. "It just seems too easy."

Kieff burst out with a laugh. "Easy? Lucky, perhaps. If you hadn't picked up on that phony syrup from the autopsy report, we'd still be holding a name, an old face, and a pair of nothings. How about a minister knocks on the door asking for help? Juna sees that it's a minister, opens the door, the minister does a push-in, the man with the Uzi steps into view, four-and-four, then the muscle man comes in and the three of them go to work."

I shook my head. "Can't buy it. They aren't exactly CSU Academy grads and all Anderson knows about being a cop is the uniform he was issued. Do you think a SWAT man, a hand-to-hand combat instructor, and a chaplain could put in three hours at a crime scene, do what was done, and leave nothing but those bogus foot impressions?"

"I still think you're wrong about the foot impressions," said Kieff.

Dock clasped his fingers over his belly and frowned. "We can't just ignore this information, Joe. I don't mind some embarrassment and a little front office heat if we roust three righteous cops. What I do mind is trying to spin away the next pair of burgered lovers we'll find someday if you're wrong." Dock's phone rang, he answered it, then handed the receiver to me. "Cab Nelson."

As Kieff and Dock muttered at each other, I held the receiver to my ear. "Hey, Cab, what's up?"

"You wanted to know the criminal history of the Seventh Street Bridge, 'Seventy-one to Seventy-seven?"

"What'd you find?"

Cab gave it to me short and not very sweet. It was a mob dump during the 'Sixties. Not really much traffic during the 'Seventies until Charlie Bonner was stabbed in the head with a stiletto or switchblade. Walter Storrow was found there the next year. He was a rapist that used to stalk his prey up in Canal Park. They found him with a knife wound in the back of his skull. His death cleared a lot of cases for Special Crimes. In fact, there was some suspicion that South River SCU might've done him. There were a couple of bums that were found there in 'Seventy-five, never identified. Those were shot with a .22. *"The only other one was Mango Bayo, a cop. He was found downstream, but the forensics showed he was done at the bridge."*

"Ice pick in the head?" I asked.

"No. He was shot in the heart with a .22. I went over the Mango Bayo file and I think I have a GQ lead. The beneficiary on his PBA insurance was one Angela Domenica."

"Thanks Cab." I hung up the phone.

"Anything?" asked Kieffer.

"Remember Mango Bayo? The uniform found on the bank of the East Branch back in 'Seventy-six?" Bobble-head nods from Kieff and Dock. "Angela Domenica, Nathan Sunday's mother, got Bayo's insurance."

"He was shot with a .22, right?" said Kieffer. "Like the Boston and Philly couple killings?"

Dock opened his mouth to ask a question when a loud pounding on his door made all three of us jump. The door opened revealing Clair Turner, still in her coat and beret, a large manila envelope in her hands. "Guess where Nathan Sunday underwent fifteen days psychiatric observation back in Nineteen Seventy-seven?" She faced the envelope toward each of us in turn. The big blue SRMHI on the envelope was a bit of a giveaway.

"Squirmhi?" I offered, using the local nickname for the South River Mental Health Institute.

"Yes. More writings." She held out the envelope revealing that she had a second, much thicker, envelope. "And guess who voluntarily committed himself there ten years later under the same name?"

"Still looking for water in the same dry hole," I muttered to myself.

Kieffer frowned at me. "What was that?"

"Where do you go when nothing works and you've been everywhere to try and fix it?"

Dock nodded toward the envelopes. "Any patient-doctor confidentiality problems with those?"

"These probably won't do much good in court," she admitted.

The frown grew profound. "You didn't—"

"No. Dr. Miklos and I agreed that he would mistakenly entrust these to my care, and once we'd finished examining them, running them through Documents, and copying them, I would suddenly realize the possible violation of privilege and return them, no harm done. I also have copies of Sunday's childhood medical records from Canal Park Hospital and the name of his family physician when Sunday was living in St. George."

"Really." Dock clasped his hands together and nodded. "Good man, Miklos. We owe him one. And Clair?"

"Yes?"

"You and the wig-picker come up with a story that can at least pass the laugh test, okay?"

"Yes, boss."

A buzz on the phone, Dock picked it up, grunted into the receiver, hung up, and looked at me. "Ward finished running alibis on everyone at Sixteen Stanton Circle. Still some additional checking to do, but right now they look good, including Julia. Meanwhile, there is work to do and poetry to process—"

His phone rang again and Clair, Kieff, and I began filing out. Dock held up his hand. "Hold it." He said to us. "Go on," he said into the phone. He listened awhile longer, his face developing a granite cast. He nodded and said, "Copies of everything, Chess. Can do?" Another nod. "Nothing I can say, man, except I owe you. We'll have some white gloves at the service, and if we get something solid, I'll let you know."

He hung up the phone, stared at nothing in particular, then shook his head. "Monkey wrench in the works. That was Chess Pattengill up in Magena. Officers Leo Martini and Teresa Morales were found dead this morning a little after eight o'clock."

Long stunned silence. I could feel my skin tingling as though I was about to pass out. Teresa Morales just didn't have that spark, did she? Maybe I should turn in my Third Eye for a pair of curb feelers.

Finally Kieff asked, "What took them so long to tell us?"

"Magena PD and the Bureau sat on it." Dock nodded at the phone and snorted out a laugh. "In fact they are still sitting on it. They don't want to risk the publicity. Chess moseyed off the reservation to give us the news. His name was never mentioned, got me?"

"Funtown problem, again," I muttered.

Dock rubbed his eyes. "Chess is sending everything he can get to me under the table."

"I don't understand it at all," said Kieffer. He was frowning, his expression just a little lost.

Dock lowered his hand and exhaled. "We haven't seen the file yet, so no jumping to conclusions." He pointed at his door. "We still have an investigation to work."

When we were back at our desks. I sat at mine staggered by the news from Magena. Mechanically I dragged my gaze over half a dozen of Nathan's poems. My attention wandered. I couldn't concentrate. I kept thinking of beautiful Teresa Morales, the woman who didn't have the spark. I had said she didn't have it. Winnie, Kieff, Dock—we all said she didn't have it. If she did have it, and the evidence seemed to suggest that, then all our assumptions regarding Sunday's motivation went out the window.

I swung around in my chair and looked at the briefing area, the rows of chairs now empty. No surveillance cameras covering MCU, or any other bullpen, office, or locker room in the Tower. The union had insisted. An attendance log had been kept, though.

Sunday or Riggs must have been there listening when we were blowing off convinced the Magena bait was no good. We had been smug, certain in our knowledge of GQ. The killer or his accomplice had either been in the room or had someone there who passed on the information about Magena and our contempt for the bait Magena PD was going to run. I was certain that GQ thought he was smarter than the police, and almost as sure that he wanted us to believe it, too. But, would GQ go all the way up to Magena and kill two cops just to show us up? The same guy who had led us to Pitone's and Casale's weapons so they didn't fall into the wrong hands? The same guy who attempted to warn the cops to stay out of his way for fear of *their* lives? It just didn't add up.

I glanced at the clock on the wall. "Man," I said to Kieff, "I can't do all this and sit on a hook, too. I got to go home and get some sleep." I looked over at Kieffer. "Give me a call if you manage to track down Anderson. You got those new poems scanned in yet?"

"Maybe in another two hours. I've been looking at Sunday's medical records from Canal Park."

"Anything?"

"Joe, over four years he was brought to the emergency room thirty-one times. Nineteen of those times involved broken bones, three of those involved serious cranial fractures. Three times Child Services removed him from his home, and three times sent him back."

"Beginning to feel sorry for him, too?"

Kieffer simply stared at the file in front of him. "You already knew all this, didn't you?" he asked me.

"Suspected. Once we manage to piece together the whole story we'll probably be amazed at how much punishment this kid absorbed before he began fighting back. Let me sync what you have in the computer now, Kieff, and I'll get the rest tomorrow. Call me on my cell once you get a look at the Magena stuff, okay?" I studied Kieffer's face for a moment. He was worried. "What?" I asked.

"The bait is still on?"

"Of course." I turned to my terminal, called up the app on my handheld, hit the sync icon. "Orders are orders. Anyway, we don't even know where Anderson is. If he is GQ, he might be in the shadows, getting ready to strike at the bait. If he isn't the guy, maybe the real GQ is." I studied Kieffer some more. Something unraveling there. "Hey, man, what is it? The case? Something at home?"

Kieffer smiled sadly. "I don't know. This Magena shit really threw me. I'm scared that GQ won't bite. I'm scared he will." The phone rang, Kieff answered it, then nodded toward me as he punched the hold.

I picked up my receiver and punched the active line. "Torio."

"Rose Pinsky over at Sherman Park, Joe. I got a line on your priest."

She had a line on Juna and Lacy Salvati's childhood priest, all right. Father Michael Cowan ran St. Helen's in the late 'Seventies and early 'Eighties and was then sent to a parish in Grove City. In between the two posts he did a tour in a treatment center, "for alcoholism and some other things." In Grove City, those "other things" popped up again, and before they came to trial, they found

Father Cowan hanging from a tree overlooking the Lyon River south of the city. His death had been ruled a "possible suicide." Then again it might have been an irate parent who had lost his faith in the system. Michael Cowan had been forty-three.

I hung up and stared at the phone. "What is it?" asked Kieff.

"I had an idea. It turned out to be true, but doesn't lead anywhere." I rubbed my eyes and stood. Letting my hand fall to my side, I said, "You know, every time I hear about a child abuser, I have this urge to beat the guy to death. When I find them dead, though, I always have this feeling that the real perp got away."

"The priest? Lacy and Juna's?"

I nodded. "Yeah. Suicide, maybe. Some time ago."

Kieffer sat back in his chair. "He sent himself to Hell. That's hard time."

"Maybe." I pulled out my cell phone and punched in Julia's private number. She answered with a hello almost immediately. "This is Joe. Tell me, lady: Are you real?"

"Very."

"I can count on it?"

"You can count on it."

"What about us moving too fast?"

"What about it?"

I looked up at the clock. "See you in a few hours."

"I count on that," she answered.

I hesitated a second, then punched off and stared at the phone.

"Joe?"

I turned and looked at my partner. "Yeah?"

"What's *your* feeling about her?" His face looked deadly serious.

"Julia?" I asked.

"No, man. Mary Freakin' Queen of Scots."

I held up a hand and shook my head. "I am in love, partner."

"You just met her night before last. How can you be in love?"

"I lost my compass and my Third Eye has a finger in it. It's thunderbolt city, Jack, just like in *The Godfather*. Love ran over me like an Abrams tank. What's worse, I really can't remember what she looks like, and half the time I'm not real sure what her name is or what planet I'm on. All of the aforementioned notwithstanding, I am in love."

Kieffer looked even more troubled. I moved my chair closer to him so we wouldn't be overheard and sat down. "How long did you know Miriam before you knew you were in love?"

"Longer than three days." He thought for a moment, leaned back in his chair, frowned, and gave a little shrug. "Maybe. We dated and saw each other for almost a year before I asked her to marry me. But in love? It might have been the thunderbolt. I ever tell you how we met?"

"No."

"It was outside at East Shore Community College, that building with the moat and all the fountains."

"The psych building: Perrin Hall."

"Right. Miriam was sitting in the sun on one of those marble benches, bent over a book, her hair gathered up in a sheer raspberry scarf, a black tank top and loose fitting shorts that matched her scarf. Those incredible legs that went from the ground all of the way to Heaven. That face. That skin."

"What shade?"

He smiled widely. "Hershey's semi-sweet," he answered with a grin.

"I'm hip."

"Joe, have you ever gotten Winnie's view on what attracts men?"

"Feathers."

"Yeah." Kieffer nodded. "Brother, I was feather struck. I felt such an attraction at that moment, even though I didn't put that word on my feelings, I knew I was in love. Hooked. Need that girl. Without her there is no future."

"That's the situation I'm in, partner. Kieff, I'm in so deep the future without her is not possible. How did you make your move?"

He laughed. "Very cool. Man, I just stood there, my mouth hanging open, staring at her like a fool until she said, 'You know, if you never blink your eyes, they dry up and fall out of your head.'"

We both laughed at that. Kieff said he took that leap into the void and asked her for a date. She said yes. When they both graduated, and Kieff got his job interning at the *Herald*, she said yes to getting married. Then Mona came along. They had just celebrated their eighth anniversary.

"As soon as this mess is settled, Joe, you and Julia are coming over for dinner. Maybe we'll all go out and go dancing. You like dancing?"

"Not by myself." I picked up my handheld, deenergized it, put it in my pocket, stood, and placed a hand on Kieff's shoulder. "You got a date, partner."

"I was talking about double dating."

"That could be fun, too." I grinned at him.

He looked up at me, his face very serious. "Backup tonight, Joe? Just me, part of the shadows?"

"What if GQ or the Sniper decides to put two in your hat and leave you beneath the Seventh Street Bridge? Who gets to tell Miriam and Mona? They'll stick me with it, man. No thanks." I headed toward the elevator.

"Only if you're still alive!" Kieffer shouted across the room, raising an eyebrow or two in the bullpen.

"No backup!" I shouted back as I stepped into the elevator car. Capt. Finn was already in the car. He nodded at me and scanned my Sonny Mirabella threads as the doors closed. "You're looking good, Joseph. It's nice to see you taking some pride in your appearance." I looked and he wasn't joking.

"Thanks, Cap."

The doors opened on the third floor, Capt. Finn patted my back and stepped out. As the doors closed again, I looked down at my wrinkled wiseguy threads. "Maybe I should upgrade my wardrobe."

As the doors opened in the lobby, I was faced by three beings who were waiting for the elevator. The one in the middle was tall, skinny, and had eyes like a meercat. The bookends were a couple of friends of ours, the one on my right being Tommy Zerilli. I stepped out of the elevator, the doors closing behind me.

"Hey, Joey D," Zerilli said. "A present from my boss." Tommy dropped a hand on the skinny guy's shoulder.

"Sorry," I said, "I'm allergic."

Zerilli turned to his right, held out a hand toward the other bookend and said, "This is Gilly Stella."

"How you doin'?" asked Stella with a deep rumbling voice as he held out his hand. We shook hands, and the man's grip was surprisingly gentle. Gilly Stella looked like Big Pussy from *The Sopranos*. He nodded toward my Sonny Mirabella threads. "They let cops dress like that?"

"Like what?"

He nodded approvingly. "Sharp."

"This," Tommy Zee said, indicating the fellow with the big eyes, "is Ahmed. He was the one called the don about Vince."

"I'm here to cooperate in any way I can," said the skinny guy. Some kind of accent. He appeared to have a great deal of incentive.

"What's your name?"

"Ahmed Shapiro."

"Ahmed Shapiro," I repeated. "You could be the answer the Middle East is looking for." I looked at Tommy. "So?"

"I am here to do whatever I can to help the police," said Ahmed. "I know my rights, I waive everything, and I don't want no lawyer. To Hell with lawyers," and then Ahmed Shapiro spat on the highly polished granite floor.

"Don't do that." I studied the man in the middle until who he was finally worked through my mental fog. "You're the guy who broke into 762 Booth Street."

"Yes, detective."

"After you broke in upstairs, did you step in a puddle of puke?"

"Yes. I'm terribly sorry. I had to work but I felt so dreadfully ill I really couldn't see straight. And then to witness what was on that bed, good god—"

"You were ill?"

"Very."

"Mr. Shapiro, was that your vomit on the rug?"

"Yes. I'm so sorry."

"You stepped in your own puke? Nobody steps in his own puke. How could you step in your own puke?"

"It was dark. I felt lightheaded. I don't know what it was. Maybe it was something I ate."

"Where did you eat breakfast that morning?"

"Jolly's 24 Hour. Very reasonable prices and they're open all night—or they used to be. I always ate there before, uh, going to work."

I looked at Tommy Zee. "I got to go someplace, Tommy. Thank Don Francesco for me, and you and Gilly take Ahmed here up to the fourth floor and get hold of Lt. Kieffer. Ahmed is just the man my partner is looking for. He'll make Kieffer's whole day."

"You got it, Joey D."

"I really like them threads," said Gilly. "Who's your tailor?"

"Benny Goodman," I said as I headed for the garage.

THE FAMILY BUSINESS

Even with the entire department on alert for the Sniper, the center of my back didn't stop itching until I got home. After changing, with Pop's CD player working its way through a few of Beethoven's *klaviersonaten,* the hangman and I were in the kitchen finishing our helpings of Caitlyn's spaghetti and meatballs. Onions, garlic, tomato, bacon, green peppers, and oregano filled the air with perfume. We were on our own, Caitlyn was seeing her sister. Later on she'd be dropping off her nephew for Pop to baby-sit.

"Pop, when are you going to quit fooling around and get married? And don't give me any of this waiting around to see the boy back into recovery. My shoulder is fine, my job is great, and I'm leaving my shrink rolling in the aisles."

"I like your job a lot better, Joe, once people stop stabbing and shooting you."

"You and me both."

"I like having you home, Joe."

"Marry Caitlyn." I tapped my plate with my fork. "Look at this, Pop: Vallone's Hot Italian Sausage? Festa Verde Tomato sauce? Arcobaleno's Parmigiano? You can't let this spaghetti get away from us."

He grinned conspiratorially. "You know the pasta she uses?"

"What? Ronzoni? Barilla? Spigadoro? She make her own fresh?"

"Mueller's."

"Mueller's? *Himmel!"* I sat back, looked down at my plate, then shrugged. "We just won't tell anybody."

We ate in silence, then the hangman put down his fork, took a sip of Dr Pepper, and leaned back in his chair. "Joe, what's it look like with your killer? Think he move on someplace else? I hear about those two cops in Magena. But the news don't say it's GQ."

"I haven't seen the crime scene reports. There's a lot we don't know about GQ, Pop. I think he knows all about what we're pulling and maybe that's even part of his plan." I frowned as the Third Eye blinked. "I keep getting this feeling, though, that he's not sure what he wants to do—or wants us to do."

"What about you and this Julia? You call it running bait?"

"Yeah." I shrugged and twirled another forkful. "I'm not sure what kind of pull GQ's victims have on him. Is he out of control when he sees those faces Julia and I have been wearing? Maybe he can resist Julia's and my irresistible performance. Maybe we just haven't given him enough time. We've only been baiting him a day."

"You still looking at cops?"

"Yeah. We must have the whole force spooked by now. Pop, you know a lot of cops. Out at the Academy, are you familiar with the chaplain, Charles Anderson?"

"I know the name and the face. He's the one who looks like Perry Como and could put riders to sleep on a rollercoaster. He was at that ceremony when Chief Harolds give you the Medal of Honor."

I tried to push back the mental cobwebs. Who pays attention during invocations? The grunts in military formations have been enduring and ignoring opening ceremonies since they stirred pigeon guts before battles back in ancient times. I couldn't remember anything except the man in the uniform, little of his face, and nothing about what he said. "We have some lame evidence that points at Anderson as GQ, possibly with the help of two other cops. The evidence thinned out considerably the past couple of hours, but there are still questions without answers."

Pop shook his head. "Can't be Anderson." He stuck his fork into the pile of pasta on his plate and began twirling the tines. "Now I do a profile, Joe. Not Anderson." He laughed and shook his head. "Never."

"How so?"

361

"You listen when he was doing that prayer? At that ceremony?"

"No. I have a mental block."

"Good thing, too." Pop looked up at me. "I talk to a lot of killers in my time, Joe. In cells, on the row, on the scaffold. Some so dumb they couldn't figure out where they were or why they were there. Some so smart they still didn't know what's going on. All kinds. Good men, bad men, rich, poor, schooled and no school, smart, stupid. Some I hate, some I pity." He nodded to himself. "Some I even love. They make me mad, happy, sad, laugh, scared, even cry. They *never* bore me. Anderson could close the eyes on the Sphinx."

I had a meatball half-chewed and in mid-swallow when Pop said that, I almost choked on it. Pop joined in—the laughing, not the choking.

"You got me there, Pop. Have to agree. I never ran into a boring killer."

"This Julia," said Pop, changing the subject. "You like her?"

I leaned forward, took a swallow of his Dr Pepper, and put the glass back on the table. "It's only been a couple of days, Pop." I looked off to the side, trying to word it so I didn't sound totally ridiculous. He didn't wait for me.

"My boy in love? For real?"

"Oh yeah. Big time and for real." I began twirling up another mouthful of pasta. "It's confusing, actually. Mostly when I've seen her she's been in a really great disguise, and it is a really great disguise, but—" and then a nagging issue poked into my awareness. "Pop, there's this piece of music: Albinoni's *Adagio*— something."

"*Adagio in G Minor*. Very famous piece of music, Joe."

"Famous?"

"You know. In South River. That was the music the Gray-eye Killer played. The big clue that caught Gerald Soams."

I pondered on that a bit. "Julia Powers took down Gerald Soams," I said. "The *Adagio* is what Julia Powers dances to when she's Margarita Azzurro. Speaking of body counts."

"Body counts?"

"Pop," I twisted the glass around, my gaze fixed to it. "I've killed four men that I know about, one at a time. Maybe one or two of the Rizzos. That night at the Rizzo brothers' garage is still a blur. Nine dead if you count the executions of Collins and Pruitt." I looked up at the hangman. "In your time you've hung a lot more than that, though. I never added them up."

"Me neither."

"Grandpop killed at least six in those two prison riots. What I'm getting at, Pop, is that our family body count is way up there. We're practically a one family population control program."

"Back when you were in high school, Joe, remember what you used to call death?"

"Yeah. The family business. Boy, was I ever a snotty pain in the ass." I put my fork down on my plate. "Anyway, there's a cop named Carlton—in fact, he's one of our suspects. But Carlton made a comment about Julia. He said that Julia Powers is a serial killer who figured out how to do it legally."

"That's a mouthful this Carlton said."

"Yeah. But, other than the law, Pop, what's the difference between us and serial killers? We take 'em out, one at a time, with plenty of cool-down time in between."

"You know the meaning is smaller than that, Joe." The hangman frowned, thought on it for a moment, then nodded gravely. "Do you need to kill someone to try and feel okay?"

"No."

"Me neither. It's been a lot of years since I stood on a scaffold, and I feel fine. Each time after those prison riots, Gaspare burned enough candles at St. Mary's for those cons he killed to change weather patterns. The killers—the pattern killers—I knew on the row were different."

"They needed to kill?" I said.

"Like a drug for some, a duty for others, one was just trying to help everybody go to Heaven. Some they couldn't tell the difference between a man's life and a mosquito's. Dead inside. Something else, too." He twirled up another load of Caitlyn's spaghetti. "The people we kill, Joe, they already dead. See, the condemned man on the scaffold is dead, no matter who springs the trap. Escaping prisoners are dead whoever's on the wall with the gun. It don't matter which cop Paul Baines aimed a gun at. He was dead. We kill the dead, Joe. Killers kill the living. More pasta?"

For desert, Gianelli's black raspberry ice cream for me and chocolate for him. "Back to the salt mines tonight?" asked Pop, an eyebrow up, a smirk on his face.

"Yeah, Pop. Back to the salt mines."

"Bad dancing and a boring wait in a fleabag?"

"Okay, okay."

"What about the Sniper, Joe?"

"He doesn't appear to be after Sonny Mirabella." I frowned and nodded. "To be perfectly honest, I don't think he's after me, either."

"Too many misses?"

"Right."

"What's it about then, Joe?"

"He's trying to frighten me off."

Pop frowned and held out his hands. "Why?"

I suddenly flashed on Billy Roth's crime scene photo, the one of his gloved right hand and the marks in the snow just beyond his fingertips. The dash and four dots wasn't the number six. It was dash dot *space* and then three dots: N S. Nathan Sunday.

Billy had been on the West Beverly rifle team. He would have met Sunday at matches. Billy knew Sunday. "He likes me," I said as I stood and dropped my napkin on the table.

The hangman studied me. "You making jokes?"

"No kidding, Pop. GQ likes me so much he doesn't want me to get hurt." I frowned, put that together with Nathan Sunday stabbing bums in the head beneath the Seventh Street bridge and Guardian popping my old enemies with an ice pick.

"What is it, Joe?"

I sat down. Pulled out my cell phone, opened my mouth, closed it. "GQ and the Guardian; they're one in the same." I called Dock and told him the same thing. He had a good question. Two wildly different signatures, two motivations about as far apart as possible, but in the same killer, and one of those motivations apparently nothing more than gratitude? *"You ever hear of anything like this before?"* Dock asked.

"Nope." I cut off the call and looked at the hangman. "Man, I know I told Lydia Jenks there are no simple serial killer cases, but this is ridiculous."

NEW ANGEL

At The Score, wearing my new Sonny Mirabella threads on a black and deep purple theme, after I left Julia off backstage and entered the club, I actually drew a small round of applause. Many of the patrons wanted to shake my hand, pat my back, buy me drinks, and inform me that my performance with the "flower girl" the night before was the hottest turn-on since Little Egypt. What were we going to do tonight?

While a hot young woman named Jade Ice did a delicious dragon-lady bit on the stage to a piece of Chinese space music, an undercover Vice cop who had a face that reminded me of a toad took me aside, flashed his tin, and cautioned me about a repeat of the hands-on violation of the evening before. Look, but don't touch. He said his name was Patterson.

I debated with myself about telling him that I was on the job, but let it drop. It wasn't just that Patterson could have been GQ or a blabbermouth. Sonny Mirabella wouldn't explain himself—not ever, not to anyone. Especially not to a goofy-looking Vice dick with dirty glasses and a bad suit. I lifted up my glass of Dr Pepper and said, "Here's looking at you, squid."

Later, I thought about Patterson. He was on the short, fat, and ugly side, but late thirties and a cop. Keeping the prude watch on gentleman's clubs would keep him up on the Angela Sunday look-alikes. While at the table, with the sounds of the music and the crowd covering my words, I called Kieffer on his cell phone to tell him to check out Patterson and any of the other Vice cops doing T&A watch at the gentleman's clubs. In return, Kieffer let me know that Sgt. Farah had been brought in. After apologizing about busting up Stan

366

Brooks and three of the uniformed officers who tried to bring him in, Farah claimed to have no idea what MCU was talking about. Anderson and Carlton were still in the wind.

An update from Magena: The stuff Chess Pattengill sent down looked very much like GQ had started but had been interrupted in mid slaughter. Martini and Morales had both been shot and killed in the hallway, but there the similarities ended. Leo Martini had answered the door and had gotten two in the heart. Teresa Morales had been in front of the living room entrance. She had been dropped with one through her neck, then while she was down the shooter put five through her face, then left both of them there, the gun on the hall floor, and the front door open. Ballistics working.

"It wasn't GQ," I said to Kieff on the phone. "Leo Martini was married, partner. I'd sure like to know where his wife was when Leo answered that door."

"You sure your third eye doesn't have some sand in it?"

"I'm sure GQ closes and locks the front door on his way out to avoid having the bodies discovered any sooner than necessary."

"Our theory is that he was interrupted."

"Kieff, those shots were in Teresa's face: her shooter hated Teresa's face. GQ loves the faces of the females he's been killing. Maybe Leo and Teresa forgot why they were there, engaged in some serious pattycake, and Leo's wife paid a visit."

"Speaking from personal experience, old sock?"

"You're going to be a great detective someday, Lt. Kieffer." I punched off and pondered the killings beneath the Seventh Street Bridge and the Guardian hits. GQ had done impulsive out-of-pattern murders in addition to his highly organized couple killings. While I pushed that around in my head, the lights faded, the *Adagio* began, and the audience noise stopped like it had been guillotined. The spot came up, aimed high this time. Instead of a flower, Julia was lowered from above, becoming a bird—

—No. An angel. A goddess. Talk about feathers. I was as close to praying, worshipping, as I had ever been in my life. In a brief moment of rebellion I swore I would stay seated and keep my lips and hands to myself. As I made the promise, though, I knew it to be a hopeless dream; an end so far out of my reach that I could have been the proverbial snowflake in Hell promising itself not to go soft, and going soft was not going to be an issue.

Someone hooted out a wolf call and was immediately thumped into silence by a nearby shadow.

After her landing, she came down from the stage and moved directly toward me, her scent, the heat radiating from her entire body, her hands touching my shoulders, my neck, my face. The insides of her thighs brushed my legs. I found myself trying to consume her, fill myself with her taste, her touch. As I drew my palms up the back of her legs, across her buttocks, and to her shoulders, I caught a glimpse of the undercover cop.

Patterson was sitting at his table, his eyes glazed behind his fogged lenses, his flabby jaw muscles twitching, helpless. He could no more have stopped what was happening in front of him than he could have pulled over and ticketed an avalanche. I drew Margarita Azzurro toward me and buried my face between her breasts. My tongue streaked up her neck until my lips brushed her ear.

Full of Caitlyn's spaghetti, Gianelli's black raspberry ice cream, Dr. Pepper, and two arms full of Julia Powers—all that was lacking was to put it on skis. If GQ truly liked me, that would have been the moment to kill me. When the spot faded to black, the applause erupted, and I was the one who said, "Good. Good."

"As Bambi used to say," said Julia, "that's why I get the big bucks."

She nibbled at my ear and she was swallowed by the dark. The lights came up, and the vibration from the deafening applause and foot stomping shook dust and bits of old confetti and glitter from the light array above the stage. I did a quick sweep as I waved at my fan club. Patterson was gone.

When she came back from the dressing rooms, Julia and I went to a booth and kissed and groped for the benefit of a killer who, for all we knew, might be lurking in the depths of the Victoria's Secret warehouse wearing a pair of peek-a-boo panties on his head and selling his soul to the Devil. Although the sweet nothings I whispered into her ear while I ran my hand up her dress concerned the Vice cop and what happened beneath the Seventh Street Bridge, as well as an update on the Magena killings, the job occupied at that moment a very low rung on my priority ladder. The feel of her skin beneath my fingertips, the pressure of her bare thighs against my lap, her hot breath in my ear, every sentient aspect of my existence was focused on touch. No sense of time. When seconds or hours had passed, my hand was gliding up the satin smoothness of her inner thigh. She took my face in both of her hands and kissed my mouth, long and slow. She at last drew back her head, those smoky eyes framed by that beautiful black hair —wig. She whispered, "How're your hemorrhoids, Sonny?"

"Like baseball bats," I croaked.

"Let's go home."

The parking attendant was a familiarly huge fellow named Mohammed Ali MacGregor, so the car was clean, and after Mo swept us, we were too. In the pimpmobile, as we pulled left onto Houlihan, we kicked around the possibility that Chaplain Anderson was GQ. Right then the strongest evidence supporting that was that no one seemed to be able to find him and no one believed it could be him.

"A minister at the door," she said. "That'd get the door open, perhaps put Vince Polizzi off guard."

"There's still the submachine gun problem."

"A modified Micro-Uzi doesn't need a lot of space." She nodded. "What could a minister be carrying that wouldn't raise suspicion? A bible?"

"Rev. Sunday comes to the door carrying a bible the size of *Webster's Unabridged*, and if I wasn't suspicious there might be something concealed in it, I'd probably be concerned that the guy was either there to sell it to me or preach a sermon."

"What about the Victoria's Secret catalogs, Joe? The missing order blanks? Someone delivering a package would at least get an open door. His weapon could be hidden in the package. He sticks his arm through a hole in the bottom or back, his finger on the trigger the whole time."

"Tough to outdraw an aimed Uzi," I agreed.

We rode silently for a moment, the street lights passing overhead, momentarily filling the interior of the car with cold blues, then plunging it into darkness. "A noise suppresser, shooting through the clothing in the package further muffling the noise. That would explain the brown wool fibers they found," Julia thought out loud. "No paper residue, though. If he fired through an envelope or a cardboard carton, CSU should have turned up bits of paper, other packaging materials."

"Nothing like that in the reports."

"Unless it was missed or considered unimportant. Then again, someone as forensically aware as GQ could have cleaned up after himself."

"Or he might have figured out a way to shoot that wouldn't leave any paper residue," I added. "Stick the muzzle through the paper before he fired."

She thought on it for a moment then shook her head. "Wouldn't Vince Polizzi be just a little suspicious of someone aiming a package at him? I don't want to engage in cultural stereotypes, but don't his people have a lot of experience with hostile violinists and florists?"

"True."

"And we still have that weekend delivery problem." She faced me. "Do you think there's any chance that Patterson might be our boy?"

"The Vice cop? I passed on Patterson's name to Kieff, but GQ announcing himself in the form of a Vice cop would be a little risky for someone who knows as much about police procedure as our killer appears to know."

"As risky as knowing about a trap, and walking right into it like we hope he will?"

"You *would* bring that up." I tapped on the steering wheel as I pushed something around in my head. "What if the top of GQ's priority list isn't getting Mom laid? What if it *is* winding up dead? Suicide by cop? Have you been reading GQ's little written glimpses of life?"

"The one where he fantasizes about getting a little girl he met in the park to put him out of his misery?"

"Yes. Think he might've given up on unqualified little girls? He knows you took down Gerald Soams, perhaps a few others. He knows my kill record. Say what you will about us, we know how to kill."

We rolled for half a block before she said, "It doesn't matter why he comes to the door, does it? For our purposes? If he wants to kill us or have us kill him, the end result is the same: whoever is quickest and sharpest comes out on top."

I shrugged. "Maybe it takes a nut to catch a nut."

"Are you a nut?"

"Indeed. So are you. Everyone's crazy."

She silently scanned the shadows, at last saying, "Joe, after we took down Gerald Soams and I left the department, I spent a few weeks in the psych wing out at Riverside General. Voluntarily."

"It'd sound worse if you didn't own the hospital."

She smiled. "It does come in handy when you want to get out of a locked psych ward."

"Just keep threatening people until you find someone who wants to keep his job."

She laughed at that. "I never had the need to test it. I knew the people there and trusted them. That and I needed help. I wasn't very experienced when we went after the Gray-eye Killer. I had all this psychology from college, but no one was teaching a course on what happens to you when you make yourself into the right kind of bait to catch a Gerald Soams. The work I did in becoming Margarita Azzurro is nothing compared to what I did in becoming a fourteen year old male whore named Julius." She shook her head and looked out of the side window. "Would you believe me if I told you that my first impression of Gerald Soams was that he was a great guy, intelligent, that he was a protector—my benefactor—that he had nothing but my best interests at heart?"

"I'll always believe you."

"He was a monster—" She faced me, her eyebrows ascendant. "What did you just say?"

"I said I'll always believe you."

She stared at me for a good five seconds and then faced the front. "Gerald Soams was a monster, but no one told me he was also a human being." She reached out a hand and squeezed my arm. "I'm still in therapy. Is that a deal killer?"

"My therapist can beat up your therapist. Maybe we can get into couples counseling and save on volume."

She laughed, then after another long silence, she asked, "What kind of man are you, Joe?"

I glanced at her and looked back at the street. "Human, mostly. What kind of question is that?"

"What do you do with truth? Do you let it live, hide from it, kill it, face it?"

I turned left on Ninth and thought on her question. What is my relationship with reality? "I'm in therapy right now on that very question."

"Found any answers?"

"I hide from some truth. There's a lot of truth I'm hiding from right now because it's a lot less confusing than rubbing my nose in it." I glanced at her. "I'm a detective, though, and truth is what I do."

"Tell me a truth you hide from."

As we crossed Pike, I pulled up in front of the main sales building of the still-operating Gallant's Nursery, put the car in park, and leaned back in the seat. A couple of dark figures approached from the shadows, determined that what they needed the occupants of the pimpmobile didn't have, and faded back into the night.

"A truth I hide from," I repeated, facing her. "Okay. I see you the way you are now, and up on that stage dancing before me, and I forget the job, why we're here, anything about everything. What I know is that you are all I've ever wanted and you have to be mine. I need you more than oxygen, but the truth I hide from? We're on the job, it's a part you're playing: a wig, contacts, a couple of really dynamite dance numbers. I really don't know much about you and I don't give a damn." Her eyes studied a point in space, her full lips pressed into a tight line. "More?" I asked.

She nodded.

"Okay, in my guts I call it love, but it seems like an addiction. I want you right now so badly that my heart actually hurts. Both times in those individual dances, you could've put a gun in my ear and I couldn't have kept my hands off you. Talk about feathers. You're not real. I only met you for the first time a few days ago. It is *insane*. Of course, so am I. But, that's another truth I hide from."

"Why do you say you're insane?"

"Everybody is. Every now and then someone defines himself out of the pack, but that's just a semantic exercise. Look what people do: They're crazy. Look what we're doing tonight: Trying to get someone to kill us. We're crazy." I held out my hands. "Look, I'm not even sure *I'm* real. My goldfish, Jaws, loves me as Santino Mirabella but he won't give me the time of day when I'm not wearing makeup. I mean I paid a woman fifty dollars to hang up my coat! That's not Joe Torio. I'm in trouble here." I stared at the street lights, watching the cold cones of mercury vapor illumination cast everything on the street in shades of steel. I faced her, reached out my hand, and placed it on her cheek. "Betty Grable says when I was a child I wasn't cuddled enough. The most recent woman I shared that with spent the rest of the night torturing me with no whales."

"Are you going to explain that someday?"

"If you're still around."

"I'll be around." She took my hand in both of hers and held it to her breast. "Joe, did you ever jump in the middle of something because you thought you had all the answers, and all of a sudden find out you don't have a clue?"

"You just described the main plot line of the autobiography I've been doing for Betty."

She kissed my fingers, raised her head, and looked through the windshield. "Let's go home, Sonny. You won't believe what I have waiting for you tonight."

The Caddy left some rubber on the road.

BROKEN DOLLS

At Margarita Azzurro's house, Julia showered first. She was wearing a green bathrobe when she came out. Cocking her head toward the bathroom, she said, "all yours." As I showered alone, my fantasies were jammed on overload. Afterward, I noticed a towel had been hung over the window for privacy. Drying myself, I noticed another green bathrobe hanging on the inside of the door. I lifted it from the hook, and beneath was a pair of midnight blue cotton pajamas. I stepped out of the bathroom wearing the pajamas and saw Julia sitting in the center of the bed, her back propped up with several pillows. She was clad in a print flannel nightgown that went all of the way up to her neck and all the way down to her wrists and ankles—a field of wildflowers. "Why do I get the feeling that I misunderstood slightly what was going to happen here?"

She smiled and patted the mattress. "Sit here." I tossed the bathrobe on the foot of the bed and sat next to her. She pulled me back until my head and shoulders were resting on her lap, her arms cradled around me, drawing me in close to her breast. "Can you hear my heart?"

"Mmm. Yeah."

"Your therapist was right, Joe. You haven't been cuddled enough. Tonight you're going to get cuddled." I began sitting up and she pulled me back down. "It doesn't matter where the cuddling comes from, Joe. Just so it's made of love."

"Am I on Candid Camera?"

"Relax. You're stiff as a plank."

"That's not the only thing that's stiff."

"Loosen up." She began rocking me slightly, stroking my face. "Relax."

"Goo, goo."

"Shut up."

Cuddling. Well, damn. I learned one thing about being cuddled: There's a big wall I had to let down first. Trust. Not a problem with babies. Mistrust has to be learned. But, what's not to trust with Julia disguised as she was as a G-club dancer named Margarita, the slayer of psycho hit man Dion Orgoglio, executioner of the Gray-eye Killer, expert markswoman and black belt butt kicker. I sighed, began letting my muscles go limp, half-suspecting I was being used to massage some sick mother fantasy of hers. As each muscle group let go, my mind wandered back to The Score, the two of us standing, writhing, touching in a bath of light before a shadow world filled with ravenous gazes, all of it to the *Adagio*, Julia's tribute to the child-killer she had slain.

My cell phone rang making me start. I brought myself back to the real world and sat up. "Too bad. I was just about to get into breast feeding." Leaning forward, I reached to the chair where I had dumped Sonny Mirabella's threads and pulled out my cell phone. "Torio."

"It's Kieff. I think you found some more ears."

"What? Say again." I held the phone so Julia could hear.

"Patterson, that Vice cop you wanted me to run?"

"Yeah?"

"Well, he's not on T&A detail, he's not in Vice, and he isn't even on the job."

"Was he ever a cop? He came across very convincing."

"Personnel says there was a Drew Patterson who was busted out of Vadalia Detectives in 'Ninety-four. Administrative reasons."

"Weenie-waver?"

"Unknown. Was he still there after Julia's performance?"

"No. He was there during it. I saw him. After it was over I looked for him but he was gone. Is he on Ward's surveillance repeater list?"

Kieffer called out off the phone and a muffled voice called out, *"Not yet,"*

"Hear that, Joe?"

"Yes."

"I wouldn't take any comfort from that. If he's any good with make up, he could have a different face every night. By the way, thanks for sending up the barfing burglar and tossing the whole case into the crapper."

"Any time."

"Ahmed Shapiro. Along with his chunk he blows the direct connection of Anderson and company to the crime scene, and IAB is done with the case. Lt. Trask thinks we're chasing black cats in the dark and he's gone, along with his help. Still there's enough that Dock says to keep after them. Anderson lives alone: Apartment at twelve twenty-four Wilson. No one in the building knows where he is. Carleton's wife doesn't know where Carlton is, either. She's worried. They had some words when they were last within shouting range of each other."

I glanced at Margarita. "Maybe he's off getting his knob polished."

"I talked to his wife, Donna," said Kieffer. *"If a honey on the side is Dave Carlton's only alternative, he has a better chance of surviving the night if he's the killer's next victim."*

"What are we supposed to do, Kieff?"

"Keep on totin' that barge, homeboy, at least until we get the cuffs on Anderson and Carlton. We're not sure of anything right now. If GQ is spooked and on the run, it's not very likely he'll come calling on you. It's out state wide and on all the stations. Every surveillance monitor at the gentleman clubs must have a copy of Carlton's and Anderson's faces by now. Roadblocks, train and bus stations covered, and the airport. If they haven't left the city, we'll get them. Ants with their faces couldn't hide in South River tonight. Is your one true love listening in?"

"Hi, Kieff," said Margarita.

"Hi, PI. Is Joe being a gentleman?"

"He's being a gentle man. Kieff, did you toss the chaplain's apartment?"

"He carries the rank of captain, so it wasn't exactly tossed. A quick peek."

"Can you describe it?"

"Stan made notes." Papers rustling. *"Nothing out of the ordinary. Two bedroom apartment, separate living room, dining room, and kitchen. Okay furniture if you're a little old lady—that's Stan's comment. The second bedroom he has set up as a home office. We have a forensic computer whiz going through the chaplain's hard drive, and the poor guy is being burnt out by sheer monotony."*

"Any password protected files," I asked.

"Nothing."

"Any porn tapes, magazines, other stuff?"

"No porn. No tapes at all. No VCR, no TV, not even a radio."

"Was he robbed?"

"Nope. That's just the kind of hairpin he is. We didn't find a gun, but in his toilet tank we did find a bottle of Bacardi Amber. Anything you two need?" he asked. *"Backup, a tank, SWAT team, a justice of the peace?"*

She glanced at me, grinning. "All we need right now is a killer and a way to go at him."

"I got it." Two beats. *"Take care of my partner."*

"For my whole life," she said into the phone. There was something resembling a stunned pause, then the connection was cut. I punched off the phone and looked at her, wondering if she could expand on that theme just a little. Before I could go into action, she said, "Joe, did you watch a lot of TV and movies when you were a kid?"

I placed the cell phone on the nightstand, and turned back. "For most of my time in school, my only friend was a TV."

"Chaplain Anderson isn't our boy, is he?"

"Not a chance. It's TV and movie addiction that hooks everything together in this case. In a way GQ is recreating the home he grew up in, and his existence was—still is—in twin orbits around his mother and the TV. Nathan Sunday was an outcast. Big athlete, top student, and no one to hang with except a TV. Chaplain

Anderson has no TV." I studied her a moment. "What about your old partner, Carlton?"

She thought about it for a moment, narrowed her eyes, and thought about it some more. At last she shrugged and said, "I can't see it. Would you grant me that I'm pretty good with undercover disguises?"

"A master."

"GQ is also very good. An expert. He can be anyone." She shrugged. "Dave would be the last on my list, though, he's such a by-the-book zombie—" Her eyebrows climbed slowly as she faced me. "Speaking of unlikely illiterate gun-toting insensitive TV addicted morons."

The light dawned. "Son of a gun." I reached for my cell phone, "If you want to hide a steak make it look like a meatball— Kieffer?"

"Yes?"

"I have a name for you, Kieff. TVs, machine guns, all kinds of cop connections, as well as a big fat connection to GQ, and you're going to laugh as soon as I say it. Look real hard at why you're laughing. Ready?"

"Do your worst."

"Scott Poleman, Baldwin Chief of Police."

Long silence which grew longer and longer. *"Jesus,"* Kieffer muttered finally. Another silence. *"Jesus,"* again. *"This isn't good. Man, we're going to have to roust Dock out of bed for this. Chief Harolds. The State Police. How come you started liking Poleman?"*

"Group effort. It's far from a sure thing, but he makes more sense than Carlton or Anderson."

"Gotta go, Joe. Decisions need to be made and everyone who can make them is in bed. I can see the headlines now: 'South River Invades Baldwin.'"

"Go for it. It'll replace high school basketball."

"Something ought to. Man, I don't know if we can get this sorted out before morning. Keep your guard up."

After he punched off, I sat there thinking about Scott Poleman. "That one machine gun on Poleman's wall. What was it?"

"The Soviet RPK-74?" she asked.

"Yeah. Too big to be concealed in anything. What size round does it use?"

"7.62mm. GQ uses a nine." She cocked her head to one side. "In certain circles, though, fully automatic weapons are like cockroaches."

"For every one you see, there are seven hiding in the walls?"

"Yes." She frowned and looked at me. "Did you lock the door?"

"Lock the door?"

"I thought I heard something."

"Don't ever say that. Don't you watch movies? Every time someone says that, sooner or later some guy with a big forehead comes crashing through the door with a butcher knife."

In four seconds I was at the door. It was locked. After a minute, between the two of us, we checked all of the doors and windows on that floor and the basement at least three times as well as peeked in all the closets. When we were done, we just stood in front of the bed looking at each other. "Tea?" asked Julia.

"Tea," I agreed and followed her to the kitchen.

Two o'clock in the morning back in bed, Anderson, Carlton, Patterson, and Poleman were still on the loose, their faces interrupting the Nite Owl Theater movie on Channel Nine every half hour. Only the reflected light from the television for illumination, Peter Lorre as the inscrutable Mr. Moto in Nineteen thirty-eight taking a last chance investigating a temple in Indochina, the sound off, our backs propped on pillows, our hands finding one another.

"What's your favorite color?" I asked her.

"Yellow. Yours?"

"Red."

"Yellow and red go together." Her eyebrows went up. "Favorite classical?"

"I'm big on Beethoven, Bach, Orff."

"Bach Orff yourself, yuk, yuk, yuk."

I poked her thigh. "What about you?"

She frowned. "Copland and Gershwin. Favorite opera?"

379

"The *Niebelungenlied* by Elmer Fudd and Bugs Bunny."

"Mine too."

"You have a favorite big band?"

"Benny Goodman," she answered.

"That guy at your place, the tailor. Is his name really Benny Goodman?"

She smiled and shrugged. "That's what it says on his carry permit and PI license."

"He's a PI?"

"Benny was the one who took me into his agency after I left the PD. He used to have offices in the Aubrey Tower on Sixteenth across from the bus terminal."

"And you paid him back by making him your tailor?"

"Benny always does exactly what he likes, and he likes tailoring clothes." She looked up at me. "What about panties?" she asked.

"What?"

"Where do you stand on thongs?"

"I make it a point never to stand on thongs," I answered. "What's your favorite sport?"

"Skiing."

"Great," I said, "I have one."

Her eyebrows descended into a mock frown. "Ready."

"The Whales of August."

Her eyebrows came back up. "What? You mean the movie?"

"Yes."

"Is this a deal-killer?"

I nodded. "My dream come true, if you come down on the wrong side of *The Whales of August* issue, we are history. Maybe not this minute or even a year from now, but eventually, in the dead of some cold, lonely winter night, one of us will take a chainsaw to the other."

She nodded and fixed the TV with a thoughtful expression. "I thought *The Whales of August* was a great setting and a splendid cast waiting desperately for a story worth telling and a screenwriter imaginative enough to tell it. While I watched, to keep myself awake, I hammered bamboo splints beneath my toenails and set them aflame."

"Such pretty toes, too. My, my, my."

"What are you thinking about, DiMaggio?" she whispered.

"I guess I'm waiting."

"For what?"

"For this appalling secret about you to be revealed that's going to blow us out of the water. You're a Satanist lesbian Mafia princess alien from outer space who likes spinach, or something. Not that any of those things couldn't be worked through, except for the spinach. Never could abide anyone eating slime."

"What about money?"

"I don't have much," I said, "but you're welcome to it."

"You know what I'm talking about," she said.

"Yeah. Okay, tycoon, how big is your pile?"

"About seven hundred million if the market doesn't trip again." She stared at me for a moment. "You don't seem phased."

"The number's too big. I can't relate it to anything." I thought a moment. "Considering the amounts the government is tossing into the black hole every second, seven hundred million is sort of chump change." I looked at her. "Money and the things it can buy me aren't super important. I mean, you've seen my car."

"I think your car says a lot more about a lack of self-esteem than it does a lack of avarice. We are going to have so much fun in couples counseling."

"I can hardly wait. Are we still an item?"

One corner of her mouth pulled back in a wry smile. "Do you know what I'm thinking about, Joe?"

"No. What."

"I've been wondering how you'll feel about me after I shuck Margarita Azzurro and go back to being Julia Powers. My fatal flaw just might be nonexistence."

"I was thinking of calling her, you know," I said.

"Who?"

"Margarita Azzurro—the real Margarita Azzurro." Dead silence. "I mean, not really. It crossed my mind, though. What happens when this investigation is over and you turn back into a pumpkin?"

She was studying me with those Margarita Azzurro eyes, and they were not amused. She got out of bed, went to the closet, pulled a handbag from it, went into the bathroom, and closed the door behind her with not quite a slam. Almost immediately the shower went on.

So much for amusing banter. While she was in the shower cooling down her fires, I was noting that once again Torio's ducks in a row managed to arm themselves. I made up and discarded about a dozen lame I-was-just-kidding lines and was about to call and wake Betty Grable up for some quick advice when the bathroom door opened.

I turned my head and saw reflected in the bathroom light Julia wearing a loose-fitting sheer robe that seemed to sparkle as though dusted by infinitely small diamonds. As graceful as a drifting cloud, she went to the bedroom door, reached out her hand, and turned on the lights.

Margarita Azzurro was gone—and a rapidly fading memory she was, too. The wig, the makeup, the manner, all gone. What was there was enough to tear out my heart and make it happily dance all over the bed. Golden hair, sapphire eyes, skin as pale as peach blossoms. It was one-hundred percent, genuine, non-shrinkable, Julia Powers. I realized I hadn't taken a breath for a while and let the air rush into my lungs as I wondered if I could measure my blood pressure with a truck tire gauge.

Her graceful fingers moved to the tie on her robe, pulled the loose end, and with a whisper she let the robe slide from her shoulders to the floor. She wasn't completely naked. She was wearing a pair of pale blue panties. Down off-the-hip Bikini panties. She turned slowly and, as her back was toward me, she looked over her shoulder.

The curve of her exposed waist moved flawlessly into the widening of her hips, that delicious dip of butt-crack at the top. My fevered gaze moved up to her face, her eyes. She had one raised eyebrow. She hooked her thumbs in the tops of the panties, bent forward slightly, and slowly pulled them down, first lifting her right foot out, then her left. Agonizingly slow, she turned until her body faced me.

"Margarita who?" I croaked.

Her eyes crinkled at the corners, she laughed, reached out her hand, and turned out the lights.

"What made GQ, Joe?" We tried for an hour but neither of us could sleep. I rolled to my right and faced her silhouette.

"He was his mother's in-between lovers lover. The boy must have been sexualized before he was even old enough to name what was going on. Sunday was the center of attention until some man came into his mother's life, then he was squeezed out. The men doing the squeezing weren't gentle about it, either. Cruel beatings, probably even to the extent of brain damage. I think he killed one of his rivals when he was still in grade school."

"Mango Bayo."

I nodded. "That ripped up his mother, and he didn't resist any of his mother's subsequent lovers until Harry Douglas. By then Nathan was big and strong, good old Gold Medal Harry looked like he was going to stick, and Nathan squeezed back. Harry left, and Nathan's mom killed herself. That pushed him the rest of the way over the edge. One way or another he's been trying to make up for it to his mom ever since."

"What about William Riggs?" she asked.

"A pawn. In college, when Nathan killed those couples in Philly and Boston, Riggs knew about them. Nathan Sunday has got something on Riggs, though. It's big. It seems big to Riggs, anyway."

"What do you think it is?"

"Nathan Sunday's thing is becoming whatever you most want him to be." I nodded and looked at Margarita. "He did that to Riggs, too. Riggs loves Nathan Sunday."

"Sex?" she asked.

"That's a stronger motive than revenge. I think Riggs likes what he's doing, though. There's a certain addiction to living on the edge of death. Nathan found another broken doll like himself and he mended it until it became a monster like himself—part-time monster. That's only one of the things that's been confusing me up until now. I feel that GQ is a loner but he keeps doing things that require more than one person, like all of these sniper stunts. Riggs is like an appendage of Sunday's. A tool. In his head, Sunday is still a lone wolf. Then there's his Guardian side." I stared at my feet, suddenly realizing that they were icy cold. I lifted my legs and sat cross-legged on the bed. Glancing at my handheld, I thought about all of those poems by Nathan Sunday.

"Julia?"

"What, Joe?"

I put my arm around her shoulders. She was cold, too. I pulled the blanket from the bed and wrapped it around us both. "You know what made my pop such a successful executioner?"

"What?"

"He was technically perfect at his job—never slow-strangled a client or tore off one of their heads. That was important. But Nicolo Torio also knew the men that he hanged. The condemned men he hanged knew that their executioner knew them—knew that he was hanging a man. That's why Leroy Brown, the man who taught me to street fight, that's why he thought he owed my old man: Nicolo Torio hanged Leroy's father. Leroy knew that Pop knew he was hanging a human being." Beneath the blanket, I rubbed her arm, warming it. "Pop knows everything about every man he ever hanged. He ought to write a book. He told me he even loved some of them."

"Honey bumps," she said, leaning into me, "What's this have to do with Nathan Sunday?"

"I think Sunday has picked me to kill him because he wants his executioner to know him." I let the statement hang in the air for a moment so I could listen to its echoes. After a minute it still sounded right. "He didn't know me except by reputation before he picked me. All he knew was that I had the department record for perps killed in the line of duty and he knew about my Third Eye. I'm guessing he wanted us both to die in some kind of Twilight of the Gods Gotterdammerung splat, but he's gotten to know me."

"He's gotten to know you?" she urged.

"Yeah. I think he's changed his mind about me being dead." I looked at her. "But his wiring is still intact."

"You mean the bait is working?"

"If it wasn't working—if he could resist what we're doing—he wouldn't be trying so hard to scare me off. He'd just leave."

I picked up my handheld and called up one of Sunday's poems that I had marked. Margarita and I read a little piece of it:

> the unwritten law
> is written
> on a thousand broken hearts
> no matter how clever you are
> no matter how brave you are
> no matter how many times
> you carry that ball
> across that goal line
> showering them all with shining victories
> you may not cross
> that other line
>
> the belonging have spoken

"Joe," she said, Margarita's large dark eyes looked at me. "Can we take him alive?"

"Being alive ourselves at the end of this is still in question. Being taken alive is not at all part of Sunday's plan."

She nodded at the handheld. "Turn it off."

I touched off the handheld, turned out the light, and settled back under the covers, Julia snuggled against me. "I wonder if all kids in school feel like outcasts," she said. "I did."

"What was your crime?"

"A good many of my classmates' fathers worked for my father. After a couple of unfortunate dates where I found it necessary to forcibly refuse amorous advances, the rumor was spread that I was a lesbian." She laughed and looked up at me. "Which, nonetheless, didn't appear to help me with the lesbians in my class, either. As one girl put it, I have money; I don't need friends."

385

I placed both arms around her and held her. "Maybe no one ever does belong. Maybe the best anyone can do is convince others that they belong." I kissed her forehead and asked, "Didn't you have any fun in school?"

"Sure. Not with other students, though. Horses, sports, academics, movies," she grinned, "our mutual old friend, the TV."

"Family? I read about your father dying some years ago. Any other family?"

"A younger sister and my mother. My sister's name is Melia. She goes to MIT." She smiled and placed a hand alongside my cheek. "Once I have my hooks in you so deep you cannot possibly get away, I'm going to bring you home to meet my mother."

"Half an hour good for you?"

She laughed once, studied me very closely, then laughed again.

About four in the morning we got a call from Kieffer that Scott Poleman was in custody. Dave Carlton and Drew Patterson were still in the wind. Margarita and I fell asleep leaving the TV on tuned to Channel Seven's Night Shift Cinema playing *High Noon*.

THIS PERFECT DAY

If you roll a ball down a slope and it hits a rock, the ball's direction will change. Left, right, it might even hop over the rock, depending upon the speed and size of the ball, it's resilience, the angle of it's descent, the nature of the slope's surface, and the size and shape of the rock. If you can see and understand all those things, you can predict the new direction the ball will take. It looks like magic to those who don't see the same things, but it's not magic. It's physics; no big deal.

Sometimes I can see the directions people will take. When the direction has already been taken, sometimes I can see why. It looks like magic or luck to those who don't see the same things I do, but it's not. It can be a big deal, though, especially when it doesn't work. Once when it didn't work I left a couple of quarts of blood on the parts room floor of Rizzo Brothers Volkswagen-Audi and died. Another time when it didn't work I had to kill a man, an old wino named Paul Baines.

I rolled over and looked at the woman sleeping there, on her left side, facing me, her eyes closed, her face relaxed. I closed my eyes and remembered what this puzzle—what Julia Powers—looked like. I wondered if GQ would survive the encounter that had to happen and wondered if this woman and I would survive it. If we did survive, I wondered if our love could withstand us stepping from behind the makeup and costumes and putting down the guns and the reasons for the guns.

Leroy Brown used to tell me it's suicide to go into a fight "thinking loser." As I looked at this woman, I was thinking that I suddenly had a lot to lose. There was Julia coming toward me, clouds swirling around us both, my gaze caressing every curve, every touch of her

387

sending me into madness. When Kieff had asked her to take care of me, she had said, "All my life." The door was before me, the doorbell ringing, Julia standing there wearing only a cloud of blue diamond dust, looking through the peephole. A new angel, her hair flaxen, her eyes blue. —The door burst open, the light from outside blinding me. As bursts of gunfire came from the light, slugs ripped through both of us and I opened my eyes.

It was morning.

I looked at Julia, her Margarita eyes wide open, not moving. Before I could calm down my heart or call Winnie at MCU for an update, I heard the slight squeak of brakes coming from the street in front of the house. Julia and I exchanged a shocked glance, she jumped from the bed, grabbed her green robe, and raced into the living room. I checked my watch: five after seven. I grabbed Santino's .44 from beneath my pillow, my pajama bottoms and green robe from the floor, and raced after her.

Inside the living room, Julia was looking through the vertical blinds at the street, her right hand holding a .38 semi automatic, her left hanging a towel around her neck against the chill in the room. When she was done, she held out another towel toward me. It was freezing, but I waved off the offer and struggled into my pajama bottoms as, back in the bedroom, my cell phone began ringing. "Julia!" I whispered. "Don't open the door even if it's the Pope. *Especially* if it's the Pope!"

"That's Margarita," she whispered back.

I waved back, turned, ran back into the bedroom, grabbed the cell phone from the night stand, punched it on, and held it to my ear as I rushed back to the living room. "What?"

"Slugger, we got Anderson." It was Dock.

"Say what?"

"The Magena PD just brought in Charles Anderson. We have him in the Tower right now. Kieffer just called to let us know the State Police will have Poleman in the Tower in a few minutes."

"Dock, I wouldn't sound the all clear just yet. I think we might be getting a visitor here. You at that command center on Randall and Houlihan?"

"Yes."

"What about Carlton and Patterson?"

"Don't have them yet."

I looked at Julia and whispered, "Dock says Anderson and Poleman are in custody, Carlton and Patterson are still out there."

She gestured with a finger toward the street. "Look at this."

"What."

"I think I just figured out who everyone in this neighborhood would welcome into their homes half-naked on a weekend no matter what time it was."

"What is it?" Dockery demanded.

"Wait one."

I rushed to Julia's side and looked through the blinds. There was a dark late model green van parked behind the pimpmobile, the words Prize Patrol emblazoned in gold on the side. There was a big man wearing a heavy chocolate colored overcoat standing on the passenger side, leaning through the window, talking to the driver. His breath was visible in the icy morning air. He was well over six feet tall, heavy, but carrying it well, much of his hair hidden beneath a brown fedora. What little of his hair that could be seen was silver. In the rear seat of the van were two or three others, keeping warm, waiting for the lucky winner to open her door before ambushing her with balloons, television cameras, and mountains of money. The man straightened up and looked over the top of the hood toward the house. I held the phone to my ear.

"Dock, what do we do? It's the Prize Patrol!"

"Pull the other one and it plays 'Jingle Bells'."

"I am *not* kidding, man! TV crew, and Prize Patrol van. This old guy coming to the door has a check in his hand."

A thoughtful silence on Dockery's end. *"Who wouldn't open the door to a man bringing you a million dollars, whatever day it was, whatever you got going on?"* he said.

"I feel like opening it now."

"Is he carrying anything?"

"Just a number ten envelope in his right hand. Thin. Nothing in the left."

"Overcoat?"

"Yeah. Buttoned all the way up. Insulated leather gloves on both hands. Dock, are you sure we have Nathan Sunday in custody?"

"I'm sure we have Anderson and Poleman in custody." A voice from the other side of the trailer. *"Ward says Stan Brooks just nailed your boy Patterson out at Temple Glen. That's everybody but Carlton."*

"And Riggs," I added.

"Should we start rolling?"

I could feel a weight climbing on my shoulders. It was imaginary, but heavy all the same. "MCU comes rolling in like an armored division, GQ sees it, and he's gone."

"Not to mention that TV crew capturing it all on tape. Hang on, Slugger," said Dock.

Julia shushed me and said in a whisper, "He's coming to the door."

"That might be Carlton," I whispered back.

The man turned from the van and began walking with a determined stride toward the door. I checked him again. His hands were gloved against the cold, his overcoat buttoned up all the way. In his gloved right hand was a letter-sized envelope emblazoned in green and gold. His left hand, gloved as well, was clenched against the cold. Julia poked my shoulder.

"That's not Carlton."

"What if he is?" I pressed.

"Then it's a great disguise," she whispered. "How did he grow five inches? I'd love to swap makeup tips with him. Where's the gun? If it's concealed in his overcoat, how does he get to it? The coat's buttoned. Heavy gloves on both hands, and his arms are in those sleeves. And look at all those people in the van. We are agreed that when he hits the crime scene GQ is a loner?"

"Any great truth is subject to amendment when contradicted by the facts."

"This guy comes with a camera crew, Joe."

Those gloved fingers couldn't fit in the trigger guard of anything smaller than a howitzer. Take off the gloves, unbutton the overcoat—even if the overcoat was Velcroed shut, Vince Polizzi could've run all the way upstairs before this guy could have pulled out his Uzi. A driver and a camera crew? "Why are they still sitting in the van?"

"Margarita stared through the blinds. "Could that be Carlton?" she said to herself. "Is it possible?"

"As a man once said to me, saber-toothed crotch crickets from outer space are possible," I whispered.

When nothing fits, I recalled Dock telling me more than a decade before, it might not be the pieces that have the problem. It might be the holes you're trying to stick them in. I moved to the peephole in the front door and looked at the approaching figure. Wire-rimmed glasses, big straight nose, fleshy face, good-natured grin.

"What if we don't answer the bell? He'll go away, right?" There was a squeaky little voice coming from my cell phone. I held it to my ear. "What?"

"Hey, Joe?"

"Dock, can you call whoever runs the Prize Patrol thing and find out if this for real?"

"Winnie's on it, but they're all over the country. You don't sound like you have the hour or two it's going to take to get an answer."

"That envelope," said Julia. "That's probably the check. He'll slip that through the mail slot and go away, unless they want to come back for the video footage. —If that's for real."

"I wonder how much it is," I said. "Margarita is going to flip." I looked through the peephole until I had a close-up of the man's blue and silver silk necktie. All my senses went numb as the focus of the universe reduced to a single point. I staggered back from the door.

"What?" Julia whispered.

I stood there, numbly shaking my head. The doorbell bing-bonged, I turned and looked at Julia.

The doorbell bing-bonged again and I put my eye back to the peephole. There was an eye looking back.

"Hello?" came the voice from outside. "Hello! Miss Azzurro? This is the Prize Patrol. Congratulations."

The voice was deep, TV rich. I glanced down at the cell phone in my left hand and Sonny's .44 in my right.

"He's not leaving," whispered Julia from the living room window.

"No one's coming out of the van, right?"

She held her right palm toward me as she shook her head, keeping her eyes on the man in brown and his van. "No one's moved."

"They never will," I whispered. "They're not real."

Five seconds passed and the doorbell bing-bonged two more times. Then the man knocked. I looked through the peephole again and as the fellow lowered his left hand, he gestured at the van with it, then turned back and pushed the doorbell again. "Miss Azzurro? Miss Azzurro?"

I cut off Dock and punched in a number, placing the cell phone on the floor and returning to the peephole, I raised Sonny's .44.

One second, two, three.

As a faint ringing came from the other side of the door, the man started and I did a rough aim with the forty-four through the door, keeping my eye to the peephole. "Freeze, Kieffer! Police! Don't move that arm! Don't move a hair! Don't even twitch!"

The man took a half step back, his mouth open.

"Freeze! Freeze! *Freeze!* Kieffer, goddammit, this doesn't—"

He took another step back and began lifting the hand holding the envelope. I jumped to my right as the front of the brown overcoat erupted, a hail of nines flying through the cheap door. The hits in my lower left abdomen felt like cannon balls, an eerie silence as though someone had punched reality's mute button.

On my side, seeing Julia running toward me into Ed's line of fire, I aimed high—one, two, three, four—I fired back through the door, the .44 jumping in my hand, deafening me. Light came through all ten holes.

"Joe!"

I gestured with my head toward the door. "He down?"

She gave a quick peek through the peephole. "He's down." Julia knelt next to me, pulled the towel from around her neck, and pressed it against my lower left side. I pulled it back and looked. Not much blood yet. No major pipes perforated. I pressed the towel back against the wounds.

"Damn, that hurts. Get more towels. I'm sure I hit Kieffer."

"Kieffer?" Her face carried an expression of disbelief.

I gestured with my head toward my cell phone. "Call Dock—"

We both jumped at the tinny sounds of the automatic voice mail, giving me the opportunity to leave a message for Miles Kieffer. I reached out, punched the end-call, and handed it to Julia. "Go on. Call Dock. Get his rolling brigade over here and a couple ambulances before the reporters show."

As she punched in Dock's number, I pulled myself up by the doorknob. Once on my feet, I unlocked the door and looked back at Julia. With my cell phone in one hand and her gun in the other, she moved to her right, crouched, and nodded back. I opened the door and peeked around the corner.

The man was flat on his back, his arms at his sides, motionless. There were three holes in the overcoat, one over his heart, one low on his left shoulder, and one large smoking one above his right waist where all of his own shots had exited. One of my rounds had gone through the left side of his neck, the fourth had made a gutter wound from his left temple to just above his left ear. The blood from his neck was pumping onto the pavement.

"He's alive. Hit in the head and the neck. You got another towel?"

"Two of them." After two seconds she handed me a clean face towel. The man on his back gasped and began moving his right arm. I rushed to that side and put my knee on his wrist. "Keep the arm down, Kieff. An ambulance is on the way. Easy does it." I leaned over and pressed the folded towel against the man's neck wound. His eyes fluttered open. He was looking at me. "Just stay quiet." I leaned over and looked at the head wound. The trough was depressed, which might mean bone fragments driven into his brain. "It doesn't look too bad. Hang on."

A wave of dizziness caused me to steady myself. I glanced to my left, noted that the Prize Patrol sign was rolling up, all on its own. By now GQ was supposed to be inside, the door closed, the butchery begun. Don't need a sign outside attracting attention.

There was what looked like an inflatable Johnny Carson doll in the van's driver's seat. Julia moved across from me on Kieffer's left side next to his head and took over holding the towel against his neck. She was still talking on the phone to Dock. Faces in doorways were beginning to appear across the street. Sonny's .44 had awakened the neighborhood. "Tell him to hurry it up," I said. "We're going to have a crowd here any second."

"The ambulances are rolling. MCU ought to be here in a minute."

As if in a dream, I placed Sonny's .44 on the pavement and unbuttoned the man's overcoat. Once I was finished, I pulled back the right coat flap revealing a layer of body armor. The Kevlar vest was cut away on the lower right, the chest and stomach padded out to create a place just above the right hip where a machined-down and noise suppressed Micro Uzi was mounted. Through a ring mounted above the weapon there was a cable attached to the trigger, the other end running into the man's sleeve through a small pulley suspended from a leather strap looped around his right shoulder. From there the cable went down the right sleeve. I ejected the clip from the weapon, pulled the bolt and picked up the round ejected from the chamber, reached up the right cuff, felt a leather band, felt around it more and found a watch. I undid the heavy strap and buckle, reached into the armpit end of the sleeve and pulled out the cable, the wrist watch attached to the end.

I nodded at Julia. "The other side."

With her free hand Julia pulled open the left flap of the overcoat. Hanging inside the flap was a keyhole saw and two knives hanging from loops, a stubby one with a thick three inch blade and one with a slender seven-inch filleting blade. A pocket beneath his left armpit contained plastic bags, soap, towels, slippers, and duct tape. I cleared the knives and saw, placing them next to the Uzi clip. An additional weight seemed to add itself to the load on my shoulders and the back of my neck. A headache.

"He'd raise his arm, an envelope full of dreams in his hand, and the tension would build in the cable, putting pressure on the trigger. The hand extends a little further out, 'Here's your prize, lady,' and he pops four caps in his mother. He lowers his hand slightly, turns ten or fifteen degrees, tightens up again, and puts another four in the boyfriend. It's bolted to his side. Makes a pretty solid platform to kill the ride. Accurate." I leaned forward and saw how the waist on the trousers went around a metal loop, allowing the discharged casings to go down his right pant leg. I looked at the stoop where he had been standing when he shot at me. Neat little pile of brass, each polished case gleaming against the concrete.

"Joe?"

"What?"

"You're pale."

Things seemed strangely detached. I glanced down at the towel at my side. It was soaked red, my hand red to my wrist. Julia said, "He's fading, Joe."

"No." I looked back at him. "Hey, Nathan? Nathan? Is he still conscious?"

"I don't know." She reached to his left wrist, put her fingers inside the cuff of his glove and took his pulse. "Thready pulse. Rapid. Way over a hundred."

"Damn." I leaned over him, dug my fingers beneath the latex appliance on his face and tore my way down to his real face. "Kieff! Kieffer? Can you hear me?"

His eyelids fluttered but remained closed. I looked up and saw that Julia was staring at me. "What?"

"So, are you channeled into Sherlock Holmes? You got a call from the Shadow, flipped a coin, what?"

I stood and looked around as the shaking from my hands grew to encompass my whole body. While she continued to hold the improvised compress against Sunday's neck wound, Julia reached back to where she'd dropped my robe and handed it up to me. Still shaking, with my free hand I threw it over my shoulders.

"TV," I said to her through chattering teeth. I picked up the third towel from Sunday's leg and held it to my side. "They all watched TV. All the vics. Lots of TV.

We're all one big TV watching family, the vics, you, me, Nathan Sunday. Everything about Sunday is TV: The prize scam with celebrities handing out big-dollar dreams. Even this stunt with the gun. I'm sure I saw something like it on TV when I was a kid. Some movie or cop show."

"That's it?"

"Doesn't sound like much, does it? TV was my best friend: blam, you're shot."

Sunday was still breathing.

"I don't know," I said as I looked around, stupidly trying to recall why I had done what I had done. The ball had gone in a particular direction and what was the rock I'd seen? "What are the chances Margarita actually won a prize from these people?"

"You don't think they really give out prizes?"

"Not to people who don't mail in their forms. Margarita's is still on the telephone stand." That didn't sound like much. I looked down at the man's necktie.

"That was it. Kieff—Sunday ties a Windsor knot with a dimple." As I said that I saw the left corner of Kieff's mouth twitch back in a tiny smile.

"That's right, Kieff," I said, "a dimple. That Army picture where Riggs stood in for you? No dimple."

Julia nodded at me. "You have good instincts, Joe."

"Where is Dock with that bus?"

Nathan Sunday's eyes opened, "Joe?" he whispered as his eyes rolled.

"Yeah?"

He whispered something and I leaned in close to hear what he was saying. "Hate me," he said, *"Hate me!"* I heard a click then Sunday's left hand punched me just beneath my right armpit.

"Joe!" screamed Julia.

My gaze wobbled about, settling at last upon Julia wrestling with Kieff's—with Sunday's—left arm. Clutched in his gloved fingers was the switchblade he had loaned me to cut the duct tape back when I found the ears, the ears he had hidden. There was blood on it. Blood on his glove. I looked down to see a growing stain on the robe beneath my right armpit. "Aw, crap! I just finished physical therapy." I fell backward, landing seated on my tailbone.

"Ow," I said, looking at my bare feet out in front of me. They were very cold. The towel on my left love handle had fallen off, my side dripping. The right was dripping, too. "I'm messing up this crime scene something terrible. Mike'll be pissed."

Above Julia's shoulder, across the street, there was someone up on the roof of a gray-painted row house, crouching in the snow behind one of the gables. He had a rifle. What was that the hangman said about Morton's Salt? When it rains . . .

"Julia, don't move, don't turn. Riggs is on a roof across the street directly behind you. He's waiting for you to get out of the way so he can finish off Sunday."

"Riggs?"

"We didn't say anything about Sunday not bringing backup." I mentally flogged the thought through the molasses of my consciousness. "On his own. Riggs is clear if Sunday isn't captured alive. A little stink on him, maybe, but no conviction. He needs Sunday dead."

"How far?" she asked.

"Thirty-five—forty yards."

She looked up at me, her gaze steady on my eyes, and she smiled brightly. "That's going to be one hell of a shot with a pistol, Deadeye." I glanced down at Santino's .44 on the stoop. I'd never fired it before today, and this target wasn't only four feet away. Julia could see what I was thinking. "Unless you use a peculiar sight picture, Joe, those sights will work for you. They're zeroed in at fifty feet. You have two shots left, unless you left an empty chamber for a hammer rest. Did you?"

"Yeah. I got one shot left. He's got us in his sights, Julia. We need to sucker punch him. A distraction."

"I'll take care it," she said. "First, get up, kneel next to Sunday, and pick up your piece."

It was a long climb back up to my knees. My ribs on my right beneath my arm hurt like sin. Grateful for it, really. It seemed to be the only thing keeping me awake. Once I was next to Kieff, I sat back on my heels, picked up the .44. by its grip, rested it on Sunday's Kevlar vest, and looked over Julia's shoulder. Riggs had us dead in his sights. All we had to do was have Julia move over six or eight inches to her left and Riggs would put a round through Sunday's head and be on his way.

Stupid sounding: Still partners: Julia, me, Kieff.

I moistened my lips, glanced at Julia, and said, "Now."

She suddenly turned to her right, pointed, and issued an atom-splitting scream that made both me and Sunday jump. Riggs, too. For a split second he took his eye away from the scope to see what Julia was pointing at. I lifted the .44 in a two-handed grip, sighted for where the part in his hair should've been, raised the front blade up a couple of degrees, and squeezed the trigger. The weapon jumped. Riggs was motionless for a tantalizing second, then the rifle fell from his hands, he slid face first into the snow on the roof, beginning a small avalanche. I never saw him fall.

Julia was saying something, her hand pressing my right side. Something against my lower left. I could smell that special surf in the air from that ocean of warm black cotton, my skin tingling. —*Dock's voice.*

"Hey, what's up, Dock?"

A mush of sounds, some questions—Winnie there. Ward and Clair— I answered some of the questions before I realized I was no longer sitting on the stoop. Somebody gave me a shot. There was already an IV in. Lying down, I coughed and noticed flecks of blood on my fingers as things seemed to clear a bit. "What's this?" I held out my hand to a fuzzy face.

"He nicked your lung with that knife, detective. You'll be okay."

"Julia?" I looked around in the swim of images until I saw her looking back. She was holding my hand.

"I'm here." She turned to fuzzy face: "I'm going with him."

Fuzzy simply answered, "Yes ma'am." It's good to be the boss.

"Did I get him?" I asked her.

"You got him, Deadeye," she said. "You did all right."

"All right, hell," said Kathleen Turner with Winnie Hewitt's face. "You drilled Riggs right in his left temple."

"Another body. Broke my own damned record. A head shot yet. Drusilla Butts will have an orgasm. What about Sunday?"

"He's critical, but stable," answered someone.

Critical but stable. I don't know. That always sounded to me like someone is in deep shit and not coming out of it. Saw someone move. Old crimes needing amends. "Winnie?"

"Yes?"

"Sorry for what I said . . . you know, about the whales."

A little sunlight on my cheek, strangely warm, a cold, dark shadow. "Det. Torio! Det. Torio!" hollered a familiar voice: Drusilla Butts. How did Dock get to the crime scene before the press?

Oh. I plugged that leak when I plugged—

Had to laugh at that. Plugged that leak when I plugged that leak—

—Coughed again. I opened my eyes, saw blood spattered all over the white blanket they had on me, all over the straps across my chest. Not good.

"We'll be at Riverside General in a couple of minutes," said Julia. Buildings streaking by. I was inside the ambulance.

"Sunday," I said.

"He's in the other ambulance, Joe." I felt Julia's hand holding mine. I looked at her. The beautiful black wig was gone. Her blond hair was close to her head, stuck full of hairpins. Her Margarita contacts were still in, looking at me. "He stuck me, didn't he? Kieffer stuck me."

"Yes."

I closed my eyes. "Son of a bitch."

Bits and pieces searched for a place to go in my mind just in case this was the way I would have to remember myself for eternity. Your life is over. Nothing can be done about that. All that is left is the dying.

I rode the chairlift up the mountain, pushed off, the gleaming white unmarked corduroy beneath my skis, the wind sharp against my cheeks, gravity tugging at me, the sun crisp and bright, dancing with the mountain. Not alone this time, though. Me and Julia, Kieff and Miriam. I'd never met Miriam, but on the phone she sounded like Gloria Grahame in *The Big Heat*. We were all flying down Rogue Angel out at Sunday River: me, Julia, Kieff, and Gloria Graham. It was a perfect day.

HEROES ALL

There's a joke they tell in Narcotics Anonymous about the difference between an alcoholic and a drug addict: An alcoholic will steal your wallet, they say. A drug addict will steal your wallet, too, but he'll help you look for it.

In the hospital meeting the rehab patients and the NAs visiting from the local groups laugh at the joke because they've all been there one way or the other: helping that poor bastard try and find his wallet. After I was patched up again and allowed out of bed, I sat in on a few of the open meetings, numbly listening to the sharing, reading the literature, trying to get a handle on addiction, trying to get a handle on Nathan Sunday, on this great weight that seemed to be driving me into the dirt. From some of his writings I could tell he'd tried some Twelve Step meetings, searching for answers.

there is no anonymous program
for my affliction
i can see why
where would we meet
what would we call ourselves
how would we let others know
where the meetings are

hi
im bob
im a killer

hi bob
ratta-tat-tat-tat-tat-tat-tat

□

Bit-by-bit over the weeks I was there, I got the details from Julia. Miles Kieffer had bailed on the State Police shortly after the Poleman bust, saying that he was heading back to the Tower. Instead he returned to some apartment he had on Eighteenth overlooking King Elementary School where he transformed into the man everyone wanted to see. Then he hopped into his money-green van and came calling on the lure he knew was a lure because he had picked it and put it in place himself. Sunday had come to get executed and stayed to wind up in a coma on life support on the violent floor at Squirmhi.

The trigger. It must have torn him in two. Kieffer had asked me if I loved Julia, and when I answered that I did, the way I did, he knew I meant it down to my core. Real love. That was the worm on the hook. On the phone, when Sunday told Julia to take care of his partner, he had given her a chance to make a joke of it, to brush off her relationship with me as a mere fling, a fantasy on my part, to state for the record that her feelings were a long way from eternal commitment. But she had answered with "All my life," and that was the hook, line, and sinker. He had to come, and he had come to kill.

Betty Grable and I talked about this weight I couldn't lift off my shoulders. "Emotionally Miles Kieffer is still your partner, Joe; your friend. With his help you and Julia took down GQ, the Guardian, and the Sniper. But you can't celebrate because you lost your partner. You miss him."

A killer. I was missing a killer and I still didn't know what I had done in my youth to earn his bloody gratitude. Maybe he had seen me defend the fat kid at Covington. Maybe not. Now I'll never know.

I asked Betty if she thought Sunday—Kieffer—was the one who had killed Carlo Rizzo back when I was running out of blood in the Rizzo Brothers parts room. She thought for a long time about that before nodding and saying, "The tourniquet on your shoulder. That too."

William Riggs had stood in for Kieffer at Quantico, giving him an alibi for the Magena killings. For the

Booth Street killings, Dock was the alibi. Dock had talked to Miriam Kieffer to establish her husband's whereabouts when Vince Polizzi and Juna Salvati were killed. Dock thought that was her on the phone. In fact, she had been the one to call Dock about something else, and while he had her on the phone, Dock asked her. Yeah. Kieffer did a good Groucho and W. C. Fields, too. He could imitate his own wife with his tongue tied behind his back.

I avoided taking any calls from Vince Polizzi's father. Don Francesco wanted to honor me for answering his son's blood with the blood of his son's murderer. As a bonus, I probably could have had any three persons of my own choosing whacked for free. I didn't think I could listen to any of that.

I watched old movies, spent endless nighttime hours writing in my room sitting in the solarium with the lights out looking at the darkness on distant Breadloaf Mountain now that skiing season was over. When I was too tired to stay awake, I went to my room and held onto Julia. Then came the nightmares and she would gently awaken me, hold my head to her breast, and tell me she was there.

Feel sorry for the victims; that's what their killer told me to do. I did feel sorry for the victims: every last one of them. And I would pace the hospital's halls, wearing myself down, trying to escape my own thinking through exhausted sleep.

One night, about three weeks after I was operated on, Dock was waiting for me in the solarium when I got back from the N.A. meeting. The light from the outside floods cast everything inside in harsh shadows. "They keep this place open for me at night so I don't have to see anyone," I told Dock.

That immense chocolate toad stood facing me, those big browns glittering above a smirk. "So, how're you doing, DiMaggio?"

"Fine," I answered with a smirk of my own. In those meetings down on the first floor, I'd learned what FINE stood for: Feeling Insecure Neurotic and Emotional.

"I talked to Betty," said Dock. "She says she can't release you for work yet."

"She's waiting for me to have a big cry. I think she has stock in Kimberly-Clark."

"Who?" asked Dock.

"They make Kleenex.

"So, what's the problem? Turn on the water works."

"I've wasted enough tears on killers, Dock. Have you been through the stuff from his home yet?"

"Not all of it. There's a lot. Maybe two or three million words worth. Clair, Ward, and Winnie have been going through them and every five minutes one or the other of them comes running into my office to show me what they've just read. I may have to put the whole unit into therapy, which reminds me." He reached into his inside breast pocket and pulled out a letter-sized sheet of paper folded into thirds. "Clair ran across this one. She thought you might find it interesting."

I opened the sheet but couldn't make out the writing in the dark. Refolding it, I stuffed it in my bathrobe pocket. "What about Miriam and Mona?"

Dock glanced off to one side. "It's all bad road, Slugger. They don't know from killers. The only person they've ever seen was Miles Kieffer, a kind, intelligent, very funny, very loving husband and father."

"Nathan Sunday's best role," I remarked. "I kind of liked it, too."

"Julia arranged for some special counseling for them. Maybe it'll help."

"Dock, is there any way . . . I mean, Miriam, at least." I looked at him.

He slowly shook his head. "No, man. Not right now." He placed a hand on my shoulder. "She still thinks we had to have made some terrible mistake." He squeezed my shoulder and let it go.

Long uncomfortable silence indicating the need for a subject change. "I heard on the news the city council passed the special budget, Dock. Considering everything, I thought we were circling the drain."

"For the time being we're heroes. MCU is fully funded."

I burst out with a laugh. "The media is going along with it?"

"The *Herald* isn't anxious to play up the fact that Sunday used to be a reporter on its own staff, and the *Herald* owns Channel Seven. Everything will come out eventually, Joe, but right now the headline is: 'MCU Stops Killer'. We did good."

"Yeah. Sure was fortunate for us the killer was on our side."

"There is that," he agreed, his eyebrows raised.

I moistened my lips. "That first night on Booth Street, Dock, you told me this case had shades all over it. What did you know then?"

"I knew about the Magena killings." He stuck his hands in his pockets. "As soon as I saw the mess at Booth Street, it felt like a cop."

"You got your own third eye?"

He laughed. "When you get to be my age you learn to call it instinct." His smile faded as he settled his gaze on me. "It felt like a cop, Kieffer agreed and said we needed you." He shrugged slightly with one shoulder. "Turned out, he was right. Joe, I want you to start thinking about a promotion—"

"No."

"I haven't even told you what it is."

"No. I am not accepting any damned promotion. Not for this."

"For something else, then."

"Not for anything. Look, Dock, I'm still working up the courage to step outside of this building."

"Lieutenant, Joe. MCU Deputy Field Commander. It's what we talked about—"

"Do you have a brain clot, Dock? Promote Winnie Hewitt. She's got the time in the unit, she's smart, trained, capable, good leadership qualities, and need I point out she's already doing the job right this minute. She also has the added advantage of not being locked up in an insane asylum."

"Neither are you, Slugger."

"That's only because my girlfriend owns the place. Look, put Winnie in, Dock. She can hit the ground running and that's what the job deserves. I'm still trying to get my legs out of the shop. I mean it." I looked up at him and smiled. "My previous recommendation worked out well, didn't it?"

Dock burst out with a laugh. "Well, hell, yes. Besides GQ, your boy took down the Guardian, the South River Sniper, a corrupt chief of police in Baldwin and got a drunken, gambling addicted, whoring chaplain fired from the Police Academy. He even tracked down that ex-cop Patterson we collared for impersonating a police officer. Clean-sweep Kieffer we used to call him."

I gestured with my head in the general direction of the South River Mental Health Institute located at the south foot of Breadloaf Mountain. "What about Sunday? Any change?"

"Still in a coma," said Dock.

"They sure? He's one hell of an actor."

"They're sure, but they also have him under lock and key and twenty-four hour surveillance."

"What about Carlton? How come he never turned up that night?"

"True love, DiMaggio. He and his wife patched up whatever it was, took everything off the hook, and went to bed. Love conquers all."

The conversation hit a snag, filling the cavernous space with an awkward silence. Somewhere an intercom was calling out a Code Blue. Crash carts would be rolling, someone teetering on the fence between this world and the next would be coaxed back, maybe. Loved ones, maybe, waiting to be told that either everything is fine or life as they knew it had suddenly ceased. Guy in the N.A. meeting that night said that it seems like every now and then God gets bored, peeks over the edge of his cloud, and drops another bag of shit in the guy's lap just to see what he does.

I looked at Dock. "Thanks for keeping Pop up to date during this."

"It's what I do during your sundry hospitalizations, Slugger. Which reminds me." He reached into the side pocket of his overcoat, pulled out a clear plastic water-filled bag. "A little something for Jaws. As near as the guy in the pet shop can tell, it's a girl."

I looked at the bag in the light reflected from the outside floods. "Thanks. Maybe Jaws will fall in love before he eats her." I could see something moving around in there, but it was hard to tell what. "Did you find out about that other thing? Sunday's feet?"

"Sunday's feet are size ten. Linear and outline match."

"Size ten," I repeated. "Size ten. He was practically bellowing at us to take him down. No wonder Kieffer got so pissed at me every time I dismissed those foot impressions. Hand match, too?"

Dock nodded.

"Damn."

The door to the solarium swung open. Julia, Caitlyn, and Pop emerged from the shadows. The hangman was bundled in his heavy black overcoat, his hands in his pockets, Caitlyn on his left arm wearing her red parka. Julia was wearing a kick-ass blue suit, black high heels, her hair up off her neck, and an orange silk scarf around her shoulders. I felt that big hand on my shoulder again as Dock said, "At least this time I don't have to pick your stuff up out of the hall."

"No sir."

"You got a family, now, Joe. Notice that?"

"I did. It took awhile, Dock, but I noticed."

"Don't fuck it up." He nodded toward the goldfish. "Her name's Lucille, after B.B. King's guitar." He patted my shoulder and walked toward the door. As he passed Julia, she stopped him, and they exchanged a few words as Pop and Caitlyn kept walking toward me. They both hugged me, kissed my cheeks, and patted my back.

"You look good, Joe," said Caitlyn.

"It's pitch black in here."

"That must be the reason. How are things?"

I looked at the hangman. "How am I, Pop?" I asked, my voice lowered. "I think they're still holding my hand. You they'll tell the truth. They find cancer or a brain tumor?"

Pop turned to Caitlyn. "Let me be alone with Joe for a bit."

She nodded as though this parting had been arranged in advance. "I'll be down in the cafeteria. She kissed Pop, turned to me, placed a warm hand on my cheek, and said, "Listen to your father." She left and walked toward Dock.

"Kinda pushy for a prospective stepmother," I remarked.

Pop nodded toward a group of chairs facing the view of the city. "Come on." He took my elbow and guided me over to the chairs. We sat down and Pop reached up to turn on one of the floor lamps.

"Leave it off, Pop." He lowered his hand. "You're making me nervous, man. What they find?"

"Everything, Joe—your side, your lung—just fine. Healing just fine. No cancer, no brain tumors, you're not pregnant."

"It's something, though. Right?"

"It's that other thing, Joe: The way you bottle things up."

"I'm nuts?" I dismissed it with a wave of my hand. "I've always been that way."

"I know!" he burst out with enough volume to make me jump. "I know," he continued more quietly. "Remember me, Joe? I watch you come home from school every day, your face all busted up, never say nothing to me. I was the one who waited a day for you to come out of your closet after the Kwan girl ran out on you. And every one of those men you killed as a police officer—and that night after Collins and Pruitt got the needle, and after the Rizzos cut you up and you died— you go into that hole of yours, plug up all the cracks, and when you think the feelings will behave, you come out again. It's no good, Joe." He rubbed his eyes and let his hand fall to his lap. "You remember Kirby Flagg." It wasn't a question.

"I'm not going to take an ax to my family, Pop."

"That's what Kirby thought. I knew Kirby Flagg for years on the row, Joe. He buried things deep. He told me the week before he killed his family, he didn't think he was crazy. He saw that little girl dead, but to him it was just another homicide victim. Then he thought he had the flu coming on. He was even taking flu medicine for it. But it wasn't flu. He worked a traffic accident a little after. Some drunk lost control of his car on the interstate and took out a van load of vacationers from New York, a father, mother, and their two girls. The drunk didn't have a scratch on him. After that, Kirby went home and killed his family." He reached out and placed a hand on my shoulder. "All but you."

I leaned forward and rested my elbows on my knees. "I know, Pop. He was hiding from his feelings—"

"The feelings hunt you down anyway, Joe. They hunted him down, caught him, and ate him alive. You think you any different?"

"Is this a private conversation?" mercifully interrupted Julia. Pop and I got to our feet. She kissed the hangman's cheek as I glanced back and saw Dock and Caitlyn fading into the dark toward the doors. A lot of people burning up a lot of time and energy worrying about Joe Torio.

Julia placed a gentle hand on my shoulder. I turned and held her. "How was the N.A. meeting?" she asked as the hangman sat back in his chair.

"Aah, the place was full of drug addicts," I joked. She leaned back and studied my face "What is it?" I asked.

"Dock says you turned down the promotion."

"Running MCU field ops takes boxcars full of stuff I don't have right now."

She looked at Pop. "What are we to do with this guy?"

"Have patience," he answered without smiling. "Maybe pray a little."

I led Julia a few steps away and handed her the bag of water containing Lucille. "Here."

She burst out with a tired laugh. "Oh, wonderful. My love is rocketing his way into a psychotic breakdown, but now I can fill his place with a—" She held the clear plastic bag up to what little light was available from outside. "—with a toad?"

"That's a goldfish. Dock brought it for Jaws."

"I'll go back to the room, toss her into the aquarium, and see if they get along."

"If they do, then Jaws will love you instead of me."

"Jaws already loves me more than you," she said. Which was true. When Julia put in the fish food, that

409

damned goldfish frolicked around like a puppy and jumped at the food like a hooked bass.

"You know, lady, you're pretty damned pushy for a gorgeous filthy-rich, high-powered tycoon."

"There's a lot of pushy women in your life for the long haul, and don't you forget it." She nodded at the water-filled bag in her hand. "This fish have a name?"

"Lucille."

"From *lucia*, 'light.' Perhaps she'll bring some to poor old Jaws. I've heard you threaten that fish with a full breaded funeral."

I touched her cheek. "Lucille is named after a guitar."

She turned her head and kissed my palm. "When you're done in here, Joe, I'll be in the room," she whispered. Julia held Lucille in her hand, looked at me for a moment, and added, "Joe, I don't cry for Gerald Soams anymore. I did for a long time. I can't imagine what the world would be like if all kids had sane and competent parents." She looked into the shadows for a long moment. Slowly she shifted her gaze until she was looking deep into my eyes. "I don't cry for the Gray Eye Killer anymore," she said. "But before I could stop, I had to start."

She kissed my cheek, waved at the hangman, turned, and faded into the same shadows that had swallowed Dock and Caitlyn, leaving me alone with the spider plants, the dragon trees, and the hangman. I lowered myself into the chair on Pop's right and looked through the wall of windows over the city lights at Breadloaf Mountain, its darkness waiting serenely for the return of the snows and the new season. Right then I missed Aunt Cella and the days when I first learned how to ski, each new thing learned, each new challenge met, each new thrill successfully experienced, another in a string of gleaming victories.

"Good sitting together," said Pop.

"Just like old times," I said. "You and me sitting together in the dark, chasing away my ghosts. All that's missing are the pancakes." I turned toward him. "You have any ghosts, Pop?"

410

"A few." He admitted. "A few, but we get along. They all know I did the best job that could be done."

I thought back to Leroy Brown and all the lessons on how to survive in an unfair world. "Pop, you know Nathan Sunday asked for help, officially, a number of times. The first time he fell into the care of a school councilor who was a pedophile. The second time he was ignored as a troublemaker. The third time—well, all we know was that either he didn't get the help he needed or it was too late. He had his broken bones and wounds in front of doctors dozens of times. Child Services fed him back into the buzz saw three times."

Pop nodded. "Julia told me." He nodded. "Tough world. What you tell me that one time about Superman?"

I nodded as I recalled. "This is the planet that put Superman in a wheelchair." I looked at the hangman. "Back when I was a kid walking around with my face all busted up, Pop, even though I didn't say anything at the time, thanks for listening. Thanks for hearing all the things I wasn't saying and for taking me to Leroy." Pop reached out and patted my knee. I leaned back and looked at the shadows. "It is dark in here, just like in my old bedroom. All we need is one of Ludwig's sonatas."

"I got something," said Pop as he leaned forward and put his hand in one of his coat pockets. "I'm going to learn to play this on the piano. Caitlyn has me taking lessons."

"Careful. Her ultimate goal is to get you on skis, Pop."

"Never happen." He held up a small player. "Want to hear?"

"Sure."

The hangman leaned to his left, fiddled with the player, there was a click, and the sounds of a tune began filling the shadows. Piano. A little string accompaniment. Simple thing. A children's song.

"That's not Beethoven."

"It's Schubert."

"Schubert? I thought you didn't like Schubert."

"If nothing ever changes, Joe, nothing ever changes." The hangman shrugged. "I like this Schubert. *'Wiegenlied'* it's called."

Franz Schubert's contribution to the lullaby genre. We sat listening to the music, looking at the lights and the few stars that could overcome the wash out from the city lights, the face of a handsome little boy named Nataniele Domenica heavy on my mind, the beautiful ghost of his mother eternally hovering just out of sight. The image of the mountain smeared and I chased away the feelings by turning on the floor lamp next to my chair, the small light startling in its contrast with the surrounding dark.

I felt for the paper Dock had given me, pulled it from my bathrobe pocket, opened it, and began reading. It was one of Nathan Sunday's poems.

joe
see him
this knight who thinks
monsters can be caught
by thinking
like monsters
they can be caught
he believes
by believing
like monsters
insanity is after all
his primary investigative tool

when gods need a god
to whom do they turn
when knights need their own defenders
who is there to face the dragon
there is joe
heroic but meaningless gestures
for the monsters always win
in
the end

Betty Grable got her good cry.

I cried. I cried not for a killer. Instead I cried for the child he used to be and the man he might have become, the tears of my own life crowding through the same opening.

I felt the hangman's hand on my left shoulder, squeezing it. The tune ended and began again, without being rewound. I looked at my father. The hangman was looking at the distant mountain and smiling. Astonishing how well he knows me.

"Pop," I said, "you are a devious old bastard."

"I know," he said patting my shoulder again. "I know."

□ □ □

If you enjoyed Barry B. Longyear's
The Hangman's Son,
please tell a friend.
Satisfied readers are our best advertisements
www.barrylongyear.com